A LITTLE LEARNING

Encouraged by her primary school teacher, Janet Travers wins a place at the local grammar school in Birmingham. Aware of the sacrifices her working class family are making, Janet is determined to do well and despite bullying from the other girls, she is soon top of her class. She makes friends with Ruth Hayman, a Jewish girl who is also an outcast and at seventeen, Janet falls in love with Ruth's brother, but a Catholic wife is out of the question for Ben. Despite love and support from her family and friends, it is many years before Janet learns to love again...

A LITTLE LEARNING

A LITTLE LEARNING

by

Anne Bennett

Magna Large Print Books
Long Preston, North Yorkshire,
BD23 4ND, England.

British Library Cataloguing in Publication Data.

Bennett, Anne
    A little learning.

    A catalogue record of this book is
    available from the British Library

    ISBN   0-7505-1755-7

First published in Great Britain 1998 by Headline Book Publishing

Published in Large Print 2002 by arrangement with
Headline Book Publishing

Magna Large Print is an imprint of Library Magna Books Ltd.

Printed and bound in Great Britain by
T.J. (International) Ltd., Cornwall, PL28 8RW

I wish to thank the following people who've helped me to write this book: Lorraine Michaelson-Yeates, Judith Kendall and Ruth Adshead for without them it would not be written at all and Josie Miery, who also works so hard for me. I would also like to thank the staff at Birmingham Central Reference Library and Erdington Library for their advice, and my close friends Bernadette Pring-Ellis, Sue Bond and her mother Renée Richards because their help has proved invaluable.

Finally I would like to thank my family for their continued support and encouragement, especially my son Simon and my husband Denis who've helped in research, and it is to Denis that I would like to dedicate the book, because he has always believed in me, and also for his love and understanding. Immense gratitude to you all.

Chapter One

'Do you really want to sit the exams for grammar school?' Duncan asked his sister, hardly able to believe she did.

Janet spun round in excitement. 'More than anything,' she said.

Duncan stared at his sister in astonishment. He couldn't understand her, and that bothered him, because he and Janet had always been very close, at least till this business. He couldn't deny she was excited, it shone out of her. He'd never thought of Janet as pretty. He was the good-looking one, with his blond curls and brilliant blue eyes. When he was younger, people were always saying he was too pretty to be a boy and what a shame his sister was so plain. He'd never looked at Janet much, she was just his sister, but he looked at her now. He noted that the mousy hair, that Mom made her keep short because of the risk of nits, seemed to have more body and was somehow fluffed out around her face. Even her eyes, usually a nondescript sort of deep grey, sparkled with excitement and transformed her whole face. Her skin had lost its sallowness and her mouth didn't seem so large, caught up as it was in a beam of happiness.

Duncan couldn't help grinning back at his sister. Janet's delight was infectious. He shook his head as he said, 'Well, I can see you're pleased,

11

Jan, but I don't see what you've got to be pleased about.'

'Oh, Duncan, it's what I've always dreamed of.'

'Well,' Duncan said, 'if it means that much to you I hope you pass, but I still think you need your head testing.'

Janet watched Duncan kicking a ball up the garden for his young twin brothers to run after, but didn't run after them. They'd all been sent to the garden because their parents wanted to talk, and Janet knew what about. Though her father had come round a bit about the exams, in the beginning he was all for not letting Janet take them at all. She knew he was worried about the expense of it all, like keeping her at school all those extra years and buying her uniform. Her mother said she'd just fix it and Janet would like to believe her, but how would she find money they hadn't got? She chewed at her thumb nail and wished she could hear what was being said inside.

'Well, say our Janet passes this bloody exam you talked me into letting her sit,' Bert said glumly, 'how the hell are we going to afford the uniform? This bloke at work told me it costs a bleeding fortune.'

Betty knew only too well that it did – she'd checked it herself – but if Janet passed, then somehow the money for the uniform had to be found.

'We'll afford it, don't you worry,' she said fiercely.

'Look, old girl,' Bert said, 'I don't want to put a damper on the whole thing, but exactly *how* are

12

we to pay for it all?'

'I'll get a Co-op cheque out,' Betty promised. 'That will do for the uniform at least, and paid in weekly, it won't be so bad.'

'And how will you pay for that?' Bert persisted. 'A five-pound cheque won't cover this.'

'I know,' Betty said impatiently. 'I suppose I could go back on the twilight shift at the sauce factory. Our Breda could put a word in, and they always said I could go back.'

'I know that's what they said, but I don't think it's right, you working nights like that just to send our girl to grammar school,' Bert said.

'Don't you see!' Betty cried. 'I'm going to work so she won't have to work like me. I'm going, to give her a chance.'

'You said all this before,' grumbled Bert, 'when you and that Miss Wentworth talked me round for her to put in for the bloody exam in the first place.'

'Yes,' Betty said, 'and that's because you said at first that education was wasted on girls.'

'And so it is.'

Betty stood up in front of Bert and banged her fist on the kitchen table. 'Listen, you blooming numbskull,' she said angrily. 'All my life I've worked. From the age of fourteen I was serving in the tobacconist's shop at the corner of Corporation Street, often for twelve hours a day. Then we wed, and when Duncan was small and Janet a wee baby, I was office cleaning from five in the morning till eight, and then again at night in the chip shop to make ends meet. Then after the war our Breda got me set in the HP Sauce

13

factory at Aston Cross. So don't you tell me about education being a waste.'

'I know you've worked, love,' Bert said soothingly. 'You're one of the best, none better.'

'Well, I want better, better for my daughter,' Betty cried. 'I don't want her working like I had to, like most women have to.'

'Yes, but when a woman's married...' Bert began, but Betty leapt at him again.

'Her life stops, is that it?'

'Not at all,' Bert declared stoutly. 'Some say it begins.'

'Oh yes it does,' Betty said. 'You've a house, a husband, children, less money than you've ever had in your life and more to do with it.'

Bert had his set face on, so Betty tried again. 'Look, Bert, I'm not blaming you. It's just the way it is. But the world's changing now. When you and all the other men were charging around Europe killing Germans, the women were holding the fort over here. They were doing jobs women had never done before!'

'I know that.'

'But you must see that that sort of experience would change a woman's outlook on things.'

'Till the men came back.'

'No,' Betty cried. 'Six years is a long time. Women won't just give up and go back to the kitchen sink. Things will have to change. Miss Wentworth was even telling me that married women will soon be officially allowed to teach. I mean, they did in the war, because they had to, and then they expected them to go back to their husbands. Only some didn't want to, and some

14

of the poor souls didn't have husbands any more, but they still had a family to bring up.'

'It's this Miss Wentworth who's filled your head with such nonsense,' Bert said stubbornly.

Betty knew he had a point, for she had listened to the teacher and to her vision of the new, emerging Britain, where women could take their rightful place alongside men.

'Women like your Janet, Mrs Travers,' she said. 'Intelligent women. The time will come when men and women will work side by side, and that will include married women. Even when they have children, they will be going back to work. It will eventually change the face of the world.'

Betty had kept quiet. She didn't say that women had been working for years and working bloody hard and yet it had changed nothing. Sarah McClusky, her own mother, had worked from dawn till dusk and for a pittance. They'd lived in Summer Lane then, the bottom end of Edgbaston. The houses were back to back with dilapidated roofs and walls, crowded around a central courtyard which housed the shared lavatory and brew'us, where the washing was done, and where the tap was that served the whole yard. Betty remembered the stench from the small industries and workshops that abounded in the area that made the atmosphere smoky and gloomy and dirty as it discharged its gases into the air to mix with the smoke from thousands of back to back house chimneys.

Betty looked at Claire Wentworth and realised she didn't know the half of it, not her Janet either; she hoped her children would never know

15

poverty like there was then. It was the threat of that that made her mother trudge across to the other side of Edgbaston to clean the homes of the gentry. Winter or summer, and often the only thing to protect her from the elements was a shawl, and the well cobbled boots on her feet might have cardboard inside them to try to keep the wet out of the soles worn through.

All day she would clean and return home weary and bone tired to a meal Betty would have to have made after her day at school. It was her job, as the elder girl, to clean and cook as best she could and, with her elder brother Conner, give an eye to the little'uns Brendan, Breda and Noel. Twice a week Sarah would bring home a large laundry basket covered with a sheet, and Betty would know her mother would be in the brew'us all the rest of the next day washing for her employers.

It was no mean feat to wash clothes then, even for a family, and yet Sarah wasn't the only woman to take on extra. She would creep from her bed at five the next morning and poke Betty awake as she slept in the attic in the bed with her younger sister. Bleary eyed, Betty would stumble after her mother in clothes hastily fastened around her and her feet in the boots given free to the poor children by the *Daily Mail*. In her hand she would carry a bucket of slack to light the copper, and inside the brew'us her mother would be filling it up bucket by bucket from a tap in the yard. Betty would begin to maid, or pound, the clothes in a dolly tub and then scrub at the offending stains. At some point her mother

16

would take over and Betty would return to the house to wake and feed her brothers and sisters and her father too.

In the brew'us, Sarah would boil all the washing in the copper and then swill the whites in a bucket tinged with Reckitt's Blue before starching. When the children returned at dinnertime, to bread and dripping they made themselves, Sarah would be mangling the clothes, and if the day had been fine and dry, by hometime she was ironing the lot with a flat iron heated in the fire, for the clothes would have dried on the lines that criss-crossed the yard. If however it was wet, the clothes would be strung above the fire and around the hearth, and the house would be cold and smell of damp washing.

But no one complained, for the washing Sarah took in to supplement her cleaning paid the rent and put food in hungry children's bellies. Even Sean who was often unable to provide for his family said little, and in actual fact, Sarah's job didn't disturb him much at all and as long as his own laundry was always done, his dinner always on the table, the fire kept up and the children seen to, he didn't moan much. The house might have got a lick and a promise rather than a good going-over, the stove might not have been blackleaded every week, nor the brass polished, nor the step scrubbed, but those were things the men didn't notice.

Until the slump, Sean McClusky had been employed at Henry Wiggins and Co in Wiggin Street which produced nickel and steel plate, but as the depression bit deeper, he was just put on short time and then out of work altogether; it was her mother who then put food on the table, Betty remembered. Yet her father would never do a hand's turn in the house and it hadn't seemed strange. Without work, he would loll on street corners with mates in the same situation, or sit listlessly in front of the fire for which his wife's money had bought the coal.

Miss Wentworth painted a view of life Betty didn't understand, or quite believe in. Her own jobs, like her mother's, had been chosen to fit in with Bert and the children.

In time life had become easier for the McClusky family. Betty married Bert which was no surprise to anyone, and the family moved from Summer Lane to the new sprawling council estate of Pype Hayes, north of the city, where Betty in time was also given a house. Money was easier as the younger McCluskys were all at work, and Sean got a job making tyres at Fort Dunlop in 1937. Then war was declared. Bert Travers was called up, along with his brothers-in-law Conner and Brendan while Noel volunteered and Breda went to work in the munitions.

'Come on, our Bet, the money is desperate, so it is,' she'd urged her sister, but Betty had shaken her head.

The years had been hard on her parents and she thought she couldn't leave them in charge of Duncan and Janet all day, whatever the lure of the money. Breda soon sported the uniform turban like all the rest of the factory girls, wore scarlet lipstick and smoked strong-smelling cigarettes. Her language, Betty noticed, was

18

pretty strong too. She'd have had her lugs scalped if she'd tried such talk, she told her sister.

'Da says that and worse,' Breda had protested.

'That's different, he's a man.'

Then Breda had laughed. 'I think you can give yourself a pat on the back for noticing that, Bet, for I'd never have worked it out on my own.'

But Betty's attitude changed when her youngest brother, Noel, was killed in the first year of the war. He was just eighteen years old. Betty thought she'd never get over it, and yet she had to cope because her parents were bowed down with grief. Eventually, anger at the waste of Noel's life replaced the sadness, and this anger was further fuelled by the blitz of Birmingham that began on 25 August 1940.

When Tyburn Road was targeted the following evening, it was dangerously close to her Pype Hayes home, threatening her family. She decided that knitting balaclavas and cowering at home was no longer good enough for her. 'I need to do something, Mammy,' she appealed to her mother, 'or I'll feel Noel has died in vain. But I can't do it without your help.'

Sarah McClusky had no wish to see another of her children exposed to danger, but she knew it was Betty's way of dealing with her brother's death. She took a deep breath to steady her own fear and said firmly, 'The weans will be as right as rain with us. Dad has the shelter that cosy, with bunks fixed to the sides and the oil heater to take the chill off, and they'll be as safe as houses.'

Betty was grateful, for she knew what it had cost her mother to react the way she did. The following day she joined up as an ARP warden.

It soon became apparent that Birmingham was ill equipped to deal with the casualties of the bombing raids, which were intensifying throughout the city. The job of the wardens included trying to arrange temporary accommodation of some sort for the homeless, plus clothes, bedding and food.

People taking shelter where they could often did not get any aid for hours, and there were some disorderly scenes among the desperate and often destitute people. In an effort to help the situation, mobile canteens were set up, and Betty elected to serve in one of these, together with her fellow ARP warden and friend Cynthia, who was the driver.

On the night of 19 November 1940, the sirens had not even died away when the first thuds were heard. Sarah McClusky felt her stomach tighten in fear as she watched her daughter struggle into her coat. She knew Betty had to go, and hoped the raid would be over soon, but she had to look after Duncan and Janet, so she began hurriedly to pack a bag to take down to the shelter. 'Take care, lass,' she said to Betty as she was about to leave.

'I will, Mammy,' Betty said. There was a sudden explosion very close and she went on quickly, 'Don't worry about me, Mammy, I'll be fine, but get the children and yourselves down to the shelter quick.' She gave her mother and children a kiss. 'See you in the morning.'

It was a long raid and a bad one. The ack-ack guns were at work as she made her way to the

ARP post in Erdington, and the searchlights were raking the skies. She sent up a prayer that her family would be safe when she returned – the children, her parents and Breda on her night shift.

Hours later, as the mobile canteen drove towards Birmingham city centre, which seemed to be ablaze, Cynthia was cut badly about the face by shards of glass from the windscreen, which had been shattered by a bomb blast. One of the ambulancemen who took the unconscious and bleeding Cynthia to hospital turned to Betty and said, 'Have to leave the van where it is, love, and hope it isn't blown to kingdom come.'

Until then, Betty had given no thought to the van, but she knew they were needed – indeed, they were a lifeline for many families, and for the rescue workers digging people out, often near dead on their feet with exhaustion themselves.

'No bloody Hitler's getting my van,' she said, climbing into Cynthia's seat. She didn't know how to drive, but she'd seen Cynthia do it often enough. She turned the key and the throbbing engine came to life. Slowly and carefully she put it into gear and touched her foot on the accelerator. She was slow and a bit jerky but she was driving, and a thrill of exhilaration ran through her. She negotiated potholes and piles of debris blown into the road by the falling bombs. The wind buffeted her through the gaping hole in the windscreen, and all around her was constant noise.

Black arrows of death were tumbling from the droning planes above, the never-ending rattle of

21

the guns seeming to make no impression on them. She heard cries and terrified screams, and saw walls crumple with shuddering thuds before her eyes, exploding in clouds of dust. The sirens of fire engines and ambulances screamed through the night. She saw the city skyline lit up with a strange orange glow, and the acrid smell of smoke was in her mouth and nose.

And she drove through it all, like a scythe cutting a swath through corn, too excited to be scared. A little while later, she was dishing out tea and sandwiches to people in an emergency rescue centre, and being described as 'an angel'.

She told no one about her driving. She told her mother as little as possible anyway. Sarah Mc-Clusky understood Betty's need to be doing something and looked after Duncan and Janet with no complaint. However, if she'd had her way, she'd have had her Betty tucked up in the shelter with the children.

Sarah was confused by the way of the world. By working her fingers to the bone, she'd been able to put shoes on her children's feet and food in their stomachs when times were bad. She'd kept them safe and healthy, she'd nursed them through childish ailments, they were well nourished enough to fight. She was proud of her fine family. But she'd already lost one son to the war, with the other two risking their lives daily, and a daughter to the munitions, for she knew that Breda – never as easy or compliant as her sister – would go her own way after this.

Then there was Betty. With her husband away fighting, she doled out nourishment, hope and sympathy to the homeless and rescuers alike in the city centre where the raids were heaviest. Betty told her mother that they took shelter when the raids were bad, but Sarah wasn't sure she'd been telling the truth. She had the idea she wasn't told about a lot of things.

'You dark horse.' Cynthia said when Betty visited her in the General Hospital later. She was swathed in bandages and looked a little pale, but she smiled bravely as she asked: 'Why did you never say you could drive before?'

'Oh, you know,' Betty said, busying herself with an imaginary stain on her skirt so that Cynthia wouldn't see the telltale flush flooding her face. 'It's a long time ago. I wasn't sure I still had the knack.'

'I think it's like riding a bike,' Cynthia said. 'You know, you never really forget.'

'Yes,' said Betty, anxious to get off the subject. She looked out of the window at the steel-grey skies and the people hurrying below huddled in thick coats, scarves and hats. 'It's bitter out there, Cynth, you're in the best place for the moment.'

'Don't you believe it,' Cynthia said. 'D'you know what they do when there's a raid? They stick us underneath the beds. Some chance if the hospital gets a direct hit, eh? I'd descend to the ground floor mighty quick, if you ask me, under tons of masonry, crushed flat by my own iron bed. No, I'd rather take my chance out on the street, where you can see the buggers coming.'

'Oh, Cynthia,' Betty said with a chuckle, 'I've missed you.'

'Well, you'll have to go on missing me,' Cynthia

said, 'because even when I'm out of here, you'll probably get a different crew now. I don't think they've got enough drivers to put two together.'

'Oh, no ... I mean, yes ... of course, you're right.' That hadn't occurred to Betty, but she enjoyed driving so much, she didn't want to give it up. She kept the truth from her mother and her husband who might have spilled the beans that she'd never had a driving lesson in the whole of her life. No one asked, and as drivers were in short supply, she was in great demand.

The war went on relentlessly. The raids eased a little, but the battle for the housewife was coping with shortages and rationing. Making do and mending was all very well, Betty thought wryly, if you had something to make do with in the first place.

Then, just before the spring of 1944, Bert came home for pre-embarkation leave.

'I think this is it, my old duck,' he told Betty, 'the big push, the beginning of the end, old girl.'

And what if, when the end finally comes, I have no husband? thought Betty, and she cried into Bert's shoulder and wouldn't tell him why. The ARP post had to do without her for two nights while she lay in Bert's arms, and their lovemaking was frantic as they realised that their time together was short. By the time Bert was treading the beaches of Normandy, Betty was getting used to the idea of another little Travers to join Duncan and Janet. She cut down on her war work as her pregnancy advanced, and gave it up entirely just before Christmas of that year.

The second telegram arrived the day the

Christmas cards were due to come down. Sarah opened it with trembling fingers, and when she read that Conner, her eldest son, was to lie beside his brother in foreign soil, she fell down in a faint. Sean McClusky envied his wife her unconsciousness, and wished he didn't have to deal with the knowledge that two of his children were dead and gone. He put his head in his hands and wept.

Betty's grief was deep and profound for the big brother she'd always looked up to. Noel's death had acted as a catalyst, urging her to take a more active part in the war that had stolen her brother. This time there was nothing she could do to lessen the hurt, for hostilities were nearly at an end and the tide of war was turning.

However, she wasn't allowed to grieve for long, for just days after they received the news about Conner, her pains began. Her labour was long and difficult and the midwife sent for the doctor. He was mystified as to why Betty should be having such a difficult time, until it was established that there were two babies, not one as originally thought. Betty couldn't believe her ears and redoubled her efforts, and on a raw January day gave birth to twin boys, both healthy, lusty and a good size.

When Sarah McClusky was told the news she dropped to her knees. 'The Lord giveth and the Lord taketh away,' she said. Betty agreed with her mother's sentiments, and the two boys were christened Conner and Noel. Sarah often looked for signs of her dead sons in the twins.

'I think Conner has his uncle's nose,' she'd say, or 'Noel is the image of his namesake. Even their eyes are the same shape.'

Betty didn't agree because in her opinion both boys looked like Bert. In their identical faces she could see Bert's hazel eyes, and his large nose. Even the shape of their faces was the same – round, with ruddy cheeks – and eventually, Betty guessed, their chins would turn craggy like Bert's. Only their wide mouths and the colour of their hair was the same as hers and Janet's. It was Duncan who resembled his dead uncles, in both colouring and build.

'Ma can't see it,' Betty said to Breda. 'Duncan is the spit of our Noel at the same age. I remember him well. I can't remember Conner as a child, because he was older than me, but I've seen photographs.'

'She doesn't want to see it,' Breda said. 'Not in Duncan. She wants the twins to look like their dead uncles because in her mind they've replaced them.' She struggled and went on, 'It helps her cope.' Betty said she supposed it did, she had neither the time nor the inclination to argue further; she was too busy dealing with the family to do any further war work, and she was just glad that things were winding down at last.

The VE celebrations and street parties were tinged with sadness for many who had loved ones not returning after the war. Betty and her parents felt sad that Conner and Noel had not lived to celebrate the day, but the twins' birth helped them all to cope. Betty knew she had much to be thankful for. Her husband and one brother were safe, and her sister, and she had her fine family, Duncan, Janet and the twins.

26

She was immersed in domesticity now, but busy as she was, she often found the days tedious. Driving around the ravaged city dealing with the destitute and the desperate had seemed important work. She had dealt with the bereaved and the sick and those in shock, and had felt useful and needed. It wasn't that she didn't consider her family important; it was the boredom of doing the same thing day after day she found hard to take. She also seemed to lack any identity now – just wife and mother, where once she'd been someone in her own right.

She knew that when Bert returned she would tell him little of the work she'd done in the war. He'd never have recognised the organised person driving the mobile canteen through the streets of Birmingham as his Betty anyway. Betty herself found it hard to remember what she'd been like then, and now the family claimed all her attention.

Duncan could have taken the eleven-plus that year, but he didn't want to and the teachers told Betty there was little point.

'An apprenticeship would be ideal, Mrs Travers,' the headmaster said. 'Or something in that line. He's not a stupid boy and he's good with his hands, but not grammar school potential. Now if it were Janet...'

The words were left hanging in the air. Betty pondered on them, but said nothing to anyone.

Duncan didn't care. 'I don't want to go to no soppy grammar school, Ma. I want to go to Paget Road Secondary with my mates.'

Janet had wished she'd had the opportunity to

27

sit the exam, and wondered if she'd ever be allowed to. She knew Duncan didn't want to go to grammar school, he'd told her often enough. He disliked school and thought it a waste of time, but realised he had to be there for a while and went without too much fuss. He was determined to leave at the first opportunity.

'But what will you do?' Janet asked.

'I reckon our dad can get me set on at Fishers with him.'

'Is that what you want?' Janet persisted. 'Make car bodies all day?'

Duncan stared at her. He'd never considered what he actually *wanted* to do. You went to school, left, got a job and had money in your pocket to spend. That was life.

'Course it's what I want,' he snapped. 'It's what everyone wants, ain't it?'

Janet didn't answer. It wasn't what she wanted, but it wouldn't help to say so.

Bert was delighted with Duncan's decision. 'Chip off the old block, eh, son?' he said, clapping him on the shoulder. He had a vision of him and his son in a few years' time, walking side by side through the factory gates.

Betty was glad that Bert was pleased, because she knew the war had robbed him of his youth. The man who returned to her had grey streaks in his dark hair, and Betty noticed that he was going thin on top. She said nothing, just being glad he'd returned safely. She didn't comment either on the haunted look that was often in Bert's eyes as he seemed to stare vacantly into space, or the times he cried out in his sleep. She could only

28

imagine the horrors he'd witnessed in the war and doubted that many of the returning heroes were untouched by their experiences.

Bert had also begun to get interested in politics again, as he had before he'd joined up. The first election of peacetime was held on 5 July 1945, but as most of the armed forces had not demobbed by then, the result could not be calculated until 26 July when all the postal votes were in and counted.

Bert was home in time to hear that Labour had been elected to government by a resounding majority, and he was cock-a-hoop with excitement. 'This will make a difference, you'll see,' he said to Betty. 'Transport and some industries will be nationalised, so the State will own them and everyone will benefit.'

'You mean like with communism?'

'Communism be damned, woman, this is socialism I'm talking about,' Bert said furiously. 'And that's not all. They've committed to taking on the Beveridge Report; that means family allowances and setting up a health service at the very least.'

'Well you seem pleased, at any rate,' Betty said. 'And if I get family allowances to help feed and clothe the children and don't have to pay every time I go to the doctor's I'll be thankful enough.'

Bert went one step further and without further delay he joined the Labour Party, and went on to run for shop steward in Fisher and Ludlow's factory where he made car bodies. All in all, Bert was well satisfied with his life and relieved that none of his family had been hurt in the war. And though he was sorry about his brothers-in-law Noel and Conner, he couldn't help feeling pleased that his wife and children were safe, and a credit to Betty who'd had most of the rearing of them while he'd been away.

Bert found little to say to his quiet, studious daughter, but he was bowled over by the twins, who looked so like him, and whose early months he'd missed. They were turned six months now, and they chuckled as Bert tossed them in the air and put them astride his bouncing foot to play 'horsy'.

He was less pleased with the job Betty had got, doing the evening shift at the sauce factory with her sister. Breda had had a good war. Despite rationing and restrictions, she had a wardrobe bursting with clothes, money in the bank and many memories, some happy, some sad. For a time it had seemed she might marry a GI and go to live in the States after the war. Mr and Mrs McClusky, in an agony of worry, had appealed to Betty, who tackled her sister.

'I'm having a good time, that's all,' Breda had snapped. 'I'm not looking for a husband. Rick's never mentioned marriage, and even if he did it's not a foregone conclusion I'd take him on.'

It was hardly satisfactory, but it had to do. Betty told her parents that Breda and her Yank were just good friends. Then there were the two dashing airmen who were both killed in action. Breda had arrived at Betty's home in tears after she'd heard about the second one.

'You see,' she'd wept, 'how can we talk about the future with this godawful war? Who's going to

30

be left alive at the end of it all?'

Betty had hugged her, rocking her almost without being aware of it. She knew what Breda meant. Each evening when she reported for duty, she viewed the desolation around her and was amazed that anyone could still be alive, or that people struggled to gain some sort of normality in it.

'I know, love,' she told Breda. 'All we can do is keep going.'

There were no attachments for Breda after that. Though she went out with many men, she never kept them for long, and never allowed herself to get involved. Betty was concerned that she might make a name for herself, but said nothing and kept her worries to herself.

Then, at the end of the war, Breda had taken up with Peter Bradshaw, a lad she'd gone out with a few times before war broke out and who now returned, one of the conquering heroes.

'Do you love him, Breda?' Betty asked.

'I'm marrying him,' Breda said, and added, 'What's love anyway, Bet? I've loved and lost enough in the last few years to last a lifetime, and I suppose me and Pete will rub along well enough.'

The munitions factory was closed and the staff dispersed, and Breda lost no time in getting herself a job in the HP Sauce factory, which was taking on a twilight shift.

'Come on, Bet, it's four nights a week, half five to half nine,' she said.

'I don't know'

'Course you know. You can cope with your

31

brood all day, give them their tea, and I'm sure our mam will do the honours till you come home.'

All of a sudden it seemed an attractive prospect to go out in the evening and talk to adults about adult things. She was restless at home and missed the camaraderie of the war years. 'If Mammy agrees to see to them, I will,' she said.

She enjoyed her job, repetitive though it was. She loved the bald, raw humour of the married women, most like herself with children and waiting for their husbands' demob. She wondered, though, how Bert would view the idea of her working when he came home. The other women also worried about their husbands' reactions, though none wanted to give up their jobs.

Betty banked her money and had a little nest egg to show Bert when he expressed doubts about her ability to cope.

'After all,' he said, 'the factory has kept my job open.'

'I know,' Betty said, 'but the children are always needing things, and with Conner and Noel it's two of everything and that's extra expense. And then of course there's the house.'

'What's wrong with it?' After years of army barracks, his home looked very comfortable to him.

'It's shabby,' Betty declared. 'There was nothing to buy during the war, but soon there will be things in the shops and new colours in paint and wallpaper, and we can do the place up a bit.'

Bert surveyed his living room. Its familiarity had given him comfort when he arrived home:

the sofa with the broken springs, and the faded lino on the floor. Now he saw it through Betty's eyes and realised how dingy and patchy the wallpaper was and how dull the brown paint-work.

It could certainly do with brightening up, he thought, and perhaps they could even get a new wireless and a carpet square eventually. 'All right, love,' he said. 'You keep your job. As long as you can manage, I'll say nothing about it.'

Things rubbed along nicely for over a year. Brendan got married to Patsy Brennan, a local girl from an Irish family, and Breda had a baby girl, Linda, but continued working afterwards. Duncan started at Paget Road Secondary Modern, and Janet began her last year at Paget Road Primary.

The autumn term was into its fourth week. Betty had been delighted when school started again. She'd been tired out coping with the demands of four children all day and working in the evening, but she'd never complained to Bert.

Bert was recounting some tale from the factory around the tea table, and Duncan was listening avidly. He was fascinated by anything to do with the world he would soon be joining. Betty was keeping a watchful eye on the twins, who were making a mess of feeding themselves but screamed if she tried to help them. She was just thankful it was Friday and she didn't have to go to work. Janet had kept her head down all through tea, and catching sight of her now, Betty realised that she'd been quiet all evening. She hoped Janet wasn't sickening for something.

There was a small silence after Bert had finished, broken only by the twins banging their spoons on their high-chair tables. Suddenly Janet said: 'Mom, Miss Wentworth would like a word with you.'

There was a hoot of laughter from Duncan. 'Why, what you done?' he said, and added in disbelief, 'Goody-goody Janet's in trouble.'

'I'm not, I'm not,' Janet declared hotly.

'That will do, Duncan,' Betty said. She turned her gaze to her daughter and said: 'D'you know what it's about?'

All eyes were on Janet now, and she stammered: 'I ... I think it's ... it's about the exam.'

'The exam?' Bert said. 'What's this?'

'The eleven-plus, she means,' Duncan said.

'Oh,' said Bert airily. 'No need to worry your head about that, pet, you don't need to do no eleven-plus.'

Janet's face flushed crimson. Betty took pity on her and said, 'Do you want to do it, love?'

'Oh, yes.'

There was a shocked silence. Even the twins were staring at her. Bert put down his knife and fork and asked in genuine puzzlement, 'Why do you want to take the eleven-plus?'

'Miss Wentworth says I have a good chance of passing,' Janet burst out. 'She says I have a good brain and . . .'

'This Miss Wentworth has been talking a lot of nonsense,' Bert said, 'and filling your head with rubbish. You've no need for a grammar school education and you can tell her that from me.'

Betty looked at her daughter's stricken face and

said, 'It will do no harm to listen to what the woman has to say.'

'Do no bloody good either.'

'Bert,' Betty admonished, with a nod towards the twins, who were reaching the age when they liked to latch on to unusual words and repeat them.

'They'll hear worse before they're much older,' Bert said, ruffling the heads of his small sons fondly. 'Proper little buggers they're growing up to be.'

Betty gave up. He'd never be any different. He stood up, scraping his chair back. 'Well,' he said, 'I'm away for a wash.'

'You going to the club?'

'I always go to the club on Friday.'

'Yes, I know.' Betty began collecting the plates, then said, almost casually, though she knew her daughter would be holding her breath for Bert's reply, 'I think I'll pop along to the school and have a chat with our Janet's teacher anyway, all right?'

'Yes, if you want,' Bert said. 'Do as you like but it won't make any bloody difference.' He chucked Janet under the chin as he went out. 'Cheer up, ducky,' he said. 'Why the long face? You're much too pretty to worry yourself over any silly exams.'

Janet didn't answer. She watched him lift the kettle from the gas and take it to the bathroom that opened off the kitchen, and a little later she heard him whistling as he had a shave.

Chapter Two

Betty went to see Miss Wentworth the following Monday lunchtime. 'You really think our Janet has a chance of passing the eleven-plus?' she asked, gazing at the teacher in amazement.

'Indeed I do,' Claire Wentworth said with an emphatic nod of her head. 'Janet has an exceptional brain. She seems to soak up knowledge.'

Does she? Betty thought. Miss Wentworth went on to describe a child Betty did not recognise as her daughter. 'She's one of the brightest I have ever taught,' she said at last.

'But she's always so quiet at home, our Janet,' Betty said.

'Assimilating all the knowledge gained, I suppose.'

'Pardon?' said Betty, not quite understanding the words the teacher was using.

'Taking it all in, you know,' said Claire. 'She's probably got too much going on in her head for chattering a lot.'

'Maybe,' Betty said. 'She often looks as though she's in a dream. She must be thinking.' She smiled and added, 'It's not something the rest of us do a lot of.'

Claire studied the woman before her. Betty Travers wasn't at all how she'd expected her to be. She was younger, for a start, and prettier, very like Janet, with the same reflective eyes and wide mouth. Her hair was the same colour as Janet's but slightly longer, and judging by the straggly curls, it had once been permed.

She looked open and approachable and did not appear hostile to her daughter taking the exam. A lot of parents were against their children bettering themselves, especially the girls.

Yet there was some obstacle, because when Claire had asked Janet that morning if she'd broached the subject at home, her eyes had had a hopeless look in them, and there'd been a dejected droop to her mouth. She'd said she'd told her mother, and that she was coming in to discuss it, and now here was the mother and proving very amenable too.

'You are agreeable to allowing Janet to enter then, Mrs Travers?'

Betty didn't answer immediately. She twisted her handbag strap round and round in her fingers. Eventually she said:

'Well ... the thing is, my husband ... he ... well, he ... he doesn't see the point.'

It was nearly always the fathers, Claire thought angrily. 'You mean her father is refusing to let her take the examination?' she snapped.

It came out sharper than she had intended and it put Betty's back up. Janet's teacher had no right to talk that way about Bert.

'He's a good man,' she said stiffly. 'It isn't that he doesn't want the best for Janet, but he sees this eleven-plus as a waste of time.'

'It's not!' Claire cried. 'It's a wonderful opportunity for her. You must see that.'

Betty stared at Claire Wentworth, but she

wasn't seeing her. The word 'opportunity' had stirred her memories. The war had given Betty the opportunity to be something other than a wife and mother. It had given her an independent life that she seldom spoke of, even to Bert, sensing his disapproval. Now an opportunity of a different kind was being offered to her daughter, and she was rejecting it on Janet's behalf.

Have I any right to do that? she thought. Will she resent me and her dad for not letting her try? She knew Bert would be furious, but she felt she couldn't deny her daughter this chance.

'When is the examination, Miss Wentworth?' she asked.

Claire smiled. 'The examination is in three parts,' she said. 'There is a maths paper, an English paper and a paper to test intelligence. She must pass all three, and the first set is held in November.'

'That's not far away, it's October already.'

'Yes, I must enter Janet's name by the end of the week. And she will need extra tuition.'

Betty was startled. 'What d'you mean? You said she had a good chance of passing, you never said a thing about her needing tuition. I can't afford that.'

'Mrs Travers, you don't have to afford it. *I* will coach Janet. She has a chance of passing now, without extra work, but the classes are large and I have no extra time to give her. I've explained all this to Janet. She is prepared to work hard.'

'You will do that for our Janet?' Betty asked, amazed.

'I would do it for any pupil who would benefit

from it,' Claire said. 'Unfortunately, most children at Paget Road junior school look no further than the secondary modern. It's what they want and what their parents want, and they see no need to take an examination.'

'But Janet's different?'

'Undoubtedly,' Claire said. 'Now, the first set of exams will be marked by Christmas; you will probably have the results with your Christmas mail. If Janet passes, she will automatically go forward to the second set of examinations, which will be more extensive and will be held at the beginning of February. It will probably be April before you hear if she has passed or failed those.'

'And say she gets through all this and passes,' said Betty. 'Where will she go then?'

'Whytecliff School in Sutton Coldfield would be my first choice,' Claire said. 'It's private but it offers scholarships to a quarter of the intake. I hear it's a marvellous school, with wonderful facilities. I'm sure Janet would love it, and provided she passes the exam, you'd pay for nothing but the uniform.'

'That would probably cost a pretty penny, I bet.'

Claire could not deny it, and Betty knew the money would have to be found somehow.

'All right,' she said. 'Put our Janet's name down for this here exam and we'll see what she's made of.'

Claire was delighted, but she didn't want to raise the child's hopes only to have them dashed again. 'I'd be only too happy to, Mrs Travers,' she said, 'but your husband...'

'Leave him to me,' Betty said decisively.

She said a similar thing to her daughter that evening. Janet had had a chat with Miss Wentworth, who told her of the outcome of her mother's visit. That afternoon, after school, she settled down in the kitchen, gazing at her mother almost shyly. Betty smiled at her.

'Went to see your Miss Wentworth today,' she said. 'I expect she told you.'

'Yes, she did.'

'Pretty young thing, isn't she? I thought she'd be a crabbed old maid.'

'Oh, no,' Janet said in the hushed tones of adoration. 'She's beautiful.'

She'd spent hours looking at Miss Wentworth. The teacher's hair was so light brown as to be almost blonde, and she tied it back from her face with a black ribbon. Her eyes were the darkest brown, and she had the cutest nose and the loveliest mouth. Her whole face had a kindness about it, and her eyes often twinkled with amusement. She had the most gentle speaking voice, that she hardly ever raised in anger, but she could get the children to listen to her just the same. Janet's dream was to look like Claire Wentworth, but her more realistic aim was to get into the grammar school, because that would please her teacher.

'She thinks a lot of you,' Betty said.

Janet said nothing, but her eyes shone.

'Thinks you have a chance of the eleven-plus if you work.'

'I know. I will if you'll let me try.'

'Well, I think you should have the chance,' Betty said.

'What about Dad?'

'Leave your dad to me.'

Janet knew it wouldn't be easy to change her father's mind, and Betty didn't try to kid her otherwise. She hadn't time to do much then anyway, for she was rushing to make tea for everyone and get to work.

'Now,' she said, getting into her coat, 'you get these dishes washed and put away before your dad comes home. Put the vegetables on at half past five for his tea, and don't let them boil dry.'

'I've done it before, Mom,' Janet protested. 'Anyway, isn't Gran coming round?'

'Yes, but she'll have her hands full getting the twins to bed,' Betty said. 'I want your dad's tea on the table when he comes in, and a tidy house. I want him in a good mood.'

'Why?' asked Duncan, puzzled.

'Never you mind,' Betty snapped. Duncan saw the glance his mother gave to Janet. He wondered why his mom was trying to sweeten his dad up, and what it had to do with his sister. He didn't ask, for he knew his mom wouldn't tell him, and she was agitated about being late for work anyway. Then Breda was at the door and he watched the pair of them scurry down the road.

When Bert Travers came in at six o'clock the house was spotless. Janet had dusted and polished and a hint of furniture polish still hung in the air. His dinner was ready, and he stood in the kitchen doorway watching his daughter dish up his meal and pour gravy over it. He felt a surge of pride for his family.

His son was a lad to be proud of and was preparing to follow in his dad's footsteps when he was fourteen. A daughter was bound to be different. Janet was much quieter than Duncan, and said to be clever, but she could produce a good meal for him just the same. She'd be another like her mom. Then there were his twin boys, washed and pyjamaed for bed. They had been drinking their milk until they saw their father, and then they threw their bottles down and began clambering all over him.

Bert was inordinately proud of the twin sons and was far more easy-going with them than he had been with Duncan and Janet when they were small. Sarah McClusky, who believed that to spare the rod was to spoil the child, watched in disapproval as Conner and Noel leaped at and climbed up their father's body.

'Leave your dad be, he's been at work all day, he'll be tired,' she admonished.

'They're all right, Ma,' Bert said good-humouredly. 'I see little enough of them.'

'They were getting ready to go to bed,' Sarah said reprovingly.

'That's what I mean,' Bert said. 'They're always nearly ready to go to bed when I get in...' But his dinner was waiting and he had no desire to fight over it, and certainly not with his mother-in-law. He was only too aware what they owed her, him and Betty, for if she hadn't agreed to come and see to the kids at night, Betty couldn't have worked, and he had to admit the money was useful.

His wages never seemed to stretch far these days, with the four children. He was constantly amazed by the way the children went through their clothes and shoes, and what they cost to replace. Then there was the amount of food consumed in one week. He was grateful for the government introducing the new family allowance, but he recognised that without the bit Betty earned, they'd often be strapped for cash. Sarah McClusky's presence meant that his life changed very little. Betty would prepare dinner before she left for work, to be cooked by her mother or Janet ready for his arrival. After he'd eaten he could go down the club for a pint, leaving his mother-in-law to keep an eye on the children.

Anyway, Bert told himself as he ate his tea, bringing up kids is a woman's job. He was looking forward to the time when him and his lad would be mates in the factory, going down the pub together and to Villa Park on Saturday afternoons. But up until that time, any decisions about Duncan's upbringing, or that of the others, he would leave to Betty, or her mother if Betty wasn't there.

Later, when he was washed and changed ready to go out, everything was much quieter. He knew his younger sons were fast asleep in their separate cots, because he'd tiptoed in to see on his way down from the bedroom. His mother-in-law was knitting placidly, while she listened to the wireless.

'You away now?' she asked.

'Yes, I'll go for a quick one.'

Sarah McClusky's eyes betrayed nothing. She

personally thought Betty wouldn't have to go to work if Bert didn't tip so much money down his throat, but that was their business. Betty had made that abundantly clear, the one time Sarah had mentioned it.

'Bert's a good man, Ma, and a good provider. He always sees to us first, and what he does with the money in his pocket is his business. Anyway,' she'd added, 'I enjoy my job.'

So Mrs McClusky kept her own counsel now, and what she said to her son-in-law was:

'You might tell young Duncan to come in on your way out.'

'Where is he?'

'Kicking a ball in the street somewhere, but the nights are drawing in now.'

'He'll be all right.'

'Betty doesn't like him out in the dark,' Mrs McClusky said. 'They get up to all sorts of mischief, she says.'

Bert thought of Duncan and his mates and knew that Betty had a point. 'I'll tell him,' he said, and added, 'Our Janet's not out there too, is she?'

Sarah McClusky chuckled. 'Not her, she's too sensible for that gang of hooligans. She's in the kitchen, doing homework.'

Bert frowned. He had no desire for his daughter to be running wild around the estate, especially with Duncan and his pals, but she was a little too sensible for his liking. It wasn't normal.

'She's an odd kid all right,' he said.

Sarah had a soft spot for her granddaughter,

much as she loved her grandsons, especially the two rips named for her dead sons. She also loved Breda's little girl Linda, cheeky monkey though she was, but between her and Janet there was a special bond.

It had grown with the resemblance she'd had to her mother as a small child, when Sarah had looked after the children so that Betty could do her ARP work during the war. Sarah was aware very early of Janet's ability to listen and absorb. She'd sit for hours and listen intently to her gran recounting an incident from her own childhood, or Betty's. Sometimes she'd interrupt with a question, but most times she'd stay still and quiet.

She'd been able to read before she went to school, because Sarah had read to her often and she'd picked up the words. They'd chosen books together from the public library in Erdington village, but though Sarah had told Betty about the trips there, she never let on that Janet could read. She told Janet to keep it to herself too, for she had an idea the teachers wouldn't like it. She hadn't been as surprised as her daughter when the teachers had commented on Janet's intelligence, but she'd said nothing. She wasn't certain now that the grammar school was the solution for Janet, and was of the opinion that men didn't like girls who were too clever. But she wouldn't let anyone put her granddaughter down either.

She looked at her son-in-law now over the top of the glasses she held on the tip of her nose in order to see the stitches on the needles, and said:

45

'She's all right, your Janet, a good lassie. Just because she finds no pleasure in running wild doesn't mean she's odd.'

'I didn't mean odd exactly,' Bert said, uncomfortable under Sarah McClusky's unfriendly scrutiny. 'Just different.'

And she *was* different, he thought, as he opened the door to say good night. She was bent over her books so intently she hadn't heard the click of the latch. Brought up as she was in a house with a brash elder brother and two younger ones prone to yelling and screaming their way through the day, she'd learnt to cut herself off from everyday noises that could distract.

So Bert had to speak before Janet jerked up from the exercise book she'd been writing in. Her eyes held a note of impatience, he noticed, and it annoyed him. But he made an attempt to try and understand this young daughter of his, who somehow held herself away from him.

'What are you doing?' he asked.

'English,' Janet answered shortly, and then, because she knew that had sounded rude, she went on, 'We have to write an essay and then I have an exercise in maths.'

'Why didn't Duncan have homework like this when he was at Paget Road Primary?' Bert asked, genuinely puzzled.

Janet shrugged. 'Maybe he didn't want homework,' she said.

'Want it! Do you mean you don't have to do it?'

You do if you want to get into grammar school, Janet could have said. She could imagine the explosion that would cause. Anyway, her mother had told her she'd handle it, so she just said:

'You can have it if you like.'

'And you like, do you?' Bert shook his head. He couldn't understand an attitude like that.

'Yes, yes, I do.'

What could he say to that? He patted his daughter's head self-consciously. 'Don't work too hard then,' he said, 'and bed by nine.'

'I know,' Janet said impatiently. She didn't understand why her dad was suddenly so interested. Her gran would tell her it was time for bed if she were to get immersed in something and forget the time. Her father was seldom at home at bedtime, but she knew if she wasn't in bed when her mother came in, she'd catch it.

'Well, good night then,' Bert said uncomfortably. He was aware that his daughter was just waiting for him to go. She was regarding him as an intrusion, he thought suddenly, and had only spoken to him to be polite. All the time he'd been in the kitchen she'd remained bent over her books, with her pen poised, waiting to continue.

Bert banged the kitchen door behind him angrily. Janet had got under his skin, but there was nothing in her manner of speaking to him that he could tell her off for. It was just a feeling he had.

Mrs McClusky looked across at him and said, 'You go slamming doors like that, I'll have the two rapscallions awake again.'

Bert glared at her. He longed to tell her to shut her mouth, but didn't dare. Instead he made his way out of the front door, deliberately banging it loudly behind him. He called out to Duncan to get himself indoors, in a voice that brooked no argument, then hurried through the cold, dark streets to the club, where he always found congenial company.

Janet heard her mother come in, and the murmur of voices between Mrs McClusky and her daughter. She heard her grandmother leave. In fact, so alive were her senses, she imagined she heard her mother filling the kettle, and the pop of the gas.

She lay and gazed at the ceiling in the smallest bedroom, which she had all to herself. She wondered if she would be able to work up here – that was, of course, if she was ever to get to the grammar school. She had a wardrobe and a chest of drawers in the room, and Mom had said she'd get her a mirror to sit on top of the chest so it would be like a dressing table. But really she needed a desk. She wondered if she could use it for homework if she cleared the top off. But it was rather high – at least it was for the plain wooden chair which was the only other thing in the room. Then there was no place to put her legs, they'd have to dangle to the sides. And then it could be very cold up there in the winter. She'd have to wear her overcoat to work up here. But she was seriously worried about working in the kitchen if she got into the grammar school and had the masses of homework Miss Wentworth had told her about.

Duncan came in every evening filthy dirty and starving hungry. Gran or Mom would make him wash at the sink and he'd splash water everywhere. Then he'd make great wads of bread and jam, smearing the table and leaving the sticky knife lying there. Or he'd make cocoa, stirring the sugar in so vigorously that the brown liquid slopped all over. Janet's books had already had more than one lucky escape from Duncan's attempts at preventing himself from starving to death.

Then there were the twins... Janet wasn't aware how they did it, but their hands were nearly always sticky, and ranged from merely grubby to filthy. She shuddered at the thought of them handling her things. They were messier than Duncan and twice as clumsy, and what if they were to get hold of a crayon and scribble over her work? No, somehow, she decided as she closed her eyes, she had to work in her bedroom.

She was jerked suddenly awake and lay for a moment wondering what had roused her. The louder buzz of voices from the living room told her that her father was home; it was him coming in that had probably woken her. It had happened countless times before, and Janet had always turned over and gone to sleep again. She prepared to do this now. Her bed was warm and she was cosy, but she couldn't rest.

She wondered if her mom would broach the subject of the eleven-plus to her father that night. Miss Wentworth had told her that the first exam was soon, and that she needed extra tuition. She knew her mother couldn't wait indefinitely, and she also knew that Mom tended to tackle things straight away, head on.

She'd loved to have heard what they were

saying, but although she could hear the drone of voices they weren't distinct enough to make out the actual words. She wondered if she should get out of bed. She'd never listened at doors before, but this was her future they were discussing.

The cold made her gasp as she stood on the freezing linoleum in her bedroom, and her bed looked very welcoming. She turned her back on it, slipped a jumper over her head and old shoes on her feet and tiptoed out to huddle on the stairs.

Bert and Betty were having a cup of cocoa before bed. Bert had had enough to drink to make him view the world with a rosy glow, and his earlier bad mood was forgotten.

Betty was glad that her husband had reached that mellow point, because she had to get this business of Janet and the exam cleared up. Her daughter and the teacher were keen enough, and she wanted what was best for Janet. She knew that speed was essential. It was also essential for another reason, but no one knew about that but Breda.

'Not again!' she'd exclaimed as Betty whispered her suspicions to her sister that evening.

'Ssh,' Betty cautioned. They'd been in the canteen, and Breda's voice carried.

'Well, I mean, Bet, really,' Breda said, though she lowered her voice considerably. 'What you trying to do? Populate the whole of the bleeding British Isles by yourself?'

'Don't be daft,' Betty said. 'It just happened.'

'Don't you be daft,' Breda retorted. 'It doesn't just happen. You know what causes it, for God's

50

sake. Didn't he take any precautions?'

'What do you mean?'

'Come on, girl, you weren't born yesterday. Don't he wear a johnny? You know what they are.'

Betty couldn't believe that such words were coming out of her younger sister's mouth.

'I ... I've never ... I couldn't ... Bert wouldn't.'

Breda looked at her sister with pity. 'You couldn't even bring it up with him, could you?'

Miserably, Betty shook her head. 'Then you have to get yourself seen to,' Breda said. 'As soon as this is over, I'm taking you up the clinic.'

'What d'you mean?'

'I thought you knew all about it, our Bet,' Breda said in amazement. She shook her head sorrowfully. 'It's like you were born yesterday. Look,' she went on, 'there's this little rubber thing that you shove up inside you and it protects you, you see.'

'Oh no, I couldn't,' Betty said.

'Course you could,' Breda retorted. 'I do. Anyway, Bet, the choice as I see it is, either you use this cap that your old man don't have to know anything about, or you tell him to keep his bloody hands to himself when he reaches out in the dark.'

'He was away six years,' Betty said, somewhat stiffly.

'I know that. So were countless others, like my Peter. Doesn't give him the right to try and populate the universe single-handed,' Breda said. 'Anyway, our Linda's one body's work, and I certainly don't want no more.'

Betty stared at her sister. Breda knew as well as

51

Betty did that it was wrong to plan one's family. The priests were telling you that all the time.

Neither of the sisters went to church very often now, but they'd been brought up as staunch Catholics and the Church's teaching went deep. Betty had been a regular attender when she was younger, and even when she was first married, and Duncan had been down to go to the Abbey Roman Catholic school, just outside Erdington village, and a short bus ride away. When war broke out, however, and Betty joined up as an ARP warden, Duncan was enrolled in Paget Road, just round the corner from where they lived, and Janet followed him there.

The priest had called to see Betty after her prolonged absence from church had been noted, but by that time, Mrs McClusky was beginning to curse the God who had taken her son from her, and was short with the priest. He came back later, when Betty was at home. 'I have to send the children to school somewhere,' she cried when the priest appeared to judge her by his very silence, 'and it's too much for Mom fetching them from the Abbey.'

'I understand it's difficult for you at the moment,' the priest said soothingly.

'Do you?' Betty burst out angrily, suddenly enraged that the priest was seemingly untouched by a war that had ripped their family apart. 'Do you really? My husband's overseas, one brother's dead, the other two are still fighting. My parents haven't time to grieve, they're too busy looking after Duncan and Janet so I can work as an ARP warden. In our own small way, we are doing our bit to win this war, and you are concerned about where my children go to school.'

The priest never came back, and Betty felt as if she'd scored a small triumph. Yes, she'd had her moment of rebellion, but a sin was still a sin.

She hesitated to broach the subject with Breda, certain that her sister would mock, but her conscience troubled her. She had to try.

'Breda, don't you worry about saying things like that?'

'Like what?'

'You know, planning your family.'

Breda stared at Betty. She couldn't understand her sister. All that carnage of war, all those people mutilated and killed, and she still believed in God and was terrified to do what the priests said was wrong. How the hell would they know anyway? she thought.

Aloud she said, 'Don't tell me you believe it's a sin, or I'll fall about laughing.'

Betty was silent.

'You do, don't you?' Breda cried. 'How can it be anyone else's business how many children people have?'

Betty didn't know. She was hazy over the reasons why the Church was against birth control; she just knew they were. The hooter went before she could think of an answer. Break was over and it was back to work for the rest of the shift, her thoughts whirling in her head.

She was on the capping machine and so was working on her own, with no opportunity to talk to Breda, or anyone else either. It was as they walked home together that Breda suddenly said:

'What did your Bert say when you told him?'

'I haven't told him,' Betty said.

'Why not?'

'I've only just missed. I mean, it could all be a false alarm.' But she knew it couldn't be. This would be her fourth pregnancy, and the bodily changes, though minimal so far, were definite enough.

'Is that the real reason?'

Betty hesitated, and then said, 'Part of it. I want to keep it a secret a bit longer anyway. I mean, he'll hardly be pleased. We have enough of a struggle to manage now, and there's this business of our Janet wanting to sit the eleven-plus.'

Breda was impressed, but not totally surprised. 'Mam mentioned something about it,' she said. 'Your Janet always was bright, though.'

'The teacher thinks so too,' Betty said. 'And she thinks Janet has a good chance of getting through the exam, but...'

'Bert's not keen,' Breda put in.

'He doesn't think it's necessary,' Betty said.

'Course it isn't necessary,' Breda said sarcastically. 'Not for him it's not. As long as he has someone to cook his dinner, wash and iron his clothes, clean up after him, look after his kids and be ready to accommodate him in bed, he's happy. He goes to work, and on Friday he tips up the amount of money he thinks you should manage on, and if you can't it's your fault. The rest is his, to spend at the club, or betting on a horse, or going to football, or any other bloody thing he likes.'

'He's not like that,' Betty protested. 'He's a

good man, he cares for us.'

'He *is* like that,' Breda replied, 'but it's not his fault. It's been that way for years. Your Bert's not used to any other way, and he's better than many. But do you think Janet will be happy with a life like that?'

Betty knew she wouldn't be. Breda didn't need an answer; Betty's silence spoke for her.

'You needn't wait for men to change things and fight for an independent life for women. It's women have got to do it for each other, or condemn our daughters to looking no further than the kitchen sink and having a baby every year.'

'It's down to me, then, to fight for our Janet?' Betty said.

'Too right,' Breda replied. 'But don't waste your ammunition. Don't fire till you see the whites of his eyes.'

'You are a fool, Breda,' Betty said, but even in the dark, Breda could tell she'd made her sister smile, and she was glad. She was sorry Betty was pregnant again. She really had enough to do now. The birth of the twins had really dragged her down. She'd not been the same since. She should have put her foot down long ago, as Breda had done with Peter.

Peter hadn't believed his luck when Breda agreed to marry him after the war. He'd adored her before he went, but she'd kept him at a distance and he hadn't even felt able to ask her to write to him. On the rare occasions he was home on leave, Breda always seemed involved with another man. But when he was demobbed, he came home to find her still single. He couldn't understand why no one had snapped her up. She even seemed pleased to see him, and told him how glad she was he'd survived the war.

In Peter's opinion, she was the most stunning-looking woman for miles, with her mane of auburn curls cascading down her back and her flashing green eyes. When she insisted that he tip his wages up every Friday and they'd work out a budget for everything – personal pocket money for each of them and a bit saved – it seemed sensible. When Linda was born and Breda said that one was enough, Peter agreed that since she'd carried the baby and given birth to it, and had the major job of bringing it up, it had to be her decision. He wasn't keen on taking precautions himself, but was quite prepared for Breda to go and get something. He also appreciated the fact that she left his dinner ready, just to heat over a pan, when he came home from work. First, though, he fetched Linda from the neighbour who looked after her for them, and put her to bed. He always had the tea mashed and a snack meal in the making for Breda when she got in. He said it was only fair.

Breda knew that Betty had a different life, because she'd seen Bert's chauvinistic attitudes. He was typical; it was Peter who was different. Breda knew it would be the next generation of women who could change things for the majority.

'When *are* you going to tell Bert then?' she asked Betty.

'I'm trying to keep it till the exams are over,' Betty said.

'When's that?'

'The first is in November, the second in early February.'

'You'll never keep it till then,' Breda said. 'Not February you won't. Christ, Betty, you swelled up like a bleeding elephant last time.'

'I was having twins then,' Betty reminded her sister. 'You'd hardly remember how I was with the other two.'

'Maybe it's twins again,' Breda said cheerfully.

'Don't. I'd go mad if I had two more like Conner and Noel,' Betty said. 'I love them, don't get me wrong, but they have me run off my feet.'

'Don't tell me, it's bad enough with one.'

'Anyway,' Betty said, 'if I can get Bert to change his mind about the first exam, before he knows about the baby and the additional expense that'll mean, it'll be something. If she passes, she automatically goes through, and if she fails, well, that's that, isn't it?'

'She won't fail,' Breda said. 'I know she won't. I've got faith in that girl.'

Betty kept that in mind as she faced Bert. She was unaware of her daughter trembling on the stairs; unaware that her words sent a shiver of icy fear down Janet's spine.

'I went to see our Janet's teacher today,' Betty said. 'That Miss Wentworth.'

'Oh, aye.' Fuddled by beer, Bert wasn't even on his guard.

'Thinks our Janet has a good chance of getting this eleven-plus.'

Bert pulled himself up in the chair. 'You told her, though,' he said, 'you told her we don't want

57

her taking no exams?'

'No,' Betty said, 'I didn't say that, because it wouldn't have been true. I said you weren't keen but that I was agreeable if that's what Janet wanted.'

Bert was astounded. His wife had never gone against him before. 'You said that,' he said indignantly, 'after I made myself clear the other evening?'

'Yes, yes, I did.'

'Am I not master in my own house now?'

'This is about Janet and her life, not yours.'

'I'm her father,' Bert thundered. 'I say what goes in this family.'

His mellowness and good humour, restored at the pub, had left him. His wife and daughter ganging up on him. He wouldn't stand for it.

'How long has this been going on?' he demanded.

'How long has what been going on?'

'This conniving between you.'

'Oh, Bert, don't be stupid.'

'Oh, it's stupid I am now?'

'Look, Bert, I'm sick of this,' Betty said. On the stairs Janet sat hugging her knees, rocking slightly as sobs shook her body. Her parents didn't hear her; they were too busy shouting at one another.

'We're talking about giving our daughter a choice in her life,' Betty cried. 'Why are you going on as if it's a bloody crime?'

'I'm not.'

'You bloody well are. Duncan had the choice, why not Janet?'

'Duncan was different.'

'Why, because he made a choice you approved of?' Betty asked. 'Or is it more than that?'

'And what do you mean by that remark?'

'Are you cross because your daughter has the chance Duncan didn't have the ability to take up, even if he'd wanted to? Do you think daughters are of no account and anything will do to occupy them until they marry and become a slave to some man?'

There was some truth in Betty's accusations, and Bert was quite ashamed of his feelings put into words like that, but he wasn't going to admit it.

'That isn't what I think,' he said.

'Isn't it, Bert Travers?' Betty said quietly, and it was Bert who looked away first.

'Let her try, Bert,' Betty pleaded. 'The first exam is in November. Miss Wentworth says that even with her being bright she'll need extra coaching. If she doesn't get in, that will be the end of it. We'll know by Christmas.'

Bert still didn't speak, but Betty knew him well enough to know he was wavering. She went on while he was in this muddle of indecision. 'The factory is probably the right place for our Duncan, he'll likely be happier there than at school at any rate, but our Janet is not Duncan. You'll have to give her this opportunity to do something better, or ... or she might hold it against us for the rest of her life.'

Bert looked at his wife, but he wasn't seeing her. He was seeing his daughter before he'd left that evening, resenting his intrusion into her life.

Was that because she imagined him to be the stumbling block in her wish to go to the grammar school? And if he stood alongside his principles and refused to let her take the exam, would she get over it eventually, or would she always hate him?

He wouldn't, couldn't take that chance. He sighed. 'All right,' he said slowly, as if the words were being pulled out of him. 'Let her take the bloody exam and we'll see how clever she is.'

Janet allowed a long, shuddering sigh to escape from her body. She felt as if she'd been holding her breath for hours. No one heard her creep back to bed, although her limbs were so stiff with cold she stumbled a few times before she reached her bedroom.

No one heard because Betty and Bert were entwined with one another. 'You won't be sorry, Bert,' Betty said. 'You'll see.'

'You could reward me for being the understanding sort tonight if you'd have a mind,' Bert said with an ogling leer.

And Betty smiled as she said, 'Maybe.'

After all, she said to herself later that night, it's a bit bloody late to make a stand now.

Chapter Three

After that, it was fairly easy. Bert had given permission for Janet to take the exam, and he accepted the fact that twice a week, Wednesday evening and Saturday afternoon, Janet would go to Miss Wentworth's home for special tuition. The rest of the week, she would work at home.

On the day of the first exam, a hollow-eyed Janet, who had slept very little, was surprised to find her father in the kitchen when she came downstairs. It was Saturday, and Bert hadn't to work. There was little enough overtime these days, and he usually enjoyed a lie-in at the weekend, but there he was, large as life.

He made no mention of the exam, no comment at all that it was a special day, but Janet was glad he was there to wish her all the best.

'Now, what would you like for breakfast this fine morning, Miss Janet?' he asked.

'Oh, nothing,' Janet said. 'I ... I couldn't eat anything, Dad.'

'Couldn't eat anything when I've got up specially to cook it?'

Betty had followed Janet downstairs. The two stared at him in astonishment. 'You!' they both said together.

'You had to do your bit in the forces, you know,' Bert said. 'I'm a dab hand with bacon and eggs.'

'You never said,' Betty said accusingly.

61

'You never asked,' Bert replied. Betty and Janet laughed, and Janet wondered why it couldn't always be like this. Suddenly, the sick feeling in her stomach eased and the lump in her throat disappeared, and she smiled at her father, who was making such an effort.

'Thanks,' she said. 'I'd love bacon and egg.'

It was a great breakfast. Every subject was discussed except the first part of the eleven-plus that Janet would sit that morning. Duncan had been primed by his mother, and the twins, of course, knew nothing anyway.

At last it was time to go, and Janet went up for her coat. 'Keep an eye on her, Bet,' Bert said. 'She looks as if she hasn't slept a wink.'

'She probably hasn't. I've tossed and turned all night myself.'

'Well, at least she has something inside her. I thought if she didn't eat this morning she'd pass out on you.'

'It was a nice thought, Bert, thank you.'

'Pity I couldn't get you to eat, though,' Bert said. 'Going out with just a cup of tea is no good to anyone.'

'I'm all right,' Betty said. 'Truth is, my stomach is churning on account of young Janet. I thought it was better to keep off the fried stuff this morning.'

Janet asked the same question of her mother on the bus. 'Why didn't you have any breakfast, Mom?'

'I didn't fancy a fry-up this morning, pet. I didn't fancy anything much.'

'You used to eat bacon and egg.'

'Can't take it now, though. Must be getting old.'

'You're not old, Mom,' Janet said, and then qualified it to: 'Not that old, anyway.'

'Watch it, miss,' Betty said with a smile.

'I heard you being sick the other morning as well,' Janet said.

'It was something I ate, must've disagreed with me,' Betty said. The bus ride wasn't helping her queasiness, and she felt her stomach give a heave as they turned a sharp corner.

'Let's leave the subject of my stomach and concentrate on getting off at the right stop, shall we?' Betty said.

'Don't be silly, Mom, we have to go right into Birmingham,' Janet said with a laugh. 'We can hardly miss the terminus.'

'You're too smart by half, young Janet,' Betty said, but she smiled back at her daughter and hoped the journey wouldn't be too jerky, for she was feeling incredibly nauseous.

She knew she wouldn't be able to keep her pregnancy a secret much longer. Only the previous evening she'd seen Bert looking at her quizzically as she undressed. She'd tell them this weekend, she decided. After all, Janet would be over the first hurdle, and it would give them something else to think about besides her results.

'We're here, Mom,' Janet said suddenly. 'This is it.'

The exam room was meant to be intimidating, with its rows and rows of single desks, and Janet was glad Miss Wentworth had warned her that it would be like that. She had to walk nearly up to the end row, because her name came late in the alphabet. She stared at the other children and they stared back, and Janet knew they were as frightened as she was.

Just before she went into the room, Betty had pressed a package into her hand.

'A lucky shamrock,' she said. 'Gran had it specially sent from Ireland to bring you luck today.'

Janet wondered if she'd be allowed to have her lucky shamrock on the table with her, and then she saw that most of the children had something: a teddy, a small horseshoe, a rabbit's foot. Her shamrock sat at the side of the desk in its little box, and reminded Janet that her grandparents were rooting for her too.

She didn't find the papers that hard. Miss Wentworth had done her work well. She'd obtained old English, maths and intelligence papers and they'd worked through them at her house. Now Janet finished those in front of her with ease. Then she looked at all the other children and was assailed by doubts. She'd made a complete mess of the tests! She must have or she wouldn't have finished in the time allotted. English was the only paper she needed more time for, and that was only because she overran on the essay.

As Janet suffered inside the examination room, Betty suffered outside it. At one point she felt she had to get out of the soulless corridor in which all the parents were waiting and had gone to look around the city shops. She seldom had a chance to visit Birmingham centre now with the demands of her family. She soon realised she wasn't taking anything in and was constantly looking at her watch, willing it to be time to collect her daughter. Eventually, she forced herself to drink a cup of coffee, but it was a struggle, for her stomach was churning more than ever.

It's not the end of the world if she doesn't pass, she told herself. It's only an examination, and she's only a child. They shouldn't be under such pressure. But she knew that for Janet it would be the end of the world, and she sent a silent prayer up to the God she still believed in and asked His help for her daughter.

On the way home on the bus, because she felt peculiarly drained and was a bag of nerves because of the strain of it all, Janet didn't speak much and answered questions as briefly as possible. What Betty wanted to say was 'How did it go?' but she looked at Janet's white, drawn face as she came out of the examination room and didn't dare. She told Bert she thought it had gone badly, and everyone kept off the subject so that Janet would not be upset.

Janet thought it odd that no one mentioned the exam. It was just as if she'd not sat it at all. They don't think I've passed, she thought, and her own confidence began to ebb away. She went to Miss Wentworth's on Sunday afternoons now, as well as on Saturday afternoons and Wednesday evenings. Sometimes she wondered why she bothered, or why Miss Wentworth still wanted to coach her.

When the Christmas cards began arriving,

Janet was in a fever of anxiety. When at last the long, thin brown envelope dropped on to the mat, she picked it up with trembling fingers and handed it to Betty.

'I can't open it,' she said.

Betty took the envelope and tore it open. 'Oh my God!' she cried, her eyes bright with unshed tears of disbelief. 'You've passed, lass, you've bloody well passed.'

Bert took his family out for a meal to celebrate, and after that began to talk at work about his clever lass who'd soon be going to grammar school. In vain did Janet tell him that this was just the first step, and that she had another exam to pass. In Bert's opinion, the result of the second exam was a foregone conclusion.

Many of the men at the factory expressed doubts as to the value of educating a girl. 'Boy or girl,' Bert told them, 'makes no difference. If they have the brains, they should have the opportunity, I say.'

'It's as if he was never against it in the first place,' Janet told Miss Wentworth, 'and he's so proud of me, it's embarrassing.'

Miss Wentworth smiled. 'Your mother won him over then. She was determined she would.'

'I'll say.'

It was a Wednesday evening towards the end of January, and Janet's last lesson before the final exam the following Saturday. It was bitterly cold and the roads were thick with ice. They'd finished work and were having a cup of cocoa and buttered crumpets before Janet set off home. Janet, who was sitting on the rug before the fire, stretched out her legs contentedly and said suddenly:

'I shall miss coming here.'

'I should miss it too,' said Claire Wentworth, 'if you stopped. But why would you?'

'What would be the point?' Janet said. 'I mean, the exam's on Saturday.'

'That just proves you have the intelligence to get into grammar school,' said Claire. 'My next job is to make you able to cope with it.'

'What do you mean?'

'I mean, my dear girl, that we will then embark on a course of improvement,' Claire said. 'We will visit the art gallery in Birmingham and learn a little of the lives of the artists; the natural history and science museums, where we will learn many interesting facts. We will take some of the classics from the library and read and discuss them. I will explain a couple of Shakespeare's plays to you so that you will understand more when you go to grammar school, and we will examine the rudiments of Latin.'

'Why Latin?'

'Because you may need it,' Miss Wentworth said. 'It is the basis of language, for one thing, and you need it to get into many universities.'

'You think I'll go to university?' Janet asked incredulously.

'Janet, you're not eleven years old yet. Who knows what you'll achieve, or where you'll end up? We must cover all the options. And when you go to grammar school, I want you to go on equal terms, not as a scholarship girl to be pitied.'

Years later, Janet would realise how wise Claire

Wentworth had been. Now, she was just thankful that her visits to her teacher's small terraced house in Erdington weren't coming to an abrupt halt.

The second part of the eleven-plus had to be taken at Whytecliff School, because that was Janet's first choice. As the school was in Sutton Coldfield, outside Birmingham's boundaries, Janet and Betty had to go on the Midland Red bus, not on one of Birmingham's yellow and blue ones. Janet had never been on one before, nor had she ever been into the small town of Sutton Coldfield itself. The bus took them along Eachelhurst Road and down the side of Pype Hayes Park, lined with prefabs, a legacy from the war. It was just past the park's perimeter and over the Birmingham border. This was the furthest Janet had ever been from her home. She looked out at the large detached houses set well back from the road, with long front gardens and drives that disappeared behind privet hedges. 'Think of the cost of all the coal you'd need to heat one of those places,' Betty whispered, seeing Janet's concentrated gaze.

'I think if you were that rich you wouldn't have to worry about the price of coal,' Janet whispered back. She wondered if any girls from the houses they were passing would be sitting the second part of the exam with her that day, but there were no girls of Janet's age at the bus stops; in fact, more often than not, nobody was at the bus stops and the bus just sailed past.

Janet began to feel nervous as they went further and further into unfamiliar territory. 'How will we know our stop, Mam?' she asked as the bus trundled along.

'The conductor will tell us,' Betty assured her. 'Don't worry.'

They passed farmland, with fields stretching out on either side, and then a few big houses scattered here and there, even larger than the first ones they'd seen. Then suddenly the conductor alerted them, and they alighted from the bus and stood looking about them. 'Whytecliff High School for Girls' was written in gold lettering above two wrought-iron gates which stood wide open. The school was in a road with other houses of similar size dotted along it, but in the distance Janet could see farmland. Suddenly she was unaccountably nervous. She moved forward cautiously and saw a sweeping gravel path which led to a large, imposing building set well back.

Now Janet saw the other girls. It appeared that no one else had come by bus. Most were getting out of private cars or taxis, and some drove past Janet and Betty as they crunched their way forward. Janet felt conspicuous and ill at ease.

As she approached the school she saw tennis courts positioned on either side of it, and a thrill ran through her as she realised that one day she might be there, playing tennis with other girls like herself. She looked up and saw the ornamental bushes decorating the front of the school and the wide stone steps that led up between them from the path. There were two newel posts at the bottom, decorated with stone balls, and a rail ran up either side and a balustrade along the top.

As Janet joined the girls going in, she almost ran back down the steps and told her mother she wanted to go home. But Betty knew her daughter and pressed her forward. 'Go on,' she hissed. 'You have as much right to be here as anyone else,' and Janet held her head high and mounted the last few steps to the front entrance hall.

Betty, however, was overawed by the whole place and only waited until Janet was taken into the hall before she wandered outside. She scarcely saw the tree-lined avenues she walked along, for her thoughts and prayers were for her daughter bent over the vital examination papers.

In actual fact, despite Janet's unease at being inside Whytecliff School, she felt quietly confident that she had done well as she laid down her pen at the end of the third paper, although she recognised that the second part of the exam was much harder than the first had been.

She talked it over with Miss Wentworth that same evening. 'I finished,' she said, 'but only just.'

'Even the English paper?'

'Even that since I've done so much work on timed essays.'

'And you feel confident?'

'In the exam room I did, but now I'm not so sure.'

'Oh, Janet, believe in yourself!' Claire cried in exasperation. 'You have a good brain. Don't use it to demean yourself.'

'I don't,' Janet protested. 'It's just that I don't know. I suppose I'm worried I'll let them all down.'

'You need to be taken out of yourself more,' Claire said. 'Come over tomorrow and we'll go out for the day.'

'If I can I will,' Janet promised, 'but it might be difficult.'

Claire's eyes met Janet's, but though they were puzzled, she didn't ask questions, and Janet didn't offer an explanation.

The following afternoon, Janet fought her way through the cold and blustery winter's day with sleeting rain stinging her cheeks. Claire opened the door. 'Come in,' she said. 'You must be freezing.'

Janet hung her sopping coat in the hall and followed Claire down the passage to the back room she tended to live in, rubbing her raw, freezing hands together.

'It's bitterly cold out there,' she was saying, and then she stopped. There was a strange woman sitting in the chair by the fire that Miss Wentworth usually occupied. One of her legs was encased in plaster and raised on a cushion.

She turned and smiled, and Janet saw she was an older version of Miss Wentworth. 'Hello, dear,' she said. 'You must be Janet. My daughter has told me so much about you. I slipped on the ice, I'm afraid, and have broken my leg. Such a nuisance, I know, but there it is. Claire has said I must stay here until I'm fully recovered.'

Janet felt a momentary flash of jealousy. She didn't want to share their special times together. It was different at school, where Miss Wentworth was so scrupulously fair and was just as hard on Janet as on the others – harder if anything, never

71

picking Janet for any particular job or privilege – but that was school; this was their special time. Here Miss Wentworth was totally hers.

She stared at the older woman, quite prepared to dislike her heartily. Then Mrs Wentworth disarmed her totally with a charming smile. 'I'm sorry that you'll have to put up with an old duffer like me, Janet. I hope I won't spoil things too much.'

Janet was prevented from answering by the arrival of Claire with a tray of tea and sponge cake. 'Good job we'd made no plans,' Claire said, 'and anyway, it's a filthy day. As it turned out, after you left yesterday, Janet, Mom's neighbour, who fortunately has a car, came to fetch me and take me to the casualty department of the General Hospital. They'd called an ambulance for Mom after they found her in the garden, unable to move, with her leg broken.' She turned to her mother and said, 'Honestly, Mom, what were you doing out in the pitch black?'

'I told you,' Mrs Wentworth said, 'feeding the birds.'

'In the middle of the night?'

'Don't exaggerate, dear, it was just after seven. I'd intended to fill the feeder earlier in the day when I saw it empty, but I'd forgotten. Birds feed at first light, you see, and they need so much food in this intense cold. And it is just outside the kitchen door.'

'Well, it's as well the Pritchards heard you, that's all I can say,' Claire said, 'because if you'd lain outside all night...'

'I wouldn't be here now, I know,' said Mrs

72

Wentworth with a hint of impatience. 'But I didn't and I am here, and surely you're not going to go on and on about it until my dying day.' She turned to Janet, gave a wink and said, 'Bossy, isn't she?'

Janet thought that she could probably get to like Miss Wentworth's mother very much, and she grinned back and said, 'Yes, she is.'

'Don't encourage insurrection in my pupils, please,' Claire said with mock severity. 'I have quite enough trouble with this one already.'

'I don't believe it, my dear,' Mrs Wentworth said, taking a large bite of sponge cake. 'Come and sit here beside me, Janet, and we'll have a chat. Either bring up a chair or sit on the rug nearer to the fire.'

Janet plonked down beside the older woman and said, 'What do you want to talk to me about?'

'Before we go any further,' Mrs Wentworth said, 'I know you have to call Claire Miss Wentworth. It's to do with rules and discipline. Apparently school would fall into a crumbling ruin if children knew their teachers' names.'

'Mother!' Claire burst out in exasperation.

Mrs Wentworth waved a dismissive hand in her daughter's direction. 'I'm not talking *to* you, Claire dear, but *about* you. I'm addressing your pupil at the moment. Now, Janet, I'm sure you don't want to call me Mrs Wentworth, do you?'

'Um, I don't know really.'

'Well, I don't want you to,' said Mrs Wentworth decisively, 'but I suppose you would feel awkward calling me Mary. Could you manage Auntie Mary?'

'Er, I suppose, I mean ... that is, if you want,' Janet said, feeling that never in her life had she met anyone quite like Claire's mother.

For all that, she sat at her feet all afternoon and talked as she'd never talked before. She told her of the tales she'd learnt from her gran, and how she and Grandad had both been born in Ireland but had had to leave to find work in England, where they met and married.

She told her about Duncan, and how they'd had to spend a lot of time with their grandparents while their mother was an ARP warden and their dad was fighting. She told of the two uncles killed and the twin boys born just before the end of the war. She didn't say that her father hadn't seen the point of her sitting the exams, but what she did say was:

'My mom's sick at the moment. I mean, she's having a baby, but she's sick with it.'

'Is she, Janet?' Claire said. 'You never mentioned it.'

'She didn't tell anyone she was even pregnant until I'd sat the first part of the eleven-plus,' Janet said. 'I knew something was wrong, because I'd heard her being sick a few times and she kept saying she'd eaten something that disagreed with her. But she still keeps being sick and eats hardly anything. That's why I couldn't come till this afternoon. I have to help out a bit.'

Mary Wentworth met her daughter's eyes over Janet's head. They both realised that the young girl was worried.

'I'm sure your mother will be fine, you know,' Mary said. 'Pregnancy takes it out of a woman,

74

and of course, if she has to look after a family too, it can be hard. I only had Claire. Her father was badly injured in the First World War and died before Claire was out of babyhood.' She added, as if to herself, 'I was glad he died before the outbreak of the Second World War. I think it would have finished him to think of all that carnage starting again.' She saw Janet's grave eyes on her and gave a start.

'Forgive me, dear, I was remembering for a while how it was. It affects one like that as one grows old.'

'Stop fishing for compliments, Mother,' Claire said briskly. 'You know you don't look anywhere near your age, and you're not half as ga-ga as you make out. Now, if you will excuse me, government guidelines or no, I must get more coal for that dying fire or we'll all freeze to death.'

Because of the national shortage of coal, people had been asked to put off lighting fires till late afternoon, and then not to pile them up with coal but to use as little as possible. It was not easy, for the winter was a particularly severe one and everyone was feeling the pinch.

Janet jumped to her feet. 'I'd better go,' she said. 'Mom went for a lie-down as the twins were having a nap. That's why I was able to come. They'll be up now, I expect, and plaguing the life out of her.'

'Where's your brother?' Mary said gently. 'The older one, Duncan, is it?'

'Yes, Duncan,' Janet said. 'He'll be playing football or something. He's no good, he's a boy. And my dad went down to the club after dinner and he'll probably be snoring his head off.'

'Ah, that's men for you,' Mary said.

'That's men all right,' Janet said fiercely. 'I don't think I'm going to bother getting married.'

'That's what Claire always said too.'

'Well, she didn't, did she?' Janet said. 'I mean, you didn't, did you, Miss Wentworth?'

'No, I didn't.' Claire didn't say that there had been somebody once who she had been willing to throw everything up for, but he hadn't loved her enough and they'd gone their separate ways. That wasn't the sort of confidence you shared with a pupil of not quite eleven years. Her mother knew. She was the one who'd picked up the pieces of Claire's shattered heart and given her back her self-respect, but she didn't want to tell the tale either.

As Janet trudged home, she determined that that was how she would be: single, independent and alone. People mocked single women, she knew that. They called them old maids and spinsters, but if you got married, you were little more than a slave.

This was further reinforced when she got home. It was just as she'd said it would be: Duncan kicking a football in the road with a crowd of mates, her father snoring in the chair. Her twin brothers had woken up from their nap, climbed out of their cots and systematically set about destroying the bedroom.

Janet popped in to see her mother, who was sleeping the sleep of the totally exhausted. Sighing, she ushered her young brothers downstairs and began to prepare tea for them all.

As Betty's pregnancy advanced, she became more and more tired. Often, Janet would arrive home to find her mother asleep and the twins with Auntie Breda or Gran. Even with Janet home, Betty seemed loath to move.

'Get me a cup of tea, pet,' she'd say, 'and I'll be as right as rain.'

So Janet would make a cup of tea and fetch the twins and make up the fire and cook a meal for all of them. Duncan would come flying in and demand: 'What's for tea? I'm starving,' and Janet wanted to hit him. Betty continued to work in the evenings, though Bert and the doctor urged her to stop.

'A few more weeks,' she'd said. 'The money's useful.'

As often as she could, Janet escaped to Claire's. It was the only place she could let down her guard. At home she had to be the one to cope and encourage her mother to rest. At Claire's she could be a child again.

'It will be worth it all when you have a new brother or sister, won't it?' Mary said one day.

Janet was a long time answering. She didn't know how to be truthful and yet not shock this woman whose good opinion she craved.

'Babies are lovely,' she said at last. 'They're sweet and innocent, but really it's better if they're someone else's and you can hold them and play with them and then give them back, like I used to be able to do with Auntie Breda's Linda.'

'Oh, surely...'

'Mom doesn't want this baby,' Janet said.

'Oh, I'm sure that's nonsense, my dear,' Mary

said. 'Sometimes grown-ups say things they don't mean.'

Janet said nothing, but she knew she was right. She'd heard her mother and Auntie Breda talking about it.

'You should have done something about it earlier,' Auntie Breda had said. 'I know people ... qualified ... you know.'

'Ah, not that!' her mother had cried, aghast. 'God in heaven, Breda, what are you suggesting? You haven't...?'

'No, I haven't,' Breda said. 'I had a good time in the war, but I wasn't a bleeding fool like some of them. I tell you, some of them in the munitions were wetting themselves to find they were expecting and their husbands overseas and been there a couple of years. Many were glad, I'll tell you, to be able to get rid of it.'

'Well, that's hardly my position.'

'No, it isn't. But you can't look me in the eye and say you want it.'

'No, God forgive me, I don't want it, but I couldn't get rid of it. I dare say I'll think enough of it when it comes.'

Poor little baby, Janet thought, no one wants it. Duncan when told just raised his eyes to the ceiling. Privately he said to Janet, 'More bloody yelling and nappies all over the house.' He leaned closer and added, 'I didn't think they did that sort of thing any more, did you?'

'What sort of thing?'

'Oh God!' he'd said. 'You do know all about it, don't you, sex and that?'

'Course I do,' Janet said, but she didn't. She

78

was totally ignorant of most sexual matters and was very vague about how babies materialised, but she wasn't letting on to Duncan.

He sneered, 'You don't know anything, do you? And you so blooming clever.'

'I do,' Janet had cried. She was aware of the hot blush that had spread all over her face and down her neck. and she'd run from her brother.

Bert had called the baby another bloody millstone round his neck.

'It's as if he had nothing to do with it,' Breda said angrily. 'He should have thought, taken a few precautions.'

'He's only worried.'

'And you're not? And that's another thing. He should do more. He can see the way you are.'

'Our Janet's very good.'

'Janet's a child. She has her own life and her future to think of.'

Too right, Janet thought. She was glad that Breda at least thought of her. It came to her with absolute clarity one night in bed that whatever sex the new baby was, it would have to share her small room. There was no more space to be found in the boys' room, nor would there be much in hers. Bang went her plans for working at night in her bedroom. Even if she could have persuaded her parents to buy her a desk, there would now be nowhere to put it.

She would work in the kitchen, where her books would be at the mercy of her messy family. She would devise an essay, or work out algebraic equations, while stale cooking smells mingled with the aroma of the damp nappies strung across the kitchen on a line. She wanted to weep, and yet she knew she was being selfish. Duncan had never complained about sharing with the twins. He'd just accepted it and asked Bert to buy him a padlock so he could lock treasures away. Janet felt ashamed of herself, but she didn't want this baby either.

She wasn't losing sight of her goal, though. Underlying all the worry of the family she was aware that one day an insignificant brown envelope would drop through the letterbox and its contents would decide where she would spend the next few years of her life. Because whether she passed or not, she'd have to leave Paget Primary in July.

Claire had decided to put off the visits to Birmingham until the spring, when the weather would be better and her mother might be fully recovered and returned to her own home. Until then, they explored Claire's extensive library. They'd read *Wuthering Heights* and *Jane Eyre*, *Silas Marner* and *The Mayor of Casterbridge* and two of Shakespeare's plays. Janet never took the books home; she read them only at Claire's. Sometimes Claire would read out loud, and occasionally Mary would.

After a chapter or two, Claire and Janet would discuss what they'd read. In the beginning, it was Claire asking the questions and Janet answering. But gradually, so gradually she had not been aware of it happening, Janet was starting to analyse what she read. She was able to talk about characterisation, the structure of the plots, how the tension was built up and the dialogue between the characters.

Sometimes, if Claire had marking to do or something to attend to, Janet would play chess or backgammon with the woman she called Auntie Mary. But what she really liked to do was talk to her about Claire, her Miss Wentworth.

She attempted to model herself on the woman who'd taken her so far. Mary realised what she was doing and told her of the fun Claire had had at school, and the gaggle of girlfriends always at the house. 'They had boyfriends,' she said, 'but nothing serious.' She hoped Claire would forgive that small lie.

'They tended to go round in groups anyway,' Mary said.

'None of them wanted to be tied down, certainly not while they were at school.'

'But after school?' Janet persisted.

'They were split up then. Most of Claire's friends went on to university, but of course they went to different ones, or were on different courses. Universities, though, are the place to make new friends. She went to Reading University near London. I had an aunt living in London then, and Claire used to visit from time to time.'

'Where did she live, Auntie Mary?'

'In the university halls,' Mary told her. 'I was rather worried about her, but I needn't have been. She said it was a marvellous experience, and it's led to a job she enjoys and independence.'

'Yes,' breathed Janet.

'And that's probably the path your own life will

take,' Mary said.

'Yes,' said Janet again. 'Yes, yes, yes, that's what I want.'

Later that same day, when Claire and Janet were discussing the merits of Keats' poetry, Janet suddenly said, 'Have you ever had anyone else pass the eleven-plus before me?'

'I haven't,' Claire admitted. 'That's not to say other colleagues haven't, but remember the disarray the country was in for six years. Many children had part-time or sporadic schooling, or none at all. You'll find now that most of the schools like Paget Road will have a steady increase in the numbers of children going through the scholarship scheme.'

'I hope so,' Janet said. She felt odd and different being the only one, and wished there was another girl to go with.

Claire didn't say that she found coaching Janet more exhausting and time-consuming than she'd thought, and it put severe restrictions on her private life. She'd already decided that any further children would be taught in extra lessons at school – she'd not open her home again, nor would she get so involved – but all these thoughts she kept from Janet.

She didn't explain either that she didn't intend to live like a nun for the rest of her life. She didn't tell Janet about David Sunderland, who she'd met at a teachers' conference after work one day, or about how he'd complained bitterly when she'd explained how her weekends were tied up. She didn't tell Janet that they'd been out together a few times and she liked him very much.

She didn't understand the pedestal Janet had put her on, and didn't know Janet assumed she would work her way through life independently and free of any man, because Janet could tell her none of this.

The Easter holidays were looming and Claire believed that the day of reckoning would come before they returned to school. Betty Travers eventually gave up work. The baby was expected at the end of May and she thought it was time. Mary had had her plaster cast removed and had returned home where the obliging neighbours, the Pritchards, would be able to take her to the hospital in their car for physiotherapy.

Claire would have missed her mother more if David Sunderland hadn't been around. Janet's presence at the house was intermittent now and she could never stay long, as her mother's confinement was getting closer.

David didn't like Claire constantly talking about the girl. 'You've done more for her than for any other child in your class,' he said. 'You have forty-nine others to concern yourself with, often from far worse homes and tragic beginnings.'

Claire couldn't disagree with David. He was right. 'You've given her a start few others have had, and certainly no one else at your school,' he went on. 'Now she's either got fed up or is needed at home, but whatever the reasons for her absence, you must let her go, Claire.'

It was true, Claire knew that. Janet was strangely elusive, even at school. She arrived often just as the bell was ringing, flew out of the door at lunchtime and left on the dot of four in the afternoon.

It was hard to find out how things were when Claire wasn't even able to snatch a quiet word with her. By tacit consent neither of them spoke about Janet's visits to Claire's house. They were well aware that the other children would make Janet's life a misery, and even the school authority might view it unfavourably. They knew, of course, that the Travers' girl was in line for a grammar school place and were pleased with that. However, Claire knew they would frown on what would be termed 'overfamiliarity' between a teacher and a pupil.

A general enquiry such as 'How is your mother, Janet?' was met with: 'She's all right, thank you, Miss Wentworth.'

A request from Claire to stay behind met with an agitated entreaty: 'Oh please, Miss Wentworth, I can't, my mother relies on me. I really must go straight home.' How could Claire argue with that? She hoped that the birth of this fifth child into the Travers house might go smoothly and that afterwards life would settle down a little for Janet, but she didn't say any of this to David.

Chapter Four

By the time the Easter holidays were a few days off, Betty Travers had been in bed for over a week with high blood pressure. The family doctor, Dr Black, had wanted her shipped to hospital, but she became so distressed that he relented, but warned, 'No slipping downstairs to peel the odd potato or do a spot of ironing, mind.'

For Bert and Duncan, life went on just the same. Sarah McClusky took on most of the housework, Breda looked after the twins a lot of the time and a heavy load fell on Janet.

One day the doctor called not long after Janet had got in from school. She'd cooked tea for Duncan, the twins and herself, prepared a tray that she was going to take up to her mother and was getting her father's dinner ready to cook while she tried to stop the twins killing one another. The doctor watched her for a few minutes, then remarked, 'You're a splendid girl, Janet, and I know you're a grand help, but don't work yourself too hard. Get Duncan to help you.'

'Duncan, Doctor?' Janet said in amazement. 'He's a boy.'

'I'm aware of that,' Dr Black said with a smile.

'Well, boys don't do anything, do they?'

'What about your father?'

Janet stared at the doctor for a minute, but didn't speak. He gave a grim smile and asked,

'Aren't you going to point out that he's a man?' Without waiting for a reply, he said, 'Tell your father I'll be round to see him this evening after surgery. I think we need to have a chat.'

When Janet reported to Auntie Breda what the doctor had told her, she said, 'About time someone spoke to him. You two better come to me for your tea. I'll ask Mammy to see to Betty and your dad and get Conner and Noel to bed, but you two had better be right out of the road. Bloody good job it's Friday and I haven't got a job to go to.'

After their tea at Auntie Breda's, Duncan and Janet were sent into the living room to look after Linda while Breda talked to Peter in the kitchen. Duncan was disgusted.

'Boys don't look after babies,' he said. 'Can't I go out to play with my mates?'

'No, you can't,' Auntie Breda told him. 'I'm not having you hanging around your house. As for boys not looking after babies, you'll probably have your own one day.'

'Yeah,' Duncan said, 'but that will be my wife's job, won't it?'

'You have a lot to learn, young Duncan,' Breda said. 'The modern woman and what she wants will be like a slap in the face to you and those like you. In this house, you'll start by doing what you're bloody well told.'

Still sulking, Duncan allowed himself to be propelled into the living room, where he kicked disconsolately at the skirting board and said to Janet:

'I don't know why they've sent us round here.

86

It isn't as if we don't know what Dr Black wants to see Dad about, is it?'

'Isn't it?' said Janet. She'd picked up that the doctor wasn't pleased with her dad, but she didn't know what it was all about.

'You really are stupid sometimes, our Janet,' Duncan snapped. 'He's going to tell our dad to stop doing it ... you know...' He looked at Janet's puzzled face and burst out 'Well, they don't want more babies, do they?'

At that moment Breda's voice came clearly from the kitchen.

'Well, someone had to speak to him, Peter, and he'd never listen to me. Someone had to tell Bert Travers to keep his bleeding hands off our Betty and put them in the washing-up bowl more often.'

Peter murmured a reply but neither of the children heard it. They picked up Auntie Breda's voice more easily, high-pitched as it was with indignation.

'Well, I don't trust him. He might do what the doc says now, but as soon as that baby's born, he'll be back to groping.'

'See,' Duncan said with satisfaction.

'Ssh,' Janet cautioned, for Breda was still talking.

'He's a man like all the rest, only after one thing. I'm getting her down that clinic, get her sorted out, as soon as that kid's born.'

'What does she mean?' whispered Janet.

'Oh, it's just women's talk,' Duncan said airily. He wasn't going to admit to not knowing.

But Janet knew Duncan didn't understand. She

didn't either, but she pieced together what she did know. According to Auntie Breda, Dr Black was going to tell her dad he couldn't touch her mother any more. That would mean he couldn't kiss her, because he couldn't do that without touching. Not that her parents went in for that sort of thing much, but she supposed they did in bed. There were lots of things people did in bed that she wasn't sure of. Groping sounded pretty awful, and Janet wondered what it was. Her father obviously used to do it to her mother, because Auntie Breda said he'd be back to it. That was probably it. This groping was the thing they did that brought the babies, and Dr Black was going to tell her dad there was to be no more of it.

Bert Travers was very subdued when the children went back after Sarah had sent word that the doctor had left. He'd been soundly told off for allowing his daughter to become a drudge.

'Considering how sick your wife is, I'm surprised you're not giving more of a hand,' the doctor had continued. 'After all, Janet's not old enough to be doing everything, is she?'

Bert hadn't even really been aware of it. He never thought about what Betty did. He knew that everything got done, but she'd never complained. He'd never considered it hard work. After all, he did the hard day's work in the factory and he wasn't keen on starting again when he came home.

'Your wife is fretting upstairs,' Dr Black said. 'She says Janet looks pasty and run-down. Worry is the last thing she needs. No wonder I can't get her blood pressure down. Go on in the selfish way you have been and you'll have a sick daughter as well as a sick wife, and then where will you be?'

Bert felt suitably chastened. He hadn't realised, he said. He'd do more, and draft in young Duncan to give a hand.

But the doctor hadn't finished. 'While we are on the subject of selfishness, you do understand that this child must be the last?'

Bert gulped. 'We hadn't intended this one, Doc, not after the twins, you know.'

'Intending is one thing, making sure is quite another,' Dr Black said grimly. 'You must ensure, if you wish to continue marital relations with your wife, that you take precautions.'

Bert stared at the doctor until he snapped irritably, 'You know what I'm talking about, man, they're on sale in all the barber's shops.'

'I'm not using them things. What do you bleeding well take me for?' Bert gasped.

'Well, I hope you're just a fool and not a cruel idiot into the bargain,' Dr Black said sternly. 'I'm telling you straight, Betty has had a hard pregnancy and she has the classic signs of a hard birth. She'll not go through another one totally unscathed and I would be worried for her very survival. Take precautions or curb your natural desires, the choice is yours.'

'Some bloody choice,' Bert said gloomily.

'Well, I'll leave you to decide,' the doctor said, walking to the door. There he turned and said, 'About young Conner and Noel...'

'What about them?'

'They seem to have boundless energy and Janet is hardly able to control them. Your wife will have her hands full in the summer with a new baby as well, and she'll need to rest at times. They could start at the Gunter Road nursery in September. There is a waiting list, but I do have some influence and I could put in a word.'

'I don't know whether Betty would like them to go to a nursery,' Bert said doubtfully.

'Talk to her,' the doctor said. 'Point out the advantages. No need to make a decision yet. I'll say good evening to you, Mr Travers, and I'll be along on Monday to see your wife.'

Bloody doctor! Bert said to himself as he watched the doctor's retreating back. Bloody interfering sod!

'Bert! Bert!' Betty called from upstairs. 'Bert, was that the doctor I heard?'

Oh, bloody hell, Bert thought as he went upstairs. He told Betty how the doctor thought he might be able to get the twins into the Gunter Road nursery in September. He had just called in to tell them so they could talk about it.

'Wonder he didn't come up,' Betty said, 'and as for the twins, I don't really know. None of the others have been to nursery.'

Looking at Betty's white, strained face, Bert felt ashamed of his behaviour. It was obvious that Betty was far from well. Her lank hair, scraped back from her face, had silver streaks in, he noticed with surprise, and she heaved herself up in the bed awkwardly. His mother-in-law, sister-in-law and daughter had been the ones running up and downstairs with cups of tea and meals for

Betty while he'd just slipped into bed at night and out again in the morning and hadn't really looked at his wife at all. Now, though, he understood the doctor's concern. Something will have to be done, he thought, because I don't want to put her through this again, and another child would cripple us financially anyway. We'll have to have a talk about it when Betty is feeling stronger.

There was a get together at the McCluskys' on Easter Sunday afternoon. Janet thought it strange going without her mother, although she liked her relations. Bert promised to bring Betty some tasty goodies from the table which, Janet knew, would be groaning with food. Satisfied, Janet was glad to visit her grandparents' house, which was almost as familiar as her own. She knew Breda would be there with Peter and Linda, as well as Brendan and Patsy. They'd seen little of Brendan since his marriage. According to Mrs McClusky, part of the reason for this was that Patsy lived too near to her own mother.

'She's there so often she might as well not have left,' she'd confided to Janet.

'Now, now, Sarah,' Sean McClusky had said. 'The lassie's only young, and sure, it's only natural. You'd have something to say if our girls didn't visit often.'

A sniff was Gran's only reply. Grandad had winked at Janet, and she'd been hard pressed to prevent a giggle escaping from her.

'Anyway,' Grandad had continued, 'isn't Brendan up to his eyes in work this minute and has been run off his feet these last months?'

Janet knew that was true, because Brendan was a carpenter and in great demand after the devastation of the war.

'Likely to be that way for years,' Bert had put in, 'with the government promising new housing for the hundreds made homeless.'

'Humph,' Gran had said. 'Governments' promises are like pie crusts – made to be broken.'

Janet liked her Uncle Brendan, and she was glad that he had plenty of work. Not everyone was as fortunate. She liked his wife too, though she'd never had the opportunity to speak much to her until that Easter Sunday.

She realised almost immediately that Patsy was pregnant, just like her mother, and must be near her time too. She was, she told Janet, a shorthand typist, and though the work was fairly interesting, she had been glad to give it up and was excited about looking after her baby when it came.

'It's a shame your mother is so poorly,' she commiserated with Janet. 'Mind you, it must be a strain having a family to cope with too.' She cast an eye over the boisterous twins, who were threatening to bring the table of goodies down on top of themselves, and remarked, 'I mean, Conner and Noel seem full of beans, enough to wear anyone out, I'd say.'

'They are,' Janet agreed wholeheartedly, watching as her grandad hauled her brothers away from the table and gave them both a little shake to remind them of their manners.

'I'll bet you're hoping for a wee sister?' Patsy continued.

Janet realised with a sudden jolt that she'd not really thought about the sex of the baby her mother was soon to have. She would be eleven years old, for it was her birthday a few days after Easter, so it hardly mattered, and yet she already had three brothers, so she turned to Patsy and said:

'Yes, I suppose so.'

'Have your parents chosen any names yet?'

'No,' said Janet, 'at least they haven't said anything.' It was odd, really. As far as she knew, names had not even been discussed. It was as if the new addition to the Travers household was not a real person at all.

'You can't expect our Janet to be interested in mundane things like names for her baby brother or sister,' said Brendan teasingly. 'Professor Brainbox she is, be above the likes of you and me before she's much older.'

Breda saw the pink flush on Janet's face and said sharply, 'Leave the girl alone, Brendan, you're embarrassing her.'

'Don't mind him,' Patsy advised. 'He's so proud of you really and tells everyone he meets about his clever niece who's off to grammar school.'

Janet was mortified. What if she should fail now? she thought. She wouldn't just disappoint herself; she'd let her whole family down. Everyone was depending on her. Breda, watching Janet, was aware of what was going through her mind.

Janet crossed over to her aunt. 'What if I fail?' she whispered.

'I don't think you will,' Breda told her confidently, 'but if you do, the earth won't stop spinning on its axis and civilisation as we know it won't come to a standstill.'

'I know, but...'

'Stop it, Janet,' Breda said. 'You can't carry the hopes and expectations of the whole family on your shoulders. Patsy and Brendan have their own dreams to build on. Do you think they'll really care whether you've passed or failed when they hold their own child in their arms in a few weeks' time?'

Janet looked across to where they stood, arms linked. 'Suppose not,' she said.

'Everyone has to follow their own star,' Breda went on, 'and have their own aims and desires to reach for. They can't hitch on the back of other people. I'll be pleased if you pass for grammar school, because you want to go. All the family will be disappointed if you don't get in, for your sake, but our lives and yours will go on as before, either way.'

Auntie Breda had a way of explaining things, Janet thought, and she felt the burden of responsibility shift a little from between her shoulder blades.

'Now then,' Breda said, 'stop thinking about your old exams and go and help your grandad choose some records to put on the gramophone.'

Sean's gramophone and record collection were his pride and joy. Betty had often told her daughter how things had been in the slump and how every article a person had that was termed 'luxury' by those who determined the means test

94

for poor relief had to be sold before a family qualified for help.

'Ma sold everything we had except Da's gramophone,' she said. 'Lots of items were pawned to pay the rent or buy food, but my ma hung on to the gramophone through all that. She said Da had lost more than a job, he'd lost his self-respect, and the gramophone was the only thing he had in his life that he cared about.'

Janet was always glad they'd been able to keep it. One of her earliest memories was of her grandfather turning the handle and the sound of the Irish music of his youth spilling out of the golden microphone that rested on the top of the spinning record and helping to drown out the sound of falling bombs.

Now she walked over to where Sean sat sorting through the record collection he kept in an old wooden box, and smiled at him. 'Hello, my lass,' he said. 'You can help me choose the airs to play.'

'Something lively,' Janet said. 'A reel or something.'

'You're on,' Grandad said. 'Something that would wear those two rips out would be welcome.' He indicated Conner and Noel, who were careering around the room.

'I think,' Janet said, 'we'd be worn out before they would.'

'You could be right, Janet, aye, you could indeed,' Sean McClusky said with a chuckle. He selected a few records. 'These will do for starters.'

Janet had said she'd stay with the record player, but Brendan wouldn't hear of it and scooped her up to gallop around the room. Janet couldn't remember when she'd last had such fun. It had been a fraught time for them all for so long, and it still was of course, for her mother was no better and Janet privately thought she wouldn't improve until the baby came. She watched her dad go off with a tray full of stuff from the table for Betty and crushed down the guilt she felt at having such a good time while her mom lay so ill.

Betty was glad to see them back from the party but gladder still at the shine in Janet's eyes as she sat on the bed and told her all about it. It was the next day before Janet remembered that Patsy had asked about the baby's name. She asked her mother if she and her dad had discussed it between themselves.

'Sort of,' Betty said. 'Your dad asked if it was a boy, would I call it Timothy, or Tim, after a mate of his killed in the war.'

'Timothy,' Janet said, rolling the name round her tongue to see how she liked it. 'That's all right,' she decided, 'but what for a girl?'

'I thought I'd call a girl Sarah after me ma,' Betty said. 'I know it would please her, and we could call her Sally while she's small.'

'That's nice,' Janet said, and added, 'I hope it's a Sally, but if it's a Tim I suppose we'll have to put up with it.'

'We have to take what God sends,' Betty said, 'but ... well, it can't hurt to hope.'

Two days later it was Janet's birthday, but no one seemed to remember it. The doctor was pleased with Betty's progress and allowed her to get up, and Janet tried to be glad about that and not mind that no one had even wished her happy birthday, let alone got her a card. She kept the hurt feeling to herself.

Duncan was now supposed to make sure there was coal in for the fire and sticks chopped up. He also had to take turns with his father washing up after the evening meal, as this was Bert's way of helping Janet out with the housework. Also, as part of the new arrangements, until school opened Duncan had to take the twins out to Pype Hayes park for two afternoons in the week, if the weather was dry, to give Janet some time to herself.

This Janet looked forward to most of all, and when Duncan suggested taking them with him that Tuesday afternoon, she was delighted and thought she might slip up to Miss Wentworth, even if she hadn't remembered it was her birthday either.

She was, therefore, furious when her Auntie Breda came round and presented her with a long shopping list. 'You don't mind getting this for me, do you, Janet love?' she asked. 'I'd go myself but Linda's got a racking cough.'

Janet glared at her, but knew she could say nothing. Respect for her elders had been drummed into her all her life. She wanted to cry. It wasn't fair. It was her birthday, for goodness' sake. Why couldn't her aunt take Linda round to her gran's and do her own shopping? But she knew she could say nothing, and she took the list and the purse with money in without a word of protest.

The shopping took simply ages. Aunt Breda wanted items from the grocer, the greengrocer, the butcher and the newsagent. Every shop had a queue and the people in front of Janet seemed in no hurry as they exchanged news and snippets of gossip with the shopkeeper, along with their order. Janet hopped from one foot to the other in impatience as she willed them to hurry up. Her fidgety behaviour only caused the shopkeeper to look at her sternly and made no difference at all to the chattering shoppers.

Aunt Breda had produced two bags for her to carry the shopping in, but the weight of them dragged Janet down. She felt as if her arms were being pulled out of their sockets. It's all right for Auntie Breda, she thought crossly, stopping for the umpteenth time to rest her aching arms. She packs the shopping around Linda in the pram, or hangs the bags from the pram handle. She doesn't have to carry anything.

Slowly she carried the bags to Breda's house, only to find her aunt was out. Rage boiled through Janet's body. Linda's hacking cough, that had prevented Breda from shopping for herself, had not stopped her going out somewhere else.

'And I bet it wasn't to the flipping doctor's,' she muttered as she bumped the bags back to her own door.

There a surprise awaited her. Everyone was there: her mom, pale but up and sitting in a chair, Auntie Breda, Gran, Grandad, Duncan and the twins, and as she entered they all shouted: 'Happy birthday, Janet!'

'Did you think we'd all forgotten, Janet pet?' Gran said, seeing the tears filling Janet's eyes.

'Sorry we had to send you for the shopping,' Breda said, 'but we had to get you out of the way.'

'There's nothing wrong with Linda then?'

'Linda's as right as rain and asleep on your bed this minute,' Breda said, 'but we wanted it to be a surprise for you.'

'You wanted what to be a surprise for me?' Janet said.

In answer, her family stepped away from the table they'd been hiding from her, and she saw the party food arranged there. In the centre was a cake with 'Happy Birthday Janet' written on in icing, and eleven candles, and arranged around the cake were parcels and cards. Janet was speechless.

'Peter will be along later, and I've phoned work and said I won't be in because I'm sick,' Breda said.

'And Brendan and Patsy will come after work,' Gran said, 'and your dad, of course.'

Janet could only gape at them all.

'Are you going to catch bleeding flies all afternoon?' Breda asked with a laugh, and Janet began to gabble.

'How did ... who ... who ... how did you do it and who did it?'

'Me and Ma,' said Auntie Breda. 'After you working so hard and all, we thought you should have a bit of a party. Mammy did some, she made the cake as well, and I did the rest. Then we had it all piled in Mammy's kitchen and we had to get you out of the way and the twins too, or they would have demolished it before you'd even seen it.'

'Oh thank you, thank you.' Janet was crying, throwing her arms around her grandparents and her aunt and her mother while tears poured down her cheeks.

'Here, here,' said her grandmother, 'less of the waterworks, girl, you'll have us drowned in a minute. Open up your cards and presents and we'll leave the food until the others get here.'

From Auntie Breda was a watch. 'You'll need to organise your life from now on,' she said to Janet as she strapped it to her wrist. Her grandparents gave her a fountain pen and a bottle of ink.

'Put it to good use, my lass,' said Sarah McClusky.

'I will, said Janet. She knew it was a good pen, and an expensive one. 'I'll look after it, I promise.'

There was a pencil, a sharpener, a notebook and a rubber from the twins, and a geometry set from Duncan.

'I asked the form teacher at school before the holidays,' he said, 'and he said you'd need one of those at the grammar school.'

'Thank you, Duncan.'

There was one more parcel, which Janet supposed was from her parents, but Betty told her that Bert was bringing their present on his way home from work. This parcel was from Gran's people in Ireland: a wooden pencil box into which all the twins' gifts fitted neatly.

They were all drinking a cup of tea Breda had made when Brendan and Patsy came in and handed Janet another parcel. Janet was almost too overawed to mutter her thanks when she pulled a brown leather satchel from the wrapping. It was so beautiful and she stroked it almost reverently.

'Oh,' she cried, 'oh, it's lovely. Oh thank you, thank you.'

Inside, despite her happiness, Janet was feeling quite desperate. Everyone expects me to pass the eleven-plus, she thought, no one has even considered the fact that I may fail.

She caught her mother's eyes on her and forced a smile. 'Shall I ... shall I make another pot of tea?' she said, and escaped to the kitchen.

'I wonder what's keeping Bert,' Betty said as they were finishing their second cup of tea. 'I won't be able to keep the twins off the table indefinitely.'

'Nor Linda,' Breda said, for Linda, awake from her nap, was toddling round the room, grabbing hold of anything she could find. Twice already she'd had to be distracted from tugging on the dangling tablecloth and bringing all the party food down on her head.

There was another knock at the door.

'That'll be him now,' Betty said. But it wasn't. It was Claire Wentworth.

Janet was totally unprepared for her entrance into the room and was so surprised that she hardly noticed Uncle Peter, who had come in after her.

Janet did not say a word as Claire strode across the room. 'Happy birthday,' she said, handing her a small parcel and card. Then she looked at Betty and said: 'I'm glad to see you up, Mrs Travers. Are you feeling stronger?'

'Yes, a little,' Betty said. 'I'll be...'

But whatever she was going to say was forgotten as Janet cried out, 'Oh, oh, but it's beautiful. Thank you, thank you.'

Dangling from her hand was a silver locket she'd withdrawn from a velvet lined box. 'I'm glad you like it,' Claire said. 'I had it inscribed.'

Janet turned the locket over. Written on the back was: 'To Janet, with love from Claire Wentworth. 1947.'

'Thank you,' Janet said again.

Claire was glad Janet liked the gift, because she'd argued with David over it.

'You can't give a present to just one child,' he'd maintained.

'Janet has become like a friend to me.'

'Even so,' David insisted, 'you're making too much of her.'

'It's a gift for her birthday, that's all.'

'You're giving her an exaggerated view of her own importance.'

'I am not,' Claire retorted. 'Surely you're making too much of this?'

'No, I don't think I am,' David said. 'I don't think you're fully aware what you're doing, buying expensive presents for...'

He got no further. He'd failed to see the anger sparking in Claire's eyes and the two spots of colour in her cheeks. But he couldn't mistake the ice in her tone as she said:

'What I do with my own money is my affair. I don't need your permission or approval. I think you'd better go now!'

She watched as he turned on his heel and left without another word, and then she took the locket to town and in a spirit of recklessness had it inscribed. It was almost worth the row to see the joy in Janet's face, though she'd spent a miserable day waiting for David to come back. She longed to make the first move herself but a stand had to be made somewhere.

There was still no sign of Bert, and the twins were becoming restless and Linda fretful, so they decided to make a start on the buffet laid out on the table. Claire Wentworth was pressed to stay and Janet was over the moon with happiness to have all her family *and* Miss Wentworth together for her birthday.

They'd almost finished eating when Bert arrived. It was obvious from his demeanour that he'd called into the pub on the way home. 'How could you, Bert?' Betty cried. 'On our Janet's birthday.'

Bert looked round the company: his affronted wife, his mother-in-law with her accusing eyes and clamped mouth, his father-in-law's calm gaze and Breda's eyes flashing in temper. He could see that Peter, Brendan and Patsy were embarrassed, and there was a young woman he'd never seen before. Janet was flushed red. She was mortified at the possibility of a scene in front of Miss Wentworth.

Bert knew he was in the wrong, so he blustered and became angry. 'What's the matter? It's a party, isn't it? I had to get the man a drink, didn't I?'

'One drink?' Betty asked sarcastically.

'We got talking, it isn't a crime,' Bert said. He winked at Janet. 'Happy birthday, pet. Come on outside, I've got a surprise for you.'

They all trooped into the front garden, and what Janet saw took away all the irritation she'd felt at her father's late arrival, for leaning against the house was a blue bicycle.

Janet couldn't believe her eyes.

'It isn't new,' her father said. 'Some chap at work bought it for his wife a year or two back, but she never took to it and I asked him if I could buy it.'

'Oh,' Janet breathed, 'I can't believe it.' She could see the bike was hardly used. Even the tyres were fairly clean and unworn, and the chrome was shiny silver. It had a basket in front and a carrier behind, and it was the loveliest thing Janet had ever seen.

In the midst of her happiness and excitement, Janet saw Duncan detach himself from the admiring crowd and slope off to the back garden. Later, after she'd thanked her parents and said that she couldn't believe how lucky she was, she took her bike round to the garden shed at the back and found him there.

Duncan had never had a bike – there'd never been money for those kind of things – and Janet felt almost ashamed that now she had one and her brother hadn't.

'You can ride it any time you want, Duncan,' she said.

'A lady's bike!' Duncan exclaimed scathingly. 'Are you kidding? I wouldn't be seen dead on it.

104

Don't you worry about me, I'll be earning in just over a year and I'll get my own bike if I want one, only mine will be new.'

'I'm ... sorry.'

Duncan didn't answer, and after a while Janet went back inside. Claire Wentworth was leaving and her father, obviously forgiven, was eating the leftovers from the table. 'We didn't cut the cake,' Gran said. 'Miss Wentworth, you can't go without a piece of cake.'

'We didn't light the candles or sing "Happy Birthday" either,' Betty said. 'We were just going to, if you remember, when Bert arrived.'

'Let's do it now.'

When the candles were all lit, there was a rendition of 'Happy Birthday' which was enthusiastic and noisy rather than tuneful. And then Breda was saying: 'Blow them out with one blow and you can have a wish.'

Janet took a deep breath. She knew it was stupid and childish, but she really felt that if she blew the candles out in one blow, it would be a perfect end to a perfect day.

The candles were out and around her they were crying, 'Make a wish! Make a wish!' Janet's eyes met those of Miss Wentworth and she closed them tight. There was only one thing to wish for; she knew it and Miss Wentworth knew it.

I wish, she thought, I wish with all my heart that I've passed the exam to Whytecliff High School.

Chapter Five

When Janet got up the morning after her birthday and saw the brown envelope on the mat, she stopped stock still for a minute and looked at it. Then Duncan was at her elbow.

'Go on then,' he said. 'Isn't that what you've been working for?'

'I'm scared,' Janet said. 'Oh, Duncan, what if I've failed?'

Duncan shrugged. 'What if you have? It isn't the end of the world, is it?'

'Isn't it?' Janet said with feeling. 'It might be for me. Look at the stuff I got yesterday. Apart from the watch, the locket and the bike, they were all for using at the grammar school.'

'Talk sense, Jan,' Duncan said irritably. 'You'd use a pen and the stuff the twins got you whatever school you went to. Even the geometry set. It's best for you to have your own stuff wherever you go.'

'At grammar school maybe, but how many have sets like that at Paget?'

Duncan hedged. 'I don't know, in the top group they might.'

'And they carry it to school in a leather satchel?' Janet said sarcastically.

'No, you know they don't,' Duncan burst out angrily. 'Now open the damned letter, can't you? Then you'll know whether you can use your leather satchel, or whether you'll have to exchange it for a book on how to survive failing the eleven-plus.'

If he expected Janet to laugh he was disappointed, so he went past her, picked the envelope up from the mat and ripped it open.

'You've done it, Janet, you passed!' he cried. 'They've offered you a scholarship to Whytecliff High School. You've got to go to see round the place Monday.' Duncan pulled a face, then grinned and went on, 'Jammy beggar, I'll be back at school by then.'

A little later, Janet was on her way to Claire Wentworth's with the letter safely in her pocket. It was a beautiful morning, she thought. Surely the sky had never been so blue, or the sun as bright, or the breeze as fresh. She wanted to leap off her bike and go singing down the road, and it was only the thought of one of the neighbours ringing Highcroft, the local mental home, that stopped her doing so. She realised it would be hard to complete a grammar school education encased in a straitjacket and housed in a padded cell.

Claire was also feeling happy that morning. David had called to see her and apologised for his bad behaviour of the previous day. He could only say in his defence that he loved Claire dearly and was jealous of Janet Travers.

Claire stared at David, amazed by his revelation. She understood his resentment of Janet – he had shown her that side of him before – but he'd never said he loved her. She wondered if he meant it, but he said nothing else and just stood looking at her.

'Well, what do you want me to say?' Claire said at last.

'You could tell me you loved me,' David said. 'Do you?'

'Well ... I...'

David's nearness was affecting Claire so much her insides were churning, yet she made no move towards him when he put his arm round her shoulders, she just snuggled closer.

'Claire,' said David, 'I love you with all my heart and soul, you must know that.'

Claire said, her voice husky, 'I wasn't sure. I love you too, David.'

'We haven't known each other long,' David said, 'but I feel so strongly about you. Claire, darling, would you consider getting married?'

'Oh, yes,' Claire said, and when their lips met she was astounded by the heat of desire that shot through her body. It was consuming her. David's probing tongue was spiriting her to peaks of passion, and even if she'd wanted to, she couldn't have stopped him unbuttoning her blouse and pushing her gently back on to the settee.

Janet shot off her bike and went down the entry to the back gate. She hadn't time to wait for someone to open the front door. She was surprised that Claire wasn't in the kitchen. She ran into the passage, pushed open the door to the living room then stood stock still on the threshold, too shocked to move or speak.

Miss Wentworth was lying on her back and her top was bare. Her blouse was open, her brassiere discarded on the floor, and a man was lying on top of her, fondling her breasts. Miss Wentworth had her eyes closed and was making loud moaning sounds. Then the man kissed her and it was as if he was eating her up, but she had her arms tight around his neck and she was moving her body under his. Eventually he broke away.

'Oh God, Claire!' he said. He spoke, Janet thought, as if he had a sore throat.

Then he bent his head and began kissing Miss Wentworth's breasts. Janet's hand flew to her mouth as she felt the bile rise in her throat. She ran out of the door and through the house, and was violently sick in the back garden. She went back to her bike, but didn't attempt to ride it. She felt too churned up inside, her legs were all shaky and she was terribly afraid she was going to cry.

She wandered aimlessly for some time, pushing her bike, until she came to Rookery Park. She slipped gratefully inside, glad to be off the streets where passing pedestrians had stared at her tear-stained face. There were lots of children in the playground, but Janet veered away from them and found an empty bench in the shrubbery at the park's perimeter. She sat down, laid her bike on the ground and tried to make sense of what she'd seen.

And suddenly Janet knew what they'd been doing – groping! That nasty word described perfectly the actions she'd just witnessed, and she could quite understand her Auntie Breda being annoyed at her dad doing it. She was sure her aunt was mistaken, though, for her mum and dad wouldn't do a thing like that. And yet, she reminded herself, Mom was having a baby and she must have done something to get it. She must have done it before too, for her, Duncan and the twins. No wonder the doctor had been cross.

Janet got to her feet. One thing she knew, she could never tell them at home, never. It must be her secret. She knew Miss Wentworth and the man hadn't noticed her. No one would get to know what she'd seen. But it was in Janet's head and she couldn't rid herself of it.

She was suddenly furiously angry with Miss Wentworth. Claire was everything Janet wanted to be – beautiful, clever and independent – and Janet's whole desire was to be like her. She'd only wanted to go to the grammar school so badly because Claire Wentworth had been for it and Janet's earnest wish was to please her. She'd enjoyed the extra tuition because it enabled her to spend time with her idol, and she worked hard in order that Claire would praise her, and not just for herself alone.

Janet put her head in her hands and wept for the woman she'd thought she knew. They'd talked for hours about everything – at least, Janet had told Claire everything, but Claire must have kept things back, big things too, judging by what she was allowing that man to do to her.

And who was he? Claire wondered, knowing that, since the previous October, Claire had had precious little time to meet men, what with her job and teaching Janet too. If she'd only just met the man, it made it even worse. Janet made her way home with a heavy heart.

110

Janet told her mother she didn't have to go to Whytecliff High School with her. Auntie Breda had offered, if Betty didn't feel up to it, but Betty told Janet not to be silly, of course she was going. Now Janet sat in the hall where she'd taken the second part of the exam, listening to Miss Phelps, the headmistress, talk to the parents of the new girls, and felt ashamed of her mother.

She was ashamed of being ashamed, but there it was. She wished her mother had accepted Auntie Breda's offer of the loan of a coat. Auntie Breda's coat was a lovely blue and would have covered her up properly. Instead, she wore her dingy old brown one that barely met in the middle and was pulled together with a belt. It made her look like a badly packed sack of potatoes. Janet saw many of the girls, and even their mothers, look with slight disgust at the swell of her mother's stomach.

And did she have to wear those old shoes, trodden down, shapeless and so out of fashion? Especially when Auntie Breda had offered her those lovely sandals with little heels. Then there was the ridiculous hat, slapped down on top of hair that hadn't seen a hairdresser for some time. The mass of unruly curls – all that was left of a very old perm – proved too much for the grips and hat pins, and the hat had been pushed up higher until it perched on the top of her head like the one the clown had worn at the circus Janet had been taken to once. The unconfined hair then escaped in untidy strands around her face, over her ears and down her back. Betty seemed unaware of her dishevelled appearance, or how embarrassed her daughter was of her outfit, and that included the bag she'd bought especially for the occasion. She thought it was smart, but Janet thought it cheap and tawdry, and it screamed 'plastic'.

Janet was amazed by the size of the school when they were taken on a tour, and wondered how on earth she'd ever find her way around.

They saw the dining hall, the science laboratories, the art and music rooms, the domestic science kitchens and the sewing rooms with their rows of Singer sewing machines. On the next floor the staff room was pointed out to them, but the sixth-former accompanying them explained that no girls were ever allowed inside. Then they moved on to the lecture theatre and the library, where they were given a uniform list.

Betty heaved a large sigh as they left. 'Thank God that's over,' she said. 'I thought it was going on all blooming day.'

'Yes, it did drag on a bit,' Janet said, but she was watching the girls playing tennis in their white skirts and shirts on the courts alongside the school, and seeing herself doing the same thing soon.

'Let's make the most of it and take a bus into Sutton and have dinner out,' Betty suggested, adding recklessly, 'Hang the expense for once. Mammy said she didn't mind seeing to the twins, and we could do with a treat.'

It was as they were eating their mixed grill that Betty said, 'You'll have to tell Miss Wentworth all about it. She'll be interested.'

Betty didn't notice Janet's reticence, though she might have done if her swollen legs hadn't been giving her such gyp. 'Feather in her cap for her as well, I suppose,' she said, 'and you can't say she hasn't worked hard with you.' She winced a bit and said, 'I did intend taking the bus to Erdington to look in the Co-op at the cost of the uniform, but if it's all the same to you, lass, I feel as if I've done enough for one day. I could do with getting home and putting my feet up.'

'Okay,' Janet said. 'We haven't got to get anything yet anyway.'

'Not a word to your dad about the uniform list, mind,' Betty warned. 'It'll only worry him to death.'

'No,' Janet said. 'I won't tell him how tired you got either. We wanted you to let Auntie Breda come with me. It was too much for you.'

She thought the same thing next morning, and before she left for school, she asked, 'Do you want me to stay at home today?' She felt guilty because it wasn't only worry for her mother that made her want to stay away from school.

She dreaded meeting Miss Wentworth, and was scared that in her mind's eye she'd see her lying underneath the man, moaning and letting him do unspeakable things to her bare breasts. She shut the image out of her mind and said again, 'Are you sure you'll be all right?'

'Yes, fine,' lied Betty, and added, 'But you could just pop into your gran's on the way to school and ask her to come round. Maybe she could take the twins off my hands.'

'All right,' Janet said, but she left her mother

113

unwillingly. She took the twins into the kitchen and gave them a big slice of bread and jam and a cup of milk each, then left them her mom's button box to play with, waved them goodbye and warned them to be good before running quickly round to her gran's.

When she got to school, the bell had gone, the children were inside and Miss Wentworth was taking the register. It was common courtesy to stand by the teacher's desk and give your reasons for being late. Some of the teachers automatically gave you a smack across the hand with a ruler or strap. Miss Wentworth only did it to persistent offenders.

However, Janet did not stand by the teacher's desk, but slunk to her own, her head bent. Miss Wentworth had seen her, but pretended not to. She noticed Janet's dejected air and wondered if she was worried because she hadn't yet heard about the grammar school. She was surprised herself; she did think she would have had the results by the time they returned to school. Or maybe Mrs Travers was ill again, she thought, and Janet was anxious about that. She'd been absent the previous day, the first day back after the Easter holidays, and it might explain why Claire hadn't seen her for a few days, since the day of the party, in fact.

She continued to take the register, and when she got to Travers, she barely heard the mumbled 'Present, miss.'

Claire looked up. 'Janet,' she said, 'were you ill yesterday?'

'Yes,' came the muffled but terse reply.

114

What's wrong with the child? Claire thought. She knows that's no way to answer. She saw the other children listening, amazed that Janet Travers had been rude to the teacher. They were watching to see what she'd do. She couldn't let it pass, it would affect discipline.

'Yes, Miss Wentworth,' she rapped out.

Janet looked at her. Claire recoiled from the look in those eyes. 'Yes, Miss Wentworth,' repeated the girl in a singsong voice that bordered on the insolent.

Claire was puzzled and a little angry. 'Well, what was the matter with you?'

Janet was staring at the floor. 'I was ill, Miss Wentworth,' she said in the same droning tone.

'Have you brought a note?' Miss Wentworth snapped.

Janet gave a shrug. No doubt now about the intended insolence.

'Well, have you or haven't you?'

'No, I haven't,' Janet said. There was a significant pause, and then she added, 'Miss Wentworth.'

'You must bring a note, you know that.'

Claire knew she wasn't handling the situation very well. If anyone else had behaved like this – and she knew the ones to watch – she'd have had them hauled before her desk and administered a few strokes of the strap to remind them of their manners.

She was aware of the amused glances and the odd titter from the class, who were delighted because Janet was sort of laughing at the teacher. The fact that it was goody twoshoes Janet Travers who was doing it just made it more interesting.

Janet was aware of the amusement, and it pleased her. She'd make Miss Wentworth suffer. She was a well-liked teacher, but if Janet was to spread around the school what she'd seen her doing, she wouldn't be quite so popular, even though Janet knew many wouldn't believe it. She didn't even like thinking about it, but she couldn't help it. Every time she looked at Miss Wentworth she saw her lying panting and moaning under that man.

'Can't get no note,' she said now. 'My mom's bad...' again that pause, 'Miss Wentworth.'

'Janet Travers, you are being impertinent.'

Janet glared at her. 'No I'm not,' she said. It wasn't exactly a shout, but she hadn't spoken quietly. There was a gasp of admiration. Claire's face flushed and two spots of anger burned in her cheeks. David hadn't recognised them but Janet did, because Janet had seen Miss Wentworth cross before. She smiled.

The smile enraged Claire. 'Come out here this instant,' she said, and banged the desk with her hand so hard the box of chalks and the board rubber jumped.

There was a moment of absolute stillness, and Claire actually thought for one awful moment that Janet would refuse. But then, slowly, so slowly, as if she had all the time in the world, Janet stood and sauntered between the aisles. There was a collective sigh, as if all had been holding their breath. The boys who were usually in trouble leaned forward eagerly. Someone else was going to get it for a change.

Claire stared into the grey eyes she thought she knew so well, but the brooding look she saw there was unfathomable. Claire's own eyes were pleading for Janet to stop this behaviour. She was more than a pupil, she was a friend, and Claire had never had occasion to censure her before, let alone strike her. She didn't want to do it now.

Janet blinked. Again the smirk crossed her face, and she said: 'Going to beat me into submission, are you?'

The other children thought Janet had gone mad. Claire thought so too. She wondered for a moment if the strain of the examination preparations and her mother's illness had been too much for her. But whatever the reasons, Claire could not tolerate behaviour like this. Already the class were moving and muttering in a way they wouldn't have dared to do the day before.

'Silence,' she rapped out. 'Get out your arithmetic and start the next exercise.'

'Please, miss,' said a boy called Williams from the back, 'you haven't finished the register.'

Claire had forgotten about the register. She was flustered, and she could see that Janet, beside her, was enjoying it.

'Why don't you just hit me?' the girl suggested, with a smile so scornful Claire longed to swipe it from her face. 'Then you can get on with the lesson.'

Right, Claire thought, I will. She's asking for it.

She took the strap from the drawer, then changed her mind and instead drew out the thin, whippy cane that whistled as it flew through the air. It was used only sparingly, and then only for serious misdemeanours, and the class murmured in disbelief. 'Hold out your hand,' Claire demanded.

She marvelled that Janet's hand was so steady and her face unafraid. But it was contempt for this woman now about to hit her that kept the shakes from Janet's hand and the fear from her eyes.

The cane whined through the air, and when it landed across Janet's palm a sympathetic 'ooh' went up from the girls in the class. Janet, however, did not flinch, or make a sound. She felt as if her hand was on fire and she had an insane desire to grab the cane from Miss Wentworth's hand and beat her about the head with it. The outstretched hand trembled slightly, so that Claire's next slash missed the mark and hit her fingers.

Oh God, it hurts, Janet cried to herself, but still she made no sound. Claire saw the spasm of pain cross the girl's face, but she didn't cry out. Suddenly it was important that she did. Claire had to establish control.

She lashed out again and again, and eventually Janet let out a strangled sob. The children by then were utterly silent, staring at the teacher. Her eyes looked wild, her hair had come undone and was tumbling around her shoulders, and sweat glistened on her face. She was crimson and panting slightly, and feeling ashamed of the way she'd lost control and laid into Janet.

Janet felt as if she was going to pass out. She saw the cuts either side of her palm and the ridges across her hand that she knew would turn to weals. She felt she would die with the pain that ran right to the top of her arm and made her feel sick. The feeling of nausea brought back the time she'd been sick in Miss Wentworth's garden, and the reason why.

It was agony to move. She wanted to sink to the floor and cry because it hurt so much and Miss Wentworth had caused that hurt. She wanted to tuck her hand under her arm for a measure of comfort. But more than either of these things, she wanted to lash out at Miss Wentworth, to hurt her back. She stared at the teacher and said, in a voice that trembled just slightly, 'Have you finished?'

Miss Wentworth leaned on the desk, her chest heaving. She knew she'd lost. 'Get out,' she said, but she was too weary and worn down to shout properly. 'Stand outside the door!'

Janet turned and walked out. Her legs were shaking but she knew that as long as she kept moving, no one would know. Her injured hand hung by her side, and everyone in the class realised that Janet Travers had guts.

She didn't wait outside the door. She walked out of the school gates and into the street, where she looked about her furtively, for the primary school opened on to Westmead Crescent, the road her grandparents lived in. Even if they were safely in the house, she could be spotted by any of the neighbours, and she knew they would feel a pressing need to tell the family they'd seen her wandering the streets when she should have been in school.

No, Janet thought, no way could she risk walking through the estate. She mustn't be seen by anyone at this time of the morning, yet if she lingered in the playground she was sure to be seen by one of the teachers, and she wasn't going back into school either. She had to find somewhere to hide out till lunchtime, when she could go home.

Westmead Crescent was the last road on the estate, and ahead of her was Woodacre Road, the start of the private houses. Janet left the playground, her eyes darting up and down the crescent. As no one was in sight, she crossed and began walking cautiously down the road.

She had to skirt carefully past the shops, because Mr Freer the shopkeeper knew everyone, and often stood at the doorway looking out, but there was no sign of him. Then she saw that the gates to Holyfields Sports Ground opposite the shop were open. She'd never seen them open before, and without thinking she slipped inside. She could hear a motor mower on the sports field and guessed the groundsman was up there cutting the grass, but she wasn't going to go that far up. There were plenty of places to hide by the steel railings, because shrubs had been planted against them on the inside, and if she crawled in amongst them no one would see her.

She had to take her throbbing hand from her armpit, where she'd held it for comfort since she'd left the school, and drop to her hands and knees to crawl between the bushes. The straggling branches caught and snagged on her clothes, thorns pulled at her hair and sharp roots dug into her knees, but she paid no heed. Not

120

until she was well hidden in the bushes did she take time to examine her hand.

It was crusted with damp earth. Janet wiped it as gently as she could with the hem of her dress, but still winced at the smarting pain of it. The slashes were deep and had cut into the flesh, where they'd bled a fair bit. The ridges where the cane had bitten into the palm were purple-red and angry-looking and hurt like hell. 'Bugger! Bugger! Bugger!' said Janet, and was surprised to find she felt better for saying it. She wondered then if she could convince her mother she felt ill and then she might give her the afternoon off school. God, she did feel ill. She'd never felt pain like this, and she just might get away with convincing her mam she felt sick.

But what could she do about tomorrow, and all the tomorrows till July? She wondered if she had the courage to defy Miss Wentworth again, but she doubted it. She knew Miss Wentworth had hit her harder than she'd ever seen her hit anyone, and she didn't think she could put up with such a beating day after day until July without dissolving into a blubbering wreck. She'd like to be able to, because she'd feel she'd scored a victory if she could. She knew Miss Wentworth had been confused and almost hurt by her defiance that morning.

She wished with all her heart that she didn't have to go back to school tomorrow. She wished that when she woke up in the morning it was September and time to begin Whytecliff High. Suddenly she remembered the priest telling them about the power of prayer. She'd gone to Mass on

Easter Sunday with Gran at St Peter and St Paul's. She didn't mind Mass. She liked the flowers, and the fancy altar with the decorated cloth on, and the smell of the stuff he swung around the church that Gran said was incense. She liked the flickering candles and the statues and pictures all along the edges and the service that was in Latin. She couldn't understand it, but she liked to listen. It was like music.

Most times she didn't listen to the sermon – that was the boring bit – but there was plenty to look at while the priest was going on. She hadn't intended to listen on Easter Sunday – she had heard the story before, after all – but the priest had captured her imagination. 'Jesus performs miracles today, in people's lives,' he said. 'Jesus said that if you have faith as small as a mustard seed, you can move mountains.'

Janet didn't know how big a mustard seed was, but it didn't sound very big. And she didn't want to move mountains either, they suited her just fine where they were. She wanted something much more important.

She shuffled on to her knees in the damp soil and prayed: 'Please, Jesus, can You fix it so I don't go to Paget Road School again. Thank You. Amen.' She wondered if that was easier to arrange than moving mountains about the place. She had no doubt it would be achieved, for her faith would have filled a whole mustard pot, but later she was to marvel and be awed and a little frightened at the power of prayer.

It was a tedious morning for Janet, and her hand and arm continued to throb. She wished she had a book to read, to take her mind off things, but she hadn't even brought her bag with her. And she realised with horror that she'd left her coat behind. Oh, she'd catch it now.

Sometime that morning she dozed off, sitting up, with her head leaning against a shrubbery bush. She woke stiff, cold and uncomfortable.

It took a minute for her to remember where she was. Then she crawled carefully out and, glancing to right and left, walked to the gates. She saw the children on their way home to dinner and realised she'd probably been woken by the dinner bell. Fortunately, few children from Woodacre Road went to Paget Road School, and none of those who passed spotted Janet hiding in the bushes. As soon as the streets were quieter again, Janet pelted home.

Gran opened the door, and Janet could tell she was cross. For a moment she imagined that Miss Wentworth had been to the house, for Sarah McClusky burst out, 'What time do you call this, miss?' Then she exclaimed. 'Mother of God! Have you seen the state of yourself?'

Janet looked down. One black stocking had a hole in the knee and the other a long tear, and Janet remembered the trailing thorn that she'd caught it on. She saw that the thorn had entered her skin and globules of blood were oozing through the stocking.

'Look at your dress, child,' Gran went on, indicating the brown soil staining the checked dress, 'and what have you done to your hand?'

Fortunately, Janet's hand was too dirty for Sarah to see exactly what had happened to it. She went on, 'Your face is all over dirt. Dear God, Janet, as if we haven't trouble enough.'

'I'm sorry, Gran, I fell over, I was running,' Janet gasped out. 'But what trouble?'

'Your mother's on her time,' Gran said. 'You're to go to your Aunt Breda's. Duncan's gone already. He's been home this long time.'

Janet felt faint. The baby wasn't due yet, not for weeks. Now she understood why her gran had kept her on the doorstep. A shuddering scream came from above.

'But I want to see Mom,' Janet cried. She attempted to rush past her gran, but Sarah was too quick.

'Oh no you don't, my girl,' she said.

Another agonising scream rent the air, and Janet almost leapt from her grandmother's arms.

'Janet, Janet,' said her gran pleadingly, 'you can't do anything for your mother. Be a good girl and go to Aunt Breda, there's a love.'

'She'll be all right, Gran, won't she?' Janet asked.

'Of course, my dear,' said Sarah, but she didn't meet Janet's eyes. 'I'll have to go back upstairs to help. You must go now.'

'Sarah! Sarah!' Janet heard the voice of Mrs Williams, the midwife, and knew her gran was needed. She turned away without another word and made her way to her auntie's.

'You took your time,' Aunt Breda said as Janet went in through the kitchen door. Then she turned and caught sight of her niece's appearance, and said, as her mother had:

'Mother of God, what happened to you?'

124

'I fell over.'

'Well get yourself washed and something inside you and you'll feel better. You'd better strip off those stockings and I'll try and darn the tears, though it's your mother who's the best darner. The teachers were always praising her for her neat stitches. She...' Breda's voice trailed away, for her eyes met those of Janet, who suddenly burst into tears.

'Oh, Auntie Breda, Mom's bad, isn't she?' she gasped.

'Oh, lovey,' Breda soothed, gathering Janet in a hug. 'She'll be all right.'

Noel and Conner were sitting up to the table attacking their stew with their spoons. They caught the seriousness of the atmosphere and it frightened them. They began to bawl too.

Duncan couldn't stand it. 'I'm finished eating,' he said. 'Can I go?'

'Take the two boyos with you,' Breda said, indicating the twins.

'Haven't I to go back to school then?' Duncan said, surprised.

'No, I might need you to give a hand,' Breda said.

'Well, I still don't see why I've got to take the twins with me,' Duncan said mulishly.

'Because I said so,' Breda snapped, 'and because they're only little and they're frightened and don't understand anything, and it won't hurt their big brother to think of someone other than himself for once.'

Duncan felt momentarily ashamed. He was a bit scared too. He knew things weren't right with

125

his mother having the baby so soon, and he was turned twelve and a half. His brothers were only babies.

'Stop snivelling,' he told them sternly. 'If you do, I'll take you up the park.'

The two little boys gulped and tried manfully to stem the tide of tears. Breda, still hugging Janet, said, 'Get a tanner from my purse on the mantelpiece and buy some sweets for you all. The sweet coupons are behind the clock.'

That brought smiles to all their faces. As Janet watched them go down the road she said:

'He doesn't care, our Duncan, he doesn't care.'

'Of course he cares,' Aunt Breda said. 'But he's a man, or nearly a man. They deal with things like this by going away and pretending it isn't happening. 'Tisn't as if they can do anything. They're best out the way.'

'Can I ... can I stay off school this afternoon too?' Janet said.

'Well, I don't think you'd concentrate much, would you?' Aunt Breda said with a smile. 'Anyway, you couldn't go in that state and I'll not darn those stockings in five minutes, nor get the stains out of your dress. You've not had a bite to eat yet either, and anyway, you're more use to me here.'

Later, as Janet washed her stinging hands and smarting legs in a bowl of hot water, she prayed silently, Not this way, Jesus, please don't let anything happen to my mom. I didn't mean You to do it this way.

Claire finished the register quickly, and leaving it

126

on the desk, went out to find Janet. It didn't occur to her that Janet had left the building. She thought she was hiding away in the school somewhere and she returned to the classroom deep in thought. The children watched her with reproachful eyes. When the boy Claire chose to take the register to the office reported that Janet wasn't outside the door any more, whispers started to go round the room. They remembered the look on Claire's face as she beat Janet. They thought she'd taken her to the Head for further punishment, and that wasn't considered fair.

Claire set the class some exercises and went off to search for Janet. She found her coat and bag on her peg, and decided that she'd pop across to the Travers' house with them at lunchtime. It was a trying morning. The whole class, Claire realised, seemed to blame her for the incident. They were silent in disapproval. No one answered the questions she asked after lessons, and no one volunteered to give out books or apparatus. There was no pleasant interchange between teacher and pupils as there had been formerly, for the children refused to play. Claire felt the barriers go up, and though they were all icily polite, by the end of the morning she was exhausted.

At lunchtime, a staff meeting was called, so Claire had to stay in school instead of going over to Janet's house. The girl did not materialise that afternoon either, and time seemed to drag slowly. Just before four o'clock Claire overheard a conversation between two mothers waiting in the playground outside her window.

'I hear Bet Travers is in a bad way. Our Elsie

bumped into Sean going for the doctor.'

'She's been bad this long time.'

'Yes, but she's been in labour all day, they say, and the screams of her can be heard down the street. She's not due for another few weeks.'

'Be the hospital for her, likely.'

'Yes, and God help them if it isn't the crematorium for one or the other.'

Oh my God, what have I done? Claire thought. Perhaps Janet's mother was in labour before she came to school, and in her anxiety she was rude to me. And I lashed out at her. Why didn't I take her from the room and talk to her? Janet's never acted that way before. Why didn't I imagine it was something like that?

She wondered if someone had come for Janet while she was outside in the corridor. Leaving her bag and coat behind seemed to suggest a headlong flight prompted by agitation. As soon as the last bell had gone, Claire caught up Janet's coat and bag and took it up to the house.

Mrs McClusky opened to her knock. 'Oh,' she said, 'you're Miss ... Miss...?' Worry had driven the name from her mind. 'Our Janet's teacher. I thought you were the ambulance.'

'The ambulance!'

Suddenly, Dr Black was running down the stairs. 'Is that them?' he demanded, then, seeing the young woman at the door, he barked, 'In or out, please, the ambulance will be here shortly and I can't have the hall cluttered with people.'

'How is she, Doctor?' Mrs McClusky asked.

'Sleeping at last,' the doctor said grimly. 'I've anaesthetised her. She was worn out.'

Claire was aware of heart-rending sobs. They came from a man sitting with his head in his hands in a chair in the living room. Through the half-open door, she recognised him as Janet's father, who had arrived late and merry at the party.

The man's grief shook her. 'She's not... Mrs Travers isn't...'

'She's very ill,' Mrs McClusky said. 'We've had the priest. He gave her the sacraments, you know. He told the doctor if it has to be a choice between the mother and the child, the Church's teaching is clear, it must be the child. I say bugger the Church, begging your pardon, miss. Where would the children be without our Betty, not to mention him there?' She indicated the sobbing Bert. 'Big gormless lump he is without my lass behind him. We need her here.'

Mrs McClusky's voice broke. 'I'm sorry,' she said to Claire, 'but we're distracted with it all. Was you wanting something?'

'No,' Claire said, thinking that they all had enough to worry about. 'I've just called with Janet's coat and bag. She left them at school.'

Mrs McClusky thought that odd, and any other time she would have questioned it, but at that moment the sirens were heard. 'You must excuse me, that's the ambulance,' she said.

Claire watched on the pavement with a knot of neighbours until she saw Mrs Travers carried to the ambulance, Bert stumbling behind her in his distress so that they had to help him too. The doctor got in his car and offered Mrs McClusky a lift.

'When we see how she's doing I'll bring you back home,' he said.

Mrs McClusky knew he meant 'if she pulls through', and with a sigh she climbed in beside Dr Black. Claire watched as they drove away.

You deserve to be flayed alive for what you did to Janet Travers today, she said to herself. And I don't know how you're ever going to make it up to her.

Chapter Six

When Dr Black called round to Breda's the next morning to tell them the news of Betty and the baby, he wasn't surprised to find that Breda had taken all the Travers children in, although only Janet was up, and drinking tea with her aunt and uncle.

'They're fine,' the doctor assured the three of them. He looked at Janet and said, 'You have a baby sister. She's small but she's a fighter. She's in the special care unit, being so premature.'

Janet felt little for the baby that had disrupted their lives and would continue to do so for years to come. 'What about Mom?' she said.

'Well, she's had a tough time,' Dr Black said, 'but she'll be all right.'

'Oh, thank God,' Breda said.

Janet felt like crying with relief. 'Can I see her?'

'Not at the moment,' the doctor said. 'They're only allowing Bert and her parents in. Later I'll see what I can do.' He nodded across at Peter and said, 'Could you tell them at the factory that Bert won't be in today. He's been up all night. I told him I'd see to it.'

'No problem,' Peter said.

'And Mammy must be bushed,' Breda said. 'I'll keep the children with me today. I'll have to go and get some clothes for them in a minute.'

'Have we to go to school?' Janet asked.

131

'Not today,' Breda said. 'I could do with you at home anyway to give me a hand with the twins and Linda, but tomorrow you should be back.'

Tomorrow could look after itself. Janet let her breath out in a sigh of relief. Dr Black glanced up at her and said, 'Thought you liked school?'

'I do usually,' said Janet. 'Only I don't particularly want to go today, 'cos I'm worried about Mom.'

'I can understand that,' Dr Black said. He stood up. 'Well,' he sighed, 'I'll have to be off or I'll have patients beating the door down.' He looked at Breda and added, 'I'll drop you at your sister's if you like, it's on my way.'

Janet saw Breda hesitate. 'I'll be here to see to the others if they wake up,' she told her aunt.

'Well, I certainly need to get them some clean clothes,' Breda said. 'The twins have gone to bed like a couple of tinkers and Janet here came home yesterday with holes in her stockings and her dress only fit for the rag bag.'

Janet, who'd been loaned a pair of Breda's pyjamas for the night, saw the doctor's eyebrows raised quizzically, and explained, 'I fell over.'

She said the same thing, just a few minutes later, when Peter had left for work and Breda had gone upstairs to change out of her slippers. Dr Black and Janet were alone. Janet reached across the table to collect the cups to rinse in the sink and suddenly Dr Black took hold of her hand and turned it over gently.

Janet looked at the blistered ridges that had appeared overnight and pulled away from the doctor's grasp. 'I fell over,' she said again. 'Auntie

Breda told you about the state of my clothes.'

'Yes,' said Dr Black, 'but Auntie Breda's not here now and you can tell me what really happened.'

'I told you.'

'Janet, I'm not a fool,' the doctor said impatiently. 'Who did this to you?'

'Did what?'

'Someone's hit you with a cane or something,' Dr Black said. Despite his impatience, he understood Janet's reluctance to speak out: she wasn't the type who was often in trouble and was probably ashamed that she'd been punished.

Janet looked at the doctor. She'd known him all her life.

She wondered what would happen if she was to tell him everything. She gave an involuntary shiver. It didn't bear thinking about.

She stared at him and said decisively, 'I fell over.'

Dr Black sighed. 'All right,' he said, 'have it your own way. But you've got dirt in it. If you don't want it to fester, it will have to be cleaned and dressed.'

By the time Breda came down, Dr Black was winding a bandage expertly around Janet's hand.

'Young Janet got some dirt in that cut on her hand,' he said by way of explanation to Breda. 'Have to keep it out of the water for a day or two.'

'What some people will do to get out of the washing-up,' Breda said with a smile at Janet.

Janet was too nervous to smile back. She'd been worried what the doctor would tell Auntie Breda and was grateful to him for saying nothing. Her hand felt much better, though it had stung like mad when he was cleaning it. But the ointment he'd dabbed on it was soothing and now it felt much easier, protected as it was by the thick wad of bandage.

Duncan, much to his disgust, was dispatched with a shopping list later that morning. Seeing the sulky droop of his lips Breda said sharply, 'Don't even bother complaining, Duncan. Janet is more help to me in the house, and anyway, she can hardly carry heavy bags with her sore hand.'

He went, only slightly mollified. Being unused to shopping, it took him even longer than it did Janet, and when he'd finished he turned for home gratefully. He was aware of his grumbling stomach and knew it must be nearly lunchtime. As he turned into Paget Road, the rain began. The early April shower was cold and stung his face, and he bent his head against it. Suddenly he cannoned into someone whose own view was obscured by the umbrella they were battling with. 'Sorry,' he said, 'I didn't see ... oh, hello, Miss Wentworth.'

'Hello, Duncan.'

Claire saw the bulging bags and realised that he'd been kept at home to help. She'd hoped that was the reason Janet was away too. 'How's your mother?' she asked. Duncan looked at her in astonishment. Although news on the estate travelled like wildfire, usually teachers were excluded from the inner circle of gossip.

'I called at the house yesterday,' Claire said, seeing Duncan's surprise. 'Janet left school in such a rush, she forgot her coat and bag.'

Duncan's eyes narrowed. Janet hadn't left school in a rush. She'd arrived at Breda's after him. But this wasn't the time to go into it. He was aware of the rain seeping into his coat, despite the umbrella Miss Wentworth held over them both.

'My mom's all right,' he said. 'She had a baby girl.'

'And the baby?'

'She's in a special baby place,' Duncan said. 'The doctor came round and told us. She's sick but the doctor seems to think she's a fighter.'

He fidgeted a little. The bags were getting heavy. 'I gotta go,' he said. 'The shopping!'

'Yes,' Claire said, 'of course.' Then added, 'Is ... is ... Janet's hand better?'

Now, how did she know about Janet's hand? Duncan thought.

'She says it feels easier now the doctor's dressed it,' he said. He watched carefully to see what Miss Wentworth's reaction would be to his words.

He wasn't disappointed. Miss Wentworth started, her eyes seemed to grow larger and her voice was a mere whisper as she said, 'A doctor! She had to see a doctor?'

'No, he came round, I told you,' Duncan said. 'To tell us about Mom. He saw Janet's hand and said she'd got dirt in it and he cleaned it and put ointment and stuff on and a bandage.'

'She'd got dirt in it?' Miss Wentworth repeated.

'Yes, from when she fell over.' Duncan said.

'From when she fell over?'

Duncan wondered if Miss Wentworth was going deaf or daft. 'Yes,' he said. 'That was how

135

she hurt it, wasn't it?' He wondered again how Miss Wentworth knew. Had she seen her fall or what? Or maybe one of the kids had said? It wasn't important. His arms felt as if they were breaking and he dared not put the bags on the soggy ground. 'I really must go,' he said.

'Of course. Tell your sister I'm sorry.'

'What for?'

'Just tell her.'

Duncan's face was creased in a frown. He was certain Miss Wentworth was going loopy. It's all that studying, he thought, enough to turn anyone's brain. He was even more certain of this when Miss Wentworth continued, 'And tell her she's sure to hear any day now about the examination results.'

'But ... well, she knows, doesn't she?' Duncan said. He'd read the thing himself, for heaven's sake, and he knew Miss Wentworth must know. He'd been sent to the factory to tell his dad, and when he got back his mom said Janet had ridden over to tell her teacher. He looked at Miss Wentworth and wondered if she'd had a knock on the head. She was staring at him as if he was the one who was odd, her eyes narrowed in disbelief and her mouth agape.

'She ... she can't know,' she said at last. Her mind didn't want to accept it.

'She does know,' Duncan said emphatically. He didn't like being disbelieved. 'I picked up the letter and opened it because she wouldn't, and it said she'd won a scholarship to Whytecliff High School. They went to see the school as well on Monday, Janet and our mom. Auntie Breda said that's what brought the baby so early, with Mom not being well and then...' He broke off and said to Miss Wentworth, 'Are you ... are you all right?'

The colour suddenly drained from Claire's face and she swayed on her feet. She felt lightheaded and tears swam before her eyes. It felt like the ultimate betrayal. Why, for God's sake? Why? her mind screamed. Perhaps, she thought, Duncan might be mistaken. She doubted it, but she had to know, and she had to get rid of Duncan before he reported that he'd seen Miss Wentworth bawling her eyes out in the street. 'I'm perfectly well,' she replied stiffly. 'I have just remembered something I have to do in school and I really mustn't keep you any longer.'

Duncan watched her walk away and shook his head. Queer kettle of fish, teachers, he thought. Nice as ninepence one minute and pulling rank the next, going all stiff and starchy. To hear Janet talking, you'd think Miss Wentworth was a blinking saint, but she was as bad as all the rest and crackers into the bargain. Less you had to do with teachers the better, he decided.

Claire's legs were shaking as she walked into the school. She went straight to the headmaster's room, knowing he was away for the day, picked up the phone and asked to be put through to the education department. As she listened to the girl's voice at the other end explaining that the letters had been sent out of the office on 24 March, she realised that Janet Travers had indeed won a scholarship to Whytecliff High School but for some reason had not had the decency to inform her teacher.

She didn't understand. She thought she knew Janet so well, but the girl seemed to have undergone a character change. Claire was willing to admit she'd hit Janet harder than she'd ever hit anyone before. In fact, she'd hit her *because* she was Janet Travers. She'd taken her insolence as a personal affront and overreacted.

Janet obviously hadn't mentioned it at home, but that wasn't unusual. Claire used the cane and the strap sparingly, but when she had occasion to resort to it the boy – it was usually a boy – took his strokes with good grace, usually knowing that he'd well deserved it. No one ever mentioned getting in trouble at school to their family. They knew they would get little sympathy, and probably another dose to remind them to behave better in future.

In the same way, no child would say what they'd seen Miss Wentworth do to Janet, for they'd have to explain why. When their parents heard the reason for her discipline, they would think the punishment justified. It was Claire herself who was having doubts.

In the worry of the Travers household that day, where the mother lay ill and in grave danger of giving birth to a premature child, little notice would have been taken of Janet's hand. When the doctor had spotted it, she'd obviously told him she'd fallen over. He must have known she was not telling the truth, but that was the story she must have stuck to, for it was all Duncan knew.

Claire wondered whether, if she'd sent the child from the room in the beginning, when she was still in control of her emotions, Janet would have

138

told her what had upset or offended her, for it was obvious to Claire, thinking it over now, that something had.

I need to talk to her, she decided, and I must do it this evening after school.

Duncan dumped the bags on the cupboard top by the sink and said, 'I'm starving, and these bags weigh a ton.'

Auntie Breda laughed. 'Come up to the table, your dinner's ready. Your dad's been round and said your mom's looking a lot perkier, so the news is good.'

'And the baby's holding her own too,' Janet said.

Duncan didn't really care about the baby, but he wished that everything was over and he could go back home. He didn't mind Breda, despite her bossiness, but he'd rather be at home, and he even thought he'd rather be at school than being sent shopping and looking after his little brothers and Linda all the time. The thought of school brought to mind his strange meeting with Miss Wentworth. 'I met your teacher coming home,' he said to his sister.

'Did you?' Janet's response was guarded and cool. She didn't ask what she'd said, or how she was. Duncan was still puzzling over this when his aunt asked, 'Did she wonder at you not being at school?'

'No, she knew, I mean about Mom. She asked about her.'

'How did she hear?'

'She said she went to the house yesterday after

school.' He looked across at Janet and said, 'You left your coat and bag behind and she took them round.'

'That was kind of her,' said Aunt Breda. Janet and Duncan looked at each other. Janet thought that Aunt Breda hadn't been a mother long enough to worry over a child losing a coat.

'She asked about your hand as well, Janet,' Duncan said. 'She asked if it was all right.'

'Did she?' Janet's eyes were trying to tell Duncan something. Asking him to be quiet. He ignored the pleading look.

'She said to tell you she's sorry.'

'What for?' Aunt Breda said.

'That's what I asked her,' Duncan said, 'and she said just to tell Janet sorry.'

'She must have seen you fall,' Breda said, but her mind was distracted because just at that minute, Noel almost tipped what remained of his dinner over his lap.

'I'm putting these little ones down for a nap,' Breda said, 'so you two deal with the dishes, and Duncan, you'll have to wash.'

'Are we going home tonight?' Janet asked.

'I'll see how the land lies,' Breda said. 'I'll pop and see your dad. If you can't, I'll have to phone in to work. They won't like me taking another night off, but they'll have to lump it.'

Janet knew her aunt's words were mere bravado. Twilight shifts were like gold dust to mothers, enabling them to bring money in without paying most of it out again in childcare. No one could afford to jeopardise their job by taking days off all the time.

Duncan waited until Breda left the room and then began swirling the soapy water in the bowl over the plates. Suddenly he turned to face Janet and said, 'Why didn't you tell Miss Wentworth you'd passed the eleven-plus?'

Janet could think of nothing to say, no excuse. 'I did,' she said.

'Miss Wentworth said you didn't,' Duncan said. 'She was upset, I think.'

Janet knew she had to tell Duncan something. 'I ... I went but she had someone with her, a friend. I'd not seen her before and I didn't want to say anything in front of her so I came away.'

'You could have gone again.'

'I didn't know how long the friend would be staying. I thought I'd wait till I got to school.'

'But you didn't tell her then either,' Duncan said. 'She knew nothing.' He stared at Janet for a minute, and then, because he knew that in some way it was connected, asked, 'What really happened to your hand, Janet?'

Janet pondered the question. Many of the kids in her class had older brothers and sisters in the secondary school and would tell them about yesterday's incident, especially as it was Janet who was caned. It was only parents they'd be wary of informing; and they'd take particular pleasure in telling Duncan. In fact, she thought, probably the only reason he doesn't already know is because he wasn't at school today. If she didn't tell him now and he found out from others, he might, from spite, fling the knowledge out in front of her gran, Dad or Auntie Breda. Again she gave her version of the truth.

141

'Miss Wentworth gave me the cane,' she said.

Duncan's mouth dropped open in surprise. He'd had the strap a few times, and a couple of strokes of the cane, usually well deserved, and he'd accepted it as one of the trials of growing up. Girls seldom had corporal punishment administered. He stared at Janet.

'Don't tell, will you?' she said.

'What do you take me for?' Duncan said scornfully. 'But what did she give you the cane for?'

'Cheeking her.'

'You cheeking Miss Wentworth?'

'Yes,' Janet burst out angrily. 'What d'you think I am, a saint or something?' She sighed and added, 'I wasn't at school Monday, was I? I didn't tell Miss Wentworth I'd be away, but Mom thought I had so she didn't send a note. Then I was late because Mom felt bad and I had to go and fetch Gran round to see to the twins. I was a bit worried about Mom and when Miss Wentworth went on about the note I gave her some cheek and she gave me a couple of strokes of the cane and sent me out of the classroom.'

She stopped there. No way was she going to say she'd run away – he'd think she was feeble – and she wasn't going to tell him how many strokes of the cane she'd had either, or how bad her hand was. He might think flogging her hand for cheek was excessive, especially if he'd seen the seeping open wounds on her palm and fingers. She blessed Dr Black and his concealing dressing as she went on.

'Anyway, that was it really, or would have been

142

if I hadn't fallen down on the way home and cut my hand and got dirt in, and you know the rest.'

Duncan doubted he did. He knew Janet a sight better than Miss Wentworth did, and he was certain he wasn't getting the whole truth. He also knew that if he talked to her till the next morning he'd get no more. She'd always been stubborn. He thought of asking her why she'd left her coat and bag behind but knew she'd come up with some other plausible lie, so he didn't bother. He knew he'd got some of the truth, and it certainly explained Miss Wentworth's strange behaviour earlier that day. Neither of them spoke of it again, and when Breda came back and said they were to return home that day, they were both pleased.

'Your gran's coming in to see to you,' she said, 'because you won't be able to cook meals and things till your hand's mended, Janet. And you'll be going back to school tomorrow. You know how much store your mom puts by education!'

Duncan made a face, out of habit. For once, he was looking forward to going back more than Janet. She had a cold pit of dread in the base of her stomach every time she thought of it.

Mrs McClusky hadn't yet arrived when the knock came on the door. Janet was by herself. Bert had gone to buy flowers for his wife and taken Conner and Noel with him, and Duncan was out somewhere. When she saw Miss Wentworth on the doorstep, she wasn't even surprised.

'You'd better come in,' she said, and Claire walked past her into the room, where they stood apart like two combatants. Neither spoke, and

143

the silence became uncomfortable. Claire felt she should apologise for hitting Janet so hard, but she also felt that Janet should apologise and explain why she'd not told her about passing the eleven-plus. Eventually the silence became too much for Claire, and she said:

'I suppose you're wondering why I've just come like this?'

'No,' Janet said. 'Duncan said he met you. I almost expected you.'

'He told me your mother's had a baby girl.'

'Yes, she has.'

'You ... you must be pleased,' Claire said. Janet was being deliberately terse and unhelpful.

'Not really,' Janet said. 'I told your mother but she didn't believe me. No one wanted this baby.'

'Oh, but I'm sure...'

'You didn't come to talk about any baby, did you?' Janet said. 'Nor my mother either.'

'Janet, why are you like this?'

'Like what, Miss Wentworth?'

'So antagonistic,' Claire said. 'What have I done, what has happened between us?'

'Nothing.'

'You're like a different person.'

Janet shrugged.

'Oh, Janet,' Claire burst out, 'why didn't you tell me you'd passed? You must have known I'd want to be told straight away.'

'I came to tell you,' Janet said. 'It was a week ago today, the morning after my party, when the letter came. Mom told me to go straight round and I cycled over after breakfast.'

'Was I out?'

'No, Miss Wentworth, you were in. But there was a man with you, and both of you were busy.'

Janet stressed the last word, and Claire flushed crimson on her face and neck. She felt faint and clutched for the back of a chair.

She remembered it so well: David's kisses driving her wild, and knowing she wanted him to make love to her more than she'd wanted anything in her life before. She'd pulled away with difficulty, and tugging her blouse around her had turned the key in the kitchen door before leading the way upstairs to the bedroom. If she'd picked up Janet's meaning correctly, the girl had arrived before she'd thought to lock up.

'You saw ... ?'

'I saw all right,' Janet said, and her voice trembled as she remembered it all again. 'I was so excited, so pleased, and I knew you would be too. I didn't bother ringing the doorbell, but went straight down the entry to the back door. You were in the living room and had no clothes on your top. You were letting him ... he was ... you were just moaning, you weren't doing anything to stop him!'

'Don't,' Claire said, 'please don't say any more.'

Janet had a lump in her throat which she swallowed with difficulty. 'Why?' she demanded. 'Are you embarrassed? I was disgusted.' She saw that Miss Wentworth was crying, and she felt tears welling in her own eyes, but she was too nauseated by the whole thing to let them fall.

'I know it must have been a terrible shock,' Claire said eventually, her voice muffled with tears, 'and I wouldn't have had you see it for the world, but David and I love each other. We are going to be married.'

'Married!' exclaimed Janet. She couldn't believe she'd heard right. 'You'll be giving up everything you've worked for, for a man.'

'No, Janet, it doesn't have to be that way.'

'It does where I live,' Janet spat out, suddenly angry. 'Only Auntie Breda and Uncle Peter are different, and everyone says Uncle Peter's hen-pecked and Auntie Breda wears the trousers.'

'More marriages will be like your auntie's in the future, Janet,' Claire said. 'Husbands and wives will both work and share the household jobs.'

'They'll share having babies too, I suppose,' Janet said scornfully. 'I mean, what if you had a baby?'

'I won't,' Claire said confidently.

'How can you be so sure?' Janet said.

'Look, Janet,' Claire said, embarrassed afresh. 'This is a conversation you should be having with your mother, not me.'

'I didn't see her doing anything.'

'Well, I'm not going to tell you,' Claire said, 'except to say there's things you can use, clinics you can go to. At the moment I don't want a baby, but I may change my mind one day, when I'm married and we decide we want to start a family.'

Janet remembered Aunt Breda's angry words to Peter the day of the doctor's visit to her father: 'I'm getting her down that clinic, to get her sorted out, as soon as that kid's born.'

That was what Auntie Breda meant, she thought with sudden clarity, and wondered if her mother had chosen to have baby Sally like Claire seemed to suggest women were able to. Somehow she doubted Sally had been planned at all.

'So,' Claire said, 'where do we go from here?'

'Nowhere,' Janet said flatly. 'I want nothing to do with you. I'll make my own way from now on.'

'Janet, listen to me...'

'No, I have listened. You made me feel I could do it, make a life of my own, and I can and will. If you've decided that's not for you, that's fine, but I don't want you to teach me any more. You let me down. It made me sick.'

'When you're older you'll probably understand a little more.'

Janet shrugged. Claire remembered the shrug of the previous day and said, 'I'm sorry about your hand. I shouldn't have reacted as I did.'

'I wanted you to,' Janet said, 'but my hand's fine now. I hated you for destroying my dream, but I won't defy you again, I don't care enough any more. And,' Janet said, 'you'd better have this back. I don't want it,' and she took the birthday locket from the sideboard and put it in Claire's hand.

It was so unfair, Claire thought. She wanted to rant and rail at Janet and remind her of how much she owed her, but that would hardly make the child like or respect her more, and that was really what she wanted. There was nothing more to say, so she turned and went out of the house and neither of them said goodbye.

Things were so hectic for the next two weeks that Janet hadn't time to think about the rift between her and Claire Wentworth. At school, she was barely polite. The first day back was the hardest, because all the kids in the class expected a repetition of Tuesday and were waiting in anticipation for an explosion that didn't happen.

Girls who had never bothered with Janet before spoke to her at playtime and she was invited to join in their games, but Janet was wary of such overtures. She knew they were only asking her because of the way she'd stood up to Miss Wentworth. Once they realised there would be no repetition, she'd be dropped again. Unfortunately, she was proved right.

No one in the family seemed to think it odd that Janet no longer went to Claire Wentworth's, and there were no questions asked. They seemed to think there was no point now, and anyway, Janet had little free time and could always see her teacher at school if she wanted to.

It was over three weeks after Betty was taken to hospital that she came home with the tiny bundle that was Sally Travers. She placed the baby in Janet's arms while she hugged and cuddled the twins, and Janet looked down at the sister she didn't want and was seized by an inexplicable and totally unexpected wave of protective love for the scrap of humanity she held.

She was so very tiny and helpless, but very beautiful. Her eyes were a vivid blue, with long dark lashes. She had a little rosebud mouth and her hair was like golden down on her head. Each day Janet thought she became more and more beautiful. She knew her sister would have the blonde curls and deep blue eyes that Duncan had and she couldn't explain the love she had for her.

Despite the novelty of the new baby, Janet was worried, for since Sally's birth Betty seemed to have forgotten all about the grammar school and the uniform list that Bert knew nothing about. One afternoon after school she tackled her mother about it.

'Give me a couple of weeks to get myself together, love,' Betty said. 'It'll be all right, don't worry.'

But Janet did worry, and it was towards the end of May before the matter was broached with Bert. Duncan, Janet and the twins were sent into the garden, and they heard Betty arguing with her husband.

Unknown to Bert, Betty had gone off on her own to town and looked in the Co-op at the prices of the uniform. She had been appalled. Gaberdine coat, barathea blazer, even the felt hats and summer boaters were ridiculous prices. She said none of this to Bert, but spoke to her sister of going back on the twilight shift, and asked the Co-op man to call and see her about a cheque. Her Janet had got this far; no one would take it away from her now.

Bert had surveyed the uniform list mournfully and asked the foreman to keep him in mind for any overtime going. With yet another mouth to feed, he found that his money didn't go as far and he was able to save nothing, and he worried about it.

'Why don't you ask about grants and things?' Breda said, knowing her sister was concerned.

'I wouldn't know who to ask.'

'Don't be so gormless, Bet,' Breda cried

impatiently. 'Go and see your Janet's teacher.'

So, unknown to Janet, because she didn't want her to be embarrassed, Betty went one lunchtime to see Claire Wentworth. Duncan and Janet had their dinner at their gran's, who also minded Sally and the twins.

She explained to Claire about the uniform list.

'We want her to go so bad,' she said, 'but I don't know how it's to be done, I really don't. I was wondering if there were grants I could get, like.'

Claire didn't know – Janet was the first child she'd got through the eleven-plus – but she promised to enquire. She knew the financial strain the family were under and was anxious to help despite Janet's feelings towards her. She spent several days getting together the relevant information and forms to fill, and because she knew Betty would probably like notice, she told Janet that she would be calling at her house the following evening.

'Why?' Janet asked, at once hostile.

'I have some business with your parents,' Claire replied, and there was nothing Janet could say.

She quizzed her mom when she got home. 'She's finding out about grants and such like to help out with the cost of the uniform,' Betty said crossly, annoyed at Janet's attitude. 'I mean, you do want to go to this school, I suppose?'

'You know I do!'

'Well then, we'll have to afford it, but money doesn't grow on trees, you know.'

'I'm not stupid.'

'Maybe not,' snapped Betty, 'but you're impertinent all right.'

'There are grants,' Claire Wentworth told them that night, 'but they're not automatic, they're discretionary. That means we have to fill in these forms about your income and outgoings and how many children there are in the family and so on, and I write a letter explaining why I think you should have a grant.'

'It's very kind of you, Miss Wentworth,' Betty said.

Bert expressed doubts about putting down his income, but Claire soothed him. 'It's confidential,' she assured him. 'No one else will know. I'll help you fill the forms in if you like, or I'll leave them for you to do on your own.'

'Oh,' Betty said, 'I'd rather have help, if you don't mind.'

Claire brought other things besides forms. Her mother, who was, she said, a terrible hoarder, had still got the white games skirt and Aertex shirt Claire had worn at her grammar school, and her old hockey boots. 'I didn't go to Whytecliff,' she said, 'but the games uniform is usually the same, and hockey boots are just hockey boots. Janet can pad the toes for now if they're too big.' She pulled the items out of the bag beside her. 'She has my old hockey stick as well, and tennis racquet, but...' she gestured helplessly, 'I'm afraid I couldn't fit them in. I'll have to bring them over another time.'

Bert and Betty laughed, and Betty looked at her daughter sternly, wondering why Janet – who'd had good manners drummed into her since the day she was born – should appear so ungrateful and sullen with her old teacher. 'Have you

151

nothing to say?' she snapped at last.

'Thank you,' Janet said woodenly. 'Please thank your mother for me.' She felt bad she couldn't be more gracious about it, but there it was.

'We're so grateful for all you've done for us,' Bert said sincerely. 'We couldn't begin to tell you, and that's not counting the extra work with young Janet.'

'She has a good brain,' Claire said. 'Janet was my first eleven-plus success and my last for a time. I'm not taking the top class next year. I didn't want the work involved, to be honest. I'm getting married and my husband wants to see something of me.'

Janet, dispatched to the kitchen to make another cup of tea, was stopped in the doorway by Miss Wentworth's news. She stared at her across the room while her parents were showering Claire with congratulations, and inside she was crying, 'Oh, Miss Wentworth.'

Chapter Seven

How was it, Janet thought, that you could long for something with all your heart, work towards making it happen, and when you achieved your heart's desire be dissatisfied and unhappy? That was how Janet felt about Whytecliff High School, and though she promised Claire she'd come and tell her how things were going, she daren't go near her, for she knew she would realise immediately how despondent Janet had become as the days passed.

She'd not met anyone at the school who even spoke as she did, and the other girls were always mocking her accent and making fun of her generally.

She was furious one day when Belinda sneered at her for calling her parents Mom and Dad. 'Mummy and Daddy, my dear,' she said patronisingly, 'or Mother and Father would be acceptable, but then good manners cannot be expected from a guttersnipe.'

Janet's hard fist connected with Belinda's nose, and she watched with satisfaction as the blood spurted on to the other girl's white shirt. But, 'Do not bring your street manners to this school,' Miss Phelps told Janet sternly, ignoring the glare she was giving her. 'Belinda was most distressed, and so, I might add, was her mother. Write out five hundred times, "I must control my temper"

153

and apologise to Belinda. That will be all.'

Janet apologised, though the words stuck in her throat. In the streets she'd been brought up in, you didn't go sneaking to adults, but she knew here she'd have to be a bit more devious. Belinda accepted Janet's apology, commenting again that such behaviour was only to be expected with her upbringing. When, the following morning, she fell heavily on her way into assembly, no one saw Janet's foot trip her, but everyone saw Janet helping her up.

'We're even now, you stuck-up pig,' she hissed as she smiled sweetly at the odious Belinda.

The grant had not provided the money for everything, and Janet's skirt had been purchased from the Co-op. It was a slightly different shade and style from those of the other girls, and the fact was seized on immediately by her tormentors.

'Where did your mother buy your skirt, council house brat?' Millicent asked. 'At a jumble sale?'

There was a peal of laughter around the room, and Annabel remarked, 'Perhaps it wasn't bought at all. It's such a rag, perhaps it was put out in the bags of rubbish even a jumble sale couldn't use.'

Janet longed to pound their stupid faces against the wall. Instead, she bided her time. Next day, in the art room, she tripped, flinging scarlet paint over Annabel's still-life picture. It dribbled like droplets of blood, causing the colours to run and merge together like a crazily patterned kaleidoscope.

'I'm so sorry,' Janet said, while Annabel wailed noisily.

Miss Masters, the art teacher, who was crossing the room to find the reason for the commotion, saw Annabel almost leap away from Janet and shriek, 'You hateful pig, you did it on purpose, but then what can you expect from someone of your type?'

Miss Masters' sympathy for Annabel's spoilt picture was wiped out by the last remark. Janet, she noted, looked suitably chastened and repentant. Janet suppressed a smile at the firm set of the teacher's mouth as she looked angrily at Annabel and remarked stonily, 'Now, now, Annabel, what a fuss over an accident. I'm sure Janet is truly sorry she spoilt your picture, and there was no need to make personal comments about her background.'

Later, Janet who was cleaning the floor of spilt paint, heard Annabel whisper menacingly in her ear, 'I know you did that on purpose, you filthy little guttersnipe.'

'Dear Annabel,' she replied, smiling sweetly, 'it takes one to know one.'

'She's getting above herself, uppity bitch,' Belinda said.

'Yes, but she's clever enough not to get caught,' said Millicent, still limping from Janet stamping on her bare toes in the changing room. That had come about because they'd made fun of her hockey stick. Despite Brendan smoothing out the dents and giving it a coat of varnish, it still looked nothing like the pristine new ones of the others, and they noticed immediately.

'A prehistoric monstrosity,' Millicent called it, and added, 'Perhaps her father fashioned it himself. After all, they're little removed from savages on these council estates.' Her feet were swollen and painful for the rest of the day.

The teachers were aware of the antagonism surrounding Janet Travers but couldn't understand it. 'She's one of the brightest girls in her year and totally attentive in class, yet she's completely friendless,' said the English teacher, Miss James, perplexed.

'No one will partner her for anything,' the games teacher reported, 'and she's the last to be picked for teams, though she's reasonably good.'

'Could be her background,' someone suggested. 'It is what the socialists would describe as "deprived", I believe.'

'Sod her background,' the maths teacher put in angrily. 'She has one of the best and most receptive brains I've had the pleasure to meet in this dump. I am fed up with teaching genteel young ladies who believe maths is "not quite the thing". Janet Travers, on the other hand, grasps new concepts almost before they leave my lips, works diligently in class and hands homework in on time, neat, legible and usually correct.'

Janet would have been gratified to hear the teachers' opinion, because she was achingly lonely. No one linked arms with her in the yard, or asked her home to tea. Keeping away from her tormentors meant skulking in the playground alone and isolated and scurrying to and from the bus stop as quickly as possible.

She could hardly confide in her family, puffed up with pride as they were that their Janet was at the grammar school, and she'd had little in common with other girls on the estate of her own age since she'd begun working for the eleven-plus. And how could she arrive at Claire's door and admit how miserable she was at the school when Miss Wentworth had worked so hard to get her in in the first place? Not to mention all the time she'd spent with Janet during the summer holidays, teaching her all sorts of things so that she wouldn't feel inadequate next to the other girls.

Even the desk she worked at at home was due indirectly to Claire, and it had also been the means of healing the rift between them. Early in the summer holidays, Claire told Betty that she had an old desk she had no use for and offered it to her for Janet, but Janet, still angry and disappointed with Claire and uncomfortable at the influence she was having in her family, refused to even consider it.

'I don't understand her and that's the truth,' Betty said to Patsy and Brendan, when she visited to admire their new baby, Liam. 'I mean, it isn't that she doesn't need a desk, and what she could have against that nice Miss Wentworth I don't know, and after all she's done for her.'

Betty's brow was puckered with anxiety, but Brendan said, 'Why shouldn't she have a new desk, a new desk for a new school, not some old, scratched thing her teacher's throwing out? I'll make her one, and if I set it into the window it will take less off the room. She'll need a bookcase too, I'd say, with all that studying.'

'Go and see Miss Wentworth and explain,' Betty said to Janet. 'Thank her for her kind offer and say your uncle is making you a desk. Tell her he's a carpenter.'

Janet stared at her. The last place she wanted to go was to see Claire Wentworth, who she'd not set eyes on since the day she'd come up with the grant forms. Also, she didn't know how Brendan was going to fit a desk in her room, for wherever he put it it would mean there was no room for Sally. 'I can't have a desk,' she cried, 'not from anyone. Sally will...'

'Sally will stay beside my bed for now,' Betty said, 'as you all did. When she's older Brendan will build her a small bed in the alcove in our bedroom that goes over the stairs, and your dad will fit a curtain for privacy later.'

'Oh,' Janet said, and her heart lightened in relief. She loved Sally, loved her with a passion she'd not felt for the twins, and she talked and read to her, even confided her worries to the baby who gurgled in her arms, but she wanted her room to herself.

'Are you sure, Mom?' she said.

'Dad and I think you need your own space and a bit of privacy,' Betty said. 'After all, it isn't every day a daughter gets to the grammar school.'

So Janet had been dispatched to Claire Wentworth. She didn't want to go and she could think of a thousand and one reasons why she shouldn't, but she knew that not one of them would satisfy her mother.

She felt a traitor to herself as she cycled up that Saturday afternoon in July. She was taking no chances and rang the front doorbell. Miss Wentworth was a long time coming, and Janet was just beginning to think she wasn't in and she could go thankfully home again when suddenly Claire stood in the doorway.

She wore a loose, flowing dress in a swirl of pastel colours with straps over the shoulders to hold it up. Her hair was coiled back from her neck and secured with a bandana to match the dress, her brown legs were bare and strappy sandals were on her feet.

Janet's heart gave a lurch. Miss Wentworth looked lovely, cool, in complete control and very beautiful. Janet was aware of the sun beating down on her head. She was hot and sticky, the palms of her hands were damp with sweat and so were her armpits, and she felt suddenly very young.

'Janet, how nice to see you,' Claire said, and though she smiled, her voice was guarded. 'Come through, we're in the garden, and I'm sure you could do with a glass of lemonade.'

Janet should have been warned by the word 'we' but she wasn't. She followed Claire, mesmerised, like a moth flutters around a light, and was unprepared for the man who lay stretched out on a blanket on the lawn.

'David, get up and meet Janet,' Claire said, and the man rose, loose-limbed and easy. Janet recoiled, but he appeared not to notice.

'Hello,' he said, 'I've heard such a lot about you.'

Janet had been prepared to despise the panting, perverted man she'd last seen lying on top of Claire Wentworth. She imagined he'd be embarrassed when they met, but Claire had not told

159

him what Janet had seen, so he was completely at ease with her. Janet couldn't believe it. She would have liked him more, she thought, if he'd shown a measure of discomfort. If he'd mumbled an apology or gone red or something, but he just smiled at her. She noticed that his face was tanned, his eyes deep brown and his jet-black hair swept back from his head. She decided that though he looked very fine, he was callous and unfeeling.

She sat there in the garden in the sunshine, feeling uncomfortable to be with them in their loose, light things. She herself felt dull and stupid and too hot in her thick, hard-wearing clothes and sturdy shoes. She told them of her Uncle Brendan and how he was building her a desk and bookcases while she drank the lemonade Claire had poured.

She suddenly noticed that, while they listened and were interested in what she said, they seemed always to be aware of one another. She saw the glances that passed between them, the soft, lingering look in their eyes, and the way they touched one another. Sometimes their fingers entwined, or David's hands would rest for a moment on Claire's shoulders and her hand would brush his arm. Janet felt excluded from this inner circle, this magic club with just two members.

She jumped to her feet. 'I've got to go.'

'Not yet,' Claire said. Janet had thought David and Claire were only aware of one another, but in actual fact Claire had been covertly watching Janet since she'd arrived. She'd sensed the girl's hostility and knew she resented being there, and she wished she knew of a way to break down the barriers she had raised.

'I've got to get back,' Janet said, and Claire knew that if she allowed Janet to rush away now she would have lost her. 'I've got a record I'd like you to listen to,' she burst out suddenly.

'A record!' echoed Janet, turning to Claire. She missed the quizzical look David threw her. Something was up. He could almost feel the tension in the air between Claire and her protégée. He wondered if they'd had a row. She'd not mentioned Janet for ages and that in itself was strange.

Then Claire turned to him and said, 'Didn't you have something to do this afternoon, darling?' Yes, he bloody did, David thought. He'd planned on lazing side by side on the grass with the woman he loved, and then slipping upstairs for a spot of lovemaking. Then later they'd go out to the pub for a few jars with their friends. He sighed. It wasn't to be, obviously, for whatever was wrong between Claire and Janet would have to be sorted before Claire would have any time for him. It was just how she was. He caught the pleading look she threw him and decided he could afford to be generous.

'Yes, I really must be off,' he said, and smiled to show her he was playing her game, whatever it was.

'What sort of record?' Janet asked flatly. She ignored David and spoke only to Claire.

'A classical piece,' Claire said, 'the sort of thing they'd probably play in the music appreciation lessons at Whytecliff High. They did that sort of thing when I was at grammar school, anyway.'

Janet said nothing. She looked anything but pleased, and David couldn't work it out. He'd hero-worshipped a master at school when he was a boy and firmly believed he would have laid down his life for him if required to do so. But this Travers girl was refusing to even be polite to Claire and he couldn't understand why Claire put up with it. He knew better than to interfere, though. He'd done that before and Claire had bitten his head off. He'd let them sort it out between them.

'Claire,' he said.

Claire tore her attention from Janet and said, 'Hadn't you better be off, darling?'

Bloody hell! David thought. He covered his bad temper with effort – maybe they'd have time together later – and regarded Claire with tolerant amusement.

'Okay,' he said. 'Are you going to see me out?'

They walked together, arms linked, to the gate, and as he bent for a goodbye kiss Claire said, 'Thanks for this, David. Come round later tonight. I'll make it up to you, promise.'

'It's okay,' David said, 'but what's up with happy Harriet today?'

'Nothing.'

'Miserable little devil if you ask me.'

'Well, I didn't ask you,' Claire said. 'She's best left to me. Go on, I'll see you later.'

Janet did look miserable, though, Claire had to admit, and out of place, embarrassed to be there. She waited for Claire to reach her and then said,

162

'I don't want to listen to any record.'

'Okay,' Claire said. 'I won't make you, but can we talk?'

'What about?'

'Oh, Janet, don't be difficult,' Claire said impatiently. 'I want you to come back and see me again. We haven't many weeks before you're off to Whytecliff, and there's a lot we haven't covered.'

Janet knew that was true, but 'I don't need to know any more,' she said.

'You don't need it, no,' Claire agreed, 'but it might help.'

'What about him?' Janet said rudely.

'Do you mean David?' Claire remarked sharply. 'He has got a name.'

'Well,' Janet said, 'I'm not coming back if he's going to be here all the time.'

Claire knew that if David was there he'd resent the time she spent teaching Janet anyway. He could get very jealous of things like that. He liked Claire's free time to be spent with him, so if she was going to coax Janet back and keep David happy, she'd have to keep them apart.

'Oh, Janet,' she said, 'what am I to do with you?'

'You can "oh, Janet" all you like, Miss Wentworth, but I'm not coming if he's going to be here,' Janet told her stonily.

Claire Wentworth was silent for a minute, and then she said: 'All right, I'll see he doesn't intrude.'

It was an olive branch that Claire was handing out, and Janet recognised it as such. Suddenly she wanted to come back and work with Claire

163

again. She hid her eagerness; she wasn't going to go overboard. 'If you want I'll come,' she said grudgingly, but it was enough.

So later, when the teachers at Whytecliff High School were staggered by the depth of Janet's knowledge, she knew she owed it all to Claire.

On their last evening together, in the middle of August, just before Claire's marriage to David Sunderland, Claire gave Janet a package. When she unwrapped it, she saw it was the silver locket she'd had for her eleventh birthday.

'Please take it,' Claire said. 'I gave it to you because you became my friend rather than my pupil. It will mean a lot if you accept it.'

Janet knew she was being asked to accept more than a locket. If she took it, she would have to try and forget the scene she had witnessed between Claire and her fiancé. She would never understand Claire's behaviour, and yet she couldn't just spurn the woman who'd given up so much time to teach and coach her.

She put out her hand. 'Thank you,' she said, and added, 'I'm sorry.'

'No,' Claire said, and Janet heard the emotion in her voice. 'Don't apologise, just come and see me in your fine school uniform and tell me how it is.'

'I will,' Janet had promised, but as the autumn term dragged on and the misery bit deeper, she confided only in her baby sister, who she seemed to draw comfort from. The others were no good. Duncan viewed anything to do with school with the patronising air of one almost done with such fripperies. He would be thirteen in November,

164

and with the world of work almost in his grasp, the gap between brother and sister widened.

Her mother was proud of her but was too busy to worry about her. In any case, in Betty's opinion, Janet was too clever to have problems. Bert was delighted with his intelligent daughter and boasted of her often, but sometimes he didn't know how to talk to her.

'All right, love?' he'd say ineffectually.

'Yes, Dad.'

'Not working you too hard at that school, are they?'

'No, Dad.'

'Still enjoying it, are you?'

'Yes, Dad.' Janet wondered what the hell else she could say. Could she admit that all that work put in by her and Claire, and the sacrifices her family had made, was all for nothing?

'That's all right then,' Bert would say, reassured.

Only the baby knew what was in Janet's heart. 'When it's your turn, Sally,' she promised her gurgling sister, 'I'll be there for you. You won't need a Miss Wentworth in your life. You'll have me.'

Claire wouldn't have been fooled by the façade of happiness she drew round herself to satisfy the family, so Janet went to see her at Christmas, only when she felt the festivities could successfully hide her dejection. She'd come top or near the top in her end-of-term exams, and though Claire was pleased, she had news of her own.

'I'm expecting,' she said, eyes shining, and Janet felt her heart plummet like a stone.

'Congratulations,' she forced herself to say, but she knew it would never be the same between them again, and her isolation, even in the midst of the Christmas revelries, felt more acute than ever.

January was bitterly cold, with snow driven into drifts by buffeting winds, and the buses were often late or full. Gales gushed around the school and icy draughts came in through rattling, ill-fitting windows and seeped under doors, freezing feet and wrapping clammily around stocking-clad legs. Faces were pinched and grey with cold, and Annabel, Millicent and Belinda began a baiting campaign against Janet.

'Funny smell in here ... oh, it's just the charity case bringing in the smell of the gutter she was dragged up in,' Annabel said one day when other jibes had failed to get a reaction.

'What is it with you?' Janet, stung at last, yelled at her. 'What's your problem?'

'You, my dear,' Millicent said, her voice dripping with sarcasm. 'Pushing your way in here where you don't belong.'

'I've as much right as you.'

'Hardly, I'm paid for.'

Janet felt the other girls' eyes upon her and knew that the mood of the class was dangerous. This was Janet Travers the scholarship girl, fair game for taunting and teasing, some fun to be had in the cold and gloom of winter.

Janet glared at them and anger flowed through her. 'You're a lot of stuck-up bleeding snobs,' she cried, and heard the shocked gasp of the girls before the cruel laughter followed her down the corridor as she fled.

The snow turned to grey sludge, the icicles melted, the winds dropped and snowdrops and crocuses pushed their heads up through the frozen earth. Spring was on its way and Janet came to terms with the fact that she couldn't fight the whole class. Her hat was snatched from her head countless times as she left school, just as a prefect was coming into view. It warranted an immediate detention with lines to write: 'I must wear my hat as it is an integral part of school uniform.'

'Why don't you learn, squirt?' one sixth-former asked her quite kindly when she'd been booked by her for the third time.

Janet shrugged. She was no telltale. When someone pulled the chair away just as Janet was about to sit down, no one knew who'd done it. In the same way, no one knew who loosened the lid of the salt cellar so that the contents were deposited on Janet's dinner, but seven pairs of glittering eyes around the table, and their explosive laughter, told her that they all knew about it.

Just before Easter, her games kit disappeared from her peg in the changing room. The games mistress was furious. 'I was going to try you out for the hockey team today,' she said. 'Judging by your previous performances, you had a good chance. Write out two hundred times, "I must not forget my games kit."'

'But I didn't,' Janet protested. Later, her kit was recovered from the drainpipe, filthy dirty and wet.

After the Easter break, it was Annabel's foot that tripped Janet in the dinner hall. As she sprawled she landed in her dinner. Mashed potato, cabbage, meat pie and gravy clung to her skirt and jumper, and a blob of something glutinous had landed on her chin. The laughter rippled and swelled in the hall and Janet wanted to die. A few days later, Millicent's hand slipped as she was pouring the water, and it flooded over Janet's plate, rendering her meal inedible.

At home, she kept to her room as much as possible, for even Betty and Bert had noticed her despondency. Betty had remarked tight-lipped one night, when she bawled the twins out for some mild misdemeanour, 'It's a pity an expensive education doesn't teach tolerance, that's all I can say.'

'I don't know where they are going to attack next,' Janet told Sally, who toddled about her room holding on to the furniture. Sally smiled and raised her arms to be picked up.

'You're no help,' Janet said, and hugged her tight. But in reality, Janet didn't know how she'd have gone on without the baby.

The next day her gaberdine coat disappeared from the cloakroom. She waited until it was emptied of people, with only the shoe bags swinging on the pegs to search properly, but no coat had fallen to the floor, or been pushed behind the pipes. She had to find it, she knew it had cost a fortune, and she scoured the classrooms and ran along the corridor in a frenzy.

'What you lost, lovey?' a cleaner asked, watching her.

'My coat. Have you seen a raincoat?' Janet asked anxiously.

But she hadn't, and Janet went off to search the playground. Remembering her games kit, she shoved her hand up the drainpipe, but it was empty. Returning to the building, she was met by the cleaner who'd spoken to her earlier. The woman was holding a bedraggled coat in her hands.

'Found it tucked behind a radiator in the toilets,' she said.

Janet took it from her in disbelief. It was grimed with dirt and very crumpled, and there was a rip in the lining.

'Playing a joke, likely,' the cleaner said, but she was seething inside and added, 'Don't cry, lovey.'

Janet hadn't been aware she had been crying and scrubbed at her eyes fiercely with her fist and she carried her coat home, for she couldn't wear it. She hoped her dad was going to the club so that she and her gran could work on it before her mom saw it.

She saw her gran glance at her strangely when she took the garment from her arm and hung it up, but Sarah said nothing. No sooner had the door slammed behind her father than Janet was down the stairs. Her gran had already taken the coat from the peg and was staring at it as if she couldn't believe her eyes.

'What in the name of God happened to it?' she asked, and glared at Janet.

'Don't ask,' Janet said wearily.

'I will ask,' Gran said angrily. 'Have you any idea what a coat like this costs?'

'Gran, please. It was a prank that went wrong. It won't happen again.'

And it won't. Janet promised herself. I've stood by long enough and let people walk over me. Tomorrow morning I'm going to dish out my own punishment.

All evening she seethed as she and Gran sponged at the stains and Gran sewed the rip. Then Janet ironed the coat and put it on a coat hanger to air in her bedroom. All night she planned, and the anger burnt and built up in her.

She strode into the playground next morning still raging inside. She had her coat on but left it flapping open, and she saw several knowing stares and nudges. The fuse was lit when a large girl called Eve shouted:

'You found your coat then, Travers?'

Janet grabbed her by the neck, and despite her considerable bulk, dragged her across the playground and slammed her head against the wall. Several girls descended on her, but Janet seemed possessed of demonic strength. Her coat flowed out behind her as one recoiled from a thump in the stomach, another from a punch in the face, another from a savage elbow jab in the ribs.

'Fight! fight!' began the swelling murmur in the playground as Janet's flailing legs and lashing feet hit out right and left. The other girls began slowly backing away, and Eve lay crumpled and crying at her feet. At that moment Miss James spotted the commotion from the staff-room window. She rushed down and right into the fray, where she surveyed the red-faced and still angry Janet, the girl at her feet and the group huddled around her.

'What is all this about?' she demanded.

'Ask them,' Janet retorted, indicating the girls in front of her. She was too cross to be cautious. 'See if they'll tell you what it's about. They might because they're all bleeding cowards, but I'm no telltale.'

Miss James' lips pressed together. Oh dear, oh dear, she thought, why does Janet have to use such a tone and such bad language? I shall have to report it to Miss Phelps. It would never do for a girl to repeat it at home and say I took no action.

It was fortunate for Janet that at that moment a dumpy, shabbily dressed figure was leaving Miss Phelps' office. All night she'd worried about the lass who owned the coat, and the look on her face when she'd given it to her.

'It's a disgrace,' she'd remarked to her husband. 'Call themselves young ladies and do that. That poor lass was so cut up. I've noticed her before. I think she's a scholarship girl.'

Her husband was shop steward at his factory. 'Hardly has parents able to afford to replace coats then,' he said severely. 'You should do something about it, Em.'

It was her husband's words ringing in her ears that lent Emma Harris the courage to walk into the office of Whytecliff High School and ask to see Miss Phelps.

While the headmistress was still digesting what the cleaner had told her, Miss James knocked on the door. She ushered before her several girls in disarray, one of them holding her head and crying noisily.

'What is the meaning of this?' demanded the headmistress sternly. Several of the girls rushed to explain, but Janet stayed silent. She saw Miss Phelps' eyes glittering with dislike. That's all right, she thought, I don't like you either.

Miss Phelps listened to the girls' garbled explanation but kept her eyes on Janet. It wasn't that she disliked Janet personally, she just didn't care for any scholarship girl. She thought they lowered the tone of the school and brought out the worst in the other girls. There had been little trouble before the scholarship scheme, but since Janet Travers had arrived ... well... And yet the teachers had nothing but praise for the girl's intelligence and diligence. Really, it was most provoking.

The girls' diatribe drew to a close eventually. It had consisted mainly of the declaration that Janet Travers had seemed to suddenly go mad, kicking and thumping, and had even banged poor Eve's head against the wall deliberately. And she'd said a bad word too.

Miss Phelps looked at Janet. 'And what have you to say?' she said.

What was the point of saying anything? Janet thought. At least if I'm expelled no one will attack me at Paget Road Secondary and rip, damage or hide my things.

'Nothing,' she said.

'Nothing, Miss Phelps,' Miss Phelps rapped out. 'You've been here long enough to know how to address a member of staff.'

'Nothing, Miss Phelps,' Janet repeated tonelessly.

172

'You've heard what the girls say you did?'

'Yes ... Miss Phelps.'

'Well, did you lash out, punching and kicking them?'

'Yes, Miss Phelps.'

Miss Phelps couldn't help a grudging admiration for the girl. Janet stood before her fearlessly, answering her defiantly, and had apparently been fighting off the others single-handed.

'Janet Travers is just one,' she said to the gaggle of girls before her, 'amongst so many.'

They shifted their feet uncomfortably. Belinda said, 'We were taken by surprise, Miss Phelps.'

'We were trying to protect Eve, Miss Phelps,' put in Annabel. 'I mean, Tra ... Janet just went wild and dragged her across the playground.'

'And yet Janet is much lighter and smaller than Eve,' Miss Phelps said, with a smile at Eve. 'Why was she able to do that, my dear?'

'I don't know, Miss Phelps,' Eve said miserably. The marks of tears were still on her face as she continued, 'She's terribly strong.'

Miss Phelps looked at Janet. She gazed back, unafraid, her face expressionless.

A bell sounded for the start of school, and Miss James started.

'Miss Phelps, I must...'

'Yes, go,' said Miss Phelps. 'I will deal with this.' She waited until the door had closed behind the English teacher and then said:

'And none of you has any idea what Janet Travers' apparent brainstorm was all about?' she asked dryly.

The 'No, Miss Phelps' was said as a chorus.

173

'It couldn't then have anything to do with a coat?'

Janet's head shot up in surprise, and the other girls showed every sign of consternation. Some flushed red, the colour drained from others; all were uneasy. Miss Phelps clicked her fingers at Janet.

'Hand me the coat,' she snapped.

She examined it carefully. She could still make out the faint marks and darker patches where someone had tried to sponge the dirt off, and she could see the tear in the lining that had been repaired. She felt angry that anyone should do such a thing.

'Is this the first time something like this has happened?' she asked Janet.

'I'd rather not say, Miss Phelps.'

Stupid, misplaced loyalty, Miss Phelps thought.

'Do you know anything about this?' she said to the others.

'No, Miss Phelps,' came the chorus again.

'I don't believe you,' said Miss Phelps, 'and if I hear about one more thing like this – just one more, do you hear? – I'll send for your parents.'

Janet was nonplussed. She wondered how Miss Phelps knew about the coat. However she'd heard, she thought, it had probably saved her from being expelled, and gave the others in her form something to think about. It was as if Miss Phelps was taking Janet's part after all. She sent the other girls back to class with five hundred lines each to write: 'I must not damage people's possessions.' As they were trooping out, she passed the coat across the desk to Janet and said,

'You shouldn't have any more trouble.'

'No, Miss Phelps.'

'Just one thing, Janet.'

Janet turned to face her headmistress, but did not speak. 'Watch that language,' Miss Phelps advised.

Janet smiled. 'Yes, Miss Phelps.' she said, and hurried to put her coat back in the cloakroom.

Chapter Eight

Janet had come top, or almost top, in all her exams. She was disbelieving and ecstatic. Her family were only faintly surprised.

They didn't see what it meant. She'd be in 2a the following year. These were the fast-stream girls who did Latin as well as French and were expected to end up at Cambridge or Oxford. To Janet's delight, her old class had been split up, and the majority of her tormentors were in the lower forms.

'Go and tell Miss Wentworth – or Mrs Sunderland, I should say – about how you did in the exams,' Betty suggested. 'It may cheer her up, and God knows she could do with something.'

'I will, Mom,' Janet said. She felt bad that she'd neglected Claire. It was because of what was happening to her at school, but she still felt guilty. It was stupid really, because going to see her wouldn't have helped her. No one could have known. She'd had a trouble-free pregnancy and labour, according to what people said. That was what made it so tragic.

Later, in Claire and David's bedroom, she looked down at the baby fast asleep in the crib beside the bed. 'Oh, Miss Went ... Mrs Sunderland, she's beautiful.'

'Yes,' said Claire tonelessly, 'she is.' She added, 'Can't you drop this Mrs thing now you're not at

Paget Road School any more? Call me Claire.'

Janet smiled. 'Okay.' She was shy with Claire after such a long time. Suddenly her exam results didn't matter as much as the mite in the cot. 'Are you sure?' she said. 'Are they sure, the doctors?'

Claire nodded. 'One doctor told me to put her into a home and forget about her. She'll never learn anything or be able to live independently; mongol children don't, apparently.'

'Put her into a home?' repeated Janet in shocked tones. 'You won't, will you?'

Claire shook her head. 'No,' she said, but her voice was so low Janet had to strain to catch it. 'Chloe may be mentally handicapped, but she needs at least the same attention as a normal child, don't you think?'

She didn't say that David didn't agree. 'So you think you know better than the doctors?' he'd railed at her.

'She's our baby, she needs us.'

'She won't know the bloody difference, you stupid fool. She'll grow up an idiot.'

Claire controlled the tears that she longed to shed and forgave the cruelty of David's words, knowing that it was deep distress and the feeling that he had been cheated of a perfect child that had made him lash out at her.

He'd crossed the room and put an arm around her shoulders. 'I know you're upset, pet. It's natural. God, I'm upset too, but the doctors know best.'

'No, they don't,' Claire had protested. 'They see her as a medical problem, a psychiatric case, not a baby to be loved.'

'Face it, for God's sake,' David had yelled. 'She isn't a baby, not a normal baby. If you do what the doctors want and put her away, we can get on with our lives. We can have another child.'

Claire had flinched away from him. Her lips had been pulled back in a snarl of disgust as she spat out, 'She's our baby, David, not a defective wireless you send back to the shop and get a new, perfect model. Chloe is our daughter. She's mentally handicapped but still our child. I can accept that, why can't you? She feels cold and hunger and pain. Later she'll feel afraid and lonely, and yet I'm advised to give her up to strangers. They are supposed to love her better than me, are they? I have an ache in my heart every time I look at her, but I already love her dearly and know she'll probably always need me much more than a normal baby would.'

'Is that your final decision?'

'Yes, David, it is,' Claire said. 'Can you live with it?'

'I don't know,' David had said.

He was still there, but the marriage was strained as David grieved for the child he might have had. It was so unfair that they should have an imperfect child. They were in good health, both in the prime of life. They'd done everything right.

As Janet looked down at the sleeping baby, Claire said, 'I couldn't give her up. Your mom couldn't have given Sally away, could she?'

'None of us could,' Janet said. 'We all love her. Even the twins are gentler round her. And I don't see why Chloe should be different.'

178

'Bless you, Janet,' Claire said, for she needed support. Janet was aware without being told that it was a lonely path Claire was embarking on. It was only as she rode home through the balmy summer's evening after tea that she wondered where David had been. She hadn't asked and Claire hadn't mentioned him at all.

All through the sunlit days of the summer holiday, Janet spent time at Claire's almost every day. Sometimes she went by bus and took Sally, now an inquisitive toddler, with her. Sally, the youngest in her family, was enthralled by baby Chloe. Claire was full of plans for the future, but throughout the long, hot summer, Janet never saw David, and Claire never excused his absence, nor did she explain it.

Not surprisingly, Janet approached the start of the autumn term with trepidation. When she walked into her new classroom in September for the first time, she felt threads of apprehension still clinging to her.

She needn't have worried. Most of the girls remaining from her first-year class were the studious and serious ones who had taken little or no part in the teasing of Janet Travers. Those who had taken part had mostly been on the periphery of the action and now wanted to forget it. They also wanted Janet Travers to forget it. A couple of months further on, their behaviour seemed to them immature and cruel.

Janet had noticed Ruth Hayman in the form room straight away. She was striking-looking rather than pretty, with thick hair so black it shone blue when the sun was on it. Yet her skin was alabaster white and only on her high cheekbones was there a tinge of pink. Her eyes were both unusual and beautiful. They were golden in colour and oval, almost oriental, in shape. In fact they looked similar in shape to Chloe's eyes, Janet realised with a jolt. She studied the girl intently and dismissed her, knowing that such an aloof, haughty girl would not be interested in a charity child.

The term began, and this time Janet was left alone to get on with her life. which was better than being tormented, but only slightly. Then, one day, she came out of school in a stream of girls, and when they'd broken up to go for their various buses, she realised that just in front of her was Ruth. She hadn't noticed before that they went the same way, and she wondered idly if she'd be able to get into conversation with her at the bus stop.

She quickened her pace a little. Ruth was striding forward briskly. Her black hair in the thick plait she sometimes wore to school bounced on her back, beneath the felt hat.

At first Janet was hardly aware of the group of three girls between her and Ruth. She knew they were there and laughing about something, but she didn't connect it with Ruth. That was, until she got close enough to hear what they were saying.

'I think our Ruthie's a chinky Chinese,' said one, pulling her eyes up at the corners in a parody of an oriental. 'They wear those plaits in China.'

'She's not Chinese,' said another. 'She's a snobby cow. Doesn't talk to the likes of us.'

'She has no reason to be snobby,' said the first girl in a loud voice meant to carry. 'She's only a dirty Jew.'

The first girl danced a little closer to Ruth and began to sing a ditty. The others soon joined in.

Jew girl Hayman what a stink,
Slanted eyes just like a Chink,
Big large nose she never blows,
Long and hooked just like a crow's,
Bandy-legged, turned-in toes,
The Jew is as ugly as a witch,
Ruth Hayman, stuck-up bitch.

Janet felt sick. The cruelty she'd experienced was too recent for her to be able to pass the girls' behaviour off as common or garden teasing.

Ruth turned round to face them, and Janet saw the stricken look on her face and her sad eyes where tears lurked behind the lashes. 'Leave me alone,' she said angrily. 'Go away and leave me alone.'

Janet recognised the fear, because she'd felt it herself, but she didn't think the other girls would know just how frightened Ruth was. Then, suddenly, Ruth looked up and saw Janet watching. Their eyes locked. At that moment Janet knew she couldn't rejoice in her own freedom and see such treatment meted out to others without doing anything.

She raced forwards, pushing past the jeering girls, who'd spread over the pavement in front of

Ruth. Then, turning to face them, she said with scornful disdain, 'What sort of cowards are you that three of you pick on one person all on their own?'

'What's it to you?' the first girl demanded. 'It isn't any of your business.'

'Well, I'm making it my business,' said Janet.

'You do know,' said the second girl with a supercilious sneer, 'that you're taking the side of a Jew?' She spat the word out. Janet didn't bat an eyelid.

'I'd take the side of a Martian against cowardly bullies like you,' she said, 'so get going or I'll make you.'

'We wouldn't fight,' the second girl said in shocked horror.

'It's so common,' said the third.

'Like me, you mean,' said Janet, and added with an ironical laugh, 'No, I don't engage in ladylike pursuits like stalking behind someone just to sneer and make fun of them. And as for your little rhyme, your English teacher would be interested in the profitable use you make of your time. Make it up all by yourselves, did you? Perhaps a copy should be sent to Miss Phelps too?'

The three girls stood in stunned silence for a moment. They understood Janet's veiled threat only too well. Then the first girl, who seemed to be the leader, said, 'You don't frighten us, you know.'

Janet leapt forward and grabbed her by the tie. 'That's a pity,' she said. 'Are you sure?'

The girl felt her friends melt away from her.

She said in a squeaky, frightened voice, 'Leave me alone, you ... you bully.'

Then Janet laughed. She pushed the girl away from her and said with scorn, 'Why don't you grow up?' Then she linked her arm through Ruth's and led her away. The other girl had stood, stunned to silence by Janet's intervention, and it wasn't until they turned the corner to the bus stop, with the bus in sight, that Janet realised that far from being upset by the incident, Ruth was amused and amazed by Janet's performance.

'You were marvellous,' she said as they climbed to the upper deck of the bus together.

'It wasn't hard,' Janet said. 'They are cowards like most bullies.'

'They were right about one thing,' Ruth said. 'I *am* Jewish, and we're an easy target to pick on.'

'In Germany maybe,' Janet said, 'but not here, not in England, surely?'

Ruth gave her a pitying look. 'Everywhere,' she said. 'There are ruthless, cruel people in every land who like a scapegoat to blame. So far, the Jews have fitted the bill for many countries. These girls picked on me today because I am a Jew.'

'I was picked on last year because I was a scholarship girl,' Janet said.

'I'm also a scholarship girl,' Ruth said. 'They have two angles on me.'

Janet's eyes opened wide in surprise. She'd never have believed that Ruth was at Whytecliff on a scholarship; she could have sworn that her family had money to pay for her place. But the fact forged a bond between them and they became friends. No one bothered Ruth after that day, but no one, Janet noticed, rushed to be friends with her either. She was a Jew and therefore not totally acceptable, and Janet realised that the aloofness, that she had thought of as unfriendly and haughty, had in reality hidden deep unhappiness and loneliness.

They'd been friends just two weeks when Janet broached the subject of meeting at the weekend. 'We could go for a ride somewhere one Saturday,' she said, having established the fact that Ruth also had a bike.

'Not ... not a Saturday.'

'Why not?'

'It's our Sabbath,' Ruth said. 'It starts with the first three stars visible on Friday and ends with the first three stars which appear on Saturday evening.'

Janet thought that with the smog and cloud around in the Birmingham skies, it would be difficult to see stars at any time, but she said nothing. She'd known that the Jewish Sabbath was on a Saturday instead of Sunday, but didn't realise that that would make any difference.

'It's a day of rest,' Ruth said gently, when questioned.

'All day?'

Ruth gave a brief nod.

Janet sighed. She couldn't imagine anything worse. 'You just sit around all day then?' she asked.

'Not exactly,' said Ruth, with a smile, but she didn't elaborate further.

Janet studied her friend for a moment as they sat on the steps leading to the gymnasium. She'd

184

thought she knew all about Jews, but she realised she'd never asked Ruth much about her Jewishness, which was obviously a major part of her life and important in a way Janet found hard to understand.

Janet's gran went to Mass most Sundays but her grandad said he could worship the good Lord just as well at home. 'Don't they tell us God is everywhere?' he demanded when Gran challenged him. 'Well, I'll chat away to Him in my own house and garden. I don't need all that bleeding carry-on at church done by prattling hypocrites, and the priest mumbling Latin mumbo-jumbo no one bloody well understands.'

Janet went with Gran quite often. Sometimes Auntie Breda accompanied them, and her mother often said she'd like to go if just to get one hour to herself, but she didn't because Bert liked his lie-in on Sunday. Besides, Janet knew her mother would hesitate to leave him with the three little ones to see to.

'When they're older I'll go maybe,' she said.

Janet thought that religion sat very easy on the women in her family and touched the men not at all. She listened astounded as Ruth told her of the synagogue and the area that men could go into, and the women's place. 'Good job it's not like that in the Catholic religion,' Janet said. 'The men's area would be near empty.'

They laughed together for a minute, and then Janet asked a question that had bothered her for years. 'Why didn't Adolf Hitler like the Jews, Ruth?'

Ruth spread her hands helplessly. 'I don't

know,' she said. 'Who knows what went on in that crazy man's little brain?'

Janet knew what Ruth meant. Hitler *had* been crazy, and personally she thought he resembled Charlie Chaplin. Her father told her he was only a small man too, and she found it almost unbelievable that a large country like Germany should have followed him so slavishly.

'Did you come from Germany?' Janet asked Ruth.

'No,' Ruth said. 'Russia.'

'Russia?' Janet repeated, amazed.

'I didn't,' Ruth went on to explain. 'My grandmother did. I was born here. My grandmother's family were wealthy until the Cossacks ransacked the towns and villages, massacring the people. My grandmother fled with her two brothers and her mother. My great-grandmother had seen her husband cut down before her eyes. She never really recovered and died in the first English winter. My grandmother married a man called Otto Heineman who had a small clothing factory. It was just before the First World War.'

Janet saw the faraway look in Ruth's eyes and realised she was recounting a tale she'd been told many times.

'They made a lot of money at first sewing uniforms. My father, Joseph, and my Uncle Saul were both small and despite the fact that Grandmother's brothers had enlisted, life was good. And then the factory was attacked and they were threatened. The last attack almost burned them to death in their beds and destroyed their business.'

'But why?' Janet asked.

'Because their name was Heineman. They only changed it to Hayman later,' Ruth explained. 'People thought they were German. Grandmother was pregnant with my Uncle Aaron; she and her husband were interned in a camp for their own safety. My Aunt Rachel was born in the camp and by the end of the war my grandmother had lost her two brothers and her business, her husband was a broken man and she had four children to bring up. Then, in the last war, Aaron was killed and Saul injured.' Ruth shrugged. 'So she is bitter,' she said.

Janet thought for a little and then said, 'But she might not have survived in Russia at all. I think bitterness burns you up inside, it's really destructive. Many people suffer unfairness or unhappiness, but life has to go on, hasn't it?'

Ruth looked at Janet, quite startled. Clearly the Travers way of looking at life was not her grandmother's. 'She has high hopes of the new state of Israel now,' she said. 'My grandmother, I mean. She says all Jews must stick together and the greatest sin a Jew can do is marry out.'

'Marry out?'

'Marry a goy, a non-Jew,' Ruth said. 'A gentile. Jews believe they are the chosen race.'

'Catholics believe theirs is the one true religion, descended from St Peter,' Janet said. 'Dad says religious differences have caused more wars than anything else and people should learn to live in peace.'

'He should maybe talk to my grandmother,' Ruth said. 'The big family secret is that my aunt wanted to marry out once. My grandmother not only wouldn't let her, but produced a Jewish man of her choice called Moishe to marry her instead.' She shrugged again and added, 'It's not a good marriage. I think your father talks sense. I really hope there will be peace eventually.'

'Me too,' Janet said fervently.

'I'd like to meet your family one day,' Ruth said, almost shyly. 'You talk about them all the time.' She'd hesitated to ask Janet to her house in case she refused. She wasn't quite sure how Janet felt about Jews. She might feel it was all right to be friends with one at school, but not want to socialise outside, or perhaps her parents would object to her having a Jewish friend to their house.

Ruth couldn't have been more wrong. Janet knew from Ruth's bearing and demeanour and her lack of an accent that she was in a different social class from herself. She wasn't ashamed of her family, or of their council house in Pype Hayes with the bathroom off the kitchen and the toilet outside the back door, but she had the feeling Ruth might feel it to be rather primitive. At school it didn't matter and they were equal.

With Claire it was different; she was her friend. When Janet had bumped into her at the library the previous Saturday morning and told her about her Jewish friend Ruth, she said she'd like to meet her and invited them both round to tea the following Sunday. 'You can meet my family later if you like,' Janet told Ruth, 'but Claire has asked us to tea. Would you like to go?'

'I don't see why not.'

'Claire was in the library reading up on children like Chloe and finding out how to stimulate them,' Janet said. 'There's exercises and things she can do, apparently. She said she'd show us when we go.' But Janet spoke without enthusiasm, feeling sure Claire was just clutching at straws. She knew it must be hard to admit that your daughter was mentally handicapped and would never be good for anything. It would be especially hard for Claire, who was a born teacher but would never be able to help her daughter learn any bloody thing.

Sunday was cold and damp with a blustery wind, and Janet and Ruth were glad to reach Claire's. She opened the door in just a thin top and trousers and the heat in the living room hit them like a furnace when she led them into it. Chloe, wearing just a nappy, lay on her back on a towel. She smiled when she saw Janet. 'I've just finished massaging her muscles. It's what the books recommend you do first. It helps relax the child,' Claire said. 'Now I've got to start on the exercises I told you about.'

'Can we help?'

'Of course, I'd hoped you would,' Claire said. She bent and turned Chloe on to her stomach. 'Her neck muscles need to be strengthened,' she said. 'Her head still tends to be a little floppy.' Claire showed Ruth how to stand above Chloe and wave something bright or clap her hands to gain her attention so that she would raise her head from the towel. Later Janet helped Claire teach Chloe to roll over. 'She will have to be taught a lot of the things that come naturally to someone without a mental handicap,' Claire said, 'but in America, where studies on mongol children have been pioneered, many children like Chloe have happy, fulfilled lives.'

Chloe was a beautiful, very placid child who gurgled and smiled whatever was done to her, and Janet felt it was almost a privilege to help her. The short winter day sped past and Chloe eventually became tired and a little grouchy.

'She needs her bottle and bed,' Claire said. 'If one of you would like to feed her, the other can help me prepare the tea.'

Ruth fed Chloe and got her ready for bed while Janet and Claire made sandwiches and cut cake in the kitchen. 'Can we come again?' Ruth asked as they sat around the tea table. 'I've really enjoyed myself.'

'Please do,' Claire said. 'It can get lonely on my own and I can achieve far more with help.'

'Claire,' Janet said, suddenly needing to know, 'where's David?'

'He ... he's gone, Janet.'

'Gone?'

'Left,' Claire said, and added, 'We're getting divorced. He's met someone else.'

Janet was shocked; no one she knew had got divorced. She felt a surge of anger – how callous and unfeeling David must be – and an incredible sense of sadness for Claire. 'Oh, Claire,' she said.

'Don't be bitter Janet, it will only destroy you,' Claire replied. 'He couldn't accept Chloe and eventually she would have sensed it. It was better this way.'

Janet could only marvel at the way Claire accepted it. 'She's all on her own,' she told her family later, 'except for her mother of course, but

Claire said she gets so upset over how Chloe is she can be more of a hindrance than a help, and she really was grateful for our help, mine and Ruth's, so can I go and give her a hand?'

'I think,' Betty said, 'it's only right considering how she helped you. But a child like that can't really learn anything.'

'Claire doesn't think so,' Janet said. 'It's based on studies from America.'

'America,' Bert said disparagingly. 'Nothing good comes from that place.'

'Oh, I wouldn't say that, Bert,' said Breda, who'd slipped round for a chat. She smiled and added, 'What about nylons and GIs?'

Janet wasn't sure that Ruth would be allowed to go to Claire's on Saturday, it being her Sabbath, but Ruth said her father had spoken up for her. 'The family is all-important to Jewish people,' Ruth said, 'and Dad was shocked that Claire's husband couldn't accept his baby. When I told the family what Claire said about being advised to put the baby in a home, everyone was upset and angry. Dad says God has touched children like that in a special way.'

'I bet Claire often wishes He hadn't bothered,' Janet said with a wry smile.

'Oh, Janet, what a thing to say,' Ruth exclaimed, appalled at Janet's audacity. 'We shouldn't question the ways of Almighty God.'

'Don't see why not,' Janet said, unabashed, 'but anyway, I'm glad you can come to Claire's with me. It will be more fun together.'

Sometimes, it seemed they took one step forward and two back, but Chloe eventually did

191

learn to hold up her head and to roll. Later she was able to crawl and clap her chubby little hands, pound a peg in a hole, and pull herself up by arms strengthened by exercises and balance on wobbly legs. Claire told Janet and Ruth as they worked with her daughter about the specialised unit called Oakhurst being built in the UK as a pilot scheme in which Chloe would almost certainly be offered a place when she was three. As the months and years went by, they were to hear more of the unit's work, and about the later one, Ferndale that was being developed from the first. They were also to hear of the Montessori apparatus and method of teaching, and the unit leader, Richard Carter, who believed that children like Chloe should not be shut away but helped to reach their potential. Claire, as she observed Chloe's achievements, came to believe in Richard's philosophy too.

Just a month after the first visit to Claire's, Ruth was invited to the Travers' for tea. Bert and Betty cared not a jot that she was a Jew and liked the pretty, well-spoken, polite child Janet had befriended, and Janet noticed that even Duncan had smartened himself up. He'd scrubbed his hands, face and neck, his fingers were free of the ingrained grime that usually lodged there and his golden curls were slicked back with Brylcreem.

Ruth liked Janet's family. She'd met Sally already, as she'd accompanied them twice to Claire's house, and she found the twins' antics funny and Duncan quite presentable. She was unnerved by the noise around the table and the way they could yell at each other one minute and burst into gales of laughter the next. But she hid her discomfort, knowing that Janet's family were very important to her, and Janet was pleased it had seemed to go off so well.

'Your dad and I liked young Ruth,' Betty told her that night. 'Pretty girl too.'

'Isn't her hair lovely?' Janet asked. 'And so long.'

Betty smiled at her. 'What are you getting at, my girl?'

'Oh, let me grow mine, Mom,' Janet burst out. 'Please. I'm not likely to get nits from Whytecliff High, am I now?'

Betty didn't answer, but she didn't say a definite no either, so Janet pressed, 'Please, Mom?'

Betty had combed Duncan and Janet's hair with a nit comb over a sheet of newspaper every Friday night since they started at Paget Road School. Nothing was ever found, but sometimes Betty had covered their hair with foul-smelling lotion anyway, 'to be on the safe side', and they had to keep it on till they had their weekly bath on Saturday. Once they left primary school, she'd not been so diligent, and was now attacking the twins' hair with gusto instead. Janet would take a bet no nits would be found on them either. Any sensible flea would find a safer location to lay its eggs than between the hair strands of a Travers child, she often thought, but even so, she had never been allowed to let her hair grow, 'just in case'.

But she was growing up. Betty smiled and said, 'You'll have to see to it yourself, I have enough to do.'

'I will, I will,' Janet promised.

The next week Janet went to visit the Haymans for the first time. Geographically they were not far apart, but socially there was no comparison, because Ruth Hayman lived in a small road off Penn's Lane in Sutton Coldfield, as different from Janet's estate as it was possible to be. The house itself was detached and set back from the road, with a high privet hedge and wide lawns to the front and side of the house. One path led to the front of the house, while another, smaller one swept through a small side gate towards the back. There were white steps to the Haymans' front door, and lions on pillars on the lower posts. The door itself was dark brown and studded, and had a brass letterbox, door handle and bell.

It was a road of silence, for no babies cried, no children screamed or laughed, no dogs barked, no wireless belted out the Home Service, no neighbours chatted amicably on their doorsteps. It was ominously quiet and the Haymans' bell seemed to jangle loudly.

The lady who stood in the doorway was a replica of Ruth, though her skin glowed with colour. Janet guessed it was from cosmetics, like the blue eye shadow and coral lipstick she wore. Her dark hair was swept back into what Janet later discovered was called a chignon at the nape of the neck. She wore a dark-blue woollen suit with a peach blouse, a peach and pale-blue scarf at her neck, black court shoes and nylons. As she bent to welcome Janet and show her in, Janet smelt perfume and remembered with a pang that

194

Betty had waved her off wearing a shapeless dress covered with an apron, her feet encased in an old pair of socks of Bert's and thrust into down-trodden slippers.

The Haymans' hall was as large as the Travers' living room and had a polished wood floor cluttered haphazardly with cream sheepskin rugs. Janet glimpsed the start of an imposing wide staircase with decorated mahogany newel posts. Naomi Hayman opened a cream panelled door to her left and said, 'Do come in.'

Janet's feet sank in the thick beige carpet. A gold brocade suite was situated around the ornate fireplace, where a small fire burned in the grate. A unit stood to one side with a wireless on top of it, a bureau of some kind to the other. To Janet's left there was a china cabinet filled with ornaments, and a man sat writing at the desk in the bay window overlooking the garden.

At Janet's entrance, he got up and extended his hand. 'I'm delighted to meet you at last,' he said.

Joseph Hayman was as Janet had imagined all Jews to be, before she met Ruth. He had dark skin and a large beard and moustache which did not quite hide his welcoming smile. His eyes were as gentle and kind as Ruth's and his nose was large and a little hooked, but his handshake was firm. 'Ruth will be with us shortly,' he said. 'These are my two sons, Aaron and Ben.'

They were both handsome boys, though Ben, the younger, was more so. He wore his curly hair longer than his brother's so that it fell across his brow and curled at the nape of his neck. They were tall like their father and had his dark skin,

195

but their noses were not so prominent and their eyes were merrier. Ben reminded Janet of a happier, less languid Byron. She knew he wanted to study medicine when he was older, because Ruth had told her, and now he smiled at her, gave a mock bow and said, 'Janet Travers, the oracle herself. If you knew how often Ruth quotes you.'

'Ben...' Joseph chided, but Janet cut in.

'Well, all I can say is, if that's true she must be hard up.'

Ben burst out laughing, and the rest were all smiling at her too when the door opened and Leah Hayman came in on the arm of her granddaughter, Ruth. The smiles slid from everyone's faces and Janet could feel tension in the air.

The older Mrs Hayman was dressed from head to toe in satiny black, with her grey hair dragged back from her face and secured in a bun. She was very wrinkled. Lines creased her sallow cheeks and her eyes, furrowed her brow and pulled at her mouth, which drooped in a disgruntled pout. Her dark eyes, as they raked Janet up and down, were as cold and penetrating as ice, and Janet sensed her disapproval and bristled.

Leah Hayman had not liked the sound of Ruth's friend and had made her feelings clear, but they'd been disregarded. Ruth had told her that Janet lived on a council estate with a clutch of brothers and sisters, and now she'd met the girl she liked her even less. She was common, but no one else seemed to see it. She knew it was up to her to show she was not welcome in her house. 'So,' she said, 'this is the friend?'

Janet was furious. She might as well have said

'the dog' or 'the cat', she thought, yet no one seemed surprised and Janet realised that she must talk like that all the time.

Bad-mannered old bitch, she thought, and she took a step forward and said firmly, 'My name is Janet Travers and I'm a friend of Ruth's. How do you do?'

The old lady's thin lips pinched together – the girl's accent grated on her nerves – and she did not answer her greeting. 'Ruth tells me you won a scholarship to Whytecliff High School,' she said instead.

'That's right,' Janet replied, and to show the sour old lady she wasn't ashamed of her family she added, 'My parents couldn't have sent me there any other way.'

'Alas, this is also the case with us,' Leah Hayman said. 'Once in Russia we had much money, a large house and servants. We came to England and...' She gave a despairing little shrug.

Joseph moved across the room, put his hand on the old woman's shoulder and led her to a chair. 'Now, Mother,' he said, 'this is many years ago.'

'Many years, but the pain is as bitter,' the older Mrs Hayman said. 'Even here, we had once a factory and a future. Both were stolen and the wrongdoers go unpunished to this day.'

'Come, Mother-in-law,' Naomi said impatiently. 'We have a guest. I'm sure she doesn't want to hear this.'

Janet knew that all this was probably a continuing theme. The older Mrs Hayman almost enjoyed raking up things that had happened years ago, over and over, in case they might be forgotten. She'd soured her own life with bitterness, and Janet guessed that she regularly reminded those she lived with of her misfortunes.

'I don't think it's very wise to dwell in the past all the time,' Janet said. 'It's best to look forward.'

Clearly no one had ever spoken to Leah Hayman in that manner before. Her eyes glittered with dislike at the child who refused to sympathise with her. 'You are not aware of the extent of my suffering,' she said.

'Maybe not,' Janet agreed, 'but with the war over and everything, the future has got to look brighter.'

'The war is never over if you are a Jew,' the old lady said.

'Come, Mother, that is enough.'

'Enough,' the old lady snapped. 'I lose two brothers to one war and a son to the next, maybe that is enough!'

Janet's eyes met Ruth's resigned ones. I told you what she's like, they said, and suddenly Janet was impatient with the embittered old woman and the family who just allowed her to go on and on all the time. 'You weren't the only one to suffer,' she put in. 'My dad's family was wiped out with TB, and I lost two uncles in the last war. Noel was the baby of the family. He lied about his age to enlist. It nearly broke Mom's heart when he died, but we can't mourn for ever and they wouldn't want us to.'

There was a stunned silence, and then Leah Hayman snapped, 'You are not a Jew, what do you know?'

'Well, anyone can understand grief, even if

they're not Jewish,' Janet said, 'and I suppose if I'm any religion at all I'm Catholic. At least, that's what I was christened and where I go sometimes.'

'Catholic,' spat the old lady contemptuously. 'Idolisers, statue worshippers.'

Janet had heard this criticism levelled before. 'My gran says they don't worship statues,' she said. 'It just helps them focus their mind on who they're praying to.'

'You focus only on Almighty God.'

'Well, maybe not everyone can do that,' Janet said. 'People should be able to choose.'

'Choose! This isn't an item we pick from the grocery shelves.'

'I know that,' Janet said, 'but I really don't see the problem. After all, it's the same God, isn't it?'

The old lady was outraged. She drew herself up in her chair, lifted her chin and said haughtily, 'The Jewish religion is a way of life. One does not choose how to worship, but does it in the time-honoured way it's always been done.'

'But not everyone could agree with you,' Janet said, 'or everyone would be Jewish.'

The older woman looked as if that wouldn't be a bad thing. She fastened her eyes on Janet and said, 'The Jewish religion is the oldest in the world and was founded by Abraham...'

Janet was unimpressed. 'It doesn't mean it's right, though, just because it's always been done that way. After all, we used to send children up chimneys and down mines, but now we know that was wrong.'

'Girl, you are impertinent.'

'I'm not,' Janet contradicted, and added angrily, 'and my name is Janet. All I was trying to say was, just because a thing has been done for years in a particular way doesn't necessarily mean it is right.'

'If you were a Jewish child, you'd be taught good manners and respect for your elders,' the old lady snapped.

What happened to you then? It was on the tip of Janet's tongue, but she held it back. She knew that to say that would be stepping beyond what was acceptable behaviour, but really, the old lady was impossible.

'I mean,' Leah Hayman went on patronisingly and with a sneer in her voice, 'what are you really but a common little guttersnipe?'

'Mother, that is enough,' Joseph snapped angrily. 'I cannot allow you to insult guests in this manner.'

It was just as if he hadn't spoken. The old lady looked across at her eldest grandson and said, 'Aaron, your arm. I'm rather tired. I think I'll go to my room.'

Janet caught her eye before the door closed and was rather startled by the loathing she saw there, and despite herself a shudder passed through her body.

'Phew,' exclaimed Ben in relief, and Joseph would have rebuked him but for the nervous laugh that escaped from Janet. She was grateful to him for lightening the tone. Ruth, Joseph and Naomi all smiled. Ben gave Janet a wink and said, 'Can I book seats for round two?' and Naomi said gently, 'Ben, really!'

Chapter Nine

Three years later Janet Travers the gauche, rather plain schoolgirl was gone. Her hair, now grown longer, fell down her back in auburn-streaked waves and it was much admired even when she had to have it plaited or tied back for school. It gave her confidence in her appearance. She also experimented with make-up with Ruth in the privacy of their bedrooms, often with hilarious results. Janet knew without asking that Bert would take a very dim view of her using make-up in the ordinary way of things.

Janet's accent had almost gone, except when she was with the family. Then she slipped into the local idiom without being aware of it. Other members of the family had changed too. As the years passed, Bert had found great pleasure in gardening. The garden had become a weed-filled wilderness while he'd been away in the war, and now he put all his spare time and energy into reclaiming it. He split it in half and left the lower part, nearest the house, just as lawns with a path up the middle. He laid flowerbeds at the sides and planted rambling roses to climb up the trellis fencing, and it was a pleasant place to sit in the summer.

At the top of the garden, he eventually dug up the Anderson shelter he described as a death trap, especially for the twins, and planted vegetables, and it had given him such satisfaction that he had taken on an allotment. An added advantage of this was the way Noel and Conner also grew to love gardening. Bert often took them with him now at weekends or in the long summer evenings, and he'd given them their own piece of ground to plant things they wanted to grow.

He was proud of his small sons, who toiled seemingly tirelessly beside him. Many of the allotment holders were amused by the two little boys who looked so alike. 'They're comical laddies right enough,' the man in the neighbouring allotment said to Bert one day. 'Damned if I can see how you tell them apart. They're as alike as the peas in them there pods you've planted.' The family couldn't help but be impressed by their earnest pride when Bert pushed the two home in the wheelbarrow clutching sacks of potatoes and peas that they'd grown themselves. On Mothering Sunday Betty was moved to tears when they presented her with a bunch of daffodils that they had been tending with special care.

Life was a little easier now for everyone. Bert had been made up to foreman, with the resultant rise in his pay packet, and with Duncan working as well, money went further. However, Betty liked the independence of her own money and the company of the other women and she kept her job on, though she did toy with the idea of looking for a part-time day shift in the factory when Sally began school. The main reason for this decision was Duncan. She felt she should keep tabs on what he was doing at night, and with whom.

She couldn't really pinpoint the moment when she realised there was something wrong with Duncan. He'd always run wild around the streets with lads on the estate, but at some point, when she was too fussed by one or another of his sisters or brothers, Duncan's attitude changed. He was downright nasty and aggressive and he'd answered both her and Bert back in such an insolent manner that Bert had caught hold of his collar a number of times.

'Don't talk to me like that, my lad. You're not too big for a bleeding good hiding.'

'Oh,' Duncan would answer cockily. 'I suppose you'll give it to me, will you?'

'I just might,' Bert would cry, but Betty knew he wouldn't. He'd never been one to hit the children, leaving that job to her. Even when she felt the twins would benefit from a stroke of the strap or a stinging slap from him, he'd never wanted to administer punishment. He'd excused their wildness as high spirits.

For the younger ones it would seem this philosophy was right, for the twins adored their father and Sally was always ready to cuddle on to his knee. Even Janet, though he couldn't really understand her passion for studying, he could talk to. Duncan, however, despite working in the factory almost alongside his father, was cheeky and insolent to him. Bert had thought they'd become mates, but now Duncan didn't even want to go to Villa Park with him any more.

Janet had seen the change in the brother she'd once looked up to and been so close to. She knew that the estrangement between them had begun when she had stated she wanted to sit the eleven-plus, and she often felt guilty about it, wondering if it were her fault in some way. She often saw Duncan, and the gang of hooligans he hung around the cafés with, as she walked Ruth to the bus stop on the nights she came to have tea with the Travers family. She knew that the gang culture hinged on the motorbikes most of them had. Duncan yearned for one, but he knew that his parents, particularly Betty, would be dead set against it.

'Blooming great death traps,' they'd all heard her say often. 'I'd not sleep nights if I had one of my own on those things.'

Later, when one of the women at work had a son killed on a motorbike and Patsy's sister was injured riding pillion with her boyfriend, her dislike became unreasonable hatred. And Patsy herself, shocked and upset by her sister's injuries, swore neither Liam nor the new toddler Patrick would be allowed anywhere near a motorbike.

Breda held the same view. 'I wouldn't allow our Linda to go out with one of those motorbike louts,' she said. 'Bringing up kids to have them chuck their bleeding lives away like they do, no thank you.'

'Easy to say when they're small,' Betty said.

'Have you asked your Duncan straight out if he wants a bike?' she asked.

'No, I haven't. I'm not bringing the subject up,' Betty retorted.

'So you don't really know anything,' Breda said. 'All this fretting might be for nothing.'

But it wasn't. Janet had seen Duncan racing up

and down the street on borrowed machines and had wondered. Then the evening after yet another blistering row with his father, she heard her brother's feet pound up the stairs. They went past her door and into the room he shared with the twins, and the door slammed. A little later, she heard the resounding crash of the front door as her father left.

First she ran to the landing window to see her father striding down Paget Road towards the allotment, the twins scampering either side of him. They looked like a couple of playful puppies and she suppressed a smile. She'd have to fetch them back in an hour or two or they'd never get up for school, and then they'd turn into whining banshees, she knew from experience.

Janet stood on the landing, undecided. She should return to her books, and yet she knew she couldn't settle with Duncan's brooding presence in the next room. She doubted anything she said would make any difference, but she felt she had to try, so she knocked tentatively on the door. There was no reply, and when Janet gently opened it she was startled to see her brother lying face down on the bed.

'What d'you want?' he demanded angrily as he swung round to face her. 'Come to spy and all, have you?'

Janet was stung by the injustice of Duncan's accusation, but she could see the marks of tears on his cheeks and didn't retaliate. Now his eyes were bright with fury and his face brick red, and she spoke quietly, hoping to diffuse the situation.

'I'm not spying.'

'Aren't you? Well, it's what you do when you go out with your prissy friend.'

'What d'you mean?'

'You know what I mean.' Duncan sneered. 'When you walk dear Ruth to the bus stop, I know you've seen me down the caff. What I don't know is why you haven't run home to tell Mommy and Daddy about it.'

Janet had wondered if Duncan had ever spotted her and Ruth. He'd given no sign and neither of them had mentioned the encounters at home, but however upset he was, he wasn't getting away with either mocking her friends or implying that she was a sneak.

'For your information, Duncan Big-head Travers,' she said, 'Ruth's bus stop happens to be just beyond the café. It isn't my fault, nor hers, we didn't position it. And what's all this "dear Ruth" business? She's done nothing to you. You nearly fell over yourself impressing her that first day, and you show off every time I bring her home.'

'I do not.'

'You do so,' Janet retorted angrily, and added in a supercilious tone that she knew annoyed Duncan, 'And as for your grubby little dealings with the hooligan element at the café, well, I'm not a bit interested in them. Mom and Dad, now that's different, they'd be worried if they knew, though why they should be concerned about a drop-out like you beats me.'

'Beats me too,' Duncan said moodily, 'because they've never done it before.'

'What a thing to say, Duncan!'

'Is it?' Duncan snapped bitterly. 'Everyone in this house is thought better of than me. Look how cute the twins are, and such a great help to their dad down at the allotment. I don't remember him having that much time for me when I was that age.'

'He was fighting a war, remember.'

'I mean before that, he never bothered with me. You won't remember, but I do.'

'Oh, rubbish!' Janet cried. 'You're making it up. Anyway, that was years ago. What's it matter now?'

'Oh, it won't matter to you,' Duncan said, 'because you're the brainbox of the family. No one ignores you, you even got special treatment from the teacher. And then there's Mom and Dad, not a word about all the money spent on your poxy uniform that Mom had to go back to work to pay for. "Our Janet's at the grammar school,"' he mimicked. 'What's it mean anyway? Dad tells everyone in the bleeding factory.'

Janet was silent, knowing that Duncan had a point. Everything had been done for her, and her parents were over the top. Every time they went to the school, dressed to kill, as they put it, so as 'not to let our Janet down', they came back puffed up with importance. Janet looked at Duncan helplessly, wondering what she could say to make it better. Before she had time to think up a response, Duncan was off again.

'And then there's the bedroom,' he snarled. 'I'm the eldest, yet I have to share with the sodding twins. Not you, though, oh no. "Our Janet needs to study,"' he continued, mimicking their parents again. "'Our Janet needs her space. Our Janet needs her own bedroom to take her friends to." Doesn't any bugger in this house have any idea I might have friends I want to come into my room? I hear you giggling with yours enough, but I have to meet mine on streets, and our Sally is pushed into a corner so that you have all the space you want.'

'Oh Duncan, I'm sorry,' Janet said helplessly, not knowing what else to say.

'Oh, you're sorry,' Duncan said sarcastically. 'That's all right then.'

'Of course it isn't all right,' Janet burst out, 'but what can I do? Why didn't you say something before?'

'And what would have been the point?' Duncan asked witheringly. 'Would you have shared with your little brothers and let me have your room?'

And Janet knew she wouldn't, couldn't have done that. She was silent, and Duncan cried triumphantly:

'See, I'm right. You'd be pig sick if you'd been expected to share with anyone, but you're all right. You're the brainbox, Sally is the baby. The twins are as naughty as hell and Mom would have scalped me if I'd done half what they get up to, but they're cute and little and Dad lets them do what they like. And when it comes to the brains in this family, there wasn't much given to me.'

'No, that *is* nonsense, you're not stupid,' Janet protested.

'No?' Duncan said. 'Well, everyone's worrying about you going to college and Noel and Conner getting into technical school and our Sally winning *Brain of Britain*, but Duncan's all right in the factory.'

'You wanted to work in the factory.'

'Yeah, well ... it isn't as if I was ever told any different.'

'You didn't want any different,' Janet cried. 'Look how you went on when you thought you'd have to wait until you were fifteen.'

'Yeah, I know,' Duncan cried. 'But Christ, I was only a kid, nothing was explained.'

'What sort of thing?'

'Any damn thing,' Duncan said. 'D'you know what the gaffer said to me the other day?' He didn't wait for Janet's reply, but continued angrily, 'He said he didn't understand why Dad didn't put me in for an apprenticeship. He said our dad is always so keen on workers' rights and stuff, him being a shop steward, and he wondered why he hadn't done more for me. My job is dead end and boring and all I've got to look forward to is doing the same bloody thing till I'm sixty-five. The only rises will be small ones, unless someone dies and I get to be a foreman or something, probably when I'm too old to care, like Dad. Well, I got to thinking about what my gaffer said and I wondered why no one had thought of apprenticing me to learn to be an electrician, or a carpenter, or a plumber – any damn thing would be better than what I'm doing now – and I found out the reason.'

'What?'

'You!' Duncan almost spat the word. 'You again. Apprentices don't get paid much and sometimes you have to pay the tradesman to take your kid on, and there was no spare money for me, was there? It was all going on brainy Janet. Then there was the cost of keeping me at school for another year, and when I started I wouldn't earn enough to give Mom much for my keep. I reckon they talked about it and how much it would cost and decided any spare money had to go on you. You were the best bet to throw the money at. You were almost certain to make something of yourself. Me, well, I'm just miserable, dumb old Duncan and I'll never amount to much. I can be thrown on the scrapheap.'

'Oh, Duncan. It's not true, really it isn't,' Janet cried, in great distress at the tone in her brother's voice. 'Mom and Dad wouldn't do that. Tell them how you feel.'

'And what good would it do?' Duncan asked. 'The die is cast now and the future set, but I'll tell you what I mean to do and that is buy myself a motorbike. Mom and Dad can say what they like, but it's my money and I'll spend it how I like and on what I want. I'll be seventeen in a few weeks and I'll have the money saved by then.'

Janet stared at her brother. She realised that nothing she could say would change his mind, and really, she had no right to criticise him for how he wanted to spend his money. Later she confided in Ruth, who asked in genuine bewilderment, 'Why do you worry so much about your family?'

'Well, Duncan's got a point,' Janet said, and she related the whole of the exchange with her brother. Ruth was silent a minute and then said, 'So, now you're going to creep around on your stomach for the rest of your life, are you? You have to keep apologising for being born at all, and beating your breast in agony because you've had the misfortune of arriving in the world with a brain in your head?'

'You are a fool,' Janet said, flinging a cushion at Ruth's head, but Ruth was right, she was feeling dead guilty. 'I don't know what to do,' she said.

'Nothing,' Ruth told her. 'Let them sort it out.'

'You don't understand,' Janet burst out in exasperation, 'you're the youngest in your family and have two brothers to take the heat off you.'

'But you're not the eldest,' Ruth pointed out.

'No, but I'm the...' Janet stopped, appalled, aware that she'd nearly said 'the cleverest'. Instead she said, 'the one they expect to know everything.'

Janet was right in that. Her mother, in particular, expected her to have all the answers. 'Have a word with your brother,' she'd urge, or 'Talk to the twins, can't you?'

Why me? Janet often wanted to cry, and yet in another way she did feel responsible for her family. She knew she owed them a lot and looking out for them was her way of paying part of her debt. Despite Ruth's words, she couldn't help worrying about Duncan and what effect his behaviour and future actions would have on the family.

On the school front, the workload increased steadily for Ruth and Janet, whose friendship remained as strong as ever. Miss Phelps

211

encouraged the older girls to take an interest in the world they would inherit, and Janet began listening to news and current affairs issues on the wireless. Ruth was particularly interested in hostilities in Korea, since Aaron, coming to the end of his university career, would soon be doing his national service.

'I said something about it the other day to Dad,' Janet told Claire one weekend. 'We'd been listening together to the news broadcast and I asked Dad if he thought the Chinese would get involved, and ... well, he was flabbergasted.'

'That you knew anything about it?'

'Yes, and that I'd *want* to know anything,' Janet said. 'I felt like an oddity, and Mom wasn't pleased. I think she sees it as just another way that I'm sort of moving away from her.' Claire said nothing, knowing that Janet hadn't finished, and eventually the girl went on earnestly, 'There's a big wedge between myself and my family, Claire and the nearer I get to achieving my goal, the bigger it becomes. Sometimes,' she mused, almost to herself, 'I'm unhappy about it, especially about my mom, you know?'

Claire felt sorry for Janet. She'd guessed that she would feel a conflict of loyalties as her education progressed. 'How are things with your father?' she asked.

'Oh, I can talk to Dad about the world situation,' Janet told her, 'and of course he's passionate about the trade union movement and the Labour Party, but even with Dad there's vast uncharted areas where I couldn't talk to him without making him feel inferior.'

'You're not sorry you went for the examination, though, are you?' Claire said. 'I mean, it's not a crime to want to better yourself. And even while your mother might regret the loss of her daughter in one sense, in another she wouldn't have it any other way.'

'No,' Janet said, 'no, I don't think she would. And honestly, I think if you could have looked into the future and seen all this and told me when I was eleven, it would have made little difference to me at the time. I was tremendously single-minded, as I remember. I thought I could go charging through life without it affecting anyone else, really. It was rather an infantile way of looking at things, especially now that I see the effect Duncan has on the family, or even how Mom and Dad worry about Conner and Noel if they misbehave.'

'Well,' said Claire, 'to quote a well-used phrase, no man is an island, and that's more particularly so with families, I suppose because they care more for one another.'

'I suppose.'

'Life changes all the time as well,' Claire said, 'and though what you do might affect your parents and so on, not everything that has happened to them and will happen to them in the future can be laid at your door.' She stopped and went on, 'As for me, I'd hate to be one of those mothers who hover in their children's shadow. Richard Carter told me it's a particular problem with the parents of mentally handicapped children. They often almost resent their children's independence, I suppose because they've made their children their life.'

'And you?'

'Well, I decided it was time for me to do something for myself,' Claire said. 'I've become fascinated with the Montessori teaching methods and apparatus that are used at Oakhurst. Some time ago I applied for the year-long course to become a directress, which is what they call the teachers at the Montessori Training Organisation. I wrote to them in London to ask if they had a branch in Birmingham. Fortunately they have, and with Chloe at the unit I'll have all the time I need.'

'What will you do then?' Janet said. 'Do you intend to go back to teaching?'

'Well, yes, and I've always got my teaching certificate. Of course, a Montessori diploma is just another string to my bow. With it I can either work in a Montessori nursery school – which are beginning to gain in popularity – or if there is enough funding to provide money for the other unit, Ferndale, which is up but not yet running at the moment as funds are low, I may find work there. But,' she said, and shrugged, 'we have a number of events planned. Perhaps Ruth would like to lend a hand, if she's at a loose end this summer?'

'I'll ask her for you,' Janet promised. 'She was really mad with her grandmother for not letting her take the holiday job in Littlewoods in Erdington with me. I was thrilled to get it. It will help me to get clothes for myself and buy books and things for school without keep asking Mom and Dad, and they say if it works out all right they'll offer me a Saturday job afterwards. Then they asked me if I had a friend who might be looking for something, and I thought of Ruth straight away and went hightailing off to her house to tell her.'

'But the news didn't please them?'

'No, well, at least not her grandmother, and she seems to be the one who matters in that house,' said Janet.

'She'll find the summer long without you being around,' Claire said.

Janet shrugged. 'One day,' she said, 'she'll have to stand up to that old tyrant, or have the whole of her life decided for her.'

'It's not always so simple,' Claire said. 'Ruth has been brought up all her life to respect and defer to her grandmother.' She saw the impatient movement Janet made and said, 'It's easier for you, you're far more independent altogether. Look at the way you stood up to me after you saw that distressing scene between David and myself, and you were only eleven.'

It was the first time Claire had referred to the intimate embrace since the day Janet had handed back the locket, and Janet flushed now with embarrassment.

'I should never have seen it,' she said, 'and I wouldn't have done if I'd allowed you any privacy at all. I was so puffed up with my own import-ance then. I thought I was the only person in your life.' She looked at Claire and went on, 'I didn't think you even had another friend besides me, never mind a lover. How conceited I was to think I was all things to you and you had no need of anyone or anything else.'

'Don't be so hard on yourself,' Claire said. 'You were only a young girl and we had a unique and very special relationship. Still have, I hope?'

'I should say so,' Janet said fervently. She wondered if Claire still loved David Sunderland, and whether the Richard Carter she spoke of so often was important to her. She decided to ask no questions. This time, she decided, it really is none of my business.

The summer sped by and then it was September and a new term for everyone. Janet was soon slogging at her books again, and now that she was working all day Saturday as well, she was busier than ever.

November, the month of Duncan's seventeenth birthday, was damp and dismal. Had Janet not been so tied up, she might have noticed the secret smile of satisfaction her brother had carried round for days. As it was, she was just pleased he'd been easier to deal with and that there'd been fewer rows than previously, and she hoped that he was settling down at last.

It was the evening of his birthday and he'd expressed thanks for the new shirts and jumpers from his parents and grandparents and the string tie from Breda. Sally shyly presented him with a bottle of aftershave and the twins gave him a tie pin, while Janet's present was a shiny leather wallet. Betty had cooked a special meal and baked a cake. She'd changed to the day shift with Breda and was glad to be at home, to enjoy a meal with the family for once. Duncan had also seemed to enjoy it and appeared to like the gifts the family had given him. Janet was pleased it had gone off so well and Duncan had been so pleasant for once.

Bert, aware of the difference in Duncan's demeanour over the last few days, and wishing to heal the rift between himself and his son, had suggested earlier that they might go for a pint to seal his birthday. Duncan said he'd rather go out with his mates. Tight-lipped but civil enough, for it was after all the lad's birthday, Bert said that that was fine, some other time maybe, and Duncan muttered something that Janet hoped was agreement before he went out of the door.

She helped her mother clear away and get the little ones to bed before returning to her books. Her room was very chilly. The oil stove on loan from her grandparents took the intense cold away and stank to high heaven, but did little for the icy draughts beneath the door that chilled the air. Her desk, under the rattling window, was the coldest spot in the room in the winter, and Janet pulled a blanket off the bed to wrap around her and shivered beneath it.

The night was blustery and wet and the rain hammered on the windows in the dark night. Janet heard music on the wireless but no sounds of her dad preparing to go out. Obviously when Duncan had turned down his invitation he'd decided to stay in, she thought.

For some reason, she found it hard to concentrate. The drone of traffic from the main road seemed unaccountably loud that night. In the middle of a maths calculation, two cats suddenly screeched at each other in the garden underneath her window and sent the figures out of her head. Somewhere a baby began to cry, loud and plaintive; she heard voices raised in argument; a dog barked and was answered by another. She heard the man next door coughing and his wife telling him to give over as the wind began to gust around the house and splattered the rain on to the window.

Janet wondered what was the matter with her. These were the usual noises of the night that she'd heard many times before while hardly being aware of them. Why should they disturb her now?

This is ridiculous, she told herself sternly. Get a grip or you'll flop your exams, and then what will you do? She bent over her maths books again.

The traffic noise had surely become louder. It wasn't a drone any more either, but a single blast of noise, as if something had detached itself from the main body of traffic.

Janet felt icy threads of apprehension trickle through her as she ran to the landing window. She saw a powerful motorbike roaring up their road, its headlights slicing through the gloom of the night. In the brilliant shafts of light, Janet saw the raindrops dancing crazily. But it was the rider who held Janet's attention, for astride the machine sat Duncan, and seeing her at the window, he lifted an arm to her in a defiant salute. Janet didn't go back to her books. She stayed shivering on the freezing-cold landing and waited for the Third World War to begin.

She hadn't long to wait, for just a moment or

two after she'd spied Duncan, she heard her father bellowing and a howl of protest from her mother. She didn't know whether her presence would help or hinder, she just knew she wouldn't be able to cower upstairs and try and pretend she couldn't hear Duncan and her parents ripping each other to pieces below.

She entered the room to hear her father bawling that Duncan wasn't too old for a bloody good hiding. Duncan was shouting back that he'd like to see him try it, while Betty, tears pouring unchecked down her cheeks, implored Janet to do something.

What? Janet thought to herself. Perform a bloody miracle?

'Stop yelling at each other,' she said as loudly as she could. It had no effect.

'Behind my bloody back, that's what I can't get over. I forbade you to get one of those death traps and...'

'Well, I got one anyway, so what?'

'You cheeky sod,' Bert said, aiming a swipe at the side of Duncan's head and missing. 'You could do as you're damn well told for once in your life.'

'Why should I?'

'You've upset your mother, upset the whole bleeding lot of us,' Bert snarled. 'But then you're good at that, aren't you?'

Duncan sneered. 'Not as good as you yet, but I'm learning.'

Fearing that Bert, purple in the face, would have a fit in a moment or two, Janet tried again, while her mother's wails rose.

219

'Do you mind?'

This time her cool voice cut through Bert's blustering and Duncan's sullenness, though her mother continued her gulping sobs. Duncan grabbed the advantage of his father being thrown off balance first.

'I don't have to do what you bleeding well tell me. I work all bloody day and tip my keep up and I can do what I like with the rest.'

'While you're under my roof...' Bert thundered, but Duncan cut in before he'd finished.

'Well, that can soon be remedied.'

'Shut up!' shouted Janet. 'For God's sake, you'll have the kids awake.'

'Oh, Janet...' Betty began, wringing her hands together while tears dripped from her chin. Bert surveyed his recalcitrant son and then turned to Janet. His face was very red now, she noticed, and his breath was coming in short gasps as he said wearily, 'D'you know what the sly bugger's done?'

Janet sighed impatiently. 'I'd have to be deaf, dumb and blind not to know,' she snapped, 'and the way you're going on, half of Pype Hayes estate will know by now.'

'Don't you take that line with me!' Bert bellowed. 'Just because you're at grammar school don't give you the right to speak to your father like that.'

'Dad, please,' Janet pleaded, 'you'll have the twins and our Sally down in a minute.'

'But he's bought a motorbike, our Janet,' Betty sobbed, and Janet knew how much her mother was affected when she added, 'a great big bleeding motorbike.'

220

'Yeah, a motorbike!' Duncan shouted, too angry to care what he said. 'I ain't committed bleeding murder, you silly cow!'

Bert cuffed Duncan on the head, sending him sprawling over the chair. 'Don't you dare talk to your mother like that, I'm telling you, or I'll take my belt off to you!'

Duncan stood rubbing his head. 'Try it and I'll knock your bleeding block off!'

'You cheeky sod,' Bert said, and made a grab for Duncan, but before he could reach him, Janet jumped between them.

Bert knocked her flying instead and as she lay there stunned, Betty began crying afresh and trying to help Janet to her feet at the same time. Bert was saying he was sorry, he didn't mean it, and it was that bugger Duncan's fault. Duncan was threatening that if his father touched him again he'd bleeding well kill him. Janet, her head swimming, stood swaying in front of them both, nearly deafened by all the shouting.

'Please shut up!' she begged. 'Please?'

Betty was still emitting great hiccuping sobs and Bert, looking sheepish, stood silent, his breath rasping in his throat. Duncan, red-faced and angry, stared stonily at her.

'I mean it,' he said.

'Shut up,' Janet retorted. She turned to her parents and said, 'Duncan's bought a motorbike that you didn't want him to have, but he used his own money to buy it and all the bloody shouting in the world is not going to change the fact that the bike is here.'

'He'll take it back,' Bert declared, 'tomorrow.'

'I'll not!'

'You will!'

'I won't!'

'We'll see about that.'

'You can't make me do any bloody thing,' Duncan said. 'That's what's really eating you, isn't it? I'm not a bleeding kid any more, to be pushed around. No one ever listens to me anyway. I'm just here to be shoved about to please others, like being sent out to work so old bleeding clever clogs could go to grammar school, and being yelled at for any damn thing. Conner and Noel are bloody awful, but not a damn word is ever said to them, and no one shouts at Sally. And as for Janet, she needs peace and quiet to study, but Duncan, he's of no bleeding use at all, you can all take your temper out on him.'

Bert and Betty were staring at Duncan in astonishment. Bert said uncertainly, almost incredulously, 'Is that ... is that really how you feel, son?'

'Yes!' Duncan snarled. 'Because that's how it is.'

Janet left them talking and made everyone tea in the kitchen. When she took it through later, Bert – a quieter Bert – was saying, 'I didn't know you felt like this, lad. You should have said. I'm not a bleeding mind-reader.'

'There wasn't any point...' Duncan began, but Bert's attention was already elsewhere.

'I can't understand how you saved all the money for a bleeding big bike like that in the first place.'

'I didn't have to,' Duncan explained. 'I just had to save the deposit and I pay the rest weekly on the hire purchase scheme.'

'Oh, I don't like that way of doing things,' Bert said, 'tying yourself down like that. And anyway, don't you have to have a guarantor if you're under twenty-one?'

Duncan went red and looked at the floor and mumbled that Mr Morland, his gaffer at work, had agreed to sponsor him.

Bert went off a bit at that, but Janet had had enough. She was tired out and her head was aching where she'd banged it on the floor trying to get between her dad and her brother. She took her tea to bed.

The next day, at work, Bert threatened to do over Mr Morland for putting a lad against his father. Morland came back at Bert and said he ought to be ashamed, there was him a trade unionist and fighting for men's rights but putting his own son in some dead-end job when anyone with half a brain could see Duncan had the intelligence and aptitude for the apprenticeship scheme.

Bert came home that evening quietly thoughtful, no longer angry, and he and Betty had a long talk. Duncan kept his bike, and for Christmas Bert and Betty and the grandparents put together to buy him a leather jacket. Brendan and Patsy gave him a crash helmet, Brendan saying he'd better protect his head, for his brain must be a bit on the small side anyway or he'd not have bought himself such a death trap. Janet bought him leather gauntlets that she got on staff discount from Littlewoods, and life settled down again, till the next time.

Chapter Ten

Duncan surprised everyone in the New Year by telling his parents he wanted to learn car mechanics. 'I was talking to this bloke at work, name of John Summers,' he said. 'His son Larry has started his national service and he's learning car mechanics in the army. I've really got interested in engines and stuff since I've had the bike.'

'But what about the prospects, son?' Bert said.

'I should say they look good, Dad,' Duncan said. 'Everyone will have a car one day, and they'll all need fixing now and again.'

Janet was astounded to hear of Duncan's ambition, and told Ruth next day on the way to school. 'I honestly didn't think he even looked ahead,' she said. 'He doesn't usually think about the future, leaving tomorrow to look after itself. He said that cars will be for everyone one day.'

'Ben says that too,' Ruth said, 'and Dad's thinking of buying one.'

'A car! Wow!'

'Not much good in us getting a car even if we could afford one,' Bert remarked when Janet told him what Ruth had said. 'I couldn't drive the bloody thing.'

'You could learn,' Janet told him.

'Yes.' Duncan agreed, 'I learned to ride the bike easy enough.'

'I could teach you,' Betty put in. 'I learnt in the war.'

There was a short embarrassed silence and then Bert gave a forced, nervous laugh and said, 'Don't be daft, Bet, you was an ARP warden.'

Betty's face unnerved him. He'd assumed when she spoke she'd been joking, but there was no trace of humour in her face, or her voice. 'And I drove a mobile canteen,' Betty snapped. 'I wrote and told you I was working on a mobile canteen. How d'you think the vans got where they were going? Think they were lowered from a barrage balloon, do you?'

'No but...'

'No but nothing,' Betty said. 'I didn't drive it, well not at first I didn't and then one day the driver Cynthia was injured and it was drive the bloody thing myself, or leave it there and have Hitler blow it to kingdom come, and I wasn't having that.'

'Mom,' Janet said breathlessly, 'I never knew.'

'Course you didn't,' Betty said. 'You were only nippers, and I had to watch what I told Ma, she worried so much, see. And,' she added with a nod at Duncan, 'when the vans went wrong, there were no army trained mechanics around for us then. We had to set to and fix our own, because if we didn't they stayed broken, and that meant letting people down, people who relied on us being there.'

Bert sat and regarded his wife with a wry smile. He hadn't been pleased at first to hear that his wife knew how to drive, but he began to see the funny side of it. 'You never said a dicky bird,' he said. 'I went on and on about my war and you said nothing.'

'No, I didn't,' Betty said, 'and I don't want to now. I was no saint and when you came back safe and sound, I just thanked my lucky stars, but if we ever are able to afford a car, I'll teach you to drive it, that's all I'm saying.'

Well,' Bert said proudly, 'all these years married and you still surprise me at times.' He suddenly put his arm around Betty and gave her a hug. It was not a thing he usually did, and never in front of the children, and Betty went red and wriggled in embarrassment, but Bert held her tight. 'Here, kids,' he said, 'I just want to say, your mom's a bleeding marvel – that's what she is.'

Janet's eyes were misted as she went up the stairs. She told herself not to be so bloody soft, but she was glad there was harmony in the family, for her end of year exams were just weeks away and that was enough for her to worry about. Despite that, most of the talk in the school and among many families was the 'Festival of Britain' based in London and planned for May of that year.

'Pity it's not later on,' Janet commented to Ruth.

'Yes, it would be nice to get the exams out of the way,' Ruth agreed. 'Still, we can give ourselves a couple of days off.'

'Mm, I suppose.'

Miss Phelps urged all the girls to go. 'Take pride in your country,' she preached in assembly one day. 'Find out what put the Great in Great Britain. Discover for yourselves that Britain is a world leader and has pioneered the way forward in things as diverse as the turbo-jet engine and penicillin. Don't languish at home while history is being made in our capital city.'

Bert Travers took the opposite viewpoint. 'Eleven thousand pounds has been earmarked for a bloody festival that won't benefit the average man in the street at all,' he said angrily. 'Thousands of people still live in sub-standard houses, hundreds in those prefab things that are little more than rabbit hutches, and yet the housing programme has slowed down. Unemployment continues to rise and prices in the shops go up daily. Boys are still fighting in Korea and the government says never mind all that, we'll have a bleeding party.' He gave a wry laugh and said, 'I read somewhere that Nero, the Emperor of Rome, played his fiddle while the city burned down, and that's what this looks like to me, a giant conga through the city of London while we pat ourselves on the back and say how bleeding marvellous we are. I know thousands who've lost everything and are struggling to survive, who'd ask what we've got to be so proud of.'

'Oh, Dad,' Janet said, exasperated, 'don't be such a grouch. People are tired of being reminded of the war all the time. Waste not, want not isn't popular any more. People want a bit of fun, light-heartedness, even more now the Korean war is threatening to accelerate. I mean,' she continued, 'if anything this will create jobs, won't it?'

Bert had to concede that, but he was upset that

227

the Labour government, that he had voted for, should waste money in such a way when so many people were still in need. 'They won't be permanent ones,' he reminded her.

'Who knows?' Janet said. 'Anyway, if we didn't have this festival, we would still have people out of work, living in bad conditions, and the Korean war would still be with us. Just for a little while, people want to forget.'

Bert had to agree with Janet in the end and was even prevailed upon to take the family on a day trip, if only, 'to see what all the bloody fuss is about!' Janet and Ruth caught the train to London from New Street like many others. People seemed to want to see and experience for themselves what Britain had to offer the world. Both girls couldn't fail to be impressed and filled with patriotic pride as they looked at the new inventions and designs. The plans and models of buildings of the future astounded them, and the colours and striking patterns in furnishings and fabrics were dazzling after years and years of bare utility and functional drabness everywhere.

The streets were thronged with people. Many were visitors, and from their accents plenty of those had come from America. A carnival atmosphere existed on the streets, and Janet smiled, remembering how her father had said it would be like a giant conga through the streets of London. He wasn't far wrong, she thought.

'Let's make for Battersea Park,' Ruth said. 'There's supposed to be lots going on there.'

As they pushed their way forward, a man lurched into them. 'Hey, I sure am sorry, ladies,' he said in a lazy Texan drawl. 'Are you okay?'

Giggling, Janet and Ruth assured him they were fine. 'D'you think it was like this in the war?' Janet asked. 'When the place was overrun with GIs?'

'Ssh,' Ruth cautioned. 'Don't let them hear you saying that, or we'll be surrounded by boastful Yanks explaining how they won the war for us, and I'm busy being patriotic at the moment.'

'Miss Phelps would be proud of you, my girl,' Janet said in the plummy voice of their headmistress, and both girls collapsed in giggles.

They had a wonderful time in the Pleasure Gardens at Battersea Park and went home tired and happy. They decided it had been a day well spent away from their studies.

'After this it's heads down until almost the end of June,' Janet said, and Ruth groaned.

'Yes,' she said. 'It's going to be worse next year.'

'Times like this, I'm not sure I want to go to university.'

'Yes, it's going to be one hard slog,' Janet said. Her dream of being another Miss Wentworth had never really faded, although it had taken a bashing when she was eleven. She'd been entered for eight 'O' levels which would be taken the following year and she knew it would be work, work and more work to get the grades she needed for a coveted university place.

However, the new term wasn't very old when one night Bert Travers came home in a foul temper and all because, 'That bleeding stupid bugger Attlee has called a general election.'

The Travers' children were pressed into service

delivering leaflets, there were endless talks and discussions on the radio and as the day grew nearer, posters appeared in windows, a large banner fluttered across the Travers' house and loud hailers toured the streets.

Election day dawned miserable and cold, with rain falling. 'Would be like this,' Bert said gloomily. 'Just the sort of day people want to stay at home in front of the fire.'

Labour Party members were already arriving as Janet was leaving for school, crowding into the small house. Outside, children released from school for the day kicked tin cans on the road, or whooped up and down in some game or other. Three cars were parked outside the Travers' door. They were needed later to transport the infirm and elderly to the polling station and chivvy the 'can't be bothered's'. Already, Janet noticed, inquisitive children had smeared the windows and dirtied the paintwork peeping inside the vehicles, for cars were still a rarity on the estate.

The yell from one of the people inside the house made her jump and scattered the children from the cars, as it was intended to do. Janet smiled grimly and slung her bulging satchel higher up her shoulder. She was glad she was getting out of the way for the day. The rest of the family were in for a cold and draughty time, for the door was open to the elements all day. The kettle was constantly on the boil for tea to be made, and Betty was going mad collecting and washing cups, only to have them filled again almost immediately. People were dragging wet mud in and out of the living room, the lino was a mess and the kitchen floor was worse. The children were complaining that they were bored and hungry, and Bert was asking if Betty could knock up a few sandwiches for the workers, or perhaps something on toast, while the loud hailers, urging people to vote for this party or that, were giving her a headache.

And it was all for nothing. The Conservatives gained power and Winston Churchill became prime minister once more.

'Bleeding stupid fools!' Bert railed. 'We'll be back to the means test, see if we aren't. And what good can that fool Churchill do? A doddering old bugger of seventy-six, and he's already had one stroke.'

'He was good in the war, Bert,' Betty reminded her husband. 'He went to a lot of the bombed out areas and spoke to the people and that. He went to the East End of London. It was in all the papers.'

'Well, people have got short memories, Betty,' Bert said, 'because before the war he turned the troops on the miners. Fighting his own people then, as there was no Germans about to have a go at. All that bloody man is any good for is writing and delivering speeches. I mean, he never got his hands dirty, did he? Spewing on about "fighting on the beaches," well, that cheered up all the blokes who'd left their dead mates behind in Dunkirk no end. Led to a massacre, we were, by people like Churchill.'

Bert was like a bear with a sore head and the house was like one in mourning. The children

231

kept their heads down.

And then in February of the following year just as Janet and Ruth were digesting the results of their mock 'O' levels, the nation was shocked by the death of George VI. Betty was in tears at the loss of the gentle man, never meant to be king, who'd conquered a stammer to lead his country.

'He could have moved out of London during the war if he'd wanted to,' Betty said, and raised a tear-stained face to her daughter. 'I mean, Buckingham Palace was hit, you know.'

'Not badly, though, Mom.'

'It could have been,' Betty snapped. 'Could have been bloody flattened with bombs flying around it all the time.' She shook her head. 'He was a great man all right, and a great king. Everybody loved him.'

It seemed Betty was right. The whole country seemed to be depressed by the death of the gentle king who'd captured everyone's hearts. Janet became irritated eventually.

'Life's got to go on, after all,' she said to Ruth. 'Thousands, even millions lost their lives just a few years ago and we go on and on about a king. I know it's sad, but he'd hardly want us to mourn for ever and we have got a coronation to look forward to.'

But long before the coronation Janet had her 'O' levels. While her mother still went on about the king whom everyone loved, Janet shut it all out and put her head down.

Bert and Betty worried about the hours she put in, her grandparents urged her to take it a bit easier and Breda reminded her that 'All work and no play makes Janet a dull girl'. Janet ignored all the well meaning advice. It was done with the best intentions, but no one knew the pressure that she was under, because they hadn't been there.

On the days of the examinations themselves, Janet was too sick with worry to eat and her anxiety affected Betty and Bert too.

'I'll be glad when it's all over,' Bert said. 'Perhaps then we'll see our lass smile again.'

But when the exams were over, Janet's principal emotion was extreme fatigue. 'Needs a bleeding holiday before she starts work in that shop all bloody summer,' Bert said.

Bert asked around, and when Janet got in one day, a week before school broke up, Betty had a surprise. 'Your dad's booked us a week in a caravan near Weston-Super-Mare,' she told Janet. 'Just as the holidays start we go.'

'My job...?' Janet began.

'You'll just have to start a week later,' Betty said. 'You need a holiday. You look worn out and that's a fact.'

Janet agreed with her mother. 'Ruth needs a break too,' she said. 'Can she come?'

'If her parents say she can,' Betty said. 'Duncan won't be coming, he's lodging with your gran,' and she gave Janet a wink. 'He's got a girlfriend,' she said.

That wasn't news to Janet. She even knew the girl's name. It was Gloria Marsden, but she didn't tell her mother that, for the Marsdens were a notorious family. Nor did she say that he roared around the streets on his bike with a shrieking Gloria clinging to him. She'd first spotted Gloria with Duncan waiting in the queue outside the Apollo cinema in Tyburn Road. She wouldn't mention that to Betty either or say that Gloria dressed as a teddy girl, for if her mother should tell Bert, it would be like a red rag to a bull. She wore the draped jacket with the velvet collar, a tight skirt, and a big beret with pearls all over it like they did. Her face had been almost orange with thick make-up with bright blue eye shadow and cerise pink on her lips. She'd looked down her nose at Janet, pulled at Duncan's arm, into which hers was tucked, and said, 'That's your bleeding brainy sister, ain't it, Dunc? She don't look that clever, does she? Bleeding drab bugger if you ask me.'

Duncan had coloured pink and muttered, 'Give over, Gloria,' while Janet lashed back with:

'Well, no one did ask you, Miss Gloria stick-your-nose-in Marsden, so keep your opinions to yourself.' She went on, 'And I hope you haven't got the idea you look good in that get up and with all that muck smeared over your face.'

She'd thought Gloria was going to hit her. Indeed, she might have tried it if Duncan hadn't held on to her, and before she was able to break away, the cinema doors had opened and they'd begun to file in. Gloria had contented herself with a lift of her chin to Janet. 'Snotty stuck-up cow,' she hissed, and Janet replied:

'Takes one to know one, Gloria.'

She hadn't told Betty about the encounter at the time, and she didn't tell her now. She was just glad Duncan wasn't going on holiday, for she had absolutely nothing in common with him any more.

The younger children were enchanted by the caravan and all its secret hiding places, and spent ages finding them. Ruth and Janet had the small bedroom, Bert and Betty the bigger one, which they shared with Sally. Conner and Noel were thrilled with the unfurled bunks they were to sleep on. 'Like real sailors,' said Noel excitedly. 'I bags the top one.'

'No, I'm having the top,' Conner said belligerently, and Bert stepped between them before they fell on each other, snarling and with their fists flying.

Janet caught Ruth's eye and laughed wryly. Some things never change, she thought. Aloud she said to the twins and Sally, 'Come on, we'll take you down to the beach and give Mom and Dad time to get straight.'

The two girls were too tired at first to do more than laze on the beach soaking up the sun, or build sandcastles and jump about in the sea with the children. The family hadn't much money to spend, though Conner, Noel and Sally had more than one ride on the donkeys. Ruth and Janet took them out one day to the fair to give Betty and Bert a day to themselves. They had as much fun as the children on the bumper cars and the waltzers and Bert and Betty were grateful for the break.

All in all, the holiday was judged a success, and they returned refreshed from the change. The summer raced by for Janet, busy with her job, but never did she forget for a minute the 'O' level results, which were due the second week in August. When they came through and she realised that she had passed every exam with distinctions, she was light headed with relief. It was congratulations all round when she discovered that not only had Ruth done nearly as well as she had, but that Claire had graduated from her Montessori course with honours.

In September Janet and Ruth joined the sixth form. As a concession to their 'grown up' status, they would be partnered by the boys from St David's Academy in their dancing lessons. They weren't an impressive bunch. Janet described them scathingly as 'A bunch of wets who are, in the main, spotty, shy and very nervous, and not necessarily in that order.'

At a nod from the teacher who'd brought them over, they would sidle across the room and mumble an invitation to dance. Janet often wondered why they bothered. Fox trot and quick step were one and the same to them as they shuffled about the room, with seemingly two left feet and no sense of rhythm.

'And why,' Janet complained to Ruth, 'do they sweat so much? Their faces positively glisten, and their hands are so sticky and clammy they make marks on my dress and I could wring out my shoulder pads.'

'My feet are crushed too,' agreed Ruth, and added, 'we're supposed to enjoy the thing.'

'Yes,' said Janet with a grin, 'it's supposed to be a treat.'

They laughed together, and then Ruth said,

'And did you find out about their hobbies and interests, like Miss Weatherstaff suggested?'

'Oh, yes,' Janet said. 'One hobby is telling awful jokes we wouldn't have found funny in infant class and they are also interested in playing tricks on people which are, without exception, in extremely bad taste.'

'What about the one who won the rugby match single handed?' Ruth said.

'You mean the mate of the one who rescued the cricket team from defeat by himself?' Janet asked sarcastically.

'Rather immature, aren't they?' Ruth said.

'Very,' Janet agreed. 'Give me a real man any day of the week.'

'Ah,' said Ruth, 'but where are they? Look at us, sweet sixteen and never been kissed.'

'Nor likely to be,' Janet said grimly, 'if the only contenders are the animals from the Academy.'

By the spring of 1953, Coronation fever had gripped the country and events to mark the occasion were planned in streets and estates throughout the land. Pype Hayes estate was no exception, but it appeared that Ruth's street was. When Janet heard that neither Ben nor Aaron were going to be home either, she urged Ruth to come to her house for the day. Leah Hayman opposed her granddaughter's decision, but Ruth stood up to her at last.

It was a special day in more ways than one, for just a couple of days before, two men had arrived at the door with a large box. Bert was the only one who didn't seem surprised, and the questions came thick and fast. He refused to answer any of them, 'wait and see,' he advised – but when the men slit the box side to slide the article out, the twins could contain themselves no longer. 'A television!' Conner said in awed tones.

'A telly, a telly, we've got a telly,' cried Noel, and began bounding about the room in excitement.

'Less of that,' Bert had admonished. 'You'll have the thing over.'

Betty stared at Bert, speechless. 'Well, lass?'

'Oh, Bert, can we afford it?'

'I wouldn't have bought it if we couldn't afford it,' Bert had said. 'I bought it the same way our Duncan bought the bike, so much down and so much a week.'

'But you said that was no way to go on,' Betty had reminded him.

'Only way for a big, expensive item,' Bert had said. 'It's all right as long as you don't go mad and just get one thing at a time.'

Betty had still looked doubtful, and Bert had draped his arm around her shoulders reassuringly. 'It's okay,' he said, 'and after all, another coronation probably won't happen in our lifetime. Surely you'd like to see it?'

They did see it, and so did the hordes of friends and neighbours who filled the Travers' house that day. They saw the milling, cheering crowds of people who lined the route the young Queen would take. 'History in the making,' Sean McClusky remarked. 'Fancy having it brought to your own living room like this.'

The people in the small room cheered with the

crowds when the first coaches and cavalry came into view on the flickering black and white screen. They saw the titled in their coronets and ermine trimmed robes, who Bert disparagingly called 'the toffs'. 'Ringside seats they have,' he commented, 'while some of the poor ordinary buggers have been camping out for days.'

'Unseasonably cold as well,' Peter said. 'Damned uncomfortable to sleep out in this.'

A silence fell as the ceremony in the Abbey began, and every eye was on the Queen. She was so small and slight, she was like a young girl. Behind her, eight maids of honour held her train.

'She's a bleeding beauty,' Bert said. But it wasn't beauty, though Elizabeth was pretty enough; it was her regalness, her dignity in the simple white linen gown that looked so right on her. She walked slowly down the long aisle and was anointed with the holy oils. They saw the heavy crown placed on the young Queen's head, and the cry rang out: 'Vivat, vivat Regina!' Bert produced a bottle of ten year old malt whisky which he'd been saving for the toast and the glasses were filled, though many of the women chose sherry as their tipple.

'Long live the Queen,' Bert said, and his words were echoed in the house and by the crowds waiting outside the Abbey.

Many of the women began crying when they saw the Queen's handsome young husband kneel before her to swear 'Life and Earthly Loyalty'.

The light, drizzling rain could not dampen the ardour of the crowds as the Queen and her husband began the return journey to Buckingham Palace. As the state coach appeared, so the roars of the crowds increased. 'Damned if it doesn't make you proud,' Bert said. 'We can put on a bloody good show when we have to.'

No one disagreed with him, for national pride was high at that time. It had begun with the newspaper headlines just days before, reporting that Edmund Hillary had conquered Everest, a fitting and apt present to bestow on the young Queen on her coronation.

The street outside the house was cordoned off and festooned with streamers and flags of red, white and blue. Most of the children had little Union Jack flags. It was a shame the day was so miserable and cold for the party fare had to be carried to the school hall. However the children did justice to the party tea the women in the street had been preparing for days, and a puppet show followed, giving the adults the chance to tidy up.

Then there were hilarious and very noisy party games before a conjuror came to do a few tricks and calm the children down before going home. Everyone stood to sing 'God Save the Queen' before they received a present to commemorate the occasion.

None of the children wanted to sleep afterwards, and anyway it would have been too noisy for them, with the adults still carousing, so eventually they were allowed to run about wild in the street. Most of the younger people, Janet and Ruth included, went back to the school hall to a party and dance organised for them there.

Tables were arranged round the edges of the

hall with table lamps, the only lights used, hiding the shabbiness of the place, as the red, white and blue tablecloths hid the scuffed and scratched school tables. Trestle tables covered in white with red and blue napkins stood at one end, filled with party fare. A bar was opened on the other side, and on the stage a band was playing 'Three Coins in a Fountain'.

'It's wonderful,' Ruth said.

Janet was pretty proud of the coronation committee. They had done well, she had to admit. Streamers decorated the walls and ceiling, a banner was pinned across the front of the stage with the first line of the National Anthem, and clusters of balloons were pinned to the walls.

'Let's find a table,' Janet advised, and they were joined a few minutes later by Peter and Breda.

'Mom's giving an eye to Linda,' Breda said. 'She's fallen asleep on her settee. She told me and Peter to come and check on you two.'

'She did not,' Peter said with a smile. 'They'll think we don't trust them.' He put his hands out and drew Janet to her feet. 'On your legs, young lady,' he said, 'and we'll take a turn around the room.'

Janet found her uncle a surprisingly good dancer. They'd not been on the floor five minutes when the band struck up a quickstep. 'Are you game for this?' she said with a grin. 'Or do you want to cry off and rest your aching bones?'

'You cheeky young scallion,' Peter said. 'I'll have you know I've tripped the light fantastic many times and I could give you a run for your money.'

'You're on,' Janet said and then gave a small

squeal as Peter caught her round her trim waist and whirled her away. This is dancing, thought Janet, not that flat footed plodding of the Academy boys.

Later as she stood over by the doorway to cool off a bit, she was startled by a voice saying in her ear, 'Hello there.'

It was so unexpected she jumped and swung round in surprise. 'Ben!' she cried. She'd hardly seen Ruth's brother in the two years he'd been away in London at medical school. The fairly rare times he was home had never coincided with the times she was visiting the family, but she'd have known him anywhere. His black hair was still worn long and the curly locks still fell over his forehead. His brown eyes were as bright and full of fun as ever, his mouth as wide and his teeth even whiter than she remembered. But Ben Hayman had gone away a boy, and yet it was a man standing before her and, she realised with a jolt, a very handsome one at that. Her heart was thudding and she was finding it hard to breathe, and she wondered if this was what people meant by love at first sight.

The room, the music, the dancing couples on the floor, even Ruth, had ceased to exist for her as she and Ben stared at one another, as if they were the only two people in the world. Ben recovered himself first. He gave a sudden start as if he'd just recollected what he was there for, and said, 'I ... I've come to pick Ruth up. I've brought Father's car.'

'Oh ... oh, yes,' Janet said. She indicated the dance floor. 'She's dancing with my uncle somewhere in there. My aunt has just popped across to see that their little girl is all right and I ... I came for some air. I was hot.'

'Oh,' said Ben. He seemed strangely nervous, Janet thought. He stood beside her by the open door, watching the dancing. Janet assumed he was looking for Ruth. She was somewhat taken aback when he suddenly turned towards her and said nervously, 'I ... I, um, was wondering, are you still hot or would you, um ... would you like to dance?'

'Yes, no. I mean, I'm fine,' Janet said in confusion, 'but haven't you got to go?'

'There's no rush.'

She fitted into his arms as if they'd been dancing together all their lives, just as she'd known she would. Many times, Janet had imagined falling in love with someone. She still wasn't sure about marriage, but most people fell in love, everyone knew that. Her mother said her Auntie Breda had been in love more times than she'd had hot dinners. She'd discussed it endlessly with Ruth: how they'd feel, what they'd say. They'd gone over and over the boys of their acquaintance (mainly those from the Academy) and decided that none of them were the type to fall head over heels for. 'I wonder which of us will be first?' Ruth had mused.

'You,' Janet had said. 'I haven't met one member of the opposite sex yet that I'd be vaguely interested in.'

'Me neither,' Ruth said, 'but doesn't it fill you with excitement to think of a world out there full of men?'

243

'Not really,' commented Janet dryly. 'I mean they're hardly all holding their breath to fall at our feet, now are they?'

'We must promise to tell each other everything when it happens,' Ruth said.

'We tell each other everything anyway,' Janet had reminded her friend, but as she waltzed, almost cheek to cheek, with Ben Hayman that coronation night, she wondered how much she would tell Ruth about it later.

'Could I see you again soon?' Ben said, almost casually, to hide his real feelings.

'What d'you mean?' Janet said stupidly. She knew quite well what he meant.

'I mean, could we go out on a date?' Ben said with a smile. 'Or if you'd prefer, would you, Miss Travers, do me the honour of meeting me one evening?'

Matching his mood and correct tone with an impish grin, Janet replied in like manner, 'Oh, Mr Hayman, thank you very much for asking me.'

They got no further, for at that moment Ruth swept past them, caught sight of her brother and descended on them both.

'Ben, when did you get here?'

'Not long ago,' Ben said, and added good naturedly, 'and I wish you'd push off for a bit, I'm trying to convince your friend Janet to go out with me.'

'You and Janet!' Ruth exclaimed. 'I don't believe it!' But the telltale blush on Janet's face convinced her that her brother was telling the truth.

'Stop it, Ben,' Janet said sharply, annoyed at what he'd said in front of her friend.

Janet watched Ruth being ushered towards the bar by her uncle, then turned to Ben and said, 'I'm afraid I can't go out with you. I'm too busy.'

'Look, I'm not here for long,' Ben said. 'Surely you can spare me one evening?'

'What do you mean, not here for long?'

'It's reading week, term hasn't ended officially yet,' he said. 'I go back in a few days and don't come home again until mid-July.'

'Oh.'

'You could put aside a night or two for me, couldn't you?'

Janet was silent. 'Oh, say yes, for God's sake,' Ben urged and added, 'We could go to the pictures if you like, I could probably get hold of Dad's car.'

'Could you?' It burst from Janet before she could stop it.

'Oh, I see,' Ben said. 'It's not me you want, it's the car.'

'That's right,' said Janet, and they laughed together.

Breda, coming back into the hall, watched the young couple and felt her stomach lurch as she remembered the men she had laughed with and loved when she was no older than Janet, men who'd marched away to war and never come back. She wished she had the power to protect her niece from heartbreak like she'd suffered, but people, she knew, had to learn from their own mistakes. Ruth too was watching them, and she felt a stab of envy that surprised her. Later, stepping outside for a breath of air, she was quite shocked to see Ben and Janet in a tight embrace, her brother kissing her friend as if he'd known her all his life. And I bet she doesn't tell me about that, for all her promises, Ruth thought, and returned to the dance in a bad humour.

Chapter Eleven

Janet never forgot the summer of 1953, the summer she fell in love with Ben Hayman. By the time early September's leaves were beginning to clutter the ground, she knew she loved him more than life itself. She thought ruefully of the girls at school she'd looked down her nose at when they'd enthused over boyfriends. They'd let their studies slip and their career goals had been dropped.

'All they want is to be a wife and mother,' Janet had fumed to Ruth on more than one occasion. 'Girls like that make it worse for the rest of us. It is pointless educating girls who marry and have babies as soon as they leave school.'

How easy it had been to say that when no one had touched her heart in that way. Now, if Ben Hayman had suggested flying to Outer Mongolia to live in a mud hut, Janet thought she'd probably consider it. Halfway through the summer, she could barely remember what she was like in the pre-Ben days. She hadn't known on their first date that this was how it would be; she only knew she wanted to meet Ben, and she was so scared of her father forbidding it that she didn't tell him and let him think she was meeting Ruth.

Bert and Betty had expressed surprise that they were going to the pictures this close to the exams, and just after they'd had a break from studying to join in the coronation celebrations too. However, they'd often wished Janet would go out more, so said nothing further about it.

She'd asked Ben not to pick her up outside her house, but at the bottom of the road. He did ask why, but she told him to mind his own business and knew by his chuckle and suggestive wink that he had guessed she hadn't told her parents about him.

'Where are we going?' Janet said. 'Which cinema?'

'Where do you want to go?' Ben asked.

'Not the Apollo,' Janet said. Tyburn Road was too close to home for comfort. Anyone could be there and see her. Even the Palace in Erdington was a little too near in her opinion.

Ben had been watching her face and guessed at some of her thoughts. He suggested, 'Shall we make for the city centre and give you a decent ride in the car?'

'Oh, yes,' Janet cried, relieved. She didn't ask what they were going to see. It didn't matter. Here she was on her first date with a boy, and she was both excited and a little scared.

As they swung into Tyburn Road on their way into town, Janet spotted Duncan and Gloria. It looked as if they were having a humdinger of an argument. She saw Gloria stamp her foot and swing her hand to strike a stinging blow to Duncan's cheek. He parried it and gripped her arms tight, and then they were passed and lost to view.

Ben had noticed her preoccupation with the couple. 'Someone you know?' he asked.

Janet nodded. 'Yes,' she answered briefly. She didn't yet know Ben well enough to tell him personal things about her family.

They had a wonderful evening. Janet had been worried how Ben might behave. She'd heard some horror stories from the girls at school about what lads got up to in the back row when the lights went down. But to start with, Ben didn't lead Janet into the back row, which she saw was almost filled with couples anyway, but to seats halfway down. And when the film began, he seemed intent on it, and eventually Janet began to relax. He'd held her hand as they sat down and continued to hold it, but apart from that he did nothing and tried nothing on at all.

Afterwards, he drove to the corner of Janet's road, parked the car and walked her to the gate, where he drew her into his arms and kissed her. Janet gave a sigh of contentment. 'Happy?' Ben asked.

'Mmm.'

'Will you go out with me again?'

Janet's eyes opened wide, happy to know he wanted another date, which meant she couldn't have bored or irritated him totally. And yet she couldn't see her way to going out again. Already she was feeling fingers of guilt stabbing at her for not staying in her room, chained to her books, that evening.

'Oh, Ben, I don't think I can manage another night,' she said.

'I go back Thursday,' Ben said, 'then you won't see me till the middle of July. I thought if I could borrow Dad's car again we could take a trip out.

We could drive across to Kingsbury, there's a place I want to show you.'

It was tempting, and suddenly Janet really wanted to go. I'll make up the time, she promised herself, I'll work like stink when he goes back.

'Okay,' she said. 'Yes thanks, I'd like that.'

She knew her parents wouldn't believe that she would go to the pictures twice in one week, so she told them she was going to Ruth's to work. She felt bad about deceiving them, especially as they didn't doubt her for a second.

'You shouldn't lie to them, Janet,' Breda said when Janet confided in her. 'If you consider yourself mature enough to go out with a boy, you're old enough to explain it to your parents.'

Janet knew she was right, but she wasn't going to take the risk and jeopardise this date with Ben. 'If he wants to see me again when he's home for the summer, I'll tell them then,' she promised, and added, 'You won't split on me, will you?'

Breda looked at her niece. She loved Janet dearly – in fact, she was her favourite of them all, and she'd hate to be the one who brought her parents' censure down on her head – but what if Bert and Betty found out and knew that Breda had been aware of it all the time?

'Do you give me your word you'll tell them?' she asked, and Janet nodded.

'I promise,' she said, 'really and truly.'

'Then I'll say nothing.'

'Oh, thanks, Auntie Breda.'

Breda looked at her a minute longer, wondering what she knew about boys and sex in general. She knew her sister's prudishness in discussing sexual matters, despite having had five children.

Eventually she said, 'Has our Betty told you about things ... you know, sex and all that?'

Janet blinked in embarrassment. 'Um, I think I know about it,' she said. 'You mean how babies are born and things like that?'

'That's part of it, yes.'

'I know all that,' Janet said. 'It's all some of the girls talk about.'

'Has your mother said anything at all?' Breda asked.

'Only when I started my periods,' Janet said. 'I didn't know what it was and I thought I was dying, and Mom told me what it was and said I must never speak of it in front of men. Then she said I would soon become a woman and I had to respect myself or men wouldn't respect me, and that could lead to trouble.'

'How old were you?' Breda asked.

'Thirteen.'

'And that was the extent of the sex talk, was it?' Breda said irritably.

'Well ... yes.'

'And a lot of bleeding good it did, I bet.'

'Well, I know what she means, sort of, and I know about sex,' Janet said defensively.

'You know how babies are made,' Breda corrected. 'There's much more to it than that.'

'Is there?'

'Janet, there will be times – maybe it will be with Ben Hayman, or maybe someone else – when a boy will kiss you and send you wild,' said Breda. 'He may touch parts of your body that, if you were thinking straight, you wouldn't let him touch, and all that talk about respect will go out of the window. You'll want him to go on and on, and if you're not careful, things will get out of hand, and before you know it you're pregnant and the boy's still fancy-free.'

Janet was embarrassed, her face flushed pink. 'I wouldn't,' she said.

'You could, easily,' Breda said. 'Tell me honestly that you're not disturbed by Ben's kisses.' But Janet couldn't, and she stayed silent.

'All I'm saying, pet, is it's the woman who has to put the brakes on,' Breda went on. 'It's unfair, but there you are. A woman has more to lose, so she has to be the one to call time. If your Ben, or any other boy, does something you don't like, or you're unhappy about it, say so and say no. And don't,' she warned, 'be taken in by the old line "If you loved me you would." That is as old as Adam and Eve and is so much bullshit, if you'll pardon the expression.'

'Oh, Aunt Breda,' said Janet, wriggling with embarrassment.

'Okay, lecture over,' Breda said, 'and to change the subject slightly, your brother seems to have gone off that girl he was so keen on.'

'Gloria?'

'If that's her name,' Breda said. 'I know she's a Marsden and as common as the rest of them.'

'I saw him with her just the other day,' Janet said, and added, 'though they seemed to be having a row.'

'She's been running around with other boys, apparently,' Breda said. 'Peter's nephew has been

252

working behind the counter at the bikers' caff for the last few weeks, and it seems young Gloria's been with nearly all of them. She's a joke among the lads. They were amazed when Duncan actually went out with her, because of how she is. Apparently she still trailed after anything in trousers, and your brother eventually came to his senses, realised what was going on and chucked her over.'

'Thank God for that,' Janet said fervently. 'Mom and Dad need never know.'

'No,' Breda said, 'and I needn't tell them about you either if you keep your word.'

'I will.'

'And remember what I told you.'

'Oh, Auntie Breda,' Janet said again.

'Don't "oh, Auntie Breda" me, just remember.'

And Janet did remember. She remembered the following night when they went on the drive and Ben seemed to know exactly where he was going. He parked the car and took Janet's hand, and they walked together down the country lane. 'Where are we?' she asked in a hushed voice, because it was that kind of place.

'Bodymoor Heath,' Ben answered in the same tone. 'We used to come here a lot when we were younger. Mother had a friend in Kingsbury we used to visit, and Dad would bring us down here when we got fed up with being polite and good. We'll come to the first lake in a minute.'

The evening was warm and still quite bright, the sun low and red in the sky, and when the path opened out and the lake was shimmering golden before them, Janet cried, 'Oh, Ben, it's beautiful.'

'Isn't it?' Ben said. 'Hard to believe the lakes are artificial.' At Janet's disbelieving face he went on, 'Oh yes, Dad told us all about it. There used to be gravel pits here and they made the lakes from the stuff they removed from the ground.' He sat on a grassy hummock, pulled Janet beside him and put an arm around her.

'It's so quiet,' she said, 'and still.' The only sound was the gentle lap of the water and the breeze riffling through the grass.

'It nearly always is,' Ben said. 'Few seem to know it's here. Often we didn't see a soul.' He smiled and pointed to the water. 'I learnt to swim in there when my dear brother pushed me in. Later, when I was a little older, I used to cycle out here to fish.'

'I didn't know you were a fisherman,' Janet said, but then, what did she know of him really?

'I'm not,' Ben said. 'I didn't do it for long, to be truthful – too sedentary for me. I haven't been here for some time, but it's a special place to me, so I wanted you to see it.'

Janet glowed inside at the way Ben had said that.

'Tell me about yourself, Janet Travers,' he demanded suddenly, holding her closer. 'Tell me about your hopes and dreams.'

'Oh, I'm very ordinary,' Janet said dismissively.

'Not to me,' Ben insisted, 'and I'd like to hear.'

So Janet talked. She told him of her scholarship and Miss Wentworth, of how she'd slaved away, of her father's initial reluctance and his subsequent pride. She told him of the dreams she had of being like Claire Wentworth one day, how she wanted to make something of herself.

Ben told her of the plans he had for his life and how he'd always wanted to be a doctor. He was fascinated by mental health and the strides being made in it since the war. 'We lag way behind America, though,' he said. 'That's the place that offers hope to parents and children alike.'

'Like Claire's Chloe.'

'Exactly,' Ben said. 'You and Ruth used to help her with exercises and things, didn't you?'

'Yes. That was based on recent studies in America,' Janet said.

'I'd like to meet Claire and Chloe,' Ben said after a minute or two of pensive silence.

'You might one day,' Janet said, and added quite sharply, protective of them both, 'If you do, you'll meet them as friends of mine, not as some sort of case study.'

'Hey,' Ben cried, 'I'm not the enemy here.'

'Sorry,' Janet said, and added with a rueful grin, 'It's just I'd hate them to be seen as some sort of peep show.'

'God, Janet, what do you take me for?' Ben burst out almost angrily. 'I'm interested in them because that's the field I think I'd like to specialise in, but I'd also like to meet them because they're your friends.'

Janet didn't speak. She didn't say that when Ben came back in July his feelings for her might have changed, but that was what she was thinking, and she shivered.

The evening had darkened as they sat and talked, and yet neither had been aware of it. Now Janet saw that the sun had nearly set and crimson shafts from it were turning the wind-driven ripples amber and sending pink-tinged clouds scudding across the sky.

'You're cold,' Ben said, pulling her to her feet. 'We've sat here long enough. Time for a drink, I think, and then I'll take you home. I bet you've never been in a pub in your life.'

Janet hadn't, but she guessed that no pubs near her home would be like the one Ben chose. The Dog and Doublet was by a canal, and though it was too dark to see the water, Janet was interested in the barges she saw moored by the sides. The pub opened on to the towpath, and inside the ceilings were white and low with black beams. Janet was charmed. It was like something from a bygone age.

'What will you have?' Ben asked.

Janet didn't know anything about alcoholic drinks except the sips she'd had of her father's beer or her grandad's stout. She'd liked neither. She knew her gran liked port and lemon and her mom sherry, but she'd never tasted them herself.

'Just an orange,' she said to Ben.

'You're a big girl now,' Ben said, 'you've turned seventeen. Be a devil and have a gin in it.'

'Oh, I don't know...'

'Go on, one small gin won't hurt you,' Ben said.

'Just one then,' Janet warned, looking at her watch, 'then we really must go. Mom and Dad will be worried.'

When Ben returned with the drinks he said, 'Where do they think you are?'

'What d'you mean?'

256

'Well, they don't know about me, do they?'

Janet stared at him for a moment or two and then gave a sigh. 'No,' she admitted. 'I was worried they wouldn't understand, and you only had a few days here.'

'I don't want a clandestine romance with you all summer,' Ben said firmly. 'I want to take you out openly, pick you up at the front door properly, not skulk round the corner somewhere. I want to meet the Travers family I've heard so much about from my sister. I want to...'

Suddenly Ben leaned across the table and grasped one of Janet's hands. 'I've talked to you more than I've ever talked to anyone before. At college, I'm always Ben Hayman, the clown, always good for a laugh. No one but you has ever really listened to me before, or taken me seriously.'

Janet could hardly believe what Ben was saying. She wondered if the gin she was enjoying was stronger than she thought. Surely this couldn't be happening to her? She was certain of it when Ben looked deep into her eyes and said, 'I really like you, Janet.'

Later, in bed, she went over and over that meeting. They'd kissed good night in the car at the corner, and Janet couldn't understand the strange yearnings in her that the kissing evoked. She wished she'd had more experience with boys and wondered if all kisses did that to you. It wasn't something you could ask anyone. She noticed that Ben seemed to be as excited as she was, but she could hardly ask him why. It sent a shock of exhilaration through her when he kissed her neck and throat, and she gave a little moan of pleasure.

'Oh, Janet, you're lovely.' She definitely hadn't imagined him saying that, though she knew his voice was strangely husky and his face was buried in her hair.

Almost immediately he'd pulled away abruptly and said in a totally different voice, 'We'd better get going, Janet, time's getting on.'

Confused and unhappy, she got out of the car. She couldn't understand how he could suddenly change his attitude like that, as if he was tired of her. But then he was walking beside her, his arm around her shoulder, and it felt so natural, so easy, it seemed as though they'd always been like this.

At the gate, he pulled her to him, gave her a chaste kiss on the lips and said, 'See you in July, funny face,' and before she'd recovered he was gone. She couldn't call out or she'd have been heard in the house. She could only look after him in the dark and wonder how she'd get through the next few weeks without him.

She realised what a good liar she was when she was able to go into the house a few minutes later and regale her parents with tales of the mountain of work she'd got through with Ruth that evening. It didn't make her feel good about herself, and anyway she wanted to be alone to think about Ben and her conflicting emotions, so pleading tiredness, she headed for bed almost immediately.

In the hallway, she met Duncan coming in. He looked her up and down and said sarcastically,

'Enjoy yourself at Ruth's house, did you?'

Oh God, Janet thought, he must have seen us. She blushed as she remembered their passionate embraces in the car. She'd hate him to have seen that. She knew he wouldn't tell on her – he wasn't a sneak – but all of a sudden it mattered that he didn't think badly of her.

'Look, Duncan...' she began in an effort to explain, but he cut her off.

'Forget it, sis, it's your life and it isn't my business. But,' he added, 'take care!'

Another one telling me to watch how I behave, Janet thought angrily. What do they think I am, a raving sex maniac? She could understand her Auntie Breda, but Duncan? He was behaving like an aged adult. She wondered if he'd behaved himself with Gloria but doubted it, if only half the tales about her were true. She nearly asked him, but knew it would lead to a row, and she didn't want to end that lovely night arguing with anyone, so she contented herself with muttering, 'Yes, Grandad' as she stomped up the stairs.

She actually had very little time to miss Ben, for the exams were frighteningly close and she really had to get her head down. Just before the day of the first paper, she received a letter. Betty was bemused and unashamedly curious.

'I wonder who it's from?' she said as she handed it to Janet.

Janet, who knew only too well, said airily, 'I haven't time to find out. I'll read it at school,' and shoved it into her satchel before her mother could have a closer look at it.

She waited only till she was round the corner

from home before ripping open the envelope.

Dear Janet,
   Missing you already. I often wish you were here to talk to. Those two dates we had were very special to me. Keep the summer free and we'll paint the town red.
   Love, Ben.

It wasn't a love letter as such, but it was the first Janet had ever received from a boy, and before the day was out she could have recited it word for word. She kept it in the pocket of her cardigan where she could touch it constantly, and it gave her comfort. She showed it to no one. Nobody, and especially not Ruth, was going to laugh over her Ben's letter, she decided.

That night she wrote a reply.

Dear Ben,
   I'm looking forward to seeing you too, although I am really very busy, nearly into my exams now. It will help the time pass quickly and all I can say is roll on the summer when we can meet again.
   Love, Janet.

Betty was intrigued by the letter Janet had received that morning, and Janet caught her mother's eyes on her speculatively a few times during the meal that night, but she made no actual mention of it, nor did she make any comment about the next two that came.

By the time Janet's exams were over and she and Ruth had more free time, Duncan had received his call-up papers for his national service.

'We're having a party,' Janet said to Ruth, 'at our house. Can you come?'

'I'll do my best,' Ruth promised. 'Probably, especially now everything's finished.'

'Yes, it's all rather flat, isn't it?'

'You bet,' Ruth said, and added, almost casually, 'Are you looking forward to seeing Ben again?' She knew her brother had been writing to Ruth because he'd mentioned it in his letters to her, but Janet hadn't let her see anything, saying they were just friendly notes, not for general debate. Ruth hadn't liked it, but decided it was not worth falling out over.

'Course I am,' Janet answered. 'He's good fun.'

'You and our Ben,' Ruth said incredulously. 'I can hardly believe it.'

'What's wrong with it?'

'Nothing, I suppose,' Ruth admitted. 'But ... well, he's my brother.'

'But not mine,' Janet snapped impatiently.

Ruth guessed that further comments would only make Janet cross, and in an effort to change the subject she said, 'Talking of brothers, is yours looking forward to national service?'

'I think so,' Janet said. 'It will probably be more interesting than the factory anyway. I know he gets sick of that every day.'

'Will his awful girlfriend be at this party?'

'No, I think he finished with her ages ago,' Janet said, 'but even if he hadn't, he'd have more sense than to ask her to our house.'

'Well, I'm glad. Your auntie certainly didn't like her.'

'I don't like her,' Janet put in, 'but it was Duncan's choice. It's his life, after all.'

'Are things better between you two now?' Ruth asked.

'We rub along okay,' Janet said. 'He doesn't snap people's heads off so much, or snarl at the twins, or make our Sally cry all the time, so I suppose it is better. You hardly think about it when things are peaceful, you just enjoy it. You only notice when things are sticky, I suppose,' she said reflectively. 'Our Duncan is growing up.'

Ruth had never seen the Travers' house so crowded as it was the night of the party. 'Who are all these people?' she asked as Janet pulled her through the throng towards the kitchen for a drink. Ruth had met all Janet's relatives, and she knew that there were many people there that night who were not family.

'They're friends of Mom and Dad's,' Janet said, 'and neighbours who've seen our Duncan grow up, and a few of his more sensible mates.' She nodded into the room and said, 'For instance, the one giving you the eye at the moment is called Robbie Palmer. He's all right. I mean, he's a bit stupid like all lads, and a biker, so he only possesses half a brain, but he's a sight better than the Academy lads.'

Ruth burst out laughing and said, 'That wouldn't be hard,' and Janet had to agree.

The party went with a swing. Ruth and Janet were out on the floor dancing to every record. Robbie Palmer was particularly attentive at getting them both food and drink, they noticed. The children went to bed fairly early, considering, with Linda tucked into the bed with Sally, and Patrick and Liam sharing a mattress in the boys' room.

Gradually the older people moved into the kitchen – the women setting about clearing away or having a good gossip, and the men guarding their beer from marauding teenagers – and the room was given over to the younger people for dancing. Janet was taken aback and rather pleased when Duncan asked her to dance, though not surprised that he had an ulterior motive.

They were barely out of earshot when he blurted out suddenly, 'My mate Robbie's dead keen on Ruth.'

Janet glanced across to where the pair were in earnest conversation. 'I know,' she said.

'He won't ask her out,' Duncan said, ''cos she's, well, you know ... a bit posh, isn't she?'

'She is not.'

'She is, Jan,' Duncan said. 'I mean, I've fancied her for years and she's never taken any notice of me.'

'That's because she's never thought of you that way,' Janet said. 'It's not because she's posh, it's because she just sees you as my brother.'

'Yeah, well, it doesn't work, the other way, does it?' Duncan objected. 'I saw you being very friendly with *her* brother, kissing and cuddling up in the car. Very cosy you looked.'

'How do you know that was Ben Hayman?' Janet said. 'You can't have seen him for years, if ever.'

'He was here Coronation Day,' Duncan said. 'He was all over you then and I asked Auntie

263

Breda who he was. Is that his own car?'

'No, his father's. He has a loan of it sometimes.'

'And why haven't you told Mom and Dad?' Duncan said. 'You're hardly a kid any more.'

Janet made a face. 'Dad thinks I am,' she said, and went on, 'It's hard to explain, but I am going to tell Mom and Dad when he's down for the summer. He's finishing his term at medical school at the moment.'

'There you are, you see,' Duncan cried triumphantly. 'He's Ruth's brother but you went out with him.'

'Well, he asked me,' Janet protested, and added, 'You've never actually asked Ruth, have you?'

'No fear,' Duncan said. 'I knew she'd bloody well refuse. Robbie won't ask either.'

But Robbie did pluck up courage to ask Ruth out, and she collared Janet in the hall to ask her what she should do about it.

'Do you like him?'

'Well, yes.'

'Say yes then.'

'But he's a biker,' Ruth said. 'Mom and Dad would have a fit.'

'I'm sure he could leave his bike at home if he cared for you enough, couldn't he?' Janet asked.

'Well, yes, I suppose.'

'Say yes then.'

'Yes, but there's something else as well,' Ruth said. 'Robbie is ... well, he's not Jewish.'

'I'm not Jewish, and Ben and I...' She stopped as she saw the look on Ruth's face, then asked, 'Has he been having a hard time because I'm not Jewish?'

'Not yet,' Ruth said. 'Mom and Dad are more liberal – well, until it comes to marriage they are – but ... well, we've kept the news of your relationship from Grandmother.'

'Bugger your grandmother,' Janet cried angrily, 'and the rest of you who kow-tow to her all the time. Now look,' she said, 'you go into that room and find out if Robbie Palmer intends taking you to a pagan festival where you worship the devil. The chances are, he will be meaning you to go to the cinema together, or for a peaceful walk in the park. In that case you can tell him you'll consider it, if he wears a skull cap.'

'Janet, you are a fool,' said Ruth, convulsed with laughter.

'Then I match the rest of you,' Janet said. 'Don't be so bloody gormless, Ruth, get in there and put the lad out of his misery.'

Shortly after this conversation, people began to drift home, and Duncan, because he was entering a true men's world in the morning, allowed women neighbours whom he'd repulsed for years to give him a kiss for luck. He shook hands solemnly with men he'd known since childhood. Everyone wished him all the best and Betty was busy dabbing damp eyes and pretending she wasn't crying.

Soon there was only the family and Ruth left, and Janet gave a sudden enormous yawn and said, 'I didn't realise how late it was. I'm for bed. How about you, Ruth?'

'If you're going I am,' Ruth said. 'Sharing a bed with you is like sharing one with an octopus. If I don't get in before you fall asleep, I balance on the edge all night.'

'Stop moaning,' Janet said unsympathetically.

She stepped forward and uncharacteristically kissed Duncan on the cheek. 'For luck,' she said, 'and for God's sake, look after yourself.'

'Can I give you a kiss for luck as well?' Ruth said. 'Seeing as your sister kisses my brother.'

They might have covered it up if Ruth, consumed with guilt for dropping her friend in it, hadn't gone brick red, clapped her hands over her mouth and said, aghast, 'Oh God, Janet, I'm so sorry!'

Bert was happily half-drunk and warmed by the true companionship of friends, neighbours and family who'd come to give his lad a good send-off. Now it seemed from what he'd overheard that there was something his Janet had been hiding from him, some lad she'd been carrying on with. 'What's this?' he thundered. The beer that had mellowed him while his world was right now made him belligerent when he felt he'd been made a fool of.

Breda tried to rescue the situation. 'It was Coronation Day,' she said. 'Everyone was kissing everyone else then.'

That was right enough, Bert knew, but one kiss after a night of hilarity and fun weeks ago would not have made Ruth behave like she had: 'Don't play me for a bleeding fool, Breda,' he said. 'I know there's more to this than that,' and he swung round to face Janet. 'Explain yourself, miss,' he demanded.

Janet raised her head angrily. She'd done nothing wrong. Her father was acting like some

Victorian parent who'd just found out his daughter was pregnant. 'I went to the pictures with Ben Hayman, that's all,' she said. 'He's Ruth's brother and I met him at the dance on Coronation Day.' She couldn't possibly tell him about the evening in the country. For one thing he'd immediately think the worst, and for another, it would land Ruth in it. Not that she didn't deserve it, Janet thought angrily, silly bloody fool.

'And why couldn't you tell us about this boy straight away?' Bert demanded. 'What have you got to be ashamed of?'

'Nothing! Nothing!' Janet cried. 'He only had a few days before he had to go back to college, and I thought ... I thought you might not agree to me going out with him.'

'You thought I might not agree, so you went anyway!' Bert snarled. 'That's showing fine bleeding respect for me.'

'It isn't like that. Ben's a nice boy. Auntie Breda and Uncle Peter have met him. He's Ruth's brother, for heaven's sake.'

'I'm well aware whose brother he is,' Bert said, 'and I have nothing against Ruth, she's not responsible for her brother. No, I'm interested in what sort of daughter I've bred. You say your aunt and uncle have met him and yet you couldn't bring him home to meet your parents. Tell me, are you ashamed of us, or of him?'

At this both Betty and Breda burst in, Betty saying she was sure it was nothing like that and she knew Janet to be a good girl, and Breda saying Bert was making a big thing about a lass going to the pictures with a lad. 'Be quiet, the pair of you!' he yelled, and banged his fist on the table so that the dishes jumped. 'It's not the fact she went to the pictures, it's the way it was done. Why, for example, didn't this lad come for her at the door properly?'

'I asked him not to,' Janet said. 'I asked him to meet me on the corner,' and because it was bound to come out later she added, 'He'd borrowed his father's car.'

Bert stared at her, horrified. In his befuddled mind he saw his daughter being fumbled by a lad out for what he could get. He knew what went on, he'd seen quiet spots where they got up to God alone knew what mischief. 'You went out with him in a car,' he said incredulously. 'The sly young bugger was cute enough to borrow it from his father to take you out, you little sl...'

'Don't you dare call me names,' Janet burst out, too angry to be careful what she said. 'D'you think I've no say in any of this? D'you think I don't know right from wrong? Don't you dare judge me. It was to avoid a scene like this that I didn't tell you in the first place. I'm turned seventeen. What age was Mom when she went out with you?'

'That has nothing to do with it.'

'Yes it bloody well has.'

'Ruth saw you canoodling,' Bert yelled. 'She said so.'

'She said she saw us kissing,' Janet yelled back. 'That's all! Kissing was all I did. I kissed Ben first on Coronation Day and she saw me!'

'Is this true?' Bert demanded.

Ruth raised a tear-stained face. She'd sat sobbing since she dropped the bombshell that had released all this anger. Dear God, it was terrible. In her house, anger was controlled by icy politeness and stony silences. She was unused to the violent outbursts of the Travers family. In the past it had always been tempered before her, and though Janet had described scenes in her home, it wasn't the same as witnessing one first-hand. She had to help her friend out of this if she could. 'Yes, Mr Travers,' she said. 'I saw Janet give Ben a kiss on Coronation Day. I assumed because I knew they'd gone out together that she'd given him a good night kiss or something. That's why I said what I did.'

'See,' Janet said. 'I suppose that's wrong too in your book.' She looked at her father in a way that could only be described as insolent, and sneered, 'I suppose you and Mom just held hands all the time, did you?'

'You cheeky bugger. Don't you dare talk to me like that,' Bert bawled, and raised his hand. Afterwards Janet was never sure if he'd intended to hit her or not. He'd never laid a hand on her before this. Betty was the first to spring in front of her daughter and held on to Bert's outstretched arm.

Condemnation was coming at him from all sides.

'Aw, man, give over.'

'Let the lass alone, can't you?'

'Bert, for heaven's sake.'

'Shut up!'

'Leave it now.'

Gran had gone across to Janet and wrapped her arms around her. Janet was crying now.

'I didn't do anything wrong, Gran, honestly I didn't.'

'I never thought for a minute you did, bonny lass. It's the beer talking. Get you and your pretty friend away upstairs. We'll deal with the boyo.' Janet watched as Bert was helped to the settee, then the two girls crept up the stairs. They heard Betty berating him before the door was properly closed.

'Fine show you made of yourself, and your son leaving this house tomorrow. From the performance tonight, I'd not hurry back if I was him. And what was it all for? Your lass, who's turned seventeen, goes out with a lad to the pictures without your express permission, because she was too scared to ask you – and with good reason, judging by your behaviour when you did know. It isn't as if the lad's a stranger. The family has been known to us for five years. Why in God's name couldn't you wait till the morning when you'll be sober and could talk about it reasonably? Oh no, that's not your way, is it? You have to make a holy show of the family and spoil our lad's last night here!'

'God, Janet, I'm so sorry,' Ruth whispered. 'I wouldn't have done that to you for anything.'

'I know, don't worry. It will be all over by tomorrow,' Janet said. 'At least it's out in the open this way.'

Ruth wondered how Janet stood such rows, but she didn't even seem particularly upset. Janet knew her father. Tomorrow, sobered up and lectured by his wife and in-laws, he would be ashamed and apologetic. In the dark of the bedroom she smiled. She could almost feel sorry for him, and she fell asleep dreaming of Ben Hayman.

Chapter Twelve

Janet was right. The day following the party, a repentant and hung-over Bert apologised to his daughter, and she was able to tell him all about Ben and what he intended to do with his life. 'He wanted to come and see you properly and ask to go out with me,' she assured her parents. 'It was just he had such a short time here and I thought ... well, I thought if you said no, I wouldn't be able to work on you to make you change your mind in time.'

Bert chuckled. 'You've got us sussed out right enough,' he said. 'And you're a sensible girl, and Ben is after all from a good home. I'm sorry I made such a fuss. It isn't that I don't trust you.'

'I know, I know,' Janet assured him. 'He'll be pleased you know, he wanted me to tell you. Can I ask him over when his term is finished?'

'You can, certainly. I'd like to meet the boy my girl is going out with.'

'Is that who the letters were from?' Betty asked, and Janet blushed and admitted that it was.

'Write and tell him he's welcome,' Betty said. 'I'm sure he's a fine young man.'

'Oh, I will, I will,' Janet said, her eyes shining.

The day he arrived home Janet was ecstatic, and Ruth was generous enough not to resent her friend's happiness. In fact the only person really unhappy about the situation was Leah Hayman.

272

It was still a whole week before Ruth and Janet's term ended, and Ben borrowed the car from his father and drove to the school to surprise them both. As he dropped Ruth at their garden gate later, he was spotted driving off with Janet by his eagle-eyed grandmother from her vantage point at the window. She pounced on Ruth as she came through the door. 'Was that the Travers girl in the car with your brother?'

Ruth was taken aback. Her grandmother was usually resting at this time and she could only surmise that Leah must have been suspicious of Ben when he said he was going to collect Ruth from school. She knew, too, that it was pointless lying; she wasn't very good at it, for one thing, and for another, her grandmother knew full well who it was in the car. 'Yes, Ben picked us both up.'

'I'm aware of that,' the old lady snapped. 'He wasn't in the house five minutes before he was hightailing over to his father's office for the loan of the car. If he went to fetch you,' she continued, 'why didn't he come in with you? If he had to pick up the Travers girl at all, he should have dropped her off first.'

'Her name is Janet, Grandmother,' Ruth said testily, 'and she lives further from the school than we do, and ... and I asked them to drop me first, I have things to do.'

She was lying and Leah Hayman knew it. Now why should that be? 'Is there something going on between your brother and that common girl?' she demanded.

Only inherent good manners prevented Ruth from yelling at her grandmother, but she spoke

273

sharply. 'Of course not, and she's not common. Now, if you'll excuse me, I have homework.' And she pushed past the astonished old woman and fled up the stairs.

But she knew her grandmother hadn't believed her, and she was waiting for Ben to warn him when he returned to the house. She told him about the conversation she'd had with the old woman, and Ben raised his eyes to the ceiling.

'She'll have Dad on my back, you'll see,' he said.

However, Joseph Hayman refused to speak to Ben about the matter. 'Mother, he's twenty years old,' he'd objected when Leah approached him with her suspicions.

'So you refuse to do anything about it?'

'I refuse to meddle in his life.'

'This girl will destroy him,' Leah Hayman said.

'Don't be so melodramatic. Mother,' Joseph said irritably. 'What do you want me to do, draw up a list of suitable girls I approve of?'

Old Mrs Hayman looked at her son out of narrowed eyes. In her day that was exactly what a father did. Sons were expected to do as they were told, and what's more they generally did.

'Look, Mother,' Joseph said placatingly, 'if he is going out with Janet Travers, where's the harm? You can't stand the girl, but the rest of us like her well enough, and she's been Ruth's very good friend for five years. As well as that, she's little more than a child...'

'She's seventeen!' the old lady snapped. 'The same as Ruth. I was married at seventeen.'

'Janet won't be,' Joseph said, 'nor Ruth either.

Both of them have things they want to do with their lives before they think about marrying. Girls are looking for careers these days.'

Leah Hayman gave a sniff. She had no time for modern girls. What Ruth should be doing was courting a nice young Jewish boy. They should visit a shatchan – a matchmaker – to go into the boy's prospects and lineage. That was how it had been done in the past. In fact, girls did not go out on their own at all before marriage.

She'd been horrified when a strange lout called Robbie Palmer had called to take Ruth to the pictures, and her parents had let her go. Naomi had even suggested it was not Leah's affair. She and Joseph had met the boy and he'd seemed nice enough. They could find no reason why Ruth should not go out with him. The old lady had been furious.

Naomi insisted Joseph hold firm and not let his mother interfere so much in their children's lives. She blamed Leah for Aaron deciding to leave home and live in a flat. He seldom even visited any more.

'I couldn't live there again, Mom!' he'd said when Naomi pleaded with him to return. 'I couldn't have Grandmother asking where I was going every minute and who with and what time I'd be in. I couldn't stand her judging my friends and looking down on my girlfriends.' He'd shaken his head, kissed Naomi's cheek and said: 'Sorry, Mom, I need my independence.'

Naomi had gone home saddened, determined to allow her younger children more freedom. 'Your mother is living in the past,' she'd complained to Joseph. 'We can't let her drive our children away like this.'

Joseph agreed with his wife. Though he'd been brought up to respect his mother, he knew Naomi had a point. His mother, he realised, had been allowed to dictate to the family. Aaron had coped with it by moving out; he didn't want the same thing to happen to Ben or Ruth. So he didn't take his son to task for dating Janet, and he allowed Ruth to see the boy Robbie Palmer.

'We need to trust our children,' Naomi said. 'We've brought them up to know right from wrong. We must let them grow up in the modern world.'

Ben and Ruth knew nothing of their parents' decision. They'd not noticed the slight shift away from their grandmother's domination in their lives. Ben had been absent from home for weeks at a time, and Ruth had been distracted by her exams. That night Ben waited for the lecture that did not come. Dinner just touched on general topics, and much to Ben's relief, his grandmother had chosen to eat in her own room, as she did on occasions.

Later he explained his confusion to Janet.

'Maybe she didn't tell your dad,' Janet said.

Ben shook his head. 'She doesn't work like that.'

'What could your dad do about it?'

'Talk to me, basically,' Ben said. 'Discuss it man to man. But nothing happened. Even over dinner the subject wasn't mentioned. Only later, when I came downstairs changed, did Mother ask me if I was going out. When I said yes, she told me to have a good time.'

'So it's all plain sailing for us then,' Janet said. 'Everyone likes everyone.'

'Well, maybe not everyone,' Ben said, 'but I'm glad your father finds me acceptable.'

Bert had been pleasantly surprised by Ben's charm and good manners. He hadn't really come to terms yet with the fact that the daughter he thought of as a schoolgirl had seemingly turned overnight into a desirable and beautiful young woman. He knew that one day soon, another man would be more important to his Janet than he was, and that took some getting used to for a father. Yet he had to concede that young Ruth's brother was a likeable lad. 'And our Janet seems fond of him, and that's what matters when all's said and done.'

So he'd shaken hands with Ben and told him to take good care of his daughter and not be too late back. Behind Ben, Janet, who'd been holding her breath, hoping that this meeting between Ben and her father would go all right, breathed easily again. She kissed her father's cheek in gratitude for his understanding and gave him a swift hug. 'Go on, lass,' he said, 'and enjoy yourself,' and his voice was gruff.

The summer belonged to Janet and Ben. Although Janet was working at the department store some days, every other free minute was spent with Ben. She loved him so much she ached. For the first time the family did not have her almost undivided attention. Ben didn't seem to know how to react to the children, and certainly didn't want to share Janet with them. Sally would have got over her initial resentment of him quicker if he hadn't occupied all of Janet's time, and her mouth was constantly drooping with disappointment.

To be fair, Janet hated to be away from Ben too. She longed for him to be near; she longed also for his hands on her body, for their lovemaking went further than kissing as the summer progressed. In fact sometimes when Ben pulled away, she had to bite her lip to stop herself crying out for him to go on. Now and again she was reminded of her aunt's warning words, but Breda could never have felt like this. she told herself. She never could have felt desire so intense it demanded to be satisfied.

She took Ben to meet Claire and Richard after he asked repeatedly for an introduction. There was no need to ask if she and Richard were an item, it had become obvious, and Claire had begun divorce proceedings against David, though no one seemed to know where he was. Janet didn't know anything about divorce, it was not recognised in the Catholic church, but Claire said she could divorce him on desertion, and Janet guessed that pretty soon there would be a marriage announced between Richard Carter and Claire, and was pleased for them.

She was also pleased that Claire was now working at Ferndale. 'I'd have hated to work with Chloe,' she said, 'it's bad enough that she has Richard, but if I worked there too it might encourage a dependency on me that I don't want.'

Chloe certainly was a different girl, far more confident than she had been, but just as happy, and Janet wondered if that was down to her home life as much as the work done at Oakhurst, for Claire was more contented in her relationship with Richard, and her mother Mary was delighted because Chloe had a pseudo-father figure who really cared about her.

Both Claire and Richard had been pleased to meet Ben and even more pleased when they learned of his interest in their field of mental health. In fact they monopolised Ben so much, Janet felt rather pushed out and resentful. She spent most of her time playing with Chloe, for though Ben seemed interested in learning about mental health and the strides being made, he did not interact with her at all. She remembered his reticence with Sally and the twins and it bothered her a little, but she told herself he just wasn't used to children. She was unable and unwilling to see a fault in the man she loved.

As they made their way home from Claire's, Ben talked about Richard enthusiastically and non-stop. 'He's so knowledgeable,' he said, 'and he said he'll open Oakhurst up on my next day over here, so I can look round.'

Janet felt a bit put out. She'd been involved with Claire for years and with Chloe since she was a baby, and yet neither Richard nor Claire had offered to open the unit for her. 'I'm sure that's the field I want to specialise in,' Ben said, and added, 'Would you like to be married to a doctor specialising in brain-injured children, Janet?'

'Married?' Janet was hardly able to believe she'd heard right.

'I know you're only young yet,' Ben said, 'but I love you and I just want to know if you feel the same.'

'I'd marry you tomorrow.' Janet couldn't believe she'd said that. What about the reluctance to marry she'd felt as a child? Marriage was like slavery, she'd said that to Claire, yet now that she loved someone, she wanted it for herself. Then she remembered Ruth. 'But I'm not Jewish,' she said.

'I'd noticed,' Ben said. They were nearly at Janet's gate and Ben suddenly pulled her close in a shop doorway that they were passing. His kisses were urgent and Janet's whole body was tingling.

'No, stop!' she protested, but reluctantly. 'Ben, we've got to discuss this. Ruth told me how it is.'

'Told you what, exactly?'

'You know, about your Aunt Rachel and how she was going to marry out and how awful it was.'

'That,' said Ben, 'was years ago. I'm not like timid Aunt Rachel who married the awful Moishe to please my grandmother.'

'But I don't want to alienate you from your family.'

'You won't,' Ben insisted. 'Look, Janet, if I loved a Jewish girl I'd be willing to marry her, but I happen to love one Janet Travers and I want her to be my wife and be by my side always.'

'Are you sure?'

Ben's answer was a kiss of tenderness which grew in intensity and sent thrills of excitement coursing through Janet. When he released her she groaned with desire. Ben held her close and murmured, 'Is that answer enough? You're marrying me, Janet, not my bloody family, remember that.'

He pulled away from their embraces aware that he was becoming very aroused by Janet's nearness to him. He took her hand and said, 'We'd better walk on.'

Janet was a little disappointed, but she said nothing. Anyway, Ben was talking again. 'Our engagement must be a secret for now, Janet,' he said. 'When you are eighteen, I'll buy you a ring. Of course we won't be able to marry for years, not until I qualify.'

'Well, I should be almost through my university course then,' Janet said, 'then I want to go to teacher training college for a year.'

'You won't need all that now, though,' Ben said.

'Why not?'

'Well, you're getting married.'

'Don't you agree with working women then?'

'Of course,' Ben said, 'until they get married, and then their full-time job is their husband and their home. Then it's the husband's job to provide for his wife and family.'

'Even if the woman wants to work?'

'Oh, come now...'

'Claire worked...'

'Not after she was married.'

'She did, till Chloe was born, and she's working again now.'

'But she's not married to Richard,' Ben explained patiently. 'Look, Janet,' he went on, drawing her into his arms again. 'Let's not

281

quarrel. I love you. I want to marry you and care for you always. I want you to have our children and look after our home. Is that wrong? Isn't that what you want too?'

And it was, of course, but Janet realised she wanted a career too. She had to make Ben see that, but he was kissing her again and the arguments were flying out of her head. She couldn't discuss it now anyway, she told herself, it was late and they were both tired. They'd discuss it some other time.

But they never did. Conscious of the passage of time, Janet hated to bring up a subject on which they might disagree. For their limited time together, she wanted harmony. There was, she told herself, plenty of time anyway before they had to make decisions.

'I don't know how I'm going to bear it when he leaves,' she told Breda. 'I love him so much.'

Breda trembled for her niece, 'Be careful, lass, and don't rush into anything.'

'We're engaged but secretly for the moment,' she confided to Claire. 'Of course, it's years till we can marry.'

'It's good to wait at your age,' Claire said. 'You have your lives in front of you after all, and you have your career to carve out too, Janet.'

'Oh yes, of course,' Janet said. How could she admit to Claire, who'd worked so hard to get her where she was today, that she needn't have bothered? How could she tell her she was casting it all aside for marriage?

Yet how could she upset the man she loved? Shouldn't his needs be more important than her own? How could she agree to marry him when they disagreed on basic issues? Yet she couldn't envisage life without him. The dilemma disturbed her sleep, where she'd lie tossing the problems in her head, but she confided in no one.

The summer rolled relentlessly on and Janet wanted to stop the clock. It had been a particularly hot, dry summer, and as often as Ben could get the car, they went to his special place by the lake at Bodymoor Heath. Their last Sunday together, they spent the day there. They'd brought a picnic with them and sat together eating it, watching the day begin to merge into evening.

Janet had a short sun dress on. It had had a bolero top but it had got hot and she'd removed it. Through the thin material, Ben could feel her pants and the buttons of her suspenders, but no brassière, and the thought excited him.

Steady, he told himself, and he took his hands from Janet's body and said, 'Shall we walk a bit?'

'Not yet,' Janet said. 'I'm too full.' She lay back and closed her eyes.

Ben got up and walked down to the lake, trying to control his feelings. He loved Janet and wanted her, but they couldn't risk anything like that. He'd had a fair few sexual encounters with girls he'd dated, and thought little of it. With some girls it was seen as a form of payment for a good night out. They knew the score as well as he did, and he'd made sure there would be no consequences of his actions. But with Janet... This was the last time they'd meet for months and he wanted her badly, but he didn't know how much Janet was aware of. He was her first boyfriend and so far she had stopped him doing nothing. She didn't seem able to say no to him, but she was so young. Ben realised that he'd have to be the one to call time in this relationship.

He walked along the shores of the lake for a while and skimmed a few stones over the water's surface. He watched the sun turn blood red and start to disappear over the horizon. They'd soon have to make tracks for home, he knew, and it was almost dusk when he returned to where Janet lay.

Her dress had ridden up while she slept and he could see the tops of her stockings. His pulses raced as he sat down beside her, trailed one hand up her leg and popped the suspender. She opened her eyes drowsily. 'What are you doing?'

'What does it look like?' Ben said.

He began to peel one stocking off. He felt as if he was on fire. This is madness, he told himself. Stop it!

Eventually his sensible self prevailed. 'Come on,' he said to Janet. 'Let's go before I forget myself.'

Instead of answering him, Janet slipped her shoulder straps down and wriggled out of her dress.

'Stop,' Ben pleaded. 'What are you doing?'

Janet wasn't sure. She just knew she had to have Ben to still the throbbing ache inside her or she'd die.

'God, Janet, you're so beautiful,' Ben cried.

Janet pulled her pants, suspender belt and

stockings off in one movement and lay naked in the dying sun. 'Love me, Ben,' she whispered.

He couldn't have stopped himself, nor could Janet have stopped him after that, but he took his time, caressing her breasts and kissing them. Suddenly she realised why Claire had moaned, because she was moaning herself. Ben went on teasing her and stroking her until she could hardly bear it and was biting on her bottom lip. Suddenly his body was on top of hers and he was kissing her throat. Then, forcing her lips open, his tongue was probing her mouth. There was a sudden sharp pain and then pleasure so exquisite she didn't want Ben to ever stop. She cried out, and then Ben gave a shout and lay across her, spent. Tears ran down Janet's cheeks.

'Don't cry, oh God, don't,' Ben begged. 'I'm sorry, I didn't mean for it to happen. Did I hurt you? I'm sorry.'

'Ssh,' Janet said, through her tears. 'I'm happy. It was ... just wonderful. Don't be sorry. They make such a fuss about losing your virginity and now I've lost mine and I feel bloody marvellous. No one tells you how beautiful it is.'

Ben rolled off her and kissed the tears from her eyes and cheeks. 'I love you, love you, love you,' he said, 'but it still wasn't meant to happen.'

'Don't be sorry. I'm not,' Janet said. 'I wanted you, I stripped off.'

'I know, but if I hadn't put my hand on your leg, aroused you like that...' Ben sat up and put his head in his hands.

'Stop it, Ben,' Janet said. 'It wasn't all your fault.' She shivered suddenly in the evening chill.

'Get dressed,' Ben said sharply, aware that her nakedness was affecting him again. 'You'll get a cold. You'd best put my jacket on till we get back to the car.'

'I'm okay,' said Janet, but she pulled on her pants as she spoke.

'I'm not,' Ben said shakily. 'I don't think you know what you do to me.'

'I have an idea,' Janet said with a laugh, 'and I'm willing again if you are.'

'God, Janet, will you please stop it,' Ben said, but he laughed. 'Here's me trying to behave like a gentleman and you encouraging me otherwise. I'm not made of bloody stone, you know.'

'No, I can vouch for that.'

What could you do with her? Ben thought. And why hadn't he realised that this might happen and brought something with him today? He knew why, because to come prepared would have cheapened her in his eyes, as if it was bound to happen, like the quick lays he'd had before in secluded parts of parks, in the back of cars, anywhere really he could find. Janet was his unofficial fiancée and had to be treated with respect. Some respect!

He groaned. 'Look, I'm really sorry...' he began again. She put her finger to his lips and said, 'Hush.'

'I can't,' Ben said. 'Don't you realise, you could become pregnant?'

Janet did know, but couldn't bring herself to care much about it at that moment.

'I should never have let myself get carried away like that,' Ben said.

286

'Don't be so hard on yourself,' Janet said. 'It just happened, and we do love each other, don't we?'

'You've no idea how much,' Ben said, and added, 'I've had trouble controlling myself this long now. We must take care to see it doesn't happen again.'

'How can we?' Janet said. 'We love each other. I know I'll probably want to do it again, won't you? Anyway, isn't there something you can use?' she asked. 'So it will be safer for us both?'

'How do you know about things like that?' Ben asked, his voice high with astonishment.

'Ben, I go to a girls' school, not a nunnery,' Janet said. 'Boys and sex is all some girls talk about. They discuss how far they've let their boyfriends go, and lots have boasted they've gone all the way. You'd be surprised, the posher they are, the worse they are.'

Ben wasn't at all surprised. He'd had experience of it himself. But he didn't want Janet to discuss what they'd done that evening with her classmates, and in particular not with his sister. 'You won't say...' he began, 'you won't tell anyone ... you know?'

'I'll never tell anyone anything,' Janet promised. This was too precious to discuss even with Ruth. She regarded Ben critically and commented, 'It wasn't your first time, though, was it?'

Ben was quiet a moment and then said, 'No, no, it wasn't, but I never loved anyone before, nor told anyone I loved them. It was just something that happened.'

'Once? Twice? Lots of times?' said Janet,

strangely hurt.

'Don't, Janet,' Ben said. 'Please believe me, it's you and only you I love. Tonight was special to me too. The other times meant nothing.' He pulled her close and kissed her gently on the lips. 'It's different for a man,' he said.

Janet wondered if it was, or if hers was a passionate, lustful nature and she'd have gone all the way with any boyfriend. But what odds? she thought. She'd lost that prized possession that many set such store by and she wasn't sorry! Strangely she felt better about Ben going back to medical school because of it. It was as if they'd signed a pact, entered into an agreement of some sort. It was more definite than their secret engagement that she had to keep mum about. No one need know about this either, she told herself.

But someone knew, or guessed at least, and that someone was her Aunt Breda, who'd noticed the slight change in Janet that she herself was unaware of. She said nothing and hoped that Janet had been sensible enough to take precautions.

For days after Ben's departure Janet was too weepy and lethargic to care about anything much, but three weeks after she began in the Upper Sixth, she realised with horror that she, whose periods were normally as regular as clockwork, was late.

If Ruth noticed her agitated, abstracted air, she put it down to missing her brother, and Janet felt she could confide in no one, least of all Ruth. She kept her worries to herself as the days ticked by. One day, alone in her room, she faced the possibility of her pregnancy. She had a letter to write to Ben but didn't know how much to tell him. Should she mention the fact that she was three weeks overdue? She knew he'd been worried, and in the first letter he'd written to her, which must have been almost as soon as he'd arrived back at his tiny bedsit, he'd asked whether everything was all right. In the next two letters he'd referred more specifically to the possible consequences of their folly. But in Janet's replies she'd ignored his concerned enquiries, and probably, she concluded now, he thought everything was fine.

How do I tell him something that might be a false alarm? she wondered. She knew that it would be the end of her career and possibly his too. How would he cope with that, dashing all their hopes and dreams for the future? We must have been mad, Janet thought, and in a way knew that they had been. It had been like a magical summer, a summer when their love for each other drove reason from their heads. And now, thought Janet, is the day of reckoning. And she put her head in her hands.

Chapter Thirteen

Janet decided she'd shilly-shallied long enough. The sooner Ben knew about her suspected pregnancy the better. Hoping it wasn't true didn't make it go away, and plans had to be made. She gave a huge sigh as she drew her writing pad towards her and picked up her pen.

She'd only got as far as 'Dear Ben' when there was a pounding on the door. She knew her father was in the bathroom having a wash and her mother round at Breda's, so she went down to answer it, wondering who it could be. Most neighbours didn't knock, but entered the house by the back kitchen door.

When she saw who stood on the doorstep, she stepped back in amazement. It was Gloria Marsden and her mother, but what a different-looking Gloria to the one Janet had had the confrontation with months before. This Gloria wore a shapeless mac, no stockings and plastic shoes on her feet. She had lank, greasy hair to her shoulders and was devoid of make-up. Her face was chalk white and her eyes red-rimmed, and there was an ugly-looking green and blue bruise on one cheek. Her lip was cut and swollen.

Mrs Marsden, beside her, was a plump woman. She had an old coat tied round her and slippers on her feet. Her red hair was streaked with grey and her eyes glittered with malice in a purplish-red face.

I wouldn't like to get on the wrong side of her, Janet thought, trying not to look at the woman's treble chins sagging below her face.

'Yes?' she said.

'Your father in?'

'Yes, he is,' Janet replied, and her manner clearly said: 'Not that you'd have any business with him.' She didn't offer any more information, and Mrs Marsden was outraged.

She stepped forward, causing Janet to take a step backwards into the hall as she said threateningly, 'You best ask me in, girl, unless you want me to shout my business over the whole sodding street.'

Janet's eyes slid from Mrs Marsden to her daughter, and suddenly she knew why they were there. It was written all over Gloria's face, the same panic and fear that Janet had been coming to terms with in her bedroom. She felt her own stomach tighten in sympathy.

God, she thought, we might be in the same boat.

She stepped back further and opened the door to the living room, and Mrs Marsden and her daughter pushed forward.

Bert was there. He'd taken off his shirt for his wash and left his vest on. His braces were hanging down by his sides and he was rubbing the towel round his neck as he came into the room. 'Was that the door I heard?' he was saying. But his sentence was cut off midstream.

'You Travers?' Mrs Marsden demanded, before Bert had time to get his breath back.

'Who wants to know?' Bert said, wishing he didn't feel at such a disadvantage dressed as he was in just his vest and sagging trousers.

'Never mind that,' Mrs Marsden said. 'Don't act bleeding awkward with me. You know who I am and if you'd got any bleeding sense you'd know why I'm here!'

'Suppose you tell me,' Bert suggested.

'I'll tell you,' Mrs Marsden shrieked. 'Oh, I'll tell you all right. Your lad's been seeing my lass, and he's took her down, the dirty bugger. I want to know what's to be done about it.'

'Took her down? You mean...'

'Only means one thing, you bleeding fool.' She jerked her thumb towards her daughter and said, 'This silly sod's expecting and your lad's responsible.'

Janet wondered why Gloria just stood with her hands by her sides, head hanging, as if all the life had been sucked out of her. Or beaten out of her, she thought, and gave a sudden shiver.

'How do I know it was my boy responsible?' Bert demanded. 'Has the lass no tongue in her head?'

'Tell him,' Mrs Marsden said, giving Gloria a punch on her arm. 'Tell him it's his son's sodding baby!'

Gloria gave a brief nod.

'What did you do, knock it out of her?' Bert said, eyeing the woman with distaste. For all his shouting and bluster, Bert wasn't one to wallop or beat his children. If anything, he was too soft.

'Well, what's a father to do when his lass is took down?' Mrs Marsden demanded fiercely.

'Let's get a few things clear here and now,' said Bert. 'First, it takes two to make a baby. Secondly, she isn't the first and won't be the last, and thirdly, if my lad's responsible, he'll do the decent thing and marry the girl.'

Marry her! Janet couldn't believe her father was saying that Duncan had to saddle himself with Gloria Marsden when the child might not even be his. Gloria had been running around with lads since she started secondary school. She was known as the estate bike, for God's sake. Their Duncan couldn't marry her!

'Go and fetch your mother,' Bert barked at Janet. 'And you,' he said, indicating the two visitors with a jerk of his head, 'best sit down and we'll discuss this.'

'There ain't no bleeding discussion needed,' Mrs Marsden was saying as Janet headed for the door. She didn't wait to hear her father's reply, but ran round quickly to her Auntie Breda's, where her mother had gone for the evening. She burst through the kitchen door and surprised them both sitting at the table. This was no time for politeness. 'You'd better go home, Mom. Dad's got visitors,' she said tersely.

'Visitors?'

'Yes, unwelcome ones,' Janet said. 'Gloria Marsden and her mother.' She looked at her aunt and said: 'Apparently Gloria is pregnant and has named our Duncan as the father.'

'Our Duncan!' Betty said in disbelief, getting to her feet. 'Our Duncan would have more sense than to get mixed up with a Marsden,' she declared.

Breda's eyes met Janet's troubled ones and she shrugged as if to say that Janet might as well tell her mother. Janet sighed and said:

'Mom, he did go out with Gloria. I saw him and so did Auntie Breda.'

'Gloria Marsden!' exclaimed Betty, and turned to Breda and Janet accusingly. 'You two knew he was going out with one of the Marsdens and never said a word to me?'

'It didn't last five minutes,' Breda said. 'By the time we knew for sure it was Gloria he was going out with, it was finished.'

'Well, it lasted long enough,' said Betty, and Janet thought, she's right, half an hour's enough if you're that way inclined.

'I'll stay here for a bit,' Janet said. 'You won't want me around.'

'No, give us half an hour or so on our own,' Betty said. 'That will be time enough to send the besom packing.'

Breda waited till the door closed on Betty then said to Janet, 'D'you think it's Duncan's baby?'

Janet shrugged. 'It could be,' she said. 'He's probably ... well, you know. But my guess is Gloria doesn't know whose it is and has just picked on Duncan.' She sighed and went on, 'You should have seen her. It was as if she didn't care any more about anything. One cheek had a huge bruise on it and her lip was split and her eyes so red and swollen she must have spent hours weeping. Old Mrs Marsden admitted her husband had beaten her to get the name of the father out of her.' She shrugged. 'If I was her, in her situation, I'd pick on the first person I'd been

294

with who came from a decent family and say it was their baby, wouldn't you?'

'I suppose,' Breda agreed.

There was silence between them for a minute. Both were busy with their own thoughts. Then Breda said, 'Well, what happens now? What does old Ma Marsden expect Duncan to do, marry the girl?'

Janet nodded. 'Dad said he must if the baby is his.'

'Poor sod.'

'Which one, Auntie Breda, Gloria or Duncan?' Janet asked.

'Both, chick,' Breda said. 'What are they really but bleeding babes in arms, the pair of them? And then what else could the girl do? She must have been desperate when you think.' There was silence for a minute or two, and then Breda suddenly said, 'And what about you?'

'Me?' Janet said surprised. 'What about me?'

'You are all right, aren't you?'

'What do you mean?' Janet snapped defensively.

'You're not in the same situation as Gloria?' Breda asked, and reached out for Janet's hand. 'Don't think I'm prying for the sake of it, because I'm not, it's only because I love you and care about you.'

'Why d'you think I should be in the same state as Gloria?' Janet asked, and Breda realised with a sinking heart that she hadn't dismissed such a possibility.

'Just something about you,' Breda said. 'A certain look you have, a different expression. Oh,

I don't know how to explain it, it's not something you can put your finger on, but it's there, and then...' Here Breda stopped, then gave a sigh and said, 'And your mom said you haven't had your monthlies for a while.'

'Oh, God,' Janet groaned, and then faced Breda and admitted, 'I am late.'

'How much?'

'Three weeks.'

'And did you ... have you...?'

'Yes, Auntie Breda, we have.'

'Without using anything?'

'Yes.' Janet's voice was just above a whisper.

'You silly sod!'

'Oh, Auntie Breda, we didn't mean it to happen.'

'Oh, you stupid bugger,' Aunt Breda burst out angrily. 'D'you think anyone in your situation means it to happen? You get carried away and that's that. "I didn't mean it to happen" could be written on most of the marriage lines on this estate at least.'

'What shall I do?' wailed Janet.

Breda gathered Janet into her arms and rocked her, saying, 'Pray girl, pray like you've never prayed before, and God might take pity on you, stupid bugger that you are.'

Later that night, Janet crept back home. Her parents were in the kitchen. Bert was wondering how to contact Duncan, who was stationed in Germany, and Betty was planning his wedding.

'It might have started in a bad way,' she said to Janet, 'but he'll have a wedding day to be proud of at any rate.'

Janet just nodded. She had cried so long in her aunt's arms that evening that she was feeling quite light-headed and faint. 'I think I'll go straight up if you don't mind,' she said. She was grateful that her parents were too interested in Duncan's problems to notice any that she might have.

She'd barely reached her bedroom when cramp-like pains doubled her over, and she lay on the bed grasping her stomach and groaning. But then, when she realised what was happening, she fell on her knees beside the bed and said fervently:

'Thank You, Jesus, oh, thank You!'

Later, Betty remarked to Breda, 'I was worried because she was late, you know, and you can't help it, with her and Ben all over one another. Not that she's not a good girl, but you can't help thinking... Still, it's all right now. It must have been that she was upset over Ben going, because she cried for days, you know. Things like that can affect the cycle, they say, don't they?'

Breda smiled, and agreed that people did say that, and made them both a cup of tea.

Janet surveyed her brother critically. He looked smart in his uniform and she could see he'd filled out since being in the army, but his face was white, with both exhaustion from all the travelling and shock. Tension lines pulled his mouth down and made deep furrows in his forehead, and his blue eyes seemed very large and darker than usual in his ashen face. He was quite a handsome lad, though Janet had always

297

known that, even though his blond curls had been shorn by the army barber.

'You look done in,' she said sympathetically.

'I am,' agreed Duncan, 'but more than that, I'm reeling with the news.'

Janet cast her eyes over to the door where her mother was making tea, to check she couldn't hear, then said:

'You did go with her, I suppose?'

'Course I did,' Duncan admitted, and added, 'But so did every other male on the estate over the age of twelve.'

'Don't exaggerate,' Janet said. But she knew her brother had a point.

'Well, okay, but you know what I mean.'

'How in God's name did you get mixed up with her in the first place?' Janet asked.

Duncan shrugged and said, 'It was one night when I'd had one of those terrific rows I used to have with Dad. I'd gone out in a mood and I found Gloria, stumbled over her nearly. She was in an alleyway near the caff, hiding from her old man.'

'Why?'

'He'd beaten her black and blue for something or other,' Duncan said. 'He's a sadistic sod and she's scared to death of him. She told me he's nasty enough when he's drunk, but even nastier when he hasn't got the money to get drunk, and he takes it out on the kids. The two lads are away now, so Gloria gets it most, as the next eldest. She says the only one he doesn't touch is their mom, because he tried it once and she gave him a punch back that nearly broke his jaw.'

Janet nodded. She could believe it. 'But she lets him hit the others?' she asked in disbelief.

'Apparently,' Duncan said. 'She's not always in, mind you. Gloria says she's at bingo a lot of the time. Anyway, this one night he'd lashed out at her and she had a right shiner, but she tried to protect her face so after that she got bruises everywhere else, all over her stomach, back, breasts, everywhere.'

'Did she show you then?' Janet asked incredulously.

'Yes,' said Duncan, adding defiantly, 'No need to look like that. Janet, it wasn't what you think. She was crying and calling her dad for all sorts, and I was a bit sorry for myself and felt sorry for her, and I put my arm around her to sort of make her feel better, but every time I touched her she winced, so I took her to my mate's house on my bike and she showed us what her dad had done to her. The man's a maniac, Janet, he should be bloody well locked up.'

'So you took her out from then?'

'Yes,' Duncan said. 'Thought it would cheer her up a bit so I took her to a few places. Then one night she said no one had been kind to her like I had, and if I wanted to ... well you know ... so I did. I mean it wasn't serious, well not for me anyway, it was just a bit of fun.'

'This is serious.'

'Well, I didn't think of her having a bleeding baby, did I?' Duncan snapped. 'I mean, most of my mates had gone with her and nothing happened. I didn't know that straight away though. They told me after we'd been on a few dates, and then they kept jeering at me and I felt a right bloody fool. So I chucked her. She kept coming down the caff and making up to these blokes in front of me. Some of the girls said it was to make me jealous, but in my opinion it just made me look stupid. And I don't know if she did anything with them or not. This kid she's carrying could be anybody's, but I've got to carry the bleeding can.'

'So you will marry her?' Janet asked.

Duncan sighed and said, 'I've got to, haven't I? After all, it could be mine, and if I don't marry her her father will lead her a merry dance, and the kid when it's born. But I'll tell you this, Janet, I'll join the regular army once I get married to Gloria. It isn't a bad life, and better than the factory all the bleeding days of my life and sitting across from Gloria in a council house on an estate like this. I had plans for my life and now they've come to sod all.'

Janet felt sorry for him, sorry for them all. It had been her first time and Ben her only lover, but it hadn't been his. What if this situation had happened to Ben?

Duncan had two days' leave to sort things out and then he was to return to his unit while the banns were called. The Marsdens were all for a quick registry office do, but Betty held firm on a church wedding for her eldest son.

'Registry office,' she said indignantly, 'as if we're ashamed of him or something. No, the job will be done properly. These registry office do's are for heathens. You're not married in the Church's eyes, living in sin you'd be.'

Sally and Gloria's younger sister Tricia were to be bridesmaids, but Noel and Conner flatly refused to be page boys.

Janet was grateful that the turmoil in the house, together with the work piling up for the A levels, kept her too busy to miss Ben. He was making arrangements to come down the weekend of the wedding, and Janet was sure that they'd be able to slip away together during some part of it if they put their minds to it.

Preparations were in full swing. Sally and Tricia had been measured up for their dresses, the cake was made and waiting to be iced, the catering organised, invitations written and Gloria's dress almost completed when the accident happened. It was early November, damp and foggy. Gloria had been shopping in Birmingham with her mother for headdresses for the bridesmaids, and hurrying from one shop to another, she stepped into the road without looking properly through the swirling mist and was knocked down by a car.

She broke a leg and an arm, had extensive bruising, damaged many internal organs and lost the baby. People said it was a mercy she wasn't killed, and if the driver had been going any faster, she would have been. Janet went to see her in Dudley Road Hospital, but she turned her face to the wall and cried. Betty tried, and her mother, and her army of brothers and sisters, to no avail. Gloria continued to cry and refused to speak to them. She left the magazines they bought unread, and the fruit and chocolates uneaten.

Duncan had compassionate leave, but Gloria

301

refused to see him and the wedding was postponed indefinitely. Duncan stayed at home for three days without once seeing his prospective bride, and then went back to the army. The hospital said they must have patience. Gloria was suffering from shock but she would eventually recover completely.

She'd been in hospital a month and everything was healing nicely, but Betty said she still refused to discuss the wedding with anyone, and it was put on hold indefinitely. Gloria's dress hung in its state of near completion in her wardrobe, according to her mother. The catering was cancelled and the invitations stayed in the Marsden house. Janet wrote to Ben to tell him the wedding was off, at least for the time being, and that she was looking forward to seeing him at Christmas, as there was no point in him coming home earlier. He might as well save the fare to have a better time at Christmas.

Janet and her parents wondered if there was ever going to be a wedding. There was now no reason for Duncan to marry Gloria. He must have had that thought himself – he wasn't stupid – but it was hardly the sort of thing they could write and ask him. Janet also knew that Duncan cared a little for Gloria. 'It's a bloody shame,' he said to her one day. 'She's had one hell of a life and when she goes back to that bully of a father, it will start all over again.'

So Janet knew Duncan felt sorry for Gloria, but she thought angrily, you couldn't marry everyone you felt sorry for. She decided to let them sort it out between them. She had enough worries of her own. Her mock exams were in January, just after the Christmas holidays, and after talking it over with her parents, she had decided not to work at the store over the Christmas period, to leave her free to revise. She also knew it would leave her time to see more of Ben, and in a fever of excitement she wrote to tell him how much she was longing to see him.

She was staggered by his reply, so staggered she didn't take it in at first. Ben had made his own plans for the holidays. 'I thought you'd be working in the shop,' he wrote in an attempt to explain, 'and I hardly see anything of you then anyway, so I didn't think you'd mind.'

Janet screwed up his letter and threw it at the wall. She complained to Ruth on the way to school.

'America,' she said. 'I haven't seen him in months and he chooses to go to America!'

Ruth looked at her friend in sympathy. She knew how crazy Janet was about her brother, for she'd talked of little else since she'd come back to school. She also knew that when Ben had first phoned his parents about the proposed trip, he had been keen to go but wasn't sure he could afford it.

'It's not a holiday, though, is it?' Ruth pointed out. 'Apparently this professor, whatever his name is, did some lectures at the medical school, and only the few who said they wanted to specialise in mental health patients and their care were offered a place on the course.'

'I know, I know,' Janet said. 'I'm being mean, I suppose, because it is what he really wants to do.

It's just that I miss him dreadfully.'

Janet had looked forward to Christmas so much after their wonderful summer together, getting more and more excited as the holidays came nearer, and now Ben would be across the Atlantic, even further from her than ever. She wondered if she was being selfish and letting her disappointment cloud her judgement. Either way, she would have a few days before Christmas with Ben, and just a couple of days after. He was flying out on 28 December and not returning till his term restarted in January.

Ruth thought that if Janet had known her grandmother was financing Ben's expenses, she would be more angry. Ben had been surprised but pleased at his grandmother's promised support. Only Ruth had seen the gleam of satisfaction in her grandmother's eyes when she put the phone down. She knew she'd offered to furnish Ben with the money he needed in order to separate him from Janet, and the course he wanted to go on was an ideal opportunity. She knew Ben wouldn't see it that way, and her parents would say she was being unjust, but Ruth knew just how spiteful her grandmother could be. Janet knew too, but to tell her the truth would hardly be helpful. Ruth feared that her grandmother would try anything to extricate her grandson from 'that insolent Travers girl' and she felt sorry for them both.

In the event, Janet had very little time with Ben at all before Christmas. He had to buy all manner of items for his trip to the States as well as arranging a passport and suchlike. Janet was also needed at home to decorate the house and tree with the children, buy and wrap presents for everyone and help her mother cook all the goodies.

Janet had explained to her mother what Ben was going to do, and though Betty could hear the disappointment in her voice and felt sorry for her, she was secretly pleased to have some time with her daughter. All too soon, she knew, Janet would be gone from the house altogether, and that would make a large hole in her life, because she'd come to rely on her elder daughter. That year, making paper chains with her younger brothers and sister and hanging the cards on strings, it had seemed as if the old Janet was back with them. And you could forget how clever she was, thought Betty, when she was working side by side with her mother, cooking and baking in the kitchen. Betty knew she was losing her daughter. In a way she had lost her years before, when the grammar school had begun to pull her away from her roots, but these few days before Christmas 1953 had brought a closeness with Janet that she'd thought she'd never experience again.

Janet knew what her mother was thinking. She'd seen it in her proud eyes, and she thought guiltily that it didn't take much to make her mother happy. But then she seldom thought of her mom without feeling guilty. She knew how much she owed her, for if Betty had not fought for her, she'd not have been given a chance. But although she recognised and was grateful for her mother's part in her grammar school education, she'd moved away from her because of it.

She had little time alone with Ben and he fretted about it. 'You're doing what you must,' she tried to explain to him one day, 'and I'm doing what I must.'

'Is that what this is all about then?' Ben said moodily. 'Punishing me?'

'Oh, don't be so silly,' Janet rapped out impatiently. 'I just have responsibilities here too.' Then she put her arms around him and said, 'I do love, you, but this is my last Christmas at home before university, which will inevitably change me. I want to make it special.'

Ben was far from satisfied. He could put up with the Travers family if he didn't have to spend much time with them, but he resented the hold they seemed to have on Janet. Even at the party Janet's grandparents gave on Christmas Day, there was no opportunity for them to be alone for more than a few minutes at a time. This time he'd come prepared for sex, and yet Janet seemed strangely reluctant. The weather was colder anyway and they'd not managed to find anywhere that was private enough.

That evening as she kissed him good night, Janet felt suddenly weak with love for this man who would soon be thousands of miles from her. 'Oh, Ben,' she said, her voice shaky with emotion, 'I know I'm being selfish, but I love you so much and I wish you didn't have to go.'

'I didn't know it would be so hard,' Ben said. 'Making the decision after the college lectures seemed easy, but I don't want to go either now.'

There was silence for a moment as they kissed,

and Janet felt her body responding to Ben's and pulled away reluctantly. They were in the doorway and it wasn't very private. 'I'd love you to come with me,' Ben said, his arms still around Janet.

'I'd love it too,' Janet said, 'but I don't have that sort of money and I know my parents haven't.'

'My parents didn't pay,' Ben said. 'My grandmother did. She was all for it when I phoned to discuss it with Dad. I was quite surprised really, because she doesn't take that much notice of what I do usually, but she encouraged me to go.

I bet she did, the malicious old bitch, Janet thought. Aloud she said, 'So she paid for everything, did she?'

'Yes, I doubt Dad would have been able to afford it,' Ben said. 'Not without getting strapped himself anyway, and he's saving every penny now for Ruth, of course.'

'Of course,' said Janet, calmly enough, despite the wild anger flowing through her against Ben's grandmother. She couldn't see his face properly in the dim light and she was glad Ben couldn't see her, because she was so angry she knew it must show. Ben, she thought, seemed unaware of the true reason for his grandmother dipping into her purse, and this wasn't the moment to tell him. She didn't want them to spend their last days quarrelling and tense with each other, but Janet promised herself she would be on her guard after this.

Janet had gone to the airport to see Ben off, glad

that he'd refused to let any of his family come too. It had been just the two of them. She was still feeling lost and a little tearful when she got home, and was glad that everyone had gone to the pantomime. The knock on the door surprised her, for she'd only been in a minute or two.

She was even more surprised when she opened the door to find Gloria standing outside. She was still very pale, Janet noticed, and was walking with the aid of two walking sticks, though her plaster casts had been removed.

'Come in,' she said, 'I'm all on my own today.'

'I know,' said Gloria. 'I waited for you.'

'Waited for me?' Janet asked. 'Why?'

'I ... I wanted to see you on your own,' Gloria said, and Janet realised the girl was frozen, shivering with cold, so that her teeth were chattering together. And this room is like an ice box, she thought, with the fire banked down for safety.

'Come up near the fire,' she said. 'I'll get it going in a minute,' and she busied herself with the poker to stir up the dying embers. As she dropped the little nuggets of coal on top of the glow she'd regenerated with the poker, she looked at Gloria sitting beside the still half-dead fire, her sticks beside her. 'I'll make us a cup of tea,' she said. 'That will warm us up.'

Gloria didn't answer. She didn't even seem to hear, and Janet hoped she was all right. When she returned to the room, the embers were brighter although little heat was coming from them as yet, and Gloria was huddled over the hearth.

'Leave your coat on till the room's heated a bit,' Janet advised, as she handed her a cup of tea.

Then she asked, 'How did you know I'd be on my own?'

'I got our Tricia to ask Sally what you were doing today, and Sally said you were going to see your young man off at the airport, but they were going to a pantomime. I didn't know what time you'd be back, so I came and waited.'

'Outside?' Janet cried. 'No wonder you're cold. It's bitter out there. Were you there long?'

Gloria shrugged. 'Long enough,' she said. 'Tell you the truth. I was glad to get out. Our dad's been at the pub since opening time and I wouldn't like to be in when he gets home. He's not touched me yet, not since I got back from hospital when I ... lost ... when I lost the ... the baby, but I've seen the way he's looked at me the last day or two and know it's only a matter of time.'

'That's awful,' Janet burst out. 'He has no right to hit you like that. Can't you stand up to him?'

'Stand up to him!' Gloria repeated incredulously. 'Don't be stupid. Can you stand up to a bleeding steamroller? Me mom probably could, but she's either out at bingo, sleeping it off herself, or not that bothered, as long as he leaves her alone.' She looked at Janet and added, 'Why d'you think I was so upset at the hospital?'

'Well, Mom said the doctors thought you were in shock,' Janet told her. 'I wondered if you were upset at losing the baby.'

'Not the baby, you silly cow,' Gloria burst out. 'Your brother.'

'My brother!' Janet cried. 'Did you love him then?'

309

'Love him,' Gloria said and appeared to consider it. 'He's the only person in my life that I have ever loved.' She was quiet a moment then added softly, 'I know my chance has gone. I'm not bleeding stupid, Janet. I know what everyone thinks, that the kid I was carrying could have been anyone's. I've been a bloody fool. But most of them couldn't have cared less. Only your Duncan was ever kind to me. The night he found me crying in the alleyway, he never touched me, even when I stripped off to show him the bruises where my old man had used his fists and feet on me.

'Later, he took me out a few times and never tried anything on. Point is, I wanted him to, to sort of pay him back for being so nice.' She looked at Janet and said almost defiantly, 'And it was bloody good, it was, and your brother – well, it was his first time of going all the way and that made it special for me as well. It was okay till his mates started pulling his leg and telling him how many blokes I'd been with, and the bloody shame of it was it was all true. Duncan couldn't take it – can't blame him – and I tried making him jealous and that, but it didn't work. Doesn't ever, I suppose.'

She gave a sigh and Janet said: 'Was the baby our Duncan's?'

Gloria nodded her head slowly. 'Bleeding right it was,' she said. 'After I'd gone with him, I couldn't seem to get it together with anyone else. It was his baby, Janet, I swear it was. Still,' she went on, 'I didn't want to tell my old man. I felt sorry for him a bit, your brother I mean, but then

310

my dad kept laying into me and I suddenly thought, why not? It would get me out of this bleeding hell hole. I knew if I'd named anyone else they wouldn't have cared, and it was Duncan's kid anyway, so in the end I said whose it was.' She looked earnestly at Janet and said, 'I'd have made him a bloody good wife, you know. I know he didn't love me or anything, but I'd have looked after him properly and not played around or anything. It would have been all right, you know.'

She looked so sad and forlorn that Janet felt tears start to sting her eyes. She wanted to put her arms around Gloria and comfort her a bit, but they'd never been friends before and Gloria didn't seem to invite affection.

The fire had become a little brighter while Gloria was speaking and the room not so bitterly cold. She drank her tea gratefully, sunk in thought. Suddenly, the fire settled in the grate and orange flames licked around the coals, and Gloria gave a start as if she'd suddenly realised where she was.

'So,' she said, 'I want you to tell your Duncan there won't need to be a wedding now. I know he didn't want one really and I ain't going to hold him to it. I did a lot of thinking in that hospital when I stopped crying. Never had a lot of time for thinking before. One thing I decided, I'm fed up being a punchball for my old man and a joke on the estate, so I'm getting out.'

'But where will you go?'

'My mom's sister,' Gloria said. 'She has the room now her youngest is married, and we've always got on. She lives by the hospital as well, and I've got to go there three times a week for physiotherapy for a bit. Later, when I can walk properly without my bleeding sticks, I'll get a job. Something worthwhile and where I can live in.' She gave a rueful smile and added, 'I thought my chance of a decent life was gone when I lost the baby and your brother too, but now I know it's all down to me. No one will know me by my auntie's, and my name won't be black as coal before I bleeding start.'

'When are you going?'

'Straight away. I've got stuff packed and hidden in the wardrobe. The old man don't know anything about it. Our mom's helping me before he kills me altogether. I've really come to say goodbye and to tell your Duncan thanks.' She got up awkwardly and with difficulty, and leaning heavily on her sticks crossed to the door. Once there she looked back at Janet and said, 'We ain't never been mates, have we, you and me? My fault, I suppose, I was always so bloody jealous of you.'

'Me?'

'Yes, you're so bloody pretty and you got brains and a bleeding marvellous family – every damn thing that matters.' She shrugged and went on, 'Never mind, perhaps there's another Duncan out there for me somewhere who'll love me as much as I loved your brother, eh?'

Later, when Bert and Betty and the children came in and found Janet weeping, they assumed she was crying for Ben. Janet herself wasn't sure whether it was Ben or Gloria she was so upset over, and she was too wearied by emotion to attempt to explain it to her family, but she wrote to Duncan and told him what Gloria intended to do.

The next day, Mr Marsden raised the house by pounding on the door and demanding to know where the bleeding hell they'd hidden his daughter.

Janet was glad then that she hadn't mentioned the matter to her parents, because their genuine surprise and concern was too convincing to be a cover-up and Mr Marsden went home none the wiser as to his daughter's whereabouts. Janet was able to tell her parents later of Gloria's revelation to her. 'Duncan was bound to think of that sooner or later,' Betty said.

'Maybe,' Bert said. 'Thank God it's not our problem any longer.'

The general consensus of the family was that Duncan had had a lucky escape, but Janet couldn't bring herself to join in the general outcry against girls like Gloria Marsden trapping lads into marriage. In Gloria's position, growing up in the violent Marsden family, she could well have been tempted to do the same thing. So while she was glad Duncan hadn't had to marry Gloria, she was immensely sorry for the girl.

Chapter Fourteen

Janet thought she'd never been so miserable. Christmas and New Year were over and her body ached with cold as she huddled over her books in her bedroom. All she could see ahead of her was a hard and dismal slog. She missed Ben like a physical pain and was depressed because all he'd sent her were a few picture postcards of the places he'd visited in the States. She hadn't been able to write to him because he hadn't been sure of where he'd be staying when he left England. He'd promised to send his address to Janet as soon as he knew it, but he'd obviously forgotten. She'd longed for a letter to say he missed her, but all she got were postcards so general they could have been read by any member of the family, and often were.

'Be fair,' Breda told her niece. 'It's his first time in America. He's bound to want to see a bit of the place. I know you're studying, but you can't work all the time, and you shouldn't sit and brood about Ben. Why don't you and Ruth go out on your own?'

'Because Ruth's in love,' Janet said disapprovingly. 'His name is Samuel Oppenheimer and he's very suitable. He's handsome and Jewish and will be starting at Ruth's college at Oxford in October – providing Ruth gets her grades, of course. He's just spent two years working on a kibbutz in Israel and bores everyone to death telling them about it.'

Breda laughed at Janet's glum face and said, 'Why don't you like him, Janet?'

'Because he's arrogant and big-headed and too smarmy for words,' Janet cried. 'Even the crabby old grandmother loves him, can you believe that? There's got to be something wrong with someone who can charm that vindictive old cow. Ruth said his mother is a widow and she and his two elder sisters run round pandering to dear Sam. Mind, she can talk, she really has got it bad, and I have to listen all the time to what Samuel said, or did, or even thought, for heaven's sake. No one else gets a look in now. Any free time she can squeeze in is for lover boy, and I hardly think she'd find time to go out with me.'

'You don't think you could be the tiniest bit jealous?'

'No,' Janet burst out, and then, 'Oh, maybe, I don't know. But she can be sickening about him. Don't laugh,' she complained, catching sight of Breda's face. 'I know I can go on about Ben, but I'm too miserable to be very understanding about Ruth's romance.'

'Oh, pet,' Breda exclaimed, 'you'll get a letter any day, you'll see.'

But when the letter finally arrived, it didn't help Janet feel better at all. 'He tells me what a good time he's having,' she fumed to Breda, where she'd fled to read the letter in peace. 'And about the skyscrapers, yellow taxis and more traffic than he's ever seen in his life. There's not one bloody word about missing me, wishing I was

315

with him or any other damn thing, and he talks constantly about a person called Therese Steinaway, who's apparently at medical school with him and is interested in mental health too, and about how he was delighted to find she had a place on the same course in New York.'

'Never mind,' Breda said, catching sight of Janet's worried face. 'She's probably fat and ugly with crossed eyes.'

She was in fact willowy and beautiful. She had black hair to just past her shoulders that shone blue like Ruth's, her skin was flawless, and she had a rosebud mouth, a small nose and vivid green eyes. Before long Ben was halfway in love with her and yet almost unaware of it.

She'd been one of the women he'd thought of as hard-faced when he first started medical school. Therese hadn't been interested in him either then, thinking him too immature, but she'd found he improved on acquaintance and set out to attract him.

'He's almost engaged to some girl in his own town,' her friend Lydia told her. She was going out with Ben's best mate Lucas and was a handy friend to have.

'Jewish, is she?' Therese asked, and Lydia shook her head.

'Lucas says not,' she said.

'Then she can move over,' Therese said. 'I'm having this man.'

She'd wangled a place on the American course and Ben, who wasn't aware she was going, was gratified to find one face that he would know amongst the sea of unfamiliar ones. It was

316

natural that they would take coffee together at break to discuss the lecture they'd just left, or have dinner in the evening. When Therese suggested they use their free afternoons and weekends to see the sights, Ben readily agreed, and when she caught hold of his hand and linked arms as they walked he thought it was a friendly gesture. Now and again, he'd feel guilty about Janet, especially after his good night kiss to Therese was more prolonged than he'd intended. Then he'd buy a postcard and send it to her.

Back in London he met Therese often, always seemed to be bumping into her, in fact. He thought it strange that he'd never noticed her around before, for now everywhere he turned, she seemed to be there. Time and again, Therese's face would be the one that floated into his mind as he went to sleep, invaded his dreams, and was there when he woke up. He couldn't understand himself. He loved Janet, had proposed to her, for goodness' sake.

Many times in the first days of term he took up his pen to write to Janet. He knew she'd be taking her mock exams and would value an encouraging letter, but he would sit staring at a blank sheet of paper and not know what to write. Sometimes he'd find it hard even to remember what she looked like. And then Lucas would be at his door suggesting going out for a few jars, and Ben would push the paper away thankfully and go with him, and promise himself he'd write soon.

He'd told Janet he'd try to get home for some weekends in the new year, and he'd meant it when he said it, but soon he found that he didn't want to go home. The weekends were when everything happened: someone would be giving a party, or a crowd were going to the cinema or a dance. Then came the trials for the football team. Ben had always been quite good at football and had played for his school a few times, but he didn't think he had a chance of getting into the university first team and he knew that the opposition was stiff. However, Lucas was very keen to try, so he went along with him and was delighted to be accepted.

He wrote to Janet:

I didn't for a minute imagine I was good enough, though Lucas is hot stuff on the field. Anyway, we're both in and that means matches every Saturday, which puts paid to my coming down at weekends until the season is over...

Ben enjoyed the football and the status it accorded him, for even at practice sessions, the field would be ringed with enthusiastic girls. Lydia always came to cheer Lucas on, and brought her friend Therese to keep her company, and they'd both cheer their heads off. Later they'd go and get the drinks in at the bar while the chaps got washed and changed.

When a few jars had been sunk and the game had been replayed again and again by Lucas, Ben and any of the other team members in the vicinity, Lucas would give Ben the nod and he and Lydia would slip away. It seemed churlish of Ben, then, to leave Therese on her own. After all, Lydia wouldn't want her tagging along any more than Lucas would welcome Ben's company, so they were both at a loose end really.

It was so gradual, that Ben was almost unaware of it happening, but a couple of months after they'd returned from the States, he realised that he and Therese were being regarded as a couple, an item. He was quite appalled at first. He knew how the rumour had begun, because they had been seen together a lot and he'd taken her to the cinema, drinks in the bar and parties, and occasionally, especially at parties, he could get quite amorous and Therese never seemed to mind. Afterwards he'd tell himself it was because he was missing Janet so much. It meant nothing, just a bit of fun, and he was sure Therese saw it the same way.

He still wrote to Janet fairly often, and was unaware of how many times Therese's name cropped up in the letters. In fact, every letter was like a dagger in Janet's heart, for in each one Ben was becoming more and more remote. Sometimes she hardly recognised him as the man who'd held her close and swore he loved her. This Ben Hayman she didn't know.

'He doesn't love me any more,' she said to her Auntie Breda one day.

'Of course he does.'

But Janet knew he didn't and she knew why. She'd been too eager for sex. She was filled with shame every time she thought of it. She'd read all about it in the women's magazines her Auntie Breda and her mom bought. Men were just after one thing, they all told you that, and lost respect for any girl who allowed them liberties too easily.

Even her aunt had tried to warn her and told her it was up to girls to put the brakes on, but she'd disregarded her advice and now Ben thought her fast. She was in despair. 'What shall I do, Auntie Breda?' she cried in anguish.

'Write and tell him how you feel,' Breda advised.

But she couldn't pour out her feelings to the man she felt she hardly knew any more. When she did put pen to paper it was because many things had happened that he needed to know about. She scoured the finished letter in case it should show any trace of bitterness or recrimination and was eventually satisfied. No one reading it, she was sure, could possibly know that she'd grovel on the floor for a crumb of attention and love from Ben Hayman.

Dear Ben,

I'm writing this to give you the news about Richard Carter and Claire, who are getting married the weekend before our school breaks up for Easter. Your terms are shorter, so you might already be finished, and of course we are both invited. The reason they are having it before the school officially closes is because of Chloe, who's had a lot of chest infections this winter. It's been found she has a bad heart, something to do with the valves – you'd probably know more than me. She needs to have an operation, but the doctors are worried the infections have weakened her and advised Richard and Claire to take her abroad somewhere where the air is dry and the temperature warm. With this in mind they are flying out to Spain after the reception.

320

Another bit of news is that Mom and Dad are getting a phone installed, so I'll be able to phone home from college (talk about counting your chickens!).

Duncan has about six or seven months of his national service left, but when he's finished him and a mate called Larry Sumners, who is also doing car mechanics in the army, are thinking of renting a lock-up workshop and garage on Tyburn Road. Dad's worried they've bitten off more than they can chew, but they both seem pretty confident.

I'm glad you're still enjoying the football and I hope you're looking forward to the Easter holidays as much as I am.

Mom and Dad send their love, as I do of course.

See you soon,

Janet.

Claire was a beautiful bride. She wore a long-sleeved cream lace dress caught in at the waist with a peach sash. Flowing layered petticoats took the skirts to halfway down her legs, and she wore cream sandals on her feet and a coronet on her head similar to those worn by Sally and Chloe, her flower girls.

Janet had seen the dress before, had asked to see it before she'd chosen her own outfit, but she'd never seen Claire wearing it, and the effect was stunning. She saw the absolute amazement and love on Richard's face as he watched her walk towards him, and it brought a lump to her throat.

She looked at Ben's profile in the seat beside her and wondered what the matter was and what she'd done to alienate him so much. She'd taken such care with her appearance. Her dress was powder blue with lace around the neckline, which was the lowest she'd ever worn. That wasn't saying much, for as the girl in the shop had commented, she was too thin to have much bosom.

'No good exposing any of it if it's not worth looking at,' she said, briskly businesslike, and then, catching sight of Janet's startled face, added: 'Make the most of what you have, my dear. Not many have the perfect figure and I know women who'd die for a waist like yours.'

Janet looked at herself critically in the mirror. 'I've got no shape,' she complained.

'Of course you've got shape, all you have to do is emphasise it,' the shop assistant said more kindly. 'We need a large belt to pull in the waist, and that in turn will raise the hemline slightly.' She caught sight of Janet's self-conscious face and said, 'Don't worry so much, dear. If I had legs as good as yours I'd show them off. Now you need a blazer-type jacket in navy, and a navy bag and a hat with a navy band. And the only type of shoe for this outfit is a navy court shoe with a stiletto heel.'

'Oh no, I couldn't wear them,' Janet said. 'I'd fall off, I couldn't possibly wear shoes like that. Couldn't I just have flat sandals?'

'What?' the assistant said, aghast. 'And ruin your outfit? My dear, it's just a question of balance.'

The shoes were surprisingly easy to wear, Janet thought. She hoped she wouldn't turn her ankle, as she'd seen some girls do. Stiletto heels had only been available for a couple of years and had caused an uproar when they'd arrived in the shops. Doctors said they would damage young people's feet and caused bunions, corns and crushed toes, and many places banned them from their establishments, fearing damage to the floors. But women loved them and they gained in popularity quickly. Janet, though, had had no occasion to wear them before, and she was astounded at the difference they made to the outfit.

Ben didn't even seem to notice either the smart clothes or the hair Breda had dressed for her or the face she'd made up with her best cosmetics. 'Hello, love,' was all he said as he gave her a swift kiss. 'Are you ready?'

Dejectedly, Janet let Ben take her arm and lead her towards the car he'd borrowed from his father.

He looked incredibly smart, she noted, in the dark navy suit, matching tie and handkerchief and pure white shirt with gold cuff links at the wrists. But he was almost aloof from her, as if he was some distant relation.

At the rather lavish reception at the Grand Hotel in Colmore Row near the city centre, Janet was pounced on by Mary Wentworth as she went through the door. 'Janet, my dear,' the old lady said, catching her arm. 'You look just ravishing.' She stood back from Janet while still holding the sleeves of her jacket, as if appraising her, and then said, to Janet's acute embarrassment, 'You are an extremely beautiful young lady, you know.'

'Oh, Mary,' Janet said. She'd dropped the

courtesy 'Auntie' a couple of years earlier. 'Stop it!'

'I can see by your face I'm embarrassing you, my dear,' said the irrepressible old lady, 'but you will have to get used to hearing compliments like that, for I'll not be the last to say it. I bet your young man would agree with me,' she went on, turning to Ben. 'I believe you are a brother of Ruth's,' she said, and without giving him a chance to reply added: 'Don't you think Janet is a remarkably beautiful girl?'

Janet wished the ground would open up and swallow her. 'Mary,' she said again through clenched teeth.

Ben was taken aback, but he rallied quickly. 'Of course,' he said, but Janet heard the flat, unemotional tone and wanted to weep.

Mary seemed satisfied, however, and said in an undertone to Janet, 'Well, I'm glad they decided to get married at last, aren't you?'

'Oh yes,' said Janet, for it was obvious just seeing them together how they cared for one another.

'Well, he's a sight better than that David Sunderland,' Mary said. 'And to be honest, my Claire could do with a bit of happiness. And little Chloe now has a new father.'

She looked across to where her little granddaughter, looking angelic in her peach satin dress with its cream sash, was smiling at everyone as she moved through the milling crowds, keeping close to Sally, the other little flower girl.

'You'll be the next down the aisle, I dare say,' Mary went on. 'Mind you, you're still so young, aren't you? I don't suppose you'll want to rush into things.'

I'm damn well blushing again, thought Janet, feeling the hot flush on her cheeks. What's the good of dressing to kill if I turn red at the slightest provocation?

She decided to steer the conversation away from herself and Mary's personal remarks which were so embarrassing. 'I think Richard is a lovely person and so dedicated to his work. Ben and he have...' She turned to where Ben had been standing beside her to find him gone. He was at the bar, in earnest conversation with the bridegroom.

She felt suddenly furiously angry. How could he walk off without a word? If it hadn't been Claire and Richard's wedding day, she'd demand that he explain his coldness towards her and his behaviour generally, but today wasn't the time. Mary's attention had been claimed by someone else and Janet stood alone, feeling awkward and conspicuous. Then she saw gratefully that people were being ushered into the dining room, and she followed quickly behind the press of guests moving forward.

Ben was seated opposite her and seemed to be studiously avoiding her eyes. Somehow, she ate the food and drank the wine, yet tasted nothing, and she managed conversation with the people either side of her. She listened to the speeches and presumably laughed and clapped in the right places, and raised her champagne glass to the toast. Inside she felt like death.

Later, Ben came up behind her and whispered in her ear, 'Janet, we must talk,' and she swung round to face him.

'Talk away,' she snapped. The band were testing their equipment for the dance which was about to start, and Janet continued to watch them as if her life depended on it, waiting for Ben to speak.

'I'll call tomorrow morning,' he said.

Janet's eyes blazed. 'No,' she said. 'If you have anything to say to me, say it now, here!' She couldn't face waiting until the next day.

She noticed a few heads turned in her direction at her raised voice, but then the band started up and people began to move past them towards the dance floor. Ben knew that Janet was angry and upset, and he took her arm and led her through the crowds until they reached the foyer of the hotel, where he was able to find a fairly private alcove.

'Don't cry,' he said, gently pulling Janet down beside him.

'I'm not crying,' she said, but she knew that tears were glistening in her eyes, and her voice was choked with emotion. She probably looked a sight, she thought. She wasn't used to make-up, and it was probably running down her face at this minute.

Ben had an arm around her shoulders, muffling her sobs. 'This isn't how I wanted it to be,' he said.

'How you wanted what to be?' Janet asked tearfully. 'There's something wrong with you, I know. What the hell is it?' Part of her didn't want to know. 'Are you tired of me, is that it?' she went on relentlessly. 'Is there someone else?'

'No, no, of course there isn't,' Ben reassured

her, and dismissed the kisses and even the more intimate lovemaking he'd enjoyed with Therese Steinaway as a bit of harmless fun. After all, he told himself, it wasn't serious and couldn't possibly hurt Janet. It wasn't as if he'd had full sex with her or anything.

'Well, what the hell is the matter?' Janet demanded, and Ben pulled himself back to the present.

'Look,' he said, 'I have some news. It's good news for me, but I didn't know how you'd feel about it.'

Janet felt threads of apprehension trail down her spine as she said, 'Well, tell me and I'll let you know.'

'I've been offered a research post,' Ben said. 'For a year initially, but there's a possibility of a permanent position later. Only, it's in New York.'

'New York!'

'With the professor I went to see there,' Ben explained. 'He liked my work and offered me a job there for a year, to see if it's what I really want to do before I have to specialise.'

'And you're taking it?'

Ben looked uncomfortable. 'I haven't yet,' he said, 'but I'd be a mug to turn it down. I mean,' he went on, 'what have I got to look forward to here? A year as a houseman working sometimes a hundred hours a week or more. I'd hardly see you at all, and if I did manage to escape from the hospital, I'd only want to sleep, so the other chaps tell me. Then there's my national service – grubbing along in the Medical Corps for two years and for damn all. Specialist posts here are

327

damned hard to get and money for research is nonexistent. If I stayed here, I'd probably end up as a frustrated, bored GP somewhere.'

'You've already decided, haven't you?' Janet said in a small voice.

'Well, yes, sort of,' Ben said defensively. 'You must see it's a golden opportunity. I have the chance of specialising in brain injury in children. It's perfect for me.'

'Yes, I see that.'

'Oh, Janet, don't go all mulish on me,' Ben complained.

'What do you expect?' Janet said. 'Where, in your great plan of life, do I fit in?'

'You, Janet?' Ben said. 'You'll be part of it, of course. Just as soon as the first year's over.'

Janet started and said, 'But I ... I don't want to live in America.'

'Well, I know it isn't how we planned things, but...'

'Ben, in a year I'll have just finished my first year at university,' Janet said.

'Yeah, but that'll go by the board when we marry anyway,' Ben said. 'We discussed it, do you remember?'

Janet remembered talking about it, but she couldn't remember any decision being reached. 'I couldn't just give everything up,' she said, amazed that Ben could even contemplate it.

Ben looked at her in surprise. 'Of course you could,' he said.

'No, I could not,' Janet said firmly. 'It matters too much.'

'More than me?'

'That's not fair,' Janet complained. 'I never thought I'd have to choose.'

'No,' Ben said, 'neither did I, but the rules have changed and now you have to make a choice. I love you, Janet, and I want to marry you.'

'I love you,' Janet said, 'but...'

She looked at the man she loved with all her heart and wondered if, for him, she could give up the dreams she'd carried around in her head since she was eleven years old. And if she gave it all up and moved to the States, would she resent him later? Would she feel unfulfilled and frustrated with her life?

'Janet,' Ben said, taking her hand, 'listen to me. I've spoken to the research firm about their offer, and after the first year they'll sponsor me through medical school. Of course I'm expected to work for them afterwards, sort of repaying the debt as it were, but it's no hardship as it's what I want to do anyway. Apparently they can fit me up with a small apartment, near the hospital. I explained about you and they were very understanding. They said I wouldn't be the only married man they'd taken on.'

'Married!' Janet cried. 'But Ben, I've already told you, I don't want to be married, not yet.'

'It's over a year away.'

'I won't be ready in a year either,' Janet said. 'I will have done nothing with my life.'

'Is marrying me nothing?'

'You know I didn't mean that,' Janet snapped furiously.

'You once said you'd marry me tomorrow if I asked.'

Janet made an impatient movement with her head. 'I didn't mean it literally,' she said. 'I'm not saying I won't marry you, just that I'm not ready yet.' She looked at Ben's stony face and went on, 'Look, Ben, you've had time to come to terms with this, but you've just sprung it on me.'

Ben refused to be mollified. 'I didn't think you'd need that much time,' he said moodily. 'I thought you'd jump at the chance of living in America.'

'But I never thought of living there. We never discussed where we'd live,' Janet said.

'Don't say it,' Ben sneered. 'You can't go because you'd miss your bloody family.'

'Yes,' Janet snapped, 'yes, of course I will, I'm not made of stone. But that isn't the only reason I want to stay here.'

'Go on, surprise me.'

'Stop being so awkward,' Janet said. 'It doesn't need much working out. This is, I admit, a dream job for you, and as you said, a marvellous opportunity, and you'd be a fool to turn it down, but not once have you given a thought to what I want.'

'I thought you wanted to be married?'

'Eventually I suppose I do,' Janet said, 'but I thought we'd have years before I'd have to think about it. I mean, I've been given a provisional place at University College in Leicester on the strength of my A level passes. It's what I've wanted since I was a child, just as you wanted to be a doctor. Claire Wentworth worked like mad with me, and my parents made vast sacrifices to make sure I had the chance to achieve my aim.'

'As my wife,' Ben said coldly, 'you wouldn't work. We discussed this, if you remember. I don't want a wife of mine working.'

'We talked, yes,' Janet said, 'but I agreed to nothing.' She felt as if her heart would break as she looked at Ben's set face. 'Oh, Ben, I can't throw it back in everyone's face,' she cried. 'Not after everything that's been done for me and just say thanks, but no thanks. And anyway,' she added, 'I'm hardly likely to get my parents' consent. You're almost twenty-one, but I'd need their consent to get married and they'd never agree.'

'How do you know, when you've never asked?' Ben demanded.

'I just do.'

Janet was right in her assumption, for just the night before Claire and Richard's wedding, Betty had confided in Breda: 'I'm worried sick about our Janet and Ben Hayman.'

'Why?' Breda said. 'She's all right, she just fancies herself in love with him.'

'That's what I'm worried about. I mean, he's a Jew, Breda.'

'I know that.'

'She can't marry a Jew,' Betty cried. 'She's a Catholic. God, to marry a Protestant would be sin enough, but a Jew ... I mean,' she went on, 'he's a nice lad and I have nothing against him personally, and I had no worries about her going out with him, but...'

'Betty, what are you fretting over?' Breda said. 'Janet is not yet eighteen. She has years of study before her and she'll not think of marriage for many a year yet. There will be more than one boyfriend before she's finished.'

'But you said she fancies herself in love.'

'And so she does,' Breda said. 'I did too, and often.'

'You don't think she'll do anything silly?'

'Get herself pregnant, you mean?' Breda said, and Betty flushed red and wished her sister wasn't so direct.

'Well,' she said defensively, 'you can't help being worried, with them all over one another.'

'That's because they see each other for a few weeks after months of separation,' Breda said.

Betty knew her sister was wise in such matters and knew also that Janet often confided in her, and so she told Bert there was nothing to worry about. But she was still concerned because she knew something was eating Janet, that she was definitely not happy. Even though she was pleased to be invited to Claire's wedding, there was just a feeling Betty had, and Janet was tense and prickly. Betty had been surprised to have been asked to the wedding at all, it was a bit posh for Bert and her. Her first reaction had been to refuse, but with Sally being a flower girl, she thought she'd better go, if just to keep an eye on her, she knew the mischief she could get up to.

She'd worried herself to death about her outfit and bullied Bert into buying her a new suit, but she still felt nervous and self-conscious. Not at the wedding which was just the registry office in Broad Street, not like a real wedding at all in her opinion, but the reception at the Grand Hotel was so smart, she just hoped none of the family would make a holy show of themselves.

Sally, however, had been angelic and it was Janet that Betty was worried about. She'd seen her talking to Mrs Wentworth and sensed her embarrassment when she turned round to find Ben gone from her side. She hoped they hadn't had words, though she knew something wasn't right, and Janet was definitely odd during the meal, she'd spoken to her twice and it was as if she hadn't heard her. And then, she came upon them in an alcove well away from the main wedding party talking earnestly and seriously together. She backed off as soon as she spotted them. It would never do for them to think she was spying on them, and she said nothing to Bert. He would only start fretting about it and probably blurt something out to Janet. No, she'd keep it to herself. There was time enough to worry when there was something to worry about. 'Probably had a little spat and it's over now,' she said to herself, but as she made her way back to the party she wondered why life didn't run smoothly for people for very long.

Every day for the week the school term had left to run, Ben was waiting for Janet when she came out of school. Ruth obligingly took herself home on the bus so that Ben and Janet could have time together. Janet was glad. She knew they needed to talk about the future.

Ben described what being a Jew meant. Janet listened nervously to the laws and dietary rules of the culture that was so foreign to her. Despite her years at school with Ruth, she hadn't been aware of how deep Jewish traditions went. She had scant knowledge of the Catholic Church, but when Ruth explained Yom Kippur or the Day of Atonement for sins, when Jews would fast and pray, Janet likened it to giving something up for Lent, and of course to the Catholic confession. In the same way Chanukah was compared with the Christian Christmas, and while Jewish boys studied for their Bar Mitzvah at thirteen, Catholic children had to study for their confirmation. It really hadn't struck Janet that despite such parallels, their religions were diametrically opposed.

'But it shouldn't matter as you hardly go to church,' Ben, pointed out.

'I do,' Janet snapped. 'Not usually when you're at home, and not every week, but I have to be married in a Catholic church.'

Ben had laughed gently. 'I couldn't do that, you must see. I mean, could you be married in a synagogue?'

Janet's mouth, agape with shock, spoke for her. 'Then,' said Ben, 'it would have to be a compromise on both sides, a civil ceremony.'

Janet could almost hear Betty lamenting, claiming that they would be unmarried in the eyes of the Church and that any children coming into the world would be illegitimate. The problems were immense. Janet knew this, and went as always to Breda. 'I love him so much I ache,' she confessed, 'and yet...' She looked at Breda and said, 'He wants me to marry him next year and then go with him to America.'

Breda's heart gave a lurch as she realised that the situation between them was more serious

334

than she'd imagined. Betty was right to be concerned, she thought. She chose her words with care. 'And what do you want, Janet?'

Janet was quiet for a moment or two and then said slowly, 'Aunt Breda, I want everything. When I think of being away from Ben, even for a day, never mind weeks or months, I feel sick. Yet ... yet I don't want to get married. I'm too young.'

'But you couldn't marry Ben yet,' Breda pointed out. 'Not for a while. You have years of study before you.'

Janet flushed and Breda said angrily, 'Ben's not suggesting you give it all up?'

Janet gave a brief nod and hurried on to explain. 'He ... he doesn't approve of married women working, and ... and he suggested I read up on the Jewish laws while he's away to find out more about his religion. But I want to do something for myself. I want to follow the dream I've had since I worked with Claire before my eleventh birthday.' She looked at Breda. 'I've wanted to teach longer than Ben has wanted to be a doctor, and certainly longer than he has had this urge to be involved in mental health care, but he thinks I'm being unreasonable.'

'You can't live on love,' Breda pointed out. 'I'm not even sure a surfeit of it is healthy at all. Tell me,' she went on, 'how is Ben Hayman to support a wife whose only occupation would be to drape herself graciously around his home and presumably wait on him hand and foot?'

Janet smiled at her aunt's terminology, knowing that that was really what Ben would like. 'He said

335

the firm will sponsor him while he trains,' she said.

'Enough to provide for himself and a wife? Enough to rent an apartment in New York? Enough to provide for any children that might happen to come along?' Breda asked wryly.

'I don't know.'

'Why, then, are you getting into this state, when Ben himself might not be able to afford to marry you? Even if he can, your parents would never agree.'

'I told him that,' Janet said. 'I really tried to reason with him. He can't or won't understand that much as I love him, I'm too young to marry, and that I want to make something of Janet Travers before I become Janet Hayman.'

'Life doesn't come to an end after marriage, you know, Janet,' Breda said. 'Not any more. Are you going to go through all that studying just to throw it away when a man puts a ring on your finger?'

Put like that it was ridiculous, Janet thought, and yet wasn't that what Ben expected? 'I suppose that's why Ben doesn't see why I should bother in the first place,' she said.

'And then what? All the studying, hard work and sacrifice of those around you so far would be for nothing. And you'll break your mother's heart.'

'I know,' Janet said, 'and I don't want that either, but I don't want to lose Ben.'

'Why should you lose him? He's been given a unique opportunity. Why should he deny you yours?' Breda asked. She reached across the table and took Janet's hands. 'Ben is, I'm sure, a fine young man, but there is one huge problem that you and he seem unable to face. He's Jewish, Janet, and that fact means that your parents will never agree to you marrying him.' Janet began to shake her head, but Breda urged, 'Hear me out, love. Someone has got to tell you this, and God help your poor mother, for if she even knew you were considering marriage, she would have a bloody heart attack.

'Now,' she went on, 'I doubt your parents would give their consent for you to marry anyone, now or in the near future, considering both your age and the years of study you have still to do. With Ben, not only would they not give their consent, but if you were to marry him when you were of age, they'd be unlikely to even give you their blessing. Added to which,' Breda added, 'Ben's parents might not be too happy with him either. In my experience, few Jews marry non-Jews. It's much more than a religion, Janet.'

Janet knew that much of what her aunt said was true. 'But I love him, Auntie Breda,' she cried helplessly.

'If you do truly love each other, this time apart will strengthen your love, and if it is as strong after the years of separation then it will also withstand parental pressure for you to part. Each of you will have to stand against your family in order to have any sort of future together.'

'I don't know if I can bear it,' Janet said.

'You must, for there is no alternative. Talk to him.'

It was hard for Janet to think of problems when Ben was around, and though she tried to discuss the difficulties that lay ahead, Ben brushed her concerns aside. Janet had no wish to quarrel with him and kept telling herself there was plenty of time.

They couldn't get enough of each other that holiday, and Janet's family were once more pushed into second place. Her home was only the place to sleep away the hours till she could see Ben again. She'd dream erotic dreams and wake throbbing with excitement and longing for Ben's arms to hold her. They were out every day, often from early morning until late at night, and made love as often as they could, and Janet glowed with excitement and happiness so that even Betty noticed. She knew what the glow meant and hoped Bert didn't guess, but she couldn't bring herself to talk to Janet. Instead she appealed to Breda. 'Please talk to her, before she does something bloody stupid.'

'Leave her,' Breda advised. 'She's sensible. She'll be all right.'

Breda prayed she was right. She hoped that the deep passion Ben and Janet had for each other would burn out, but in fact, every time they made love, Janet was filled with such intense emotions that she found it hard to breathe. What matter if he is a Jew? she told herself over and over. Love can conquer anything.

On Janet's eighteenth birthday, Ben presented her with an engagement ring on a chain. 'As neither set of parents has been consulted about our marriage,' he said, 'this must be an unofficial engagement for now, but wear it around your neck and remember that I love you.'

'Oh, Ben, it's beautiful.'

'It's only small,' Ben said, 'and all I could afford at the moment, but one day I'll buy you a better ring, with a huge diamond in it.'

'I don't want a huge diamond,' Janet said. 'This is perfect.'

Ben returned to medical school a couple of days after that, and Ruth sought Janet out. She knew that her grandmother was subsidising Ben's trip to the States and giving him a healthy allowance while he was over in America. Ben himself was pleased but puzzled, because Leah was not known to be generous, but one day she made plain to him the reason for her benevolence. 'I'm glad to see that you have broken off that unsuitable alliance with Janet Travers,' she said, and he realised that her dislike of Janet was as strong as ever.

Ruth, who'd overheard, was astounded when Ben said nothing in defence of Janet. She tackled him about it, but he said it was no concern of hers. She wondered how much Janet was aware of and was surprised when Janet told her that Ben had proposed. 'You won't be allowed to marry,' she said.

'We love each other.'

Ruth thought that if Ben truly loved Janet he should have told their grandmother. He could have survived without her money. But she didn't tell Janet what she'd heard, for it would have served no useful purpose.

Janet glanced across at Ruth and said, 'Can't

you be happy for us?'

'I'd like to, but I see problems ahead for you. It's not just a religion, Jewishness, it's a different way of life.'

'I know.'

'No shiksa can know, not really,' Ruth said.

'We can't get married for years anyway,' Janet said, 'and by then your family and mine will be used to it.'

Ruth shook her head sadly. Janet was fooling herself, she knew. Many Jewish parents would prefer their children to die than marry out – the ultimate sin. She'd heard them say there was honour in death. She went home troubled, but Janet fingered the engagement ring nestling in the hollow between her breasts and smiled. She knew that Ruth was wrong. Love would find a way for them to marry in time.

'Did you talk to Ben?' Breda asked the next day.

'No,' Janet admitted, 'I couldn't seem to find the right moment.'

'Well write to him,' Breda suggested. 'It's only fair. Put your case to him and say you can talk it over in the summer. Then perhaps you can get back to studying.'

Janet flushed guiltily. Breda had a point, for Janet had elected not to work at the shop during the holidays in order to have more time to study. In fact, she'd seldom opened a book, and the decisions she'd come to under her aunt's guidance were preying on her mind. 'I'll do it at once,' she promised, and went home composing the letter in her head.

Chapter Fifteen

Dear Ben,
I miss you already and can hardly wait for the
summer when I'll see you again. I love you so much
and I was really glad we were able to spend such a lot
of time together at Easter. I wear the engagement ring
all the time, though I've told no one about it but my
Aunt Breda.

She thought she'd better not mention the
conversation she'd had with his sister too.

I had to tell her. I wanted her advice because we
didn't ever finish the discussion we began at Claire
and Richard's wedding about the research post you
were offered, and no decisions were ever reached. My
aunt assured me, as I thought, that my parents would
never give their consent to a marriage while I was so
young. She also said they would be furious if I
suggested giving up my university place, and to be
fair, I don't want to give up my plans either just yet.
She believes as well that we'd meet stiff opposition
from our parents and possibly our churches if they
found out we were intending to marry.
In view of all this, it would seem that the most
sensible option and the only alternative is for us to live
apart for a while, however hard that will be for both
of us. Meanwhile, I will be able to gain my BA and
teaching certificate while you get established in New

York. *It will break my heart to have such a long separation, but as Aunt Breda said, if our relationship can survive that, it can survive anything, including parental opposition.*

Please remember I love you dearly, but we must be realistic in realising that our marriage cannot happen for some years. I hope you understand my position and look forward to your reply.

All my love as always,

Janet.

Janet surveyed the letter critically. It was her third draft and she was still not happy. She knew the tone had to be firm to convince Ben that this was how it must be, and yet she had to assure him of her love and explain that she wasn't trying to be deliberately awkward or endeavouring to punish him in any way. In the end she sent it as it was, because although she was dissatisfied, she felt it was better to open the lines of communication between them and state her opinion on the matter of their future together.

Ben read the letter almost in disbelief. He couldn't believe that Janet had written it, and phrases swam before his eyes. He recounted it to Therese at the party Lucas had dragged him to, the day the letter arrived. 'She hasn't even begun university yet, though, has she?' Therese asked.

'No,' Ben said, 'then she wants to do a conversion course to teach.'

'So we're talking about four years!' Therese said, shocked and surprised. She took hold of Ben's hand and led him to the settee. 'Tell me about it,' she said.

Ben was flattered by Therese's attention and had drunk enough to want to talk to someone who would sympathise with him. 'I wouldn't want to wait four years to marry someone I loved,' Therese assured Ben when he'd finished.

'What about not fulfilling your ambition?'

'My ambition would be my husband,' Therese said. 'As for being offered a life in the States as well, to be frank, most girls would just jump at the chance.'

'Would you?'

'You bet I would,' Therese said, pouring Ben another beer from the bottles at their feet.

'You wouldn't go on about missing your family?'

Therese omitted to remind Ben that her parents lived in New York. Instead she said firmly, 'A wife's duty is to follow her husband.'

'We make a good team, you and me,' Ben said, pulling Therese closer to him.

'We sure do.'

His fuddled mind was trying to get things straight. 'Pity really I love Janet,' he said, 'because if I didn't, then you and me...'

'She doesn't love you,' Therese said.

'Oh, I'm sure she does,' Ben said. 'She wrote it in the letter.'

Therese kissed Ben's lips and he felt his pulse race as she went on, 'She's trying to let you down gently, d'you see? No woman who truly loved a man would say she wasn't ready for marriage and would rather go to university.'

Ben gulped his beer and thought moodily that what Therese said made sense. 'It was shit, her

343

letter,' he said, 'all shit!'

Therese poured more beer and agreed that it was.

'And all about her, what she wants, what her aunt says and what her parents think. I mean,' he said, 'she's not even sodding well asked them.' Therese noted with satisfaction that Ben's words were beginning to slur. 'I could have talked them round,' he said, 'her parents, they liked me.'

'But darling, she doesn't want to marry you. She said so, didn't she?' Therese reminded him. 'Not ready yet is just another way of putting it. Take it from me, a woman is always ready when she meets Mr Right.'

'Yeah,' Ben said, 'she did say that.'

Therese began kissing Ben's neck while her hands moved over his upper body, and suddenly Ben's arms were around her and he was kissing her with passion. She felt desire flow through her and knew Ben was aroused, but she wasn't ready yet. She drew away reluctantly, though she stayed in the circle of his arm and let her hand stroke the upper part of his leg slowly and sensuously. 'She's setting you free to see other people,' she told Ben. 'That's how women work.'

Ben thought she was probably right. He didn't really care at that moment. Janet was miles away and Therese was in his arms. He wanted to kiss her again, and in fact do more than kiss her. Their lovemaking before had always stopped short of full sex, and often, he had to admit, it was Therese who pulled away first. She'd even said on more than one occasion, 'What about Janet? Think of Janet!'

But now Therese had said that Janet had released him. She wanted her freedom and had handed him his. He was free to make love to any damn woman he liked.

Another beer was in his hand. He was having trouble focusing and realised he was very drunk. Drunker in fact than he'd ever been in his life. He was sitting caressing a beautiful, desirable woman, and if he wasn't much mistaken, he was in for a good night with her.

Therese stopped nuzzling his ear to speak again. 'Also, darling, Janet has a point in one way, for after all, she's not Jewish. What does any goy really know of us? Is she really worth you being cast out by your family? And would she be happy if she was disowned by her own if she's as devoted to them as you say?'

'No,' Ben heard himself say. 'It would never have worked.' He didn't want to talk about Janet any more and was ready to agree with anything Therese said. He was breathing heavily as his hands slid under her blouse and made their way to the hooks of her brassière. But a fumble in a dark corner of a crowded party was not what Therese had in mind.

'Stop it,' she said, pushing his hands down.

'Come on,' Ben said urgently, 'you've let me before.'

'There's always been Janet before,' Therese said. 'Anyway, I don't do things like that in public.'

'Then where?'

'Perhaps nowhere,' Therese said sharply. 'I was comforting you, not offering to sleep with you.'

'God, Therese, you must know what you're doing to me,' Ben said huskily. Janet had never refused him anything. This last holiday he imagined he could have stripped her naked and taken her on the living room floor with her family watching had he wanted. She'd been so anxious to please him, and though she was apparently not ready for marriage, she'd been ripe for sex all right. He felt a stab of regret for what might have been between them, but there were, after all, plenty of other women, and if Janet felt like she did, well, that was that.

Therese guessed some of his thoughts. She knew he'd slept regularly with Janet. Really, she thought, the girl had made herself a virtual doormat, and a doormat, after all, was just there to be walked over. Therese, on the other hand, had slept with many men, for she had a high sex drive and was used to getting her own way. But her encounters had always been on her terms and she'd never lost her heart to anyone. With Ben it was different because she was attracted to him too. Eventually she would allow him to have what he wanted, but first he had to be brought to the point of no return, and she also had to make him believe it was his decision.

She kissed him long and lingeringly, and Ben clasped her tighter as he felt her tongue in his mouth. But then it was over and she leapt swiftly to her feet. 'Wait,' Ben cried.

'You can't monopolise me all night, darling,' Therese chided. 'I'll be back soon. Drink your beer.'

All night she teased and tantalised Ben and

plied him with more drinks, until he didn't know whether he was coming or going. By the time she was ready to call it a day, Ben was unable to stand. 'I'd better see he's okay,' she told her room mate. 'Don't wait up.'

Lucas and Lydia shared the taxi and helped Therese carry the unconscious Ben to his bedsit. 'You do know what you're doing?' Lydia asked urgently.

'Course I do,' Therese answered. 'I've been waiting for a moment like this for months. I'm not going to waste it now.'

When Ben Hayman opened his eyes the next morning, the throbbing in his head made him shut them again. He'd never felt so ill, and he wondered if he were dying. 'Hello,' said a voice beside him.

He peered out through half opened lids. His mouth felt like sandpaper and his voice was husky. 'What are you doing here?' he said, realising in that moment that he was in bed with Therese Steinaway and that both of them were naked. 'I brought you home in a taxi,' she said. 'You asked me to.'

'I did?'

'Don't you remember?'

Ben shut his eyes against the light. 'I can't remember anything,' he admitted. 'Was I very drunk?'

'Pretty far gone,' Therese said, and added, 'We both were, I guess.' In fact, she'd drunk very little, but she considered the lie a necessary part of her plan.

'Wh ... what else did I say?'

'Lots of things. You told me you loved me, that I was a great girl and we were a great team together. Then you asked me to go to the States with you and suggested we go back to your room to cement our relationship,' Therese said, getting out of bed and slipping into a bathrobe.

'Oh, God!' groaned Ben. 'And did ... did we?'

'We sure did,' Therese said, 'and it was bloody marvellous.'

Ben lay in bed, trying to make sense of what Therese had told him. What was he doing having sex with Therese when he was engaged to Janet? But *was* he still engaged? He shut his eyes tight and then vaguely remembered the letter, the one that said she wasn't ready to marry him, the letter Therese said was a brush-off. He wished that his head would stop its pounding and he didn't feel quite so sick.

Therese came back into the bedroom at that moment with two steaming mugs of coffee, and Ben had to admit she looked wonderful and not at all hung-over. She saw the confusion he was in and decided to hit him while he was vulnerable. 'You said some awful things about Janet last night,' she said. 'It's maybe a good job you can't remember those, even if you don't love her any more.'

'Did I say that?'

'Of course you did, and you said you loved me,' Therese said, adding indignantly, 'I hope you don't think I go to bed with anyone. It was only because you said you wanted to marry me, and I told you I'd join you in America later, that I agreed to come back to your room. I wouldn't have done it if I'd thought you hadn't meant what you said.' She lowered her eyes and looked hurt. 'I knew you'd had a bit to drink and so had I, but I really believed what you said. After all, it was my first time.'

Ben felt a heel. He'd obviously taken advantage of Therese. He put his arm around her and drew her down beside him. 'I do love you,' he said, and at that moment he did.

He remembered that Janet had rejected him, while Therese... Therese had agreed to marry him and follow him to America. He didn't know if he wanted that, he didn't know what he wanted. Suddenly, Therese's arms were around him, her lips seeking his, and in minutes she'd slipped off the robe and they were making love again.

He accepted a cigarette from Therese, and she nestled drowsily into the crook of his arm. He felt almost stupefied by what had happened and he inhaled the cigarette slowly, trying to get his head together.

I wasn't drunk that time, he thought to himself, and I wanted Therese as much, perhaps more than I've ever wanted Janet. He felt Therese stir and move against him as he wondered how he'd break the news to Janet that he loved someone else.

They stayed in bed most of the day, something Ben had never done before. Any sexual experience he'd had had been snatched stolen moments, and he'd met no one like Therese before. She lowered her eyes demurely and thanked him for making lovemaking special for her and he swelled with pride.

Later, with his headache almost gone and his stomach settled, she made scrambled eggs and brought it in on trays for them to eat in bed. Rejuvenated, they made love again afterwards and Ben was brought to heights he hadn't known existed. They slept entwined together, and when they woke it was dusk. They dressed and sped through the darkened streets hand in hand to buy fish and chips and a bottle of wine, then returned to the flat and the bed with the steaming parcels and two glasses.

'This is to us,' Ben said and raised his wine glass. 'To us and our future.'

Therese held back. She had to know where she stood. 'What about Janet?' she said. 'I don't play second fiddle to anyone.'

Ben looked at her and knew he didn't want to lose the girl who obviously loved him so much and so very satisfactorily. Little had been denied to Ben in his life and he didn't like people opposing him, and yet he felt bad about telling Janet there was someone else in his life. He would have felt worse had she not written that letter that Therese seemed to think meant she was getting tired of him. 'Janet needs to be told about us,' he said, 'and yet I hate to write to her about it, especially now, because she'll be taking her A levels soon.'

'Well, we've got exams too,' Therese reminded him. 'Perhaps it would be better to wait a while.'

'I'll write to her afterwards and tell her how things are,' Ben promised.

'She'll be pleased,' Therese assured him. 'You'll be releasing her to be free, which must be what she really wants or the tone of the letter would have been different.'

Ben thought Therese was probably right. After all, he reasoned, a woman would know these things. 'So,' he said, 'Janet Travers is history.'

Therese smiled and raised her glass. 'To the future,' she said, 'and us.'

By the end of that weekend Ben knew he couldn't risk losing Therese. He couldn't seem to get enough of her. She'd shipped many of her clothes from the flat she shared to Ben's bedsit. It was crowded but as they spent most of their time in bed, it hardly mattered. Life was more comfortable for Ben anyway, as Therese cleaned and tidied, cooked nice meals for him and collected the washing and took it to the launderette in the town. She said she enjoyed looking after him and it was no trouble to her.

Ben wrote a note to Janet explaining that they had much to discuss, but that they were both busy with exams and he'd get in touch later. He signed it, 'Love, Ben' and Janet was delighted.

'He's obviously coming round to my way of thinking,' she told her aunt thankfully.

'I thought he would. He's a sensible chap,' Breda said.

Janet agreed happily and shelved Ben for the moment, putting all her energies into her A levels. This was what she'd strived for. The results of these exams would determine whether she'd made it to university or not. The whole house crept about on tiptoe, the television and wireless were turned low so they didn't intrude on her study time, and Betty and Bert took her snacks and drinks that she seldom wanted and often forgot. Drinks would cool by her side as she struggled with revision, her appetite slashed by anxiety until Bert said there would be nothing left of her by the time the exams were over.

She didn't exactly fade away, but at the end of it all she was very skinny. Her eyes had blue smudges beneath them and seemed very big in her face, which was so thin it was almost gaunt. But it was over at last. Now, for better or worse, the exams were finished, and so were her school. days.

She went to see Claire, who she'd neglected slightly, and was upset to see Chloe ill again. The child's face was as pale as Janet's own and she could hear her breath rasping in her chest. Janet, who knew Claire well, realised she was worried, but no one else would have picked it up. Certainly not Chloe, as Claire explained to Janet, while the child listened, that she was on the waiting list for an operation that would make her as 'right as rain' again.

Later, with Chloe asleep, Janet asked Claire how dangerous the operation was, and Claire shook her head. 'Dangerous enough,' she said. 'Any heart operation is, of course, but you see how she is now. Without an operation she has no future. This way at least she has a chance.'

Janet didn't tell Claire anything about America, thinking she had enough on her plate, and was surprised when she asked if Ben had accepted the research post. Then she recalled seeing Ben discussing it with Richard at the wedding. 'Yes, yes, he has.'

'Richard had some idea he was anxious for you to go with him next year,' Claire said. 'I told him you had too much sense to throw away everything you'd ever worked for.' She was quiet for a moment then added, 'I nearly did that once.'

'You did!'

Claire nodded. 'Head over heels I was. I would have gone anywhere, done anything for the lad concerned. Then I woke up one morning and realised that not once had he considered what *I* wanted out of life. It was as if it was of no account and I'd have no identity but that of being his wife. He honestly thought he was bestowing some great gift on me and couldn't believe it when I refused to ride off into the sunset with him without so much as a backward glance or a qualm.'

Janet thought uncomfortably that the man Claire had rejected sounded a lot like Ben. He didn't think her life was important except as an extension of his own. 'I told Ben I wanted to get my qualifications before I made any decisions,' she said.

'Quite right,' Claire said.

'I'm expecting a letter any day,' Janet said. 'He said he'd be in touch when the exams are over and we both have more time.'

But when the letter finally came, Janet read it with hands that shook. Then, unable to believe it, she read it again and again, though she could scarcely see the words for the tears that blurred her eyes. Then she threw herself on the bed and wept until she could weep no more, muffling the sound in her pillow. She couldn't believe the evidence of her own eyes, and phrases kept returning to torment her mind.

Obviously, wishing to defer plans for years is showing a reluctance to marry me at all. You are very young yet and maybe I was wrong to press you. Perhaps you are right, your parents would be unlikely to give their consent to our marriage, but I think it would be wrong to commit ourselves so far in the future, so I think it would be fairer to terminate our engagement. You can keep the ring if you wish.

Ben had thought about adding 'Perhaps we should see how we feel about things later' but Therese told him there was little point in lying to her.

Breda read the letter and handed it back to Janet with a grim face. 'This is a guilt letter, Janet,' she said. 'He's met someone else. That's what this "fairer to terminate our engagement" means.'

'No,' Janet breathed softly. She wasn't able to bear that.

And then, as her aunt continued to stand in silence, watching, Janet asked, 'How do you know? How can you be so sure?'

Breda shook her head sadly and said, her voice full of sympathy, 'Lass, for all the world I'd spare you the heartache that's to come, but it's no good. I've seen enough "Dear John," letters in the war to recognise this as one in the same mould. My guess is that someone who's had her eye on Ben for some time has slipped into your place, and he's welcomed her.'

'Oh, Auntie Breda, what shall I do?'

'Live your life without him, what else.'

'I can't.' The anguished cry burst from Janet's soul.

'You must,' Breda said, almost roughly. 'You have your life in front of you and it can be a good life, a fulfilled life. Don't say it's not worth living without Ben Hayman, because that's bullshit.'

'Auntie Breda,' Janet cried, 'have you ever felt like me? I can't believe I can survive feeling this bad.'

'Course you can,' Breda said briskly. 'Yes, I felt just like that with a man I loved who went to war and never returned. Somewhere out there will probably be a man who appreciates Janet Travers for who she is and not who he'd like her to be.'

'But how will I cope now?'

'With your head held high and a spring in your step,' Breda said firmly. 'You'll cry in your bed and maybe in my house, but not in your own and not in public. You'll show that bastard you don't care about him if you have to drag up every ounce of self-respect to do it.'

The words were easy, but the deeds were harder, and yet Janet did it. She told her parents about Ben's post in the States. 'Four years is a long time,' Janet said, 'and we both feel we should be free to meet others.'

Betty breathed a sigh of relief and thanked the God she still prayed to nightly for delivering her daughter back to her and preventing her marrying a Jew.

Janet returned the ring and wrote to Ben thanking him for the good times they'd shared. He was surprised, but pleasantly relieved, that she'd taken it so well.

'I told you,' Therese said, slipping the returned ring on to her own finger.

Ruth was embarrassed to see Janet and wondered how much she knew about this Therese Steinaway, who'd been introduced to them as the future Mrs Benjamin Hayman. The families had met and approved of each other and everything was fine, except that Janet was the loser. Ruth reminded herself that she had warned Janet she wouldn't be allowed to marry Ben, but her friend hadn't seemed to take it seriously. Ruth hoped she wasn't too upset, but being unable to help, she did not call to find out.

Janet felt bowed down with depression and a sense of deep loss. Ben, like Claire's lover, wanted everything his own way. He hadn't been able to see things from her point of view and wasn't even willing to give their separation a try. Apparently he could not even wait until they met in the summer to discuss it.

Later, when she looked back on that summer, it appeared that the world had gone on without her, while she, trapped in unhappiness, hovered on the edge of it. In July Patsy miscarried a very much wanted baby, in August her grandad's chest was so bad her gran had to have the doctor in, and as the summer drew to an end Chloe's condition worsened and the operation was now of critical importance. Yet none of these things seemed to affect Janet. It was as if they were happening to people she didn't know, she cared so little. The exam results came in the third week of August, and Janet opened the envelope to find she had her three passes, two A's and a B. The way ahead was clear for her, but she felt no elation, nothing, and was almost frightened of the deadness inside her.

That night, Ruth knocked at the Travers' door. She had something to tell her friend and she owed it to her to be the one to break the news. They sat in Janet's bedroom, as they'd done so many times before, and discussed their A-level passes and their future plans. Janet longed to ask about Ben, but would not. She'd never done it and wouldn't do it now. It was Ruth who brought his name up.

'He's getting married,' she said, 'the beginning of September. The girl is called Therese Steinaway and she's pregnant.' Ruth had to turn away from the anguished misery in Janet's face, and yet Janet was not totally surprised that Ben had thrown her over for Therese Steinaway, whose name had appeared so frequently in his letters to her. She wondered how long he'd been in love with her and how long they'd been sleeping together. Had he gone straight from their magic place by the lake into the other girl's arms? Or the previous Christmas, when he'd complained of Janet's neglect, had he sought solace from Therese in New York?

She wondered also how they could have messed up so badly, allowing Therese to become pregnant when she'd not finished her course, but it hadn't been an accident.

Ben had been concerned at first that their frantic lovemaking without taking precautions might have repercussions. 'I'll get something,' he promised, but Therese shook her head. 'I've got something,' she said. 'I've been to the clinic and got a cap.'

'What's that?'

'Nothing you need to know about,' Therese assured him.

That had been in April; by July she'd decided he was enough in love to marry her. The exams were over, Janet Travers was out of their lives and so the cap stayed in Therese's handbag. She fell pregnant straight away, as she guessed she would, and told Ben as they snuggled in bed together one night.

Ben was shocked at first. 'You said you'd deal with it.'

'I know, I'm sorry,' said Therese, looking contrite. 'It was the night of the end-of-term party, I think. I was tired and rather drunk and I didn't think you'd want to ... you know... Anyway, I forgot to put it in and it was too late.'

Tears squeezed out of her lovely eyes and trickled down her cheeks, and ashamed of his initial reaction, Ben gathered her into his arms. 'Darling, I'm sorry. How could I be so thoughtless? Of course we must get married.'

Their parents were slightly shocked at them pre-empting their marriage vows, and yet it wasn't too bad, they were at least engaged and had intended marrying. It just meant bringing the wedding forward a little. Daddy Steinaway, who had a business as well as a house in New

York, would sort out an apartment for them as a wedding present. And Ben realised that having Therese by his side and in his bed was far preferable to mooning around on his own for a year, yearning for her. Really it was better all round, and soon he would have a son, Ben Hayman junior, to hold in his arms.

Ruth didn't know about Therese's scheming yet she knew things weren't right, and she'd resented the triumphant look Therese had thrown her one night as she said to her, 'I believe you were friends with Janet Travers?'

It was not what was said, but the way it was said, and Ruth felt the hackles on the back of her neck rise as she replied, 'Yes, I was, and I still am.'

She didn't mention this to Janet, for her friend was still reeling from the news she had just delivered. She was also feeling used, for she'd stayed faithful to a man who'd begun a sexual relationship with someone else. Janet vowed then that no man would ever again get close enough to her to hurt her so much.

As a child she'd never wanted to get married; she'd wanted to be free and independent. She'd thought Claire was the same, but now her friend had found a good man in Richard. But Janet imagined there were few Richards around; most men were like Ben Hayman or David Sunderland and, she told herself, she could do without either. She'd make her way from now on as Janet Travers, and if it was a lonely path, at least she'd walk it with her heart intact.

She thanked Ruth coldly for telling her about Ben's marriage and Therese's pregnancy and said she needed to be alone to think things through, but she didn't ask Ruth to call again.

Ruth knew that in some way Janet was making her the scapegoat for what Ben had done, and though it wasn't fair, perhaps she had to have someone to blame. She knew that she could never just call at the Travers' house again, because without actually saying anything, Janet had made it clear that she would not be welcome. She hoped the rift that had been created by her brother would soon be mended. She said goodbye sadly and left knowing that if they were to remain friends, the next move had to come from Janet herself.

Janet wasn't able to grieve openly for what might have been with Ben Hayman, for her parents were ecstatic about her A level results. Bert went around with a smile plastered to his face for he was tickled pink at having a daughter brainy enough to go to university, and he told everyone who'd listen. 'Not of course that I'd ever doubted it,' he said. 'It was obvious she was clever, even from a nipper.'

Betty was also pleased for her daughter, and yet her joy and pride in Janet's achievements was tinged with sadness. Janet had been moving away from them all for years, and she knew once she began university that the gap between her and the family she was reared in would be even greater.

But it wasn't the time to think of herself, for Janet had done well, and she couldn't and wouldn't let her own feelings of the loss of her lass spoil the moment of glory. Janet herself didn't seem as pleased as she might have been anyway, Betty thought, and wondered if she was yearning after Ben Hayman. Breda said it was bound to be a wrench for them both breaking up after they'd been so close, although it had been the only decision with them being so young and with their lives spread before them.

Neither Janet nor Breda, who Janet had confided in, told Bert or Betty about Ben's marriage. Janet couldn't bear to and Breda felt it wasn't her place. Instead Janet dragged up every ounce of enthusiasm she could for the family who came en masse to congratulate and share in her good news. Her good health and bright future were toasted again, and though Janet thought her future looked bleak indeed, she smiled with the rest and raised a glass and drank with their best wishes ringing in her ears.

Bert took the family for a celebratory meal and embarrassed Janet by explaining to the waiter and in a loud voice that reached the ears of all the other diners, what they were celebrating. Again congratulations came from all around. 'You see, love,' Bert said, reaching over and patting Janet's head, 'everyone's rooting for you and wishing you the best, and you deserve it.'

Janet felt tears in her eyes. She'd made everyone so proud and suddenly she felt a rush of love for her family and knew how much she'd miss them all. How could I possibly have gone to New York, she thought, when the idea of living a few miles away horrifies me? She squeezed her dad's hand and said 'I love you, Dad,' and Bert, caught unawares, had to wipe his eyes surreptitiously.

Janet went to see Claire the morning before she

set off for University College, Leicester. Claire was pleased to see her and Janet realised she would have been hurt if she hadn't come, and they spent most of the afternoon and early evening reminiscing about the times they'd spent together.

'A lot of water has gone under the bridge since I suggested you take the exam,' Claire said. 'You were ten. Do you remember?'

Janet smiled. 'I remember my dad sounding off about educating girls being a waste of time. I thought I wouldn't ever be given the chance to sit the eleven-plus. In the end, I think Dad turned out the proudest of anyone.'

The day grew dusky as they talked and remembered, and eventually Janet got to her feet. 'I must get back,' she said. 'I said I wouldn't be late. They'll all be in to wish me the best, you know. Not that they haven't done it already, but that's as they are.' She smiled in embarrassment and went on, 'You'd think I was emigrating.'

'Janet, it's a big thing for them,' Claire said. 'I'm surprised they didn't suggest a party.'

'They did,' Janet said. 'I said no.' She looked at Claire bleakly and said, 'Who would I ask? Ben and his new wife? Ruth? Duncan is waiting to be demobbed and most of his friends are doing their national service or are scattered about. I told Mom and Dad not to fuss, I'd be home at Christmas, possibly before.'

'You haven't seen Ruth either?' Claire asked gently.

'Not since she told me about Ben getting married. I thought it best,' Janet said. 'I can't

362

understand why people change like Ben did. He was crazy about me one minute, and the next he's with someone else.'

Claire sighed. 'Look at David,' she said. 'I thought we were so much in love, we'd be able to take on the world, yet he wasn't able to cope with one small daughter who wasn't quite as he imagined.'

'Do you ever see him?' Janet asked.

Claire shook her head. 'It's just as if Chloe and I have never existed in his life. He used to pay maintenance, but that stopped some time ago and he disappeared. We'd have been under some financial strain, despite my pay cheque, if I hadn't met Richard. He applied to adopt Chloe when we got married, but our solicitor hasn't been able to trace David. He doesn't even know how ill Chloe is.'

Janet knew. She'd seen the pallid child lying in bed struggling to breathe. She'd sung her her favourite songs, read her favourite stories and eventually tiptoed from the room when her eyelids fluttered shut. 'What's the news on that front?' she asked now.

'We wait daily for a summons to the hospital. I've given up work indefinitely to be with her and I just pray it will be soon.'

So did Janet, but she said nothing. It was time she was off. At the door she turned and put her arms around Claire. They'd never done that before, but it was strangely unembarrassing.

'Thank you,' Janet said. 'Thank you for everything. I'll be back at Christmas to tell you how it is.'

The next day she met Shirley Tate and Lou Burrows, who were to share her dormitory in Greystones Hostel for Young Females. It was used to house many students when the halls of her dormitory in residence were full. It was quite a large place and noisy, for as well as students, the hostel was home to working girls. Janet's dormitory was on the third floor, and though there was a fourth bed, it was never occupied. They were given a set of rules when they entered; these were also plastered on every available surface and dealt with such things as when and how often to use one of the two bathrooms, which were shared by everyone on the floor, who numbered about eight. Light snacks only were to be made in the kitchenette adjoining the dormitory, the rules said. The rest of their meals were prepared and they ate with everyone else in the dining room.

It was all rather grim and not at all welcoming for girls who'd left home for the first time, and like Janet, both girls were half excited and half terrified. During induction week the three rallied one another's spirits and by the end of it were firm friends and they toured the district around the hostel which was on Howard Road in the Knighton Fields area of the city. It was a little way from the city centre they found, although the bus service was good and the university itself backed on to Victoria Park. The girls found that in fact there was a lot of countryside around Leicester and the three went on many a ramble at the weekend in the first few weeks.

Janet soon realised how wise Claire had been when she'd advised her not to apply to universities too close to her home. 'Universities are more than lectures and essays,' she'd said. 'The social scene is very important and you really need to be on site. Also, at university you learn to look after yourself, stand on your own two feet and often make lifelong friends.'

So Janet had applied to Leicester, too far to travel daily, but near enough to make a dash for her own hearth if homesickness became unbearable. At first as Janet, Lou and Shirley helped each other cope, Janet's room mates became intrigued by her attitude to men.

'What is it with you?' Shirley asked Janet one night as they sat on their beds removing make-up and discussing the evening.

'Nothing!'

'Nothing?' Shirley said indignantly. 'Well, you were pretty shirty with that gorgeous man with the blond hair.'

'I didn't like him, okay?'

'He was dishy,' Shirley protested.

'What about the man who wanted to buy us all a drink last night?' Lou put in. 'You nearly bit his head off.'

'He wouldn't take no for an answer,' Janet said.

Just then there was a knock on the door, and when Janet opened it one of the girls from the ground floor was there.

'Phone call,' she said, 'for someone called Janet Travers.'

Janet's heart was racing as she followed the girl down the stairs. Something must be wrong. No one would phone just for a chat; her mother was afraid even to use the phone. The booth was in the hall. Janet had only ever heard the phone ring twice, and she'd never taken any notice of it, certain that it wouldn't be for her.

'Hello,' she said tentatively.

'Janet?'

'Mom!' Janet's voice was high with surprise. She knew it wouldn't be a social call. 'What is it?' she asked.

'Janet,' Betty said, her voice heavy with sadness, 'you'll have to be very brave, pet. I thought you should know straight away. Little Chloe died at five o'clock this evening. Richard phoned us from the hospital. Claire had to be sedated. It was a complication with her heart from the operation...'

Janet dropped the receiver, cutting off Betty's flow of words, as if by not hearing them they'd cease to be true. They couldn't be true, she told herself, Chloe couldn't be dead, she was only a little girl.

The small hall began to tilt and sway, and the walls refused to stay still. Janet put a hand to her head to try and stop the dizziness. Her eyes were rolling in their sockets as she tilted forward, and she lost consciousness before she hit the concrete floor. From the dangling phone came Betty's agitated disembodied voice: 'Janet! Janet! Are you there? Say something! Janet! Janet, for God's sake!'

Shirley and Lou found their unconscious room mate and replaced the receiver, but by that time Betty Travers had rung off.

Chapter Sixteen

The church was packed and there was a lot of sniffing and nose-blowing, but apart from that, the place was hushed and silent. There was no whispering or chattering, just an immeasurable sadness across the whole congregation.

Janet couldn't believe she was here, sitting with her parents, dressed head to toe in black. Chloe would hate this, she thought, she liked bright colours and happy music she could sing along to. Janet hardly listened to the service, for she couldn't keep her eyes away from the tiny white and gold coffin in the centre aisle. It seemed somehow obscene that soon it would be laid in the black earth and piled over with dirt.

When Janet had been roused from unconsciousness by her room mates and had tearfully told them the news from home that had caused her to faint, they had been a tower of strength to her. Shirley had helped her pack a few things in a holdall, while Lou enquired about trains, organised a taxi and phoned her parents with news of Janet's plans. She'd eventually arrived home at around five o'clock in the morning. She let herself in quietly and, too churned up to sleep, sat in the kitchen trying to come to terms with the tragedy and drinking endless cups of tea.

She'd gone to Claire's as early as she decently could. 'What will you say?' Betty had cried, and

Janet had shaken her head helplessly.

In the end she'd said nothing. She had hugged Claire only once before, in gratitude for what she'd done for her, but the Claire she saw that morning looked so lost and so sad that she put her arms around her instinctively, as she would have done with a child, and they cried together. Richard found them later, entwined and weary from their combined sorrow, and tried to rally them with tea and toast. He was glad Janet was there; he had things to do and hesitated to leave Claire alone. Janet, glad to be of any help, readily agreed to stay. Claire seemed unable or unwilling to talk, and Janet didn't try, for she had nothing to say either.

Claire sat staring into space, her eyes red rimmed and puffy. She held Thumper, Chloe's white toy rabbit, turning the ear round and round in her fingers as Chloe used to do. She seemed unaware of anything. Janet wondered if she'd ever recover from the tragedy that had taken the light from her eyes and pinched the skin tightly across her face, tugging at her mouth and hollowing her cheeks.

Mary Wentworth came when Janet had been there about an hour, and she was shocked by the older woman's appearance. Richard had told her that Mary had been with them at the hospital till the early hours, and it looked, Janet thought, as if she hadn't slept since.

She had never seemed old to Janet, exuding an attitude of youthfulness. It wasn't only her beautifully set hair arranged in waves and curls around her face and carefully rinsed so the auburn highlights showed not a hint of grey; nor was it her skilfully made-up face with its rouged cheeks and pink lipstick: it was her whole demeanour. Now she walked with a heavy step and her face was ravaged with grief. Her hair looked as if it hadn't seen a comb that morning and her face was ashen grey. Janet noticed for the first time that Mary's mascara-free eyelashes were auburn like her hair, and today the blue smudges round her eyes were due to tiredness rather than make-up. She saw for the first time the broken veins on her cheeks that powder had hidden, as it had hidden the wrinkles around her eyes and mouth.

Mary smiled at Janet, but before either of them were able to speak, Claire called out. Janet was hardly able to recognise her voice. Before it had always carried the authoritative tone of a teacher, but the 'Mom' she wailed now could have come from a child as young as Sally.

Mary sprang forward and held her daughter, rocking her as she sobbed. 'There, my love,' she was saying over and over, 'there, my lamb.'

Janet couldn't bear it. She felt stifled by sadness, and Claire and Mary no longer needed her, so she went home. She found the house quiet and her mother sitting motionless in the kitchen. It was odd to see Betty still, and Janet sat down opposite her heavily. 'How was it, love?' Betty said, and Janet answered tearfully:

'Awful, Mom, I've never seen Claire like that. I don't know if she'll ever get over it.'

'No, poor lass.'

'And Chloe, Mom. It's so bloody tragic.'

'I know, pet.' Betty put her hand over Janet's and went on, 'The point is, you must believe that young Chloe has gone to a better place.'

'Do you really believe that?' Janet said. 'Not just as something we tell the children?'

'I must believe it,' Betty said. 'How else would we make sense of anything? You think little Chloe lived six short years and when her life is snuffed out there's nothing but a big black hole she's dropped through?' Betty put her hand to her head. 'God, girl, that's an awful thought. Isn't it better to think she's gone to Jesus and is in His arms now?'

'But is it true?'

'The Church tells us it is.'

'Yes, but...'

'No one knows, lass, not really, but what's the alternative when all's said and done?'

Janet shook her head.

'Your dad and I will be going to the funeral,' Betty said. 'We didn't know the little girl but we know her mother and we'll go to show our support.'

Janet was surprised and touched. 'Thanks, Mom,' she said.

'Breda is seeing to the children after she gets in from work today,' Betty said. 'I didn't think you'd welcome them leaping all over you when they come home.'

'No, no, I wouldn't.'

'Sally knows,' Betty said. 'Not that she understands death, of course, but you know how sensitive she is.' Not waiting for Janet's nod, she went on, 'She picked up that I was upset this morning. I thought of palming her off with some excuse, but she's that knowing, she'd probably tumble to the fact I was codding her. Then, of course, there's always the worry that someone might tell her at school. I thought it best to be straight.'

'You did right,' Janet said, and then was overcome with a huge yawn and was aware suddenly of how weary she was. She wanted to put her head on the table and sleep and sleep, and yet she doubted she'd get any rest with her mind jumping about as it was.

'I'm off to St Peter and Paul's to have some masses said for wee Chloe,' Betty said, heaving herself to her feet.

'She's not a Catholic, Mom,' Janet snapped.

'I don't suppose the good Lord minds about that,' Betty retorted, 'and it can't do any harm, now can it?'

'No, no, it can't,' Janet said, suddenly sorry for her short temper. 'Take no notice of me, I'm so tired I don't know what I'm saying.'

'Try and rest,' Betty advised, 'or you'll make yourself ill.'

Janet did go and lie down on her bed, but though her eyes were smarting, every time she closed them her head was filled with visions of Chloe and she'd jerk them open again. Two or three times she told herself to get up, find something to do, but a strange lethargy filled her body and she stayed beneath the covers. When Betty woke her, she realised she had dozed, but it had been an unrefreshing, fitful sleep and she felt worse, rather than better.

371

By the day of the funeral, she was so bone tired she was finding everything an effort. Somehow she got through the service, flanked as she was by her parents.

She followed the cortège out of the church, head bowed, aware of the mass of people who had come to pay their respects. In the porch, the vicar stopped Richard and Claire's progress for a moment to express his deepest condolences. Janet was right behind them, level with the back seats of the church. Idly, she glanced across the pews, and came face to face with Ben Hayman.

She was stunned with shock. He was the last person she'd expected to see; he should, she reasoned, have been in America by now. Her eyes blurred with tears. It was too much to see him at Chloe's funeral, and with Ruth standing alongside him. The procession was moving again and Janet gave neither of them a sign of recognition but followed behind the funeral party with her eyes once more cast down.

Outside the sky was leaden grey and oppressive. Rain dribbled from the heavy cloud through the cold damp air. They shivered through the service by the graveside and the vicar's breath trailed mist from his mouth as he intoned prayers for the dear departed Chloe.

Raindrops skittered on the opened umbrellas and plopped on the coffin being lowered gently into the tiny grave. The trees sighed around the group as if moved by some great sadness, and their leaves dropped giant teardrops. People stepped forward one by one to take handfuls of earth and drop them on the coffin with a dull thud, while the mud around the feet of the mourners turned to slimy sludge.

All around Janet, people were weeping, but not Claire, who seemed too weak to cry. She was almost incapable of walking and Richard half carried her to the waiting cars. 'I'll see you back at the house,' he said to Janet as he passed.

'Are you sure?' Janet asked, and Mary Wentworth pressed her hand gently.

'Please come my dear.'

Betty and Bert said they wouldn't intrude so Janet went alone, packed in someone's car with people she didn't know. It didn't matter; she was in no mood to make conversation and sat in silence until they reached the house.

Once there, in Chloe's own territory, she could hardly believe the little child she'd loved was gone forever. Never again would she run flat-footed across the room to throw herself against Janet and put her plump arms around her knees. She'd tried so hard to control the lisp she had but had never quite mastered it. 'Thing,' she'd say to Janet with her endearing smile. 'Thing thome-thing to me,' and Janet would go through all the nursery rhymes she knew, always finishing with 'Daisy, Daisy' because it was the song that Chloe had liked best.

Suddenly the loss seemed almost unbearable. It was like a physical ache and Janet could feel the tears welling in her eyes and a lump in her throat that threatened to choke her. This wouldn't do, she thought, she had to be strong for Claire. She didn't know how she'd stand it. How did people cope with sorrow as extreme as this? she wondered. Mary Wentworth saw that Janet was almost overwhelmed by grief and took her hand in a gesture of support. 'Bear up if you can,' she said, 'because we need you,' and she pressed a tray of sandwiches into her hands.

Janet was glad to have something to do and busied herself replenishing the food on the table and dispensing drinks. It was as she turned with another laden tray that she heard her name called. She knew who it was, for hadn't she heard him call her many times, and she swung round to face Ben Hayman. She had a sudden urge to throw the tray in his face. She restrained herself with difficulty, but she was angry.

What the hell are you doing here? What right have you got? The words were screaming in her head. For a second she thought she'd said them aloud, and then she saw Ben's puzzled face looking at her and realised he was waiting for her to speak. Did he think he could swan in and out of her life, taking advantage of her and casting her aside, then greeting her like an old and trusted friend?

Ben was glad to have the opportunity to see Janet again before he left, though he bitterly regretted the situation that had brought them together. Therese's assurances that Janet would welcome her freedom from the engagement, plus the letter she'd written, had convinced him that she couldn't have been upset about the ending of their relationship and that she'd be mature and sensible about the whole thing should they meet again.

He was not unduly perturbed that she had

appeared not to recognise him in the church, or respond to the hand he'd raised in greeting. The lighting was dim for a start, Janet's mind would possibly be elsewhere and she would not have expected to see him there, so he was glad to have the chance to meet up at the house.

He wondered if she knew he was married. He presumed Ruth had told her, but he'd only arrived home days before his wedding and Ruth had been strangely elusive. Therese had demanded most of his attention. With one thing and another, he never got to have a quiet word with his sister and he did wonder if she thought he'd let Janet down, though of course, he reasoned, she didn't know the whole story.

But whichever way it was, there was no time for quiet talking at the wedding itself and then he and Therese were off on honeymoon. When they returned for a few days at home before leaving for America, Ruth had already started at Oxford. And then came the call to the Hayman household from Richard Carter, and when Ruth arrived home after a frantic phone call from Naomi, she could only talk about the tragedy of it all. Therese couldn't understand why Ben felt bound to go to the child's funeral at all.

'She's nothing to you, not related or anything,' she said.

'You don't understand.'

'It's not as if you'll do any good.'

'It's a mark of respect for her parents.' Ben's tone was placatory. He knew from bitter experience on the honeymoon that if he were to inflame his wife's temper, the resultant tantrum would be fierce, frightening and exhausting.

He resisted Therese's sulks, however, and contacted his American firm to explain the position. They readily agreed to postpone his starting date. Therese had refused to go with him to the funeral, for which he was grateful, but he hid his relief from his moody wife and accompanied his sister.

He was unprepared for the disgust he saw now in Janet's eyes, and the ferociousness of her verbal attack. 'You shouldn't have come here. She was nothing to you, Chloe, just an interesting case. Go back to your wife and study other children in America who I'll never know and grow to love.'

'You're not being fair, Janet,' Ben said, and Janet almost laughed aloud. 'I did care about Chloe and I have great respect for her parents.' He added, 'I postponed my passage to the States. I told them the circumstances and they quite understood I had to be here.'

'Bully for them,' Janet said sarcastically, 'and for you too, but you needn't have bothered, you wouldn't have been missed.'

'Janet, don't let's be like this,' Ben said and put his hand on Janet's arm. To her shame, she felt her insides begin to tremble and her heart start to thud against her ribs. She forced herself to speak harshly to keep any note of longing out of her voice.

'Get your hand off me, Ben Hayman.'

Ruth, seeing Janet speaking to her brother, had crossed the room and now said placatingly to Janet, 'Don't, Jan, we only came to ... you know,

376

to say we're sorry.'

'Huh!' Janet exclaimed. 'You're sorry? We're all bloody sorry.' She added witheringly, 'Get out of here. You've no place here today.'

Ruth was hurt. 'It's not for you to say,' she said, but Janet retorted savagely:

'Sod off, the pair of you, before I forget this is a funeral and throw something!'

Ruth's eyes widened and she might have argued further, but Ben saw that Janet was very near the end of her tether and he pulled his sister towards the door. Outside she was inclined to be indignant with Janet.

'I know Claire was a personal friend of hers,' she said, 'but I helped with Chloe as much as she did. I even helped Richard and Claire at fundraising events in the holidays when Janet was working, so she had no need to be like that and act all high-handed.'

Really, Ruth knew that it had little to do with Chloe and the issue of their right to be there. She'd seen the way Janet looked at Ben before she had the chance to put on the mask of indifference she wore. She'd seen the glimpse of longing on her face, and realised that her friend still loved her brother. She hoped Ben was unaware of it. He seemed sunk in thoughts of his own, and such deep thoughts he seemed unaware she'd spoken.

'Don't you think she was out of order?' she said.

Ben didn't answer. He was wondering what had happened to him when he put his hand on Janet's arm. He'd meant it as a gesture of support, but he hadn't imagined the spark that had jumped between them. It had caused the blood to pound in his veins and brought a weakness to his legs, and he'd had an insane desire to crush her to him and kiss her and beg her forgiveness and say he'd been a bloody fool. A fine kettle of fish that would have been.

At home, surrounded by crates and boxes, was his sulky, temperamental wife, a slight swell in her stomach already betraying her condition. She was a beautiful woman, always ready for sex – sometimes almost too ready. He longed to plead tiredness, but he'd seen the evidence of her temper when she was thwarted in anything and he would be ashamed to let his parents witness her uncontrolled fury. She'd been the darling daughter the Steinaways had doted on and had had her own way in everything, and now she demanded it of Ben, though her selfish, possessive and jealous streak had not been apparent till after the honeymoon.

He decided that the best thing he could do was get out to the States as soon as possible and work until he was tired enough to sleep. That was the only way to deal with this madness. He'd make a life of sorts with Therese, and it was no good complaining; he'd married Therese with his eyes wide open and she was carrying his child. In time he'd forget about Janet Travers.

Lou and Shirley were very worried about Janet when she returned to the hostel after the funeral. She was white-faced with strain and exhaustion and thinner than ever, but it was the aura of

sadness she held around herself that most concerned her two room mates.

Janet herself wished she could break out of the
apathy that seemed to be burrowing inside her,
but she seemed powerless to stop the images of
Chloe that flitted unbidden into her conscious
moments.

'Time heals' was such a trite remark for such
sadness, and yet it was true. Janet wasn't aware of
when she started to feel that she was not quite so
consumed with sadness – and began slowly to
emerge as the girl Lou and Shirley had known
before the tragedy.

The term was drawing to a close, the last essays
were in, the last lectures given. Janet eventually
felt strong enough emotionally to drop a line to
Claire inside a Christmas card. As arranged
before she'd left for university, Betty had
managed to find Janet holiday work at the sauce
factory, but as it wasn't full time she'd still be
able to visit Claire, and she told her she'd see her
soon.

She didn't expect a reply to this at the hostel,
but she was surprised on arriving home to find
nothing from Claire at all. She would have liked
to have gone over to the house straight away, but
the family claimed her attention as always, and
her mother advised caution.

'It's her first Christmas without the little one,'
she said. 'She's bound to feel it.'

'Yes, that's why I...'

'I think it's best to leave her and Richard on
their own, don't you?'

'I don't know what to do,' Janet said helplessly,

but she didn't go near, afraid her presence might make matters worse.

She was incredibly lonely, despite her family, who were delighted to see her, and her job. She missed Claire, her friend and confidante, and yet she could not contemplate visiting Ruth. Ben's betrayal still hurt like hell and she felt that if she was to get over it, she had to keep away from the Haymans.

She tried not to let her family see her restlessness and threw herself into the festivities with a will, decorating the room and the tree with the children. She helped Sally and the twins choose presents for the family and then wrap them and hide them in secret places all over the house. She felt guilty that she couldn't be more content, especially as she knew her mother had missed her so much, and she tried not to be irritated by her. Not being able to understand Janet's course, Betty busied herself with practicalities.

'Hostel okay?'

'Fine, Mom, yeah, great.'

'Get on with the other girls, do you?'

'Oh, yes, they've become good friends.'

'I hope you're looking after yourself properly. You do cook good food, I hope, and not fill up on junk.'

'Most of it is cooked for us, Mom,' Janet said, in an exasperated tone she tried hard to disguise. 'And we take it in turns to cook snacks and things like that.'

'Not damp or anything, the bedrooms?'

'No, no, they're okay. In fact, everything's okay.'

Betty shook her head. 'I don't like to think of

the place empty all this time with you all away on holiday. The beds could really do with an airing before you go back in January. You'd better take a couple of hot-water bottles back with you.'

'Oh, Mom, don't fuss,' Janet muttered and took herself off to her grandparents. She was shocked to find her grandad ill in bed.

'Sit up here, bonny lass,' he said, patting the bedspread, 'and tell me how it goes,' and Janet dredged up incidents from her first term at university to interest and amuse him. She could see that Sean was sinking fast.

She told him of the miserable old caretaker, Mrs McPhearson. 'She's a big, dour Scottish woman,' she said, 'with a face on her like she'd sucked a lemon. And she's got this sniff, when she disapproves of anything, you know, and she seems to disapprove of everything we do. She's always snooping round to see if someone is smoking, which we're forbidden to do in our rooms, and she's against us having a drink, and after all we're all over eighteen.'

'A drink never did anyone any harm yet,' declared Sean.

'She wouldn't agree, Grandad,' Janet said. 'We end up sucking peppermints when we come in at night, so that if she's lurking in the hall she won't smell our breath.'

Janet was pleased to see her grandad chuckle and hear his wheezy laugh. 'Does she do that?' he asked. 'Hang about to catch you?'

'You bet she does. In case anyone should come in rolling drunk, or try to creep upstairs with bottles of something, or, worst of all, try to sneak up with a man! I tell you, Grandad, you haven't a hope of getting past her!'

'Perhaps she was a sergeant-major in the war?' Sean suggested with a smile.

'Oh, she would have been at least a general,' Janet cried, and went on, 'One day she came up to inspect the kitchen, it's little more than a cupboard, and she's always trying to catch someone doing something they're forbidden to do. We got word she was coming up and went to town, cleaning the place in the little time we had. Lou had this disgusting black cloth she cleaned everything with, and not finding anywhere else to put it, she threw it in the teapot. Anyway, when McPhearson had gone, after poking into everything and sniffing at our attempts at cleanliness, we all had a cup of tea together. Only we'd forgotten the dirty cloth still in the teapot and made the tea on top of it. Point was, we could have been poisoned and yet it was the best cup of tea I'd ever had!'

Sean McClusky laughed so much the tears ran down his face and he had to mop them away with the big hanky Janet found for him. 'You're a marvel, young Janet,' he said, 'but,' and he touched her arm lightly, 'don't tell your mother about that last incident. I'm not saying a word against her, mind, she's a fine woman in her way, but she'd not have found that amusing.'

Later she kissed him goodbye and was surprised how paper-thin and lined his skin appeared. 'You've cheered him up no end,' Sarah told her granddaughter. 'You're a grand girl to bother about us old ones.'

'I love you both, Gran, you know that,' Janet protested.

'I know that, but some in your position would be too high and mighty for the likes of us.'

'Don't be silly, Gran,' Janet said, giving the old lady a hug. 'Why, what would I do without you?'

Everyone was at the Travers' house on Christmas night as Sean McClusky was too ill for them all to call there. 'You're looking well,' Patsy said to Janet as they were both taking a breather in the kitchen from the noise and the children.

'And you,' Janet said, not at all sure that the slight bump in Patsy's stomach was what she thought it was.

Breda, coming in at that moment, caught Janet's quizzical gaze and said, 'You might well stare, young Janet, the bloody woman's on again. I told Brendan he'd be best tying a knot in it. It might help.'

Patsy laughed. 'Oh, Breda,' she chided, 'you're awful, and anyway, I wanted another after losing that one in the summer. Point is,' and Patsy leaned forward confidentially, 'I'm only on three months and the doctor says I'm so big it could be twins.'

'Holy Mother of God,' Breda said. 'You'll be grey before you're much older if you have a couple like Conner and Noel, added to the two rips you have already.'

Janet listened to the shouts and screams of the lads in the living room and thought Breda had a point. 'It could be twin girls, though,' she said. 'Our Sally wasn't much bother, nor your Linda either, of course,' she said and added loftily, 'Or it could take after me, the perfect child!'

'And the most big-headed,' Breda commented with a laugh.

'Well, let's hope if it is a girl it's nothing like her Auntie Breda!' Brendan commented, coming into the kitchen at that moment. 'Or she will be bad-mouthing the whole world as she comes out!'

'You cheeky sod,' Breda said in mock indignation as the laughter swelled around them.

Only Janet heard Patsy say quietly, 'I don't really care, boy or girl, as long as it's healthy.'

The comment jogged Janet's memory, and two days later she went to see Claire. Perfect strangers opened the door. They were leasing the house, they told Janet. They knew nothing of the previous occupants as all transactions had been done through a letting agent, and any correspondence which had arrived at the house had been sent to them too.

The agent couldn't help Janet either. Mr and Mrs Carter had gone abroad, he'd said. He understood Mrs Carter had been ill. He was sure they would contact her in due course, and in the meantime she could write and he would forward any correspondence to Mrs Carter.

Janet had to be satisfied with this and went home dejected. Claire's disappearance had left a great void in her life. She hadn't realised how much she had depended on her. She tried not to let her loneliness show and was annoyed with herself for being dissatisfied with her lot. Everyone had been pleased to see her home, even

Duncan. Now finally demobbed, he was older, wiser, much nicer to know and working long hours in the garage with his partner Larry Sumners. With her family all around her, she was sure it was wrong to miss Claire, but miss her she did, though she tried to hide it.

It was nearly time to return to university when she remembered Mary Wentworth. She had her address, and though she'd never visited her before, there was no reason why she shouldn't.

But Mary's house was empty and a 'Sold' sign flapped in the wind. Neighbours either side couldn't help. 'She went so quick, you see,' one said.

'Went quick?' Claire repeated, shocked. 'You mean she's dead?'

'No, I mean went off – to see her daughter, so I heard. Not that she doesn't look ill herself, never been right since the little girl died.'

Janet remembered her the day after Chloe's death and the day of the funeral, and knew what the man meant. No one knew anything really, but the neighbours were only too willing to speculate. 'I heard she had bad nerves, the daughter,' said one man.

'She went mad, tried to do her hubby in,' said another.

'No, it was herself she tried to do away with,' corrected his wife.

'She had a breakdown after losing the kiddie,' said the woman at the end of the row, and added, 'Not that it wasn't for the best, her dying like that. After all, she was only a halfwit. But when all's said and done, she was the child's mother.'

Janet had thanked them and gone home and told no one where she'd been. She'd felt as if she'd been cast adrift with no one to talk to or confide in, and wondered how she'd manage without Claire. At first, after she returned to university for the spring term, things would happen and Janet would find herself wondering what Claire would think or say about them, and then she'd remember that she wasn't part of her life any more. She wrote at first via the agent, but it was hard to write and receive no answers, so in the end she stopped. She often discussed with her flatmates why Claire had just left like that without telling anyone, and could only conclude that she'd been too upset to contact people. Perhaps she and Richard wanted time on their own. Lou and Shirley said that Janet shouldn't try so hard to find her; they both said it was up to Claire to contact Janet when she felt able to do it, and they were unwilling to let Janet brood.

Janet was very glad of her deep friendship with the other two girls, and the whole social scene at the college, that ensured no one had to be by themselves unless they chose to be. Not that the dates she had or the parties she attended could be called unqualified successes. Afterwards they would often sit, drink coffee and discuss the night. Lou and Shirley thought Janet's attitude to men a scream. 'What was wrong with Jim?' Lou wanted to know after one party. 'I saw you talking to him for hours.'

'Hardly hours,' Janet objected. 'Ten minutes I'd say, if that. That's just about my boredom level.'

'Oh, that's not fair, Janet. He's very sought

after. He's in the first eleven, you know.'

'Of course I know,' Janet snapped. 'He told me at least twenty times.'

'Well, what about Clive, the studious one with the hornrimmed glasses?' Shirley asked.

'And the groping hands,' Janet added. 'He held me so close, I could feel every bit of him against me, and his hands were everywhere. He even tried to undo my zip till I threatened I'd undo his manhood if he didn't keep his hands to himself.'

By this time Lou and Shirley were convulsed with laughter, and Janet went on, 'And before you ask, the creep on the stairs, whose name I didn't catch, thought fetching me a warm martini from the kitchen entitled him to put his hand up my skirt.' She paused a moment and then added pensively, 'I wonder if martini washes out of a white shirt.'

'Oh, Janet, you didn't throw it over him?' squealed Shirley.

'No, course not, I tried to bloody well drown him. What do you think? Honestly,' Janet said, looking at her two friends, 'some of these boys who think they are men aren't much better than the Academy fodder our school used to draft in to dance with the senior girls.'

Lou and Shirley were always falling hopelessly in love with one man or another, whereas Janet, while accepting dates from many people, refused to get emotionally involved with any. She held herself aloof, frightened to let anyone capture her heart again and smash it into a million pieces.

There were endless late-night discussions in their room about sex and men, and the issue of how far to let chaps go was under constant deliberation and discussion. 'You never get lessons in this sort of useful information at school, do you?' Lou complained. 'You learn a whole heap of crap you won't use if you live to be a thousand, but everyone goes through this.'

'Bit difficult to teach, though,' Janet put in.

'And men don't go through it, do they?' said Shirley. 'I mean, they don't worry about it like girls do. Classes for them would be easy, wouldn't they? "Go for it, lads, and see if she'll let you." That's all they'd need!'

'Too right,' Janet and Lou agreed, and though they were all amused, Lou noticed that Janet's laugh was a little forced. Janet saw Lou's eyes on her and forcing herself to speak lightly she suggested, 'We could set up a pointer system and pin it up on the wall, and you could look at it going out and check it coming back in and see if you stuck to it.'

'Yes,' said Lou, 'how about: "First date – kiss on lips, no tongue. Second date – kiss with tongue. Third date fondling outside clothes."'

'Hang on,' Shirley protested. 'I'd be ninety-five at that rate before I let Stuart go the whole hog. I can hardly spend my youth and middle age fending him off because of a bloody chart on our wall.'

'Well, what do you use now to fend him off?' Lou asked.

'Every bloody excuse I can think up,' Shirley said, and the girls burst out laughing again.

'You see the problems,' Janet said.

'Well, on Lou's chart you'd have no fun at all,

Janet,' Shirley said. 'Your dates never last that long.'

'Maybe she has a secret lover back home,' Lou suggested.

'Some hopes,' Janet said.

'Have you ever had?' Lou persisted. 'Or is it a secret from your dark and murky past?'

'You are a fool,' Janet said, but Lou noticed she didn't answer so she asked again: 'Have you ever had a steady boyfriend, Janet?'

'Of course,' snapped Janet and tried to curb her irritability at Lou's questioning. 'I wasn't a bloody nun.'

'No?' queried Lou sarcastically, with a wink at Shirley.

The pillow caught her on the side of the head and she collapsed on the bed, writhing in mock agony as she cried, 'I'm mortally wounded! Poor Michael will never have his wicked way with me now.'

'Wouldn't that be the worst thing?' Shirley said. 'To die without doing it and never know what all the fuss was about.'

'Maybe it's all about nothing anyway,' Janet said, too quickly.

'Maybe,' Shirley agreed, 'but it would be nice to decide for ourselves.'

Lou was watching Janet's face again and suddenly said, 'You know something you're not telling, Janet.'

'No I don't.'

'Yes you do, you bloody dark horse.'

Janet felt her hands growing clammy and knew she was overreacting. 'Sod off, Lou,' she said, but

Lou wasn't giving in so easily.

'You've done it, haven't you?' she said.

Shirley joined in. 'God, Janet, have you actually gone all the way?'

Janet should have parried the questions – she'd done it before – and the outburst was her own doing. 'Piss off, the pair of you,' she shrieked suddenly, furious with them both. 'Get out of my bleeding life, can't you, and get one of your own.'

Lou and Shirley exchanged glances. Janet had never reacted that way before about anything. They knew they'd touched her on the raw, and that could only mean she had indeed gone all the way with a boy. Janet was ashamed of the outburst she'd unleashed against her friends and knew that her face and neck would be crimson with embarrassment. She took herself off to bed knowing she'd made a fatal error by blowing her top and aware that the subject had only been postponed, not cancelled altogether.

However, it didn't happen straight away, for the university was breaking up for the Easter holidays and Janet was glad to get away from her inquisitive flatmates for a few weeks.

Chapter Seventeen

Unfortunately, that Easter holiday of 1955 was not the peaceful idyll Janet had promised herself. Despite her regular phone calls home, she had been sheltered a little from what was happening in the world, and especially from her father's passionate interest in the Labour Party, for whom he'd worked tirelessly in their years of opposition while they waited to be elected to government.

But many were happy being ruled by the Conservatives. There was almost full employment and the welfare state was being maintained, and both Janet and Bert knew that the government would probably go to the country fairly soon from this position of great strength.

Churchill was eighty years old and knew he couldn't lead his party through an election, for his health was failing. He stepped down, to be succeeded by Anthony Eden, which was no surprise to anyone. Eden, though upper-class, appealed to the middle-of-the-range voter, who had risen in prosperity since the war.

'Damned poppycock,' Bert said, 'spouting all about what he'll do for the ordinary man. What does a bleeding toff like him know anyway?'

Janet felt sorry for Bert, for she knew the Labour Party was in disarray. The austere post-war years under Labour had been succeeded by four years of prosperity under the Conservatives.

'It had to be that way, girl,' Bert answered angrily when Janet expressed her opinion. 'For God's sake, the country was in a state. We'd just fought and won a bleeding war. There were all the returning forces men to find jobs for, and we were committed to starting up the health service.'

'I know, Dad.'

'We'd have been in a fine mess if we'd not had the family allowance when you were all growing up, and how in God's name could we have afforded the doctor's bills all these years?'

'I was just saying...' Janet began, but Bert was in full spate.

'People have short memories. My own mother had to sell every damn thing so we could eat in the years of the bleeding slump when my father couldn't find work. And when they became sick and my two brothers and sister as well there was no money for doctors, medicines or even any bleeding decent food, and TB took them all. Only my sister Maggie and me survived when we were sent to our grandparents at the start of the sickness.'

Janet knew this and still thought it sad that her father had no one to call his own but a sister who had married young and moved to Scotland and who they only heard from at Christmas, when cards were exchanged. But it was all past and done with, as she tried to explain to her father.

'The point is, Dad, life was hard for everyone then, not just one or two, and hard times were followed by six years of war, but people want to forget the bad days now and look forward. It's no good reminding people what Labour did for them in the past; they want to know what Labour will do for them in the future.'

However much Bert might bluster and grumble, the fact was that Janet was right. Most middle-income families wanted a car, a home of their own and the possibility of a grammar school place, leading to a white-collar job, for their children. These were Conservative ideals, while Labour, many thought, was in thrall to the unions. Labour played into Conservative hands by having a very public and damaging disagreement among themselves about nuclear disarmament in the run-up to the election.

The Travers' house was used again on election day, though Betty and Janet were at work in the sauce factory during the morning and early afternoon. Bert and his Labour friends had to fend for themselves for the day, and Bert had to also give an eye to the twins and Sally and Linda. Usually, on holidays from school, Sarah McClusky looked after the children, but Betty said her mother had her hands full tending her father and it wouldn't hurt Bert to do a stint for once.

The feverish excitement had died down by the time the women came home. The banner still fluttered across the front of the house, and loudhailers continued to tour the streets, but much of the early impetus had gone from the day.

The smell of fish and chips lingering in the kitchen and the stack of newspaper in the bin betrayed what they'd had for dinner, and there was a host of strange men in the living room.

They huddled in groups and talked earnestly together, while Janet and her mother dispensed tea and biscuits.

Janet thought you could almost smell defeat, and disappointed as she knew her father was, she couldn't sympathise totally with his despondency. She knew that her grandfather was nearing the end of his life, and when the Conservative Party romped home victorious, it suddenly didn't seem so important. She prepared to go back to university miserably aware that she might never see her grandad again.

'Phone me Mom,' she'd urged, and Betty didn't insult her intelligence by pretending she didn't understand her.

'It won't be long,' she said, 'and I really don't know how Mom will cope without him.'

'Maybe I could move in with Gran holiday times,' suggested Janet. 'After all, Sally's cubicle is getting a little cramped now. She could do with her own room, and I'll only be round the corner from you all.'

'It would be a load off my mind, Janet,' Betty admitted. 'And it would buck her up to have you in the house, if you're sure.'

'Course I'm sure,' Janet said, giving Betty a peck on the cheek and boarding the train. 'See you in the summer, unless something happens sooner.'

Lou and Shirley recognised that Janet was subdued over something and sympathised when she explained what it was. They'd learnt enough of the Travers family over their two terms together to understand what a close-knit unit they were.

Not long after term began again, Lou and Shirley both had dates for the evening, and though both urged Janet to go with them, she refused.

'Neither Michael nor Stuart would like me tagging along,' she said.

'Stuart will find a friend,' Shirley promised airily.

'I'm really not in the mood,' said Janet. 'Honestly, I'd be company for no one tonight.'

She was still bent over the books she'd neglected over the Easter holidays when Shirley returned, earlier than Janet had expected and rather dishevelled.

'All right?' Janet asked her.

Shirley nodded, but her eyes were very bright. 'Fine,' she answered shortly.

'Good,' Janet said, knowing she was anything but fine, but she didn't contradict her. Instead she said, 'Good job you didn't meet Mrs Mc-Phearson on the way up. Your blouse is fastened up wrong.'

'Oh, God,' Shirley said, and blushed as she began attending to it, looking suddenly very young and vulnerable.

She gave a shudder, and a convulsive sob escaped her, and Janet said, 'What is it, Shirl?'

'Oh,' Shirley burst out, 'I'm so miserable. Stuart is furious with me. He says I'm a tease, but truly I didn't mean to be.'

'What happened exactly?'

'We were...' Shirley began, 'we were ... you know, Janet.'

'Necking?'

'Well, yes, and I was letting him ... well, we got a bit carried away. I mean,' she said defensively, 'I have been going out with him for ages.'

Janet hid her wry smile. Shirley didn't go out with anyone for ages. But she had to admit she'd been keen on Stuart the previous term and had gone out with him, and only him since coming back to college.

'You don't have to justify yourself to me,' Janet said. 'Did you...'

'No,' Shirley broke in, 'that's the point. I wouldn't and Stuart said it was bad for a man to be frustrated. He said he could damage himself.'

Janet burst out laughing. 'As my aunt would say, that's bullshit,' she said.

'Is it?'

'Course it is. It's what men say to get you to do the things you'd rather not do.'

'How do you know these things, Janet?' Shirley asked. 'I mean, how do people get to know? It's not something you can ask your mother.'

'God, no,' Janet replied with feeling, 'but I had an aunt who was quite good at telling me things.'

'I've been told damn all,' Shirley said, 'and you're the only one who I could ask. I mean, you're the only one I know who's done it, gone ... like, all the way ... you know. You have, haven't you? You haven't just touched it or anything?'

And Janet, knowing denial was useless, nodded her head. 'Yes,' she said, 'I've done more than touch it, I have done it with someone.'

'Did you like it?' Shirley said, and went on before Janet had a chance to reply. 'See, me and

Lou talked about it, and decided that's why you only go out on one or two dates with people and never get involved.'

'What d'you mean?' Janet asked, puzzled.

'Because you didn't like it,' Shirley said, 'and don't want to have to do it again.'

'No one has to do it again if they don't want to,' Janet said, smiling at Shirley's naivety. 'Okay, we've established what Stuart wants. Now what about you? Do you want full sex?'

'God, no,' Shirley said. 'I'm bloody scared to death.' Then, more honestly, she added, 'At least I can say that now. It's different when Stuart's kissing me and stuff. I don't always think straight then.'

Janet remembered her time by the lake with Ben and their joyous, rapturous lovemaking. She knew only too well what Shirley meant. 'What exactly are you scared of?' she asked. 'Getting pregnant? The act itself? What?'

'Everything,' wailed Shirley.

'If it's pregnancy you're concerned about, there is something men can get. Barbers and places like that sell them.'

'I ... I suggested that,' Shirley said, 'but Stuart said it was no good for men with one of those things on.'

'Now I know why my aunt said "bullshit" so often,' Janet said. 'It's the only word to describe the crap your chap is feeding you.'

'Then that isn't true either?'

'Nope,' Janet said. 'Tell Stuart it's either use a rubber thing or keep his trousers on.'

'Oh, Janet.'

'Don't be so soft,' Janet said with a smile. 'What else?'

'Well, I'm scared. People say it hurts like hell and you bleed all over the place.'

Janet sighed. Really, she thought, all joking apart, someone should tell girls something besides advising them to keep their legs crossed. Cast adrift as they were, fed crap by creeps like Stuart, it was small wonder so many girls became pregnant.

'Does it hurt?' Shirley asked again.

'A bit the first time, but you hardly notice it,' Janet said. 'Some people bleed, not everyone and not that much.'

Shirley's eyes widened as she realised that Janet had done it more than once. 'How many times did you...'

'That's none of your bloody business, is it?' Janet said tersely.

'Okay,' Shirley conceded quickly, hesitant of making her angry again. 'But was it good?'

'For me, yes, it was very good,' Janet said.

'Well, what was it like?'

Janet closed her eyes for a moment. 'I couldn't describe it,' she said at last. 'It was wonderful and magical for me and it's really no one else's business. I suppose,' she went on, 'it's different for everyone.'

'What ... what happened to the boy you went with?' Shirley asked.

Janet considered telling Shirley that that was her own affair, but eventually she shrugged and said, 'We were engaged. I loved him very much and thought he loved me.' Her voice had dropped to just above a whisper and Shirley leaned closer. 'But,' she went on, 'he didn't love me enough. He married someone else.' She was surprised at the stab of hurt it still gave her to say that.

Shirley nodded. 'My mother said all men are bastards, just after one thing, and if you let them do it they lose respect for you.'

Janet considered Shirley's words and then said, 'I think Ben was more weak than wicked, and probably manipulated. But you,' she said, 'must either put the brakes on before Stuart gets too excited, or, if you decide to go for it, make sure he uses a Durex, or you'll be left holding the baby.'

After that the three girls' relationship shifted a little. Shirley asked Janet if she could tell Lou, and they both looked at her with more respect. She was an experienced woman who they thought could help them with their tangled love lives. Eventually, Janet threatened to start charging for her services if they didn't start thinking for themselves for a change, and they began to treat her almost as they had before.

They applauded and agreed with her decision not to get too serious too quickly after such a bad experience, and though they continued to ask her out, they didn't try to press her if she said no. They arranged girls-only nights, when they found they could have riotous fun without a man dancing attendance. Then one or the other would find the love of their life again and the girls' nights would be curtailed – till the next time.

They were flat-hunting at this time, having had

their fill of Mrs McPhearson, but it was proving more difficult than they had imagined to find accommodation that would satisfy all three of them. It was also time-consuming looking at flats when the end-of-year exams were looming ever closer.

But before the problem of finding somewhere to live had been solved, Janet received the phone call she had been dreading.

'The doctor says he has only days to live,' Betty told her, 'and he's asking for you.'

It was two weeks before the official end of term, but the exams were over and Janet's essays were in. She packed her stuff and set off for home, stopping only to press her parents' phone number into Lou's hand at the station. 'Keep me informed,' she urged, and both girls promised they would.

Janet waited downstairs, knowing that soon her grandfather would relinquish his faint hold on life. She'd sat and held his hands for hours, talking to him, for although he was unconscious, the doctor had told her that hearing was the last sense to go and he might be aware that she was there. In case he was, she talked as she had never talked to him when he was hale and hearty. She discussed university and her courses and finding somewhere else to live, and she told him how much she loved him. She wondered if she was doing any good, for even if Sean could hear her, he made no sign and couldn't answer her in any way. But death was a lonely path to tread and, Janet told herself, maybe it gave a person comfort to know that they were not alone.

They'd all been to see him, all the grand-children: Duncan, the twins, Sally, Linda and Brendan's two boys. Janet was the last and the one who stayed the longest.

The priest arrived while she was there to give Sean the last rites, and Sarah, Betty, Breda and Brendan came in to be with him. Janet watched the priest anointing her grandfather with holy oils and mumbling Latin prayers, and doubted that Sean would have given his consent for the last rites if he'd been conscious.

'Bloody mumbo-jumbo' he would have called it, and tears stood out in Janet's eyes when she realised that she'd never hear him say that again. Eventually the priest was done, and Janet went down with him and made him a cup of tea, leaving her grandad surrounded by his wife and children. It seemed right that way. Long after the priest had left she sat on, her cup of tea untouched beside her.

Shortly after the keening of her grandmother signalled that it was all over, there was a knock at the door. Patsy's pains had started and Brendan had to set off for home.

Once before, the birth of twins had eased the pain of death. Now two girls, Finolla and Mairead, were born fine and healthy, despite being three weeks early, and everyone, while still grieving for Sean McClusky, knew that life went on. Gran, though, was like half a person without her man by her side, and Betty knew it would take her a long time to get over it all.

The funeral was well attended. Sean McClusky

had been a respected, well-liked man and St Peter and Paul's Church in Pype Hayes was chock-a-block for the requiem mass.

The brown mahogany coffin, so different from Chloe's, seemed to dominate the church, the top almost covered with mass cards. The incense left a musty smell in the air and the Latin responses were like incantations, soothing to the soul.

Afterwards, Gran's house seemed to be heaving with people, and Janet saw the food she'd helped her mother and Breda prepare disappear at speed. Drinks of every description were piled in the kitchen, where Brendan was doing his best to dispense them. Muted voices rose and fell. Sometimes one or two voices would become very loud, and then they would be hushed, as if they'd suddenly remembered where they were, and the murmur would begin again.

The house was full of unfamiliar faces. Many, Janet knew, were her grandparents' people from across the water, relatives spoken of often but never seen. They spent a long time exclaiming over Janet and the other grandchildren and deciding amongst themselves who looked the most like Sean McClusky, talking in brogues so thick it was often difficult to make out what they said. Tearful women enveloped Janet in hugs, while their menfolk pumped her hand up and down, kissed her cheek or patted her shoulder. All told her that her grandad was one of the best – as if she needed telling.

Later, when everything had returned to normal, the visitors gone back home, the children finishing the summer term at school and the adults back at work, Janet broached the subject of moving in with her gran during the holidays. She didn't say they were worried about her, that they didn't think she could look after herself or perhaps wouldn't cook proper meals, for that, Janet knew, would cause her gran's hackles to rise. Instead, she made it sound like a favour Sarah would be doing the Travers family as Janet explained how cramped Sally was now she was growing up, and how pleased Betty would be to find a solution to the dilemma. Her grandmother was delighted to have company, even if it was only sporadic, but hid her pleasure and said, almost grudgingly, that she didn't mind if everyone else was agreeable, and Janet moved her things in almost immediately.

Janet's presence in the house seemed to cheer Sarah McClusky. There were times, though, when certain things – the sight of an odd sock, a certain tune or song, or coming upon one of Sean's discarded pipes – would remind her of her devastating loss and bring tears to her eyes. She hid them from Janet, who was finding it hard enough herself to cope with the fact that her grandad was gone forever. He'd been so quiet and unassuming, and yet he'd been the king pin of the family, and no one had quite realised it till he was gone.

Janet was bored. The children still had a few weeks of school left. Her summer job at the factory was not yet available. Breda and her mother were at work most of the day and Gran had gone to Brendan's to look after the family.

403

Patsy was home now, but unable to do much, and Mrs McClusky said that good as the neighbours had been, it was time the family took a hand. She was glad to do it, Janet knew. There was no time for moping, for she was too busy.

Janet longed for the children to be home and wandered aimlessly round the shops or visited the library, missing Claire as she never imagined she would.

She'd wondered often how Claire was, and where she was. Disappearing the way she did had left a big hole in Janet's life that no one could fill totally, and yet she knew Claire wouldn't have just gone without even getting in touch unless she'd had a good reason. She often wondered if she'd become ill; she'd even thought she might have died, given up as it were. After Chloe's death she must have felt she'd lost everything dear to her, and though Richard had been a tower of strength, she wondered if Richard alone would be enough for Claire without her daughter. Could you die from a broken heart? Janet didn't know, and there was no one to ask. She longed for news. Just a short note to say that Claire was fine would help to still the fear in Janet that something had happened to her special friend and adviser.

Then one day she had a call from Lou to say they'd found a flat in the last few days of term, and that made her feel a little happier. 'It's on the London Road,' Lou told her. 'Everyone knew we were on the lookout and we heard about it on the grapevine.'

Janet was cheered a little by the knowledge that

she wouldn't have to go back to the hostel and sourpuss McPhearson. She'd told Breda more about her room mates and McPhearson than anyone, except perhaps her grandad.

'What are they like, the girls you share with?' Breda had asked.

'They're great,' Janet said enthusiastically, and went on, 'Shirley's a scream. She's got orange hair. I don't mean auburn like yours, I mean orange, like a carrot, and there's a lot of it, it sticks out like a bush. She's always complaining about it, and yet she's stunning-looking, with this super skin and not a spot in sight and deep-brown eyes, and she's tall and slim, with a figure like a model.'

'And she can't see it, I suppose,' Breda said.

'No, she can't,' agreed Janet. 'All she can see is her hair, which isn't that awful either. Anyway, Lou got fed up hearing about it and offered to put a rinse on it to tone it down a bit. Only we all forgot about it and she came out glowing like a Belisha beacon.' Janet was laughing at the memory as she went on, 'She washed her hair about fifty times, didn't speak to Lou for weeks and had to go about with a hat on for a fortnight.'

'I've been there,' Breda said. 'I was forever doing things to my hair. My mother always said I'd be bald by the age of thirty.'

'She was wrong,' Janet said, but added with a mischievous grin, 'though I do think it's thinning out on top a bit now.'

'You cheeky bugger,' Breda said good-naturedly, giving Janet a swipe.

She was pleased to see Janet in such good

405

spirits and so obviously enjoying herself. For years her niece worried about the family, and then there was all that business with Ben, the tragic death of Claire's daughter and now her beloved grandad, yet Janet had seemed to rise above it all.

'No one stolen your heart yet, Janet?' she asked.

'No,' Janet said, 'and I haven't met anyone I'd like to give it to either.' She might have added 'since Ben' but thought better of it.

'What's the other girl like that you share with?' Breda asked. 'Lou, is it?'

'Oh, she's small, with short dark hair and freckles. She's always up to something, always in a hurry, and she's attractive rather than pretty. Her mouth is like mine and her nose is bigger and her eyes a sort of nondescript hazel, and yet you forget all that when you talk to her. Her face gets all animated, and when she smiles or laughs – and she does both often – it lights up.'

'I'm really glad you get on so well,' Breda said. 'It's nice to see you making friends.'

And Janet realised that Lou and Shirley *had* become friends, and that part of the reason she wasn't enjoying her holiday was because there was no one for her at home any more. There was no Claire and no Ruth. The family had found out that Claire and Richard had left the area, but they knew no more than Janet of why or where they had gone, and they'd accepted that she and Ruth had naturally grown apart. Yet Janet would have loved to knock on Ruth's door as if they were still friends, as if she'd never spoken those words at Chloe's funeral.

But it would never do for anyone – and most especially perceptive Auntie Breda – to guess at her unhappiness. So she smiled back at her aunt and said, 'Lou nearly got us all in terrible trouble one night. It was turned midnight and she wasn't in and you need a late pass to stay out after eleven.'

'Dear God,' Breda exclaimed. 'They treat you like schoolchildren.'

'Worse,' said Janet, and added thankfully, 'But at least we won't be so restricted next term.'

'Well, what did she do when she found herself locked out?' Breda asked.

Janet laughed before she said, 'She tried to wake me and Shirley by throwing gravel at the window, but I thought it was just rain. I was half asleep, you know, and just lay there thinking how wet Lou was going to get, and then I heard scrabbling on the wall and we leaned out the window, me and Shirley, and saw Lou trying to climb up the ivy, only she fell and cricked her ankle. There was no way we could get her in the front door without rousing Mrs McPhearson and so we rushed down to let her in through the downstairs bathroom window. Only trouble was, in her haste to clamber in the window, Lou knocked all the stuff off the ledge with her handbag and made such a clatter the whole hostel was woken up and McPhearson came to investigate.

'We hadn't time to invent a good story and couldn't risk McPhearson seeing Lou, so Shirley, who was fairly decently clad in her dressing gown, went to the bathroom door. We hid behind it and prayed she wouldn't just barge in, while Shirley explained to McPhearson that she'd fallen off the toilet and that was what had caused the noise. McPhearson took one look at the stained and crumpled dressing gown Shirley had hastily tugged around herself and the orange hair standing out on her head and her face crimson with embarrassment, and asked, with a very expressive sniff, if she'd been drinking. I mean, it was hardly any of her bloody business. Shirley said afterwards that she thought falling off the toilet stone-cold sober was something Mc-Phearson might find suspect, so she said she'd had a few, even though she'd had nothing stronger than tea all night. McPhearson said she'd see her in the morning.

'Then we tried to get Lou up the stairs quickly, which wasn't so easy as she was unable to put any weight on one ankle and was biting her lip to stop herself giving little yelps of pain as we stumbled unsteadily from step to step. Next morning McPhearson gave Shirley a lecture on the demon drink. "Not only were you so drunk you fell off the toilet," she said in this high, disapproving whine of hers, "but as if that wasn't enough, I heard you later, making your way to bed, almost too intoxicated to climb the stairs. And," she added, "if I ever see you in that state again, I will consider it my bounden Christian duty to write and inform your parents."'

'The interfering old bitch,' Breda burst out. 'You're best out of that place.'

'I know,' Janet said fervently. 'She sees sin everywhere.'

Only a couple of weeks after her chat with Breda, Janet was thankfully packing her suitcase under the watchful eye of her grandmother, who, she realised, would probably feel very lonely when she had gone back to university. 'Bye, Gran, see you soon,' she said, kissing the crinkled cheek.

'Bye, my bonny lass, it's back to your real life now,' said the wise old lady, and Janet marvelled that her gran, above all others, knew that her granddaughter had just been marking time.

'I love you,' Janet said, and Sarah McClusky smiled.

'I know, lass,' she said. 'I know.'

Chapter Eighteen

Janet was glad she'd arranged with Lou and Shirley to go back a little earlier than the official start of term so that they could give the flat a good clean. It wasn't in all honesty terribly dirty, but Janet, surveying it, said, 'It's a bit dingy.'

Lou and Shirley agreed. 'Maybe it will look better after a clean,' Shirley suggested.

They set to with a will with lots of soapy water, scrubbing brushes and great enthusiasm, and at the end of it, the place didn't look much better. The paintwork was dull brown and reminiscent of the pre-war years, and the hideous cheap paper was yellow and patchy with age. The lino was stained, pitted and cracked and the curtains were filthy dirty. 'I'd be afraid to wash them,' Janet said. 'I think the dirt's holding them together.'

Shirley's parents came to inspect the place. Shirley's father had put up key money and the first month's rent the landlord had demanded to secure the flat, and though the girls were able to pay him back later from their grants, he wanted to see the place too. 'It's a bit grim,' Shirley confessed to her mother.

'Not at all, darling,' her mother said reassuringly. 'Many people start out with much worse.'

'But it's all so dull.'

'Nothing a spot of paint won't put right,'

Shirley's father said. 'It just needs brightening up.'

'Rugs can cover the worst bits of the lino,' Shirley's mother said. 'And shelves in the alcoves for your bits and pieces, and of course new curtains.'

Janet stared at them in amazement. They hadn't got that sort of money. Then Shirley's mother, who was over at the window, suddenly said, 'I'll make new curtains for you if you'd like me to. It will be a gift to you all, my moving-in present.'

By the time term began, the flat was almost unrecognisable from the one they'd first visited. The walls were painted white, the woodwork sunshine yellow. Curtains with large yellow sunflowers on them fluttered at the kitchen windows and those of the bedroom the three girls shared. The curtains in the living room were gold and muted green in swirling patterns, and Shirley's mother had made a matching throwover to hide the sagging three-piece. They'd paid the landlady's son a small amount to put natural-wood shelves in the alcoves, and Shirley's parents had found a number of rugs they said they had no use for that covered the worst bits of the lino. The girls pooled their resources, for while Lou and Shirley got an allowance to eke out their grants, Janet had her wages, and went hunting for things to make the flat more homely.

They bought a carpet remnant that nearly covered the bedroom floor, a second-hand wicker ottoman to hold their jumpers, and colourful bedspreads to make their beds look better. They searched the junk shops for cheap lamps for muted lighting in the living room and bedroom, and filled the place with plants. Shirley had brought her record player and collection of records and put it in one alcove, while the other housed books, with a large desk built beneath them.

They were all incredibly proud of having their own place. It was rather daring of them and some of those they left behind in the hostel said they thought they were rather fast. Lou said they were just jealous, and Janet thought if she hadn't have got out when she did, she'd have given Mrs McPhearson the length of her tongue or worse. She had to admit though that without Shirley's parents' contributions, the flat wouldn't have been so nice. It was on the third floor, like their room in the hostel, but they had their own kitchen and bathroom, and two other rooms which they used as a living room and communal bedroom. The place was so central, too, just a short walk away from the town centre and the railway station, and yet within easy reach of the university as there was a short cut across Victoria Park.

Excitedly, Janet described it all to her parents in the pay phone on the ground floor, but their enthusiasm was muted, not really sure whether it was the done thing for young unmarried girls to live alone. However, the girls had no such qualms and threw a house-warming party. It was a great success and many were envious of the place they had entirely to themselves. Janet wished her parents could see it, she just knew they would be

412

so proud of her.

The day after the party there was a knock at the door, and Janet opened it to a young man she remembered talking to the evening before. He had light-brown hair that went back in a quiff, and deep-hazel eyes, and he was tall and slim. She remembered that he had a ready laugh.

'Hello,' he said, 'remember me?'

'Of course,' Janet said. 'Simon, isn't it?'

'That's right, Simon Webster. I've brought the book I told you about.'

'Come in,' Janet said. She remembered they'd discussed literature for a long time and Simon had told her about *The Diary of Anne Frank*, which had been published that year. She'd remembered Ruth's story of the Russian pogroms and said she'd like to read it.

She made coffee and they sat in the kitchen and talked. Janet couldn't remember talking like that for ages. It was the way she'd once confided in Claire and Ruth. Now she was discussing every subject under the sun with a young man she'd just met and who she felt completely at home with.

She agreed to go to the cinema with him the following evening, and once he'd gone, she settled down to read the book he'd brought, glad that for once she had the place to herself. As she read, she sensed the agitation of the young girl hiding with her family and a few friends in Amsterdam. It was such an unnatural and fear-filled adolescence she was forced to endure because of her race and religion.

Janet could only imagine the terror that would

have possessed them all when the Gestapo screeched to a halt outside their hiding place. There would have been screams and shouts from those below as they sought to pretend ignorance of the sealed-up room. How did a young girl cope with the dread feeling that would descend on her as she heard the storm troopers' boots pound on the stairs and kick open the room to their little sanctuary?

When Janet finished the book she lay back, overcome with sadness at the futility of it all. She'd severed her friendship with Ruth solely because she'd had an association with her brother, who'd let her down and married another, and she was ashamed of herself. I'm like the kings of old, she thought, who'd kill the messenger who brought bad tidings. She realised that Ruth had a point about the persecution of the Jews; even the embittered old grandmother maybe had just cause to feel hard done by.

Knowing that it was up to her to heal the rift between them, Janet took up her pen twice during the next fortnight to write to Ruth, but couldn't find the words.

The matter still had not been resolved by the time she returned home for Duncan's twenty-first birthday party. He expressed surprise to Janet that Ruth hadn't been invited, and Janet admitted, 'I don't see her any more.'

'Why not?'

'Well, we ... sort of drifted apart ... you know, with going to different universities...' Janet's voice faded away and Duncan could recognise her floundering and feeble excuses only too well.

414

'Don't give me that, Jan,' he said. 'I was away over two years, but when I came home on leave, my mates were still my mates, and now we're all together again.' He stopped a minute and said: 'This isn't anything to do with Ben, is it?'

The denial was on Janet's lips, but she could not deliver it because she knew she could not do it emphatically enough to be believed. Her silence was equally damning.

'God, Jan,' Duncan burst out. 'Ruth's hardly her brother's keeper.'

'I know,' Janet snapped. 'Why do you have to be so ... so ... oh, I don't know, such a Mr Big Head?'

Duncan burst out laughing. 'Me, Janet Travers?' he exclaimed. 'You've got a nerve. That's the cap that fits you nicely, Miss Clever Clogs 1955, and still you can't give me a decent reason why your good friend Ruth Hayman's in the dog house.'

Because I don't have a good reason, Janet might have said.

Betty and Bert were confused by the girls never meeting again once university started. Janet had kept a lot of the unpleasant things about Ben's defection from them, and they were unaware of his marriage, or what had happened at Chloe's funeral. They knew the girls had drifted apart and considered that natural, but didn't realise the split was so final.

In issuing the invitation to Janet, Betty had said, 'Bring someone if you like.'

'What kind of someone?'

'You know, if there's anyone special.'

415

'There isn't,' Janet said, and thought of Simon. He was special, she supposed, and she was very fond of him, but she couldn't just present him at her home, not yet. Anyway, she thought, the Travers *en masse* were enough to frighten anyone to death. Simon would have to be introduced slowly, if at all. He'd been quite annoyed with her when she'd told him that she was going to her brother's twenty-first alone.

'Aren't I invited?' he'd asked.

'No,' Janet answered. 'Why should you be?'

'Well, we are going out together.'

'Yes,' Janet said, 'just that, not yet joined at the hip.'

'Look here, Janet,' Simon said, 'if you were to tell your parents...'

'Tell them what?'

'That we're an item, for Christ's sake,' Simon burst out. 'I'd like to meet them, and your brothers and sister.'

'You don't meet people at a party,' Janet said.

'Well, let me come and meet them the weekend before.'

'No.'

'Christ, Janet, you can be damned obstinate.'

'What's this thing about my bloody family?' Janet cried. 'We're only going out together, for God's sake.'

Simon shrugged. 'You talk about them all the time and I'd just like to put faces to the names, that's all.' He'd forced himself to speak casually. What he would have liked to say was that he loved Janet, was crazy about her and would like to meet the family he might one day be related to. Lou had warned him that to declare his love and serious intent was a surefire way of putting Janet off.

Janet looked at him, considering what he'd said, and commented, 'I might take you one day.'

'Great,' Simon said sarcastically. 'Don't put yourself out.'

'I won't.'

'Do you know how annoying you are?' Simon asked, and added threateningly, 'You'll push me too far one of these days.'

Janet's eyes narrowed. 'Well, if you don't like the way I treat you, you know the way out.'

Lou and Shirley shook their heads over Janet and her treatment of Simon Webster, but Janet was unrepentant.

'He can take it or leave it,' she said.

Lou and Shirley weren't invited to Duncan's party either, though Betty had suggested Janet ask her flatmates.

'They have a pretty heavy social schedule,' Janet explained, not altogether truthfully. She couldn't understand why she didn't want Lou and Shirley at that party. It was as if she was trying to keep her two lives separate, and yet it wasn't only that. If they were to meet her family, she wanted them to do it on an ordinary weekend, not one with a party in progress which might give them the wrong impression of everyone.

'Well, ask Ruth then,' Betty suggested. 'I'm sure she'd like to come and wish Duncan all the best on his coming-of-age.'

'Mom, I haven't seen Ruth since I began

university,' Janet said.

'Yes, but that was just circumstances, wasn't it?' Betty said. 'You know, with you both going to different universities and so on.'

'Not entirely, Mom, no.'

'Yes, but...'

'Mom, Ruth won't be coming,' Janet said, and Betty didn't argue further, but she did say to Bert and Duncan that evening:

'Has our Janet had a fall-out with Ruth, do either of you know?'

'They've never had a real fall-out, have they?' Bert said. 'Thick as thieves they were as youngsters.'

'So she's said nothing to you?'

'No,' Bert said. 'I know she sees less of her now, but that's just growing up, isn't it?'

'I'm not sure,' said Betty. 'What I am sure of, young Duncan, is that Ruth won't be over for your party to wish you well.'

'I'll survive,' Duncan said lightly, but he'd been determined to discover from Janet what it was all about.

He found out very little, except that Janet's unfriendliness with Ruth was somehow connected with her brother. All Duncan knew was that Ben had become engaged to his sister and then changed his mind, because he had the offer of a job in America. It seemed eminently sensible to him not to hold someone to a commitment when they were going to live on another continent for a while. Anyway, Janet wouldn't have been able to marry for years and years. She'd been just at the start of her university course.

Duncan stopped trying to work out his sister's love life and gave himself up to enjoying his party, and within a few hours he couldn't remember anyone having a problem at all.

Simon was livid when Janet announced on her return that she would be going back home for the next two weekends.

'But why?'

'My young brothers are sitting an exam to get into technical school,' Janet explained. 'I found out in the summer when I was home. They have extra homework and I said I'd give them a hand weekends, till the exams are over.'

'Why you?' Simon asked. 'What about their teachers?'

'They can't give them extra time. The classes are too large,' Janet said. 'And I had the chance. My teacher gave up her free time for me, and without her help I'd never have got to grammar school and wouldn't be here now today. I promised my sister when she was just a baby that I'd help her, but now my two brothers are down for it first.'

'It's a problem she has,' Shirley told a lonely Simon the first weekend. 'She feels almost guilty about the educational opportunity she had offered to her, and has spent the rest of her life making it up to her family.'

Janet was so busy with her university course, working with her brothers and seeing Simon as often as he could convince her to go out with him that she put aside her worry about Ruth, and what, if anything, she could do about her, until the end of November. Then she broached the problem with her flatmates.

'Simon said I should contact her,' she said. 'What do you two think?'

'Send her a Christmas card with a note inside,' suggested Shirley.

'She's Jewish.'

'Oh yes, so she is.'

'Well,' said Lou, 'send her a note anyway. Something low key but friendly.'

Janet tried, but the notes came out either too stiff and formal or too inane for words. The term was coming to an end. There was the usual end-of-term flurry and last-minute things to do, and when Janet set off for the Christmas holidays, she still hadn't made any contact with Ruth Hayman.

The Haymans' house had never struck her before as unfriendly, nor the door as forbidding. But two days into the Christmas holidays, Janet stood before it with her knees quaking. She almost turned around and went home, but she knew that would be a stupid thing to do when she'd got so far. She hoped and prayed that the crabby old grandmother wouldn't answer the door. Not that she'd ever seen her do that – she would deem it beneath her – but still she waited with clammy hands and a dry mouth.

Relief flooded through Janet when she saw that it was Ruth who stood in the doorway. She didn't seem pleased to see Janet, though her mouth dropped open in surprise. She wondered what the other girl wanted, for their last encounter had been pretty awful, but she said nothing and just waited for Janet to speak.

'Hello, Ruth.'

'H ... hello.' Ruth stared at the girl she'd been friends with since they were both twelve years old. She noticed she was shivering, and was suddenly aware of the icy chill of the day.

'Come in,' she said, throwing the door wide.

'Is it all right?' Janet said. 'Your parents? Your grandmother?'

'My grandmother has broken her hip,' Ruth said. 'She slipped last week on the ice. My parents are visiting her in hospital at the moment. I'm on my own.'

'Oh' Janet said. 'Is she badly hurt, your grandmother?' She felt she had to ask.

'Bad enough, I think,' Ruth said, 'but why should you care?'

'Well, I ... I mean, you...'

'I don't care really,' Ruth said. 'I'm more relieved she's out of the way for a while. It's been so peaceful these last few days. I don't want her to die or anything awful, just stay out of our hair for a bit and give Mom, in particular, a bit of a rest.'

Janet didn't know what to say to that. She'd be worried to death if it was her own grandmother, but then Mrs McClusky was nothing like the elder Mrs Hayman. Ruth was watching her, and the silence became uncomfortable. Eventually Janet said, 'Can we talk, Ruth?'

'What about?' Ruth was defensive.

'Ruth, we were once good friends.'

'Yes,' Ruth said flatly, 'we were.'

The draughty hall was cold and Janet suddenly gave a shudder. 'It's always cold in here,' Ruth

421

said apologetically, and added almost grudgingly, 'We could go in the kitchen. It will be warmer, and I suppose I could make us a drink.'

It was on the tip of Janet's tongue to say 'Don't strain yourself' but she managed to stop herself. What did you expect! she told herself as she followed Ruth along the passage to the kitchen. That she'd fall on your neck in base gratitude that you've deigned to remember her existence again?

She waited until Ruth had made two cups of coffee, pushed one across the table and indicated that they should sit down. Then she spoke. 'I wanted to say I was sorry. I was out of order and wrong to say what I did at Chloe's funeral. I was overwrought.'

'Ben said you were,' Ruth said. 'I was annoyed with you, and upset, but he said we should make allowances.'

'Ben did?'

'Yes,' said Ruth, and then burst out, 'This is all about Ben, isn't it, all this antagonism towards me?'

'Well ... yes, yes, it is – or was,' Janet agreed. 'I was annoyed with you because you came and told me about his marriage. I know it was illogical and stupid. It seemed as if you were on his side.'

'I couldn't have been on yours if I'd wanted to,' Ruth said. 'I couldn't get near you. You froze me out that night in your room. Really I'm on no one's side. But if we're going to become friends again – and I'd like that – we can't ignore Ben as if he didn't exist, and go round the Wrekin to avoid using his name, as if he's some kind of pariah. He's my brother and your ex, and a lot of the unhappiness you carried around was because of him. We probably need to talk about it.'

'I don't want to talk about Ben,' Janet said firmly.

Ruth shook her head. 'Maybe you don't want to talk about him,' she said, 'but I bet you've often wondered about him and what he's been doing since he walked out on you. It's only natural.' Janet didn't answer. She wasn't going to admit how often she'd wondered, certainly in the early days. 'The company he did research for are sponsoring him at medical school,' Ruth said. 'He's specialising in mental illness and they have a job for him when he's finished. His son Jacob Eli was born in May.'

'Jacob?' Janet said in surprise. 'I would have thought a first son would have been called for his father.'

'Ben would have liked it that way, but Jacob Eli is the name of Therese's father,' Ruth explained. 'He's provided the apartment in New York and a nanny for the baby, because Therese was screaming and complaining that she couldn't cope. Ben's salary alone at the moment wouldn't keep her the way she wants to be kept. As it is, Mr Steinaway's sizeable allowance enables Ben and Therese to live in high-society New York and therefore gives him a big stake in their lives and that of their son.'

There was a short silence, and then Ruth said suddenly, 'He's not terribly happy, Janet.'

When Janet had first learned of Ben's marriage,

she wanted him and his new wife to rot in hell together. Now, she was sorry it hadn't worked out, but it mattered to her no more than that. She shrugged. 'That's life. We don't always get what we want, what we hope for.'

Ruth let out a sigh. 'Or what we deserve,' she said. 'Yet I'd want to murder someone if I'd been just left like you were, and in such a cowardly way.'

'What about Sam Oppenheimer?' Janet said, glad to change the subject a little.

'Oh, he's history,' Ruth said. 'It was all right till we began university. Then he made it plain that there was no commitment on either side and we were both free to see other people. I felt a bit of a fool and for a while mooned after him, but I soon saw what a flirt he is. He's gone through most of the girls in my year already.'

'Oh, Ruth, I'm sorry.'

'I'm over it now,' Ruth said, 'yet if he'd crooked his little finger at one time, I'd have done anything he wanted. I even toyed with the idea of giving up my course and everything, if he proposed marriage and wanted me to. Not that he ever mentioned the word marriage, it was just a fantasy I had. Anyway,' Ruth gave a definite shake of her beautiful black mane of hair, 'I'm over it completely now and I've had quite a number of romances, but I've kept it light.'

'Me too,' Janet said. 'Once bitten, twice shy, as they say.'

'It's awful here at home at the moment as well,' Ruth said. 'Ben's miles away and Aaron might as well be.' She was silent a minute and then said.

424

'My grandmother is eaten up with bitterness and hatred, and Mom and Dad are so worn down by her ... oh,' she said almost impatiently, 'they have no life either. Grandmother pushed Ben and Therese together and refuses to see the cracks opening up in their marriage, and yet she won't even speak to Aaron, because he married out.'

'Married out?' Janet said in a high, surprised voice.

'Yes, to a lovely girl called Lisa,' Ruth said. 'Aaron told Mom and Dad he loved her and that was that, he wasn't marrying someone he didn't love because she was the right race or religion. Grandmother kept screeching about disgracing the family name, and she told Dad he should disown Aaron and cut him out of his will as she had done. Mom said she wasn't prepared to lose her son pandering to an old woman, and poor Dad was caught in the middle.'

'Who won?'

'If I'm honest, it was Aaron,' Ruth said with a smile. 'For while all this mayhem was going on in our house, Aaron and Lisa just carried on serenely planning their wedding. Eventually their happiness won Mom and Dad over, but my malicious old grandmother has continued to carry on a hate campaign.'

What's new? Janet thought, but she didn't say it. She didn't want to rock the boat in this new friendship she was building with Ruth. It wasn't quite the same between them as before; once they could say anything to one another, and now they were cautiously feeling their way, anxious not to annoy or offend. But it was a start. They met again and again over the Christmas break and discussed many things, especially the English degree they were both studying for.

'What do you want to do eventually? Still teach?' Ruth asked one day.

'I think so,' Janet replied. 'What about you?'

'I'm not sure,' Ruth said, 'but I think I'd like to have a shot at journalism. It's a tough world to get into for a woman, so I'm learning shorthand and typing too in the evenings, as it might give me a greater chance.'

Bert said he imagined Ruth would have a hard job to prove her worth. 'Not many women journalists,' he said, 'and yet it was often women who kept the papers going during the war, so there's no logical reason for it to be male-dominated. Good luck to the lass, if that's what she wants.'

Both Betty and Bert were pleased that the two girls seemed to be friends again, and they told Janet that Ruth was welcome at their house any time. The pair never seemed to run out of things to say, and Janet was glad to have someone to talk to about Claire's odd and worrying disappearance. Ruth had also discovered that Claire had left, but knew no more than that, and they discussed the whys and wherefores endlessly, both anxious about her safety.

The younger children took Ruth's reappearance in their stride. The twins were at any rate basking in the praise from the family at passing the first part of the eleven-plus, and it was hard to get them to do any more of the work Janet had prepared for them in the holidays. 'The second

426

part's harder,' she scolded, 'and you'll need to work for it.'

The twins grumbled, refused to settle and were unable to concentrate. They were delighted to see Ruth when she began visiting the Travers' house again, knowing that Janet's attention might be taken up by the friendship long enough for them both to slip away.

Sally regarded Ruth solemnly with her large blue eyes and asked, 'Why haven't you been to see us for such a long time?'

Both girls were embarrassed, not knowing how to answer. They began gabbling excuses about being busy, living away from home and the pressure of their university courses, but Sally patiently waited till they'd finished and then asked searchingly:

'Did you fall out?'

Janet wondered how her little sister just seemed to know things. She looked across at Ruth, and with a grin and a shrug admitted, 'Yes, Sally, yes we did.'

Sally looked from one to the other. She loved them both and had missed Ruth's presence, and yet had said nothing. She shook her head sadly as she remarked. 'That was rather silly of you, wasn't it, considering you're almost grown up?'

Janet burst out laughing as she put her arms around her sister and hugged her. Sally was unsure about why there was such hilarity, but she didn't mind being cuddled by Janet, which she considered her right anyway, and she put her arms around her big sister and gave her a kiss.

Ruth felt a sudden stab of envy. Janet's home

seemed so full of fun and laughter and noise, and though they all shouted and swore, she knew they cared for each other. Her home seemed sterile in comparison. She dreaded her grandmother returning home. She'd been bad enough before she broke her hip, and worse after Aaron's defiance, carping, demanding, finding fault. She'd blamed Joseph and Naomi for allowing their eldest son the freedom of living away from home in the first place. She'd insisted Joseph forbid the marriage, but he'd refused to do so, and she'd chided and ridiculed him until Naomi, goaded out of her customary respect and good manners, turned on her.

Now there was an uneasy peace, but no one was happy, Ruth thought, except perhaps Aaron and Lisa. She certainly wasn't. Her parents had little energy left for her, and desperate though she often was for companionship, she had always avoided her grandmother's company. She had made friends at Oxford, but not such good friends as Janet's flatmates seemed to be. Janet, despite her undoubted ability, had rejected both Oxford and Cambridge, much to Miss Phelps' chagrin. The school's success was judged by the pupils who gained a place at Oxford or Cambridge, but Janet had refused to consider either.

'I'd not fit in at either place,' she'd maintained, and despite all the pressure applied by the school she had not been moved in her decision. Ruth wished wistfully that she'd gone with Janet to Leicester University. It seemed to be a great deal more fun than Oxford.

'I'm so glad we're friends again,' she said on

their last night together, as Janet walked her to the bus stop. 'I often wanted to call on you, but I was afraid you wouldn't want to see me.'

'I was a bloody fool,' Janet said cheerfully. 'I shouldn't have spoken to either of you the way I did that day at Chloe's funeral.'

'You were upset,' Ruth said. 'I should have tried to see you again, or write to you. Your mom would have given me the address. But in the end I did nothing. I'm afraid I'm not as brave as you, Janet.'

'Forget it,' Janet said. 'We're friends again now, that's all that matters.'

'You'll write, won't you?'

'Of course,' Janet said. 'And you be sure to write back.'

And when she waved Ruth off on the bus, Janet went home with her heart lighter than it had been for some time.

Chapter Nineteen

The three girls were always buying things to make their flat more homely, but it was Shirley's parents, far richer than Lou's or Janet's, who made such a difference donating things they said they had no further use for. They'd taken to driving Shirley down in their car at the beginning of term or if she'd gone home for a weekend, and she seldom came in empty-handed.

'A set of pans Mum said we might find useful,' she'd say, or 'A large casserole dish Mum doesn't ever use.'

The fluffy pink bath set that looked rather incongruous in their cupboard of a bathroom appeared new to Janet but 'It's an old one,' Shirley assured her. 'It hasn't had much wear, because it was always in the guest bathroom.'

'Oh, the guest bathroom, of course,' Lou mocked in her plum-in-the-mouth accent, and the girls fell about laughing.

They took turns to cook and had tremendous fun trying out recipes on one another. They threw the odd party, or just invited friends round for the evening, but had strict rules on each girl having the place to herself one night a week, when the other two would guarantee to make themselves scarce. Shirley, after Janet's talk, had finished with Stuart and had a fling with a few others before settling with someone called Paul.

Janet knew that, although Lou and Shirley weren't actually sleeping with their boyfriends, they were going much further than she was prepared to go with Simon. She didn't have to ask them, as they still discussed things in great detail together. Simon couldn't understand her reluctance to go further, and sometimes she couldn't understand herself.

'Do you love him?' Lou asked one night.

'I *think* so.'

'Don't you know for sure?' Shirley said.

'No, not really,' Janet replied. 'How do you know if it's love or not? I loved Ben, I do know that. I couldn't think about anything else but him, day and night. I only had to see him to start trembling, and when he kissed me...'

'Yes?' Lou and Shirley said together, leaning forward. Janet gave a grin and said:

'Mind your own business.'

'Ooh, Janet,' complained Lou, 'as soon as it gets interesting you go all coy on us.'

'Anyway,' Shirley said loftily, 'that sounds like infatuation to me, not love.'

'You'd know all about it, of course.'

'Maybe not, but I suppose I am entitled to an opinion.'

'Oh, don't go all stuffy on me,' Janet complained.

'Stop arguing,' Lou commanded. 'Come on, Shirley, we're trying to establish if Simon's in with a chance. Now, Janet, how do you feel when Simon kisses you? And don't tell us to mind our own business, we're trying to help.'

Janet shrugged helplessly. 'It's all right, I

431

suppose,' she said. 'I mean, pleasant enough, but I don't hear a full orchestra playing or anything.'

'Don't tell me that happened with Ben, because I won't believe it,' said Shirley.

'Well, not exactly,' Janet said, 'but you know what I mean. And when he ... when we ... well, anyway, the earth doesn't move or anything.'

Lou fairly rocked with laughter. 'God, Janet, you are green,' she spluttered through her hilarity. 'It's not the earth that moves.'

There was no more sensible discussion after that, as one ribald comment followed another. It clarified nothing for Janet, but cheered her no end, and she was grateful for Lou and Shirley's friendship and sense of fun.

She went home for the Easter holidays and for the first time really missed Simon. She wondered if she was beginning to fall in love with him or whether he was just becoming a habit. She decided to test him on her home ground, and when he phoned one day, just after the holiday had begun, she asked him down for the weekend.

'Don't get excited,' Janet warned her mother. 'He is a boyfriend, but nothing special, just someone I go round with.'

'All right, love,' Betty said, but she was still as pleased as Punch that her Janet was asking a lad to stay. There had been no one since Ben, and that had worried Betty a little. It wasn't that Janet didn't seem to be having a good time, but both of her flatmates had steady boyfriends and Betty was glad there was someone on the horizon for her girl. She was determined that no one should spoil the weekend for her. She threatened the twins what she'd do if they misbehaved, but Janet, knowing that threats were useless on her young brothers, promised to give them the money to go to the cinema if they were good.

It went surprisingly well. Janet couldn't but be impressed at how calmly Simon took the Travers clan at mealtimes, which she often thought resembled feeding time at the zoo. Gran was there too, as she ate with Betty and the family most weekends anyway.

Eventually the talk got round to university and the course, and then the flat Janet shared with her friends. 'They've made it lovely,' Simon said to Bert. 'It's a pity you haven't seen it.'

'You've seen it then?' Bert almost snapped, and Simon realised from Bert's tone, and Janet's foot that had come into sharp contact with his ankle under the table, that he'd better be careful how he answered.

'Oh, a number of times,' he said breezily. 'Lou and Shirley and Janet are very popular girls, and they've thrown a number of very good parties.'

'Ah,' said Bert, who wasn't so worried about crowds at parties. It was the thought of what the young man – however nice he seemed – might do to his daughter alone in a flat that brought him out in a cold sweat. 'Our Janet's always enjoyed a good party. Maybe,' he added, turning to Janet, 'maybe we could come up and see this place after term starts. We could go one Saturday, just your mother and me?'

'Course you could,' Mrs McClusky said. 'I could look after the children.'

'We don't need looking after, Gran,' Conner said.

'No,' Noel added, 'we'd look after you instead, Gran, and our Sally.'

'I can look after myself,' Sally retorted. 'I'm nine now, not a baby any more.'

'You'll all do as your gran bids you,' Bert said, 'if we go at all, and we haven't decided yet.' He nodded at the twins and said, as a form of explanation to Simon. 'These two have been getting above themselves since they heard they've both passed their eleven-plus.'

'Dad!' The complaint from Noel and Conner was simultaneous, but before Bert could reply. Simon was saying:

'That's great. Congratulations to the pair of you,' and went on to tell them about his own eleven-plus success and the fun he'd had and scrapes he'd got into at his grammar school. He soon had the whole family laughing.

Later, as Simon and Janet walked arm in arm to the pictures, Janet said, 'Thanks for coming today and praising Noel and Conner like you did. They're little devils at times, but I'm beginning to think that a lot of what they did when they were little was to get attention.'

'They're okay. I think I was much the same.' Simon told her. 'They're just lads, that's all. Your family's all right, Janet.'

'I'm not apologising for them,' Janet snapped, stung by the implied criticism. 'I'm just explaining. It's easy to get ignored in a big family.'

'Ssh.' Simon said, raising his hands in a gesture

of surrender. 'Peace. I'm a friend not an enemy.' His words brought back an echo of the past, something Ben had said about not being the enemy, something that concerned Claire and Chloe. The vague memory disturbed Janet, so that when Simon attempted to draw her into his arms to kiss her, she wriggled free.

'What's up?' he said, and she shrugged.

'Nothing, I don't want to be late for the film, that's all.'

Simon gave a sigh. Sometimes he couldn't get to grips with Janet. He seemed to be going one step forward and two back all the time. He wanted to come clean, to tell her how much she meant to him, and wondered if he'd ever be able to tell her. He felt his heart thud against his ribs and sighed because he knew he could say nothing, for if he spoke those words he might lose her. So he tucked his arm inside hers and they made their way to the cinema in silence.

Janet thought it felt terribly grown up to have your parents for a meal in your own place. Everything had been wonderful, from the minute she'd picked them both up at the station in a taxi. Bert had been pressed into a suit and was hot and uncomfortable in it, for although it was only May, the day was sultry and warm. He'd also been warned about swearing.

'Don't you be bad-mouthing and letting our Janet down in front of her posh friends,' Betty had warned. 'And don't you dare take off your jacket and show your braces, and I don't care how hot you are.'

So Bert had sat in Janet's flat prickly with the heat, feeling his shirt collar tightening on his sweating neck with the unaccustomed tie and tried to make polite conversation with Lou and Shirley. They'd agreed to stay in for a little while to meet Bert and Betty and then go off and do their own thing so that Janet could have some time alone with her parents.

Despite the fact that Bert liked Lou and Shirley, he breathed a sigh of relief when they'd gone, for Janet immediately said, 'Take your jacket off, Dad, it looks like a straitjacket on you, and your tie if you like, and loosen your top shirt button, I can see you are sweating like a pig.'

Bert did as his daughter advised, with a smug look at his wife. Janet was a bit of all right, he decided, and he didn't need to be so particular about his language either, for she wouldn't faint from shock if she heard him swearing. She was, after all, more than used to it.

Bert and Betty were very proud of their Janet's flat. 'You have it really nice, pet,' Betty commented more than once. 'Well, it isn't just mine, remember,' Janet said, 'and Shirley's parents have helped a lot.'

'Are they well off, lass?'

'Oh, yes,' Janet said, 'but they're the sort of rich who don't mind spreading it about a bit, and they're very nice.'

'Well, their daughter seemed pleasant enough,' Bert conceded. He patted his stomach, for they'd just eaten, and commented, 'And you're a decent little cook as well, almost as good as your mother.'

Later, as they were about to leave, Betty hugged her and said, 'It's smashing, pet, better than I thought, and it's good to see it. Now when I think of you, I'll be able to place you in your bedroom, or kitchen, or whatever. It helps somehow.'

Bert didn't say it helped him too, or tell her it had been bad enough for him she'd left home to go to university. He thought the hostel had sounded a little strict, and the caretaker a battleaxe, but at least while Janet was there he felt she was being looked after. If he was totally honest, he knew that a woman like Mrs McPhearson would not tolerate any sort of carry-on in her house, and therefore it had been a bit of a shock to him when Janet said she wanted to find a flat of her own.

His mind had worked overtime. 'What d'you think she wants a flat for, Betty?' he'd asked.

'Well,' Betty had said, 'I expect she needs her own space more. She's matured in the year away from home. It's probably time for a change.'

'What if she ... she takes men up?' Bert said tentatively.

'What if she does?' Betty said. 'Our Janet does know right from wrong, and she is sharing with two other girls.'

'Well, I know that, but...'

'Look, Bert, you've got to face it, she's growing up. She might take her young men up to the flat but so what? We were always looking for lonely spots to do our courting.'

'Yes, but they were bloody hard to find, weren't they, girl?' Bert burst out, knowing that often it was the lack of privacy that had kept his feelings in check. He was tortured, at first, by the thought that his Janet had all the privacy she wanted.

But now he'd seen her flat. She'd been delighted they'd come, pleased as a child to point out the things they'd bought for the place and show them around. He'd met Janet's flatmates and knew them to be nice, pleasant girls from good homes. It set his mind at rest, but if he told Janet any of it she'd be angry with him. So, when he caught her eye over the top of Betty's head, he smiled, as if at his wife's foolishness, and leant over to kiss his daughter goodbye.

All through the late summer of 1956, the news was dominated by what was happening in Egypt, where President Nasser had nationalised the Suez Canal. 'He could hold the world to ransom over this if he liked,' Bert said. 'If he cuts off the oil supply.'

'Well, I'm just glad our Duncan has finished his national service,' declared Betty.

'That won't save him if this blows up,' Bert said. 'If there's call-up, he'll be one of the first to go.'

Janet looked at her mother's stricken face and wished her father had kept quiet. Nothing definite had happened by the time she returned to college, though most thinking people knew that the world was hovering on the edge of a crisis.

Shirley's father struggled up the stairs with a large box the day he returned his daughter to the flat. It was a box that Janet had seen only once before on Coronation Day and could hardly believe her eyes. 'A television!' she shrieked. 'You've never actually got a television set?'

'It was supposed to be for my birthday,' Shirley said, 'but Daddy said I ought to have it now and installed here, so that we can keep up with what's happening in the news.'

The television was marvellous and had the commercial channel as well as the BBC. They were all watching it when they heard the news of the insurrection in Hungary which began with the destruction of the hated Stalin's monument in the centre of Budapest. The Hungarians had few weapons but those they pilfered, and no trained armies; just Molotov cocktails and great determination. The world seemed to be holding its breath, and the occupants of the flat, and many friends who'd crowd in every evening, watched the patchy smuggled newsreel footage almost in disbelief.

Danny Benedicti was a name they heard often, as the charismatic leader urged his comrades, some only teenagers, to cause disarray among the Russian troops. Then, at the end of October, British, French and Israeli troops invaded Egypt. The general opinion was that it was just a small skirmish and Egypt would soon be brought to heel. Meanwhile, Hungary had won a wonderful victory, for on the last day of October the Russian tanks and troops rolled out of Budapest.

The joy of the Hungarian people was infectious. They could barely believe they'd beaten a superpower and a carnival atmosphere existed in the streets. Their prime minister declared Hungary to be a neutral country.

However, at the same time, Egypt's military targets were bombed by British and French aircraft, and it was obvious that the skirmish was escalating. Britain prepared for all-out war, troops were on alert and reservists, including Duncan, received their call-up papers.

The flat was crowded every evening at nine to watch the news, then they'd drink endless cups of coffee as they discussed the issues. 'Thank goodness that at least Hungary's problems are over,' Shirley said one evening in early November.

'I'm not so sure,' Janet said.

'Don't be silly, they've won,' Lou said. 'The Russians have pulled out.'

'Yes,' Janet said, 'but if I were in charge of Russia now, this would be the time to counter-attack, wouldn't it, with the world's weapons and troops concentrated in Egypt? And Dad always said that Russians weren't to be trusted.'

'Janet Travers and her father, the perpetual pessimists,' Simon said with a chuckle. He pulled her on to the settee beside him and advised, 'Stop worrying about the whole world and worry about me for a change.'

But over the next few evenings, it was obvious from the scrappy news items smuggled out of Eastern Europe that all was not well, although it was some days before the world knew the scale of the carnage. They learned that 150,000 troops and 3,000 tanks had been sent into Hungary to quell the embryonic revolution, and a reign of terror ensued, with people gunned down indiscriminately as they queued for basic foodstuffs and not even Red Cross vehicles given immunity.

The Western world urged the Hungarians to hold on, but could offer no support. Anthony Eden appeared on television to explain Britain's position and why it was necessary to invade Egypt. Everyone knew there was nothing to spare for Hungary and that the people hadn't a chance. Refugees poured out of the city and thousands of people, many of them only children, disappeared altogether.

Meanwhile Duncan was preparing to leave for Egypt. French and British paratroopers had been flown in, and their navies had attacked by sea, when President Eisenhower intervened and a ceasefire was agreed upon. Janet was glad that a major catastrophe had been averted and Duncan was safe, but no one could be really happy when they saw the pictures of the Hungarian refugees, many of whom reached Britain, cold and destitute.

Janet was frustrated by her own helplessness and was glad of Simon's comforting arms around her and the feeling of safety they gave her. She suddenly felt stifled by the flat and the noise of everyone in it. She knew they would linger for hours and talk on and on about a desperate situation that all the words in the world couldn't alter. Simon was beginning to recognise many of the moods that he read in Janet's expressive face and eyes, and taking her hand, they escaped from the crowded flat and walked the damp and cold November streets together.

Janet had been badly affected by what she'd seen, and much of the abrasive shell she wrapped around herself had been softened by the tears she'd shed. She welcomed Simon's presence and didn't object when his arm tightened around her, nor did she say anything when he kissed her passionately in the partial privacy of a shop doorway. She responded ardently, and perhaps because her emotions had already been touched in a deep and special way that evening, she became violently aroused by him. She'd been affected by his lovemaking for some time, but never with the intensity she felt then. She wanted him to make love to her now, urgently, and it was a revelation about her feelings for him. Had the flat been empty, she might have suggested going back.

Simon, though not privy to Janet's thoughts, was aware of something happening between them, some spark that had been missing previously. He felt Janet trembling in his arms and decided that if he didn't speak of his feelings now, he might never do so. 'Janet,' he began, 'I love you. I think I always have, ever since the housewarming, when I promised to bring that book round just so I could see you again.'

'Oh, Simon.'

'How ... how do you feel about me?'

Janet didn't know how to answer, for she'd scarcely come to terms with the new, fragile feelings she had just become aware of. She pulled his head down and kissed him with a passion that surprised herself. The strong yearnings in her body reminded her of her romance with Ben, and she tried to push her memories away and concentrate on the man who'd just told her he loved her.

When, eventually, they broke apart, they were both breathless. 'Oh, Janet,' Simon said, holding her close, 'God, Janet, I love you, and I want you so badly.'

'I love you too, Simon,' Janet said, and she meant it. 'And I want you too.'

Simon gasped, scarcely able to believe he'd heard right. Janet, while aware of the change in their relationship, knew that to agree to sleep with him was a giant step forward, and yet she couldn't just keep refusing Simon, especially when her own body was crying out too. But first, she thought, in all fairness she had to tell him about Ben.

She began the tale in the flat much later, when they'd eventually made their way home. Most people had drifted away and Lou and Shirley took themselves off to bed, recognising Janet's need to be alone with Simon. She made coffee and they sat on the floor before the fire, and she told him about Ben Hayman.

Simon understood much more about Janet and her reluctance to commit herself to anyone again as he listened to the tale of Ben Hayman's betrayal. He saw the hurt that lurked in her eyes still. He wanted to kiss it away for her, he wanted to lie beside her and make love on the rug before the fire. He could feel the stirrings of Janet's body against his and guessed she felt the same, but both were aware of the two girls sleeping only a few feet away, the other side of the paper-thin walls of the flat.

'How do you feel about this Ben Hayman now?' Simon asked when Janet had finished speaking. 'I mean, you were hurt by what he did and perhaps angry, but do you still feel anything for him now?'

'He was... Ben was in a different life,' Janet said. She couldn't tell this man who loved her that she still felt there was something between her and Ben. Anyway, she reasoned, maybe there isn't. I was so upset at Chloe's funeral my emotions were bound to be mixed up.

Should she tell Simon all this when she couldn't understand it herself? What purpose would it serve, and did it really matter if she still felt something for Ben? He was married and living in America. So she smiled at Simon and said, 'He means nothing to me, Simon, nothing at all. It's you I love.'

In the following weeks, till the term ended for Christmas, Janet often felt there was some sort of conspiracy to save her immortal soul from damnation, for she and Simon never seemed able to be alone at all for more than a few minutes at a time. The rules about each girl having the flat to herself one night a week had gone by the board. In the flurry of Christmas end-of-term, when essay deadlines and lectures had to be juggled with the parties that someone always seemed to be throwing and a flat that never seemed to empty of people, finding time for themselves was impossible.

By the time term was breaking up, both Simon and Janet were getting desperate. Their lack of privacy and subsequent curtailed lovemaking had increased their desire for one another, and Janet knew something would have to be arranged before she went home for Christmas.

Janet told her parents that term finished two days later than it actually did, and she'd barely waved Lou and Shirley off before Simon, as arranged, was knocking on the door.

They thought it would be easy. The kisses that Janet had once described as 'pleasant' now lifted her to heights of excitement, and their subsequent lovemaking had become more ardent. But this had been in stolen moments, the excitement increased by the small amount of time they had available and the possibility of discovery.

But they lay on the bed, wide-eyed and embarrassed, in an empty flat with no one to disturb them and felt almost shy with one another. Janet, modestly clad in a nightie, said, 'Shall I turn the light out?'

Simon, in borrowed pyjamas beside her, answered, 'D'you usually have the light out?'

Janet stared at him. 'Of course I do to go to sleep. I don't know what I do about making love, because I've never done it here before. D'you think I'm in the habit of taking men to bed?' The ridiculousness of the situation wiped out her embarrassment and she began to giggle.

'What's so funny?' Simon asked.

'We are,' Janet said. 'Two liberated college students at the very end of 1956 and we're behaving like we're at a Sunday school outing.'

She snapped off the light, leapt into bed and kissed Simon, long, lingering and hungrily. After that it was all right and basic instincts took over, and she gave herself up to the pleasure so exquisite they both cried out and then lay back, spent, on the bed.

Do I really love him? Janet asked herself later. Or is it just that my body wants sex? She lay wide awake listening to Simon's even breathing beside her, trying to marshal her thoughts. She wondered if it were normal to have had sex with two men by the age of twenty. She knew that Lou and Shirley would say she shouldn't think about things so much. She almost wished they were here; they would have laughed and joked her out of her doubts.

But despite the doubts, Janet enjoyed her two days with Simon, just the pair of them in the flat. She was sorry when it was time to pack to go home, though the pull of the family had made her anxious to see everyone again. She put her arms around Simon. 'Oh, I'm going to miss you,' she said with a sigh.

'Let me come and see you?' Simon said.

'I don't know,' Janet said uncertainly.

'What is it? I got on all right with your family last time.'

'I know, it's just...' It was such a family time at the Travers house, and by including Simon Janet knew she would be placing their relationship on a more intimate level. But then it *was* more intimate. She loved him, she knew that now, and he said he loved her. He would be looking for commitment – marriage – he was that sort of man. That frightened Janet a bit, but when they married he would be part of her family too.

'Yes,' she said, 'yes, I'd like you to come.'

'When?'

'Give me a couple of days at home,' Janet said, 'and let your parents see something of you first, and then I'd be delighted for you to come.'

Simon was so happy and excited by the new feeling between them he felt he would burst, and he crushed Janet to him in a passionate embrace. She responded ardently to the man she had just discovered she loved with all her heart.

Janet went round to Ruth's that Christmas holiday as soon as she decently could. She was particularly interested in seeing her as Ruth had mentioned in her last letter that Ben thought he'd caught sight of Richard Carter at a conference in America. Janet wanted to know if there was any more news.

But Ruth couldn't enlighten her further. 'I wrote and asked Ben all about it,' she said, 'but he hadn't been aware that Claire had virtually disappeared without trace since the day of the funeral, or he might have tried harder to catch hold of Richard. He thought he saw him walk out of the hall they were in and assumed he'd be at the bar, but there was no trace of him, and though he asked a few people, no one recognised the name. He said it might not have been Richard, he could have been mistaken, and if it was him, he'd aged a lot.'

'Did he say how?'

'Well, he only caught a glimpse of his face, but he said his hair at the sides is grey.'

'But he's not old,' protested Janet.

'No,' Ruth agreed. She paused a minute and then asked: 'Do you think Claire was sick, Janet,

I mean nervous collapse type of sick?'

'I think that's the only explanation for her virtually dropping off the planet with no trace,' Janet said. 'Otherwise I'm sure she would have contacted me or you – someone at least. I think Chloe's death pushed her over the edge. God, I was upset enough, I can't even begin to imagine Claire's pain.'

'Well, now Ben knows, he'll keep an eye out for Richard – well, for either of them, of course.'

'Yes, but he's unlikely to see them, isn't he?' Janet said. 'If we look at it all realistically, for a start, America is a big place, and we don't even know if they're there or not.'

'It's a chance, that's all,' Ruth said. 'The conference was on mental health, which is the field they're all interested in. Ben travels all over America now and he says that in time he might be coming to Europe.'

Janet didn't answer. She didn't want to talk or think about Ben Hayman, but Ruth continued, 'He works really hard, but then he hasn't got anything else. His marriage is a sham, Janet. Therese's left, or virtually left. She's moved herself, baby and nurse to her parents' house. Ben rattles round in an apartment in New York. He says nothing, of course, but you pick it up in his letters.'

Janet snapped, tight-lipped, 'I'm not interested, Ruth, I don't see why you should think I am. He's not the only one with a less than ideal marriage, but he has to make the best of it like everyone else. You feel sorry for him if you like, but don't ask me to, because I save my pity and

448

sympathy for those who deserve it, and that's not Mr Ben Hayman.'

Ruth was sorry she'd upset her friend, who was obviously still hurt and angry over what had happened. She decided to keep off the subject of her brother and his awful marriage altogether. 'I'm sorry,' she said, 'really. I wasn't thinking. I know that what he did to you was terrible. He must have been seeing Therese at the same time as going out with you.

'Yes, and sleeping with both of us.'

Ruth's mouth dropped open. 'You slept with him?'

'What do you think?' Janet said. 'I was crazy about him, and despite what you thought, we were going to get married. He'd bought me a ring and everything, only I had to wear it on a chain around my neck.'

'Have you still got it?'

'No, I sent it back,' Janet said. 'It's probably adorning Therese Steinaway's finger now.' She shrugged and said, 'Life goes on. I have someone else now, have you?'

'Sort of. He's a reporter on the Evening Mail and I met him last holidays when I wrote and asked if I could work on the paper in a voluntary capacity, just to see if I liked it. The paper was fine, Phillip was gorgeous, but he has yet to realise how ravishing and irresistible I am.'

'I'm a bit further on than that,' Janet said, but didn't elaborate further.

Later, in bed, what Ruth had said concerning Ben and his marriage kept crowding her mind as she tried to settle to sleep. She wondered if

Therese was really as bad as she was painted. Although she owed the girl no favours, she found it hard to imagine that the faults were all on one side. Therese had been halfway to being a doctor when she left medical school, she reminded herself, and could probably have specialised in America as Ben had, especially as they had a nanny for the baby. That wouldn't, of course, have suited the chauvinistic Ben, but perhaps Therese's frustrations at being unable to continue with her career might be at the root of her dissatisfaction in her marriage, thought Janet.

Lou and Shirley were aware almost immediately of the changed relationship between Janet and Simon, but hesitated to tease Janet about it. Janet was grateful for their sensitivity, for she and Simon were still feeling their way. They had grown much closer after their two days together after term had ended, and Simon had spent most of his Christmas holiday at the Travers' house.

They spent much of that spring term talking together, finding out about one another and their views on things. Simon had no objection to Janet taking a conversion course in order to teach after she finished at university. 'I'll be doing my national service anyway,' he said. 'By the time I'm out, you'll have finished your probationary year and we can get married.'

'I'm not sure I'm ready for marriage yet,' Janet said. 'Don't rush me.'

Simon saw the panic in her eyes and kissed her lips gently. 'No rush, sweetheart,' he said. 'I'm not suggesting it immediately, it's just something to think about.' And Janet promised she would think about it.

Simon, Lou and Shirley were invited to Janet's twenty-first birthday party, which fortunately fell in the Easter holidays. Janet felt more confident about her friends now, and the very ones she hadn't wanted at Duncan's, she was determined to have at her own.

It was the best party she could ever remember, and everyone agreed. One of the most important things was that Shirley and Lou got on so well with everyone. Janet had thought there might have been some resentment, almost jealousy, from Ruth when she was introduced to them, but there was none. Later, Ruth explained to Janet that she'd described the two girls so well and often she felt she'd known them all her life.

The others felt the same way. Lou told her afterwards that she would have known her Auntie Breda anywhere, and her gran was just as she'd described. Even their boyfriends, Michael and Paul, blended well into the company. Ruth had obviously made her conquest, for as she introduced Janet to Phillip Williams, her reporter boyfriend who she said worked on the local paper, she gave her a huge wink.

Much, much later, Simon and Janet waved their friends off before walking round to Sarah McClusky's, where they were both spending the night, though Simon would be sleeping on the couch.

'I can't believe it,' Gran said for the umpteenth time that night. 'Twenty-one, our Janet.'

Janet smiled and passed Sarah the cup of cocoa

she insisted on drinking every night. 'Yes, Gran, twenty-one. I can do what I like now,' she said.

'You always did, bonny lass,' Mrs McClusky said with a wheezy laugh.

She looked from her granddaughter to the young man across the table and knew she was in the way. They'd be polite as long as she cared to stop, but really they could easily do without her presence.

'Well,' she said, heaving herself to her feet, 'you'll not be wanting me hanging around spoiling your fun. I'll be away to my bed.'

Janet protested, as Sarah had known she would, but it was a courtesy gesture.

'Nay, Janet,' she said, 'you'll not believe it, maybe, but I was young and courting myself once. It might be a while ago, but I remember enough to know I'd not want my old gran sitting between myself and Sean – God rest him – the whole night long.'

'She's a character, your gran,' Simon said, when the door had closed behind the old lady.

'She's lovely,' Janet agreed.

'And is she broad-minded?' Simon asked with a sly grin. 'Would she be up to me sneaking to your bedroom, or you sneaking down to share my couch?'

'Forget it,' Janet said with mock severity. 'I'm locking my door firmly against drunken, marauding students, bent on rape and the odd pillage, and I don't roll around on a couch with anyone.'

'I'm not asking you to do it with anyone, foolish girl,' Simon said. 'I'm asking you to do it with your beloved.'

'Ah, Simon,' Janet said softly, and put her arms around his neck and kissed him. Then, hand in hand, they moved into the living room and sat cuddled on the settee.

Simon took Janet's hand and said, 'I have something special for you.' He drew a ring box from his pocket. 'I had to give it to you when we were alone.'

Janet gasped when she saw the sapphire glinting in the light, surrounded by tiny diamonds set in a golden band. 'Oh, I couldn't, I couldn't,' she was crying. 'Simon, it must have cost you a fortune. I couldn't accept it and I don't want to be engaged yet. I'm not ready.'

'It's not an engagement ring, and it cost me nothing,' Simon said. 'Let me explain. I was asking my mother what I could give you for your twenty-first as I wanted something decent and I'm a fairly impoverished student, and she produced the ring.'

'Your mother's ring!' Janet cried.

'Not in the way you mean, no,' Simon said. 'It's a family ring and has been passed on through the eldest son for ... oh, I don't know how many generations.'

'That's what I mean. It's too valuable.'

'My mother asked me if you were special to me,' Simon said, ignoring Janet's outburst. 'I said yes and told her I loved you, and she said that the ring is given as a token of regard, and is later replaced by an engagement ring when the girl has accepted a marriage proposal.'

'But, Simon...'

'Please take it,' Simon said. 'I can't return it to my mother now, and it won't fit her anyway. I had it altered for you.'

'How?' Janet asked in astonishment. She took the ring out of the box and slipped it on to the third finger of her right hand. It fitted perfectly. 'How did you know the size?' she asked again.

Simon laughed at the look of surprise on Janet's face and said: 'Shirley lent me a ring that she said you'd borrowed a few times, and we went from there.'

'So they're in on this too?'

'Well, yes,' Simon agreed, 'but don't make it sound like some dastardly plot.' He took Janet's hand in his and said, 'You will accept it, won't you?'

'Well, I don't know,' Janet said. 'I suppose, but I'm not ready for commitment yet, not even an engagement. I seem to have been studying most of my life and I haven't finished yet, and then I want to live a bit before settling down.'

'I know,' Simon said, 'and I understand that, but in a few months we'll be apart from one another. I just want to stake my claim, I suppose, before I leave, and tell you how I feel about you, and while you wear the ring, you'll never doubt it. We can write to each other and see each other when I get any leave, then, when I'm finally demobbed, we'll talk again.'

'I'm a bit scared of marriage, Simon,' Janet said, and gave a shudder.

'You won't be in two years,' Simon assured her. 'You just want to do something with your life first, that's all. I can live with that.'

Janet thought it astonishing that Simon should understand her so much better than Ben had, and realised that it was because Simon had really listened to her and how she felt. 'Thank you, Simon,' she said. 'It's a beautiful ring and I'll be proud to wear it.'

Simon was relieved. He hadn't been at all sure that Janet would accept it. He loved her very much, and it was only the thought of the old lady upstairs that forced him to put the brakes on his lovemaking.

They eventually broke apart, breathless. Janet was aware that if she stayed downstairs with Simon much longer, the inevitable would happen, so she reluctantly kissed him and made her way upstairs. Simon gave a sigh, wrapped himself in the blankets left ready and settled himself on the settee.

Chapter Twenty

Janet obtained a first-class honours degree, but her parents didn't notice how elated she was about it, nor how hard she'd had to work. They were used to Janet's successes by then and they said it was only to be expected. Lou and Shirley had done nearly as well, and had previously decided to take the conversion course to teach like Janet. 'Daddy would love me to work in the family firm,' Shirley said, 'but I'd hate it, it would just be like I'd never left home, his little girl again. Anyway, I want to do something for myself for once, and I've always liked children.'

'I agree,' Lou said. 'Anyway, I don't see people lining up to employ graduates and I really can't think of what I want to do with my degree now I've got it, and a teaching certificate at least fits you to do a decent job, and I've always liked telling people what to do.'

'We've noticed,' Janet and Shirley said in unison, and they all burst out laughing. Janet was pleased with her flatmates' decisions and glad they would have another year together. She knew neither Lou, nor Shirley had the same burning desire to teach that she had, but then there had never been a Claire Wentworth in their lives and they'd probably make more than adequate teachers just the same.

She wondered if her mother was disappointed

with her decision to stay in Leicester for at least another year. Possibly Betty would have preferred her to take a job locally and live back at her gran's, but Janet knew that that part of her life was over and she'd probably never live on the Pype Hayes estate ever again, except perhaps for holidays. It was sad, but there it was, her life was going in a different direction.

But Betty had accepted that years ago before Janet had even begun university and she was anyway more concerned about the relationship between her and Simon. After all, passing exams was all very well, but it wasn't what life was all about. Now even Duncan had decided to settle down, getting engaged to his girlfriend Frances just weeks before, and Betty asked her daughter if she and Simon had made any plans. It had been in her mind ever since Simon had given Janet the ring after her twenty-first birthday party. To Betty's mind, there was only one reason for a man to give a lass a ring, and for all Janet's claim that it was not an engagement ring and because of that she wore it on her right hand, a ring was a ring and it meant something between a couple. 'I was just wondering,' she said to Janet, 'now you're finished and everything.'

'But I've not finished, have I?' Janet said. 'I have another year and Simon's got nearly two years' national service to complete.'

'I know all that. I just wondered if there's some sort of understanding between you.'

'Oh, Mom,' Janet burst out impatiently. 'Don't rush me. I do love Simon and we enjoy being together. Can't you leave it there?'

'Let the girl be,' Bert said firmly. He wasn't keen for his daughter to get hitched to anyone just yet. He knew the day would come when another man would be more important than him in Janet's life, but no way did he want to rush her into anything.

Betty said nothing more, but she was worried. Janet had said she loved Simon, but wasn't keen to marry him yet. She hoped she wasn't going to suggest living together like some youngsters did these days, or she'd get a bad name for herself.

By the end of September, Simon was in uniform, Sally had started in the eleven-plus class at Paget Road School. Ruth had begun as a cub reporter on the *Evening Mail* and Janet and her friends were beginning their conversion year at teacher's training college.

There was a desperate shortage of teachers throughout the country at that time and many certified teachers were taken on for just two years. It was strange for graduates to take the conversion course, but the three girls held firm that this was what they wanted to do. It fulfilled Janet's burning ambitions, but she knew as well that a degree was not a passport to meaningful employment, either.

Teaching, however, was an area in which women could do well, for everyone knew looking after children was a woman's job, and with the national shortage there would be plenty of work for them when they left college. That's what Janet needed, a chance to earn and try to repay her parents for all the years they'd given her, often at the expense of others.

The training college was situated in disused ARP offices on Humberstone Road, further away from their flat than the university. The college had its own hostel-style accommodation, but Janet, Lou and Shirley rejected it out of hand. They decided, despite the distance, that the freedom they had in the flat was worth it and they elected to stay where they were.

Janet, like her friends, found the training course very exacting and there was little free time. She was to find it even harder during the weeks of teaching practice that would finish just before the college broke up for Christmas. However, as she'd promised Sally years ago, she went back at the weekends to help her with the extra work for her eleven-plus, and despite the fact that Sally was a bright and receptive child, by the time the Christmas term drew to a close, Janet was beginning to feel the strain.

Bert and Betty both noticed how drawn she appeared, though she told them she was fine when they asked. She hated fuss and was glad she was now living with her gran, who was so pleased to have company in the house again she failed to see how worn out Janet was.

Bert was always glad to see his daughter come home. He missed talking over the items in the news with her. Although Duncan was turning into a better mate than he'd ever thought possible at one time, it was Janet who'd always had an opinion about things. Sometimes they didn't agree, but still Bert valued another viewpoint.

The next evening he brought up the news

459

about the satellite that the Americans had failed to launch. 'It could be sabotage,' he said. 'I mean, these sputniks of the Russians went up all right.'

'It's not the same thing, Dad.'

'Maybe not, but what do them Russians want with sputniks in space anyway, except to spy on us and the States. Bloody sods, the lot of them. And an inter-ballistic missile – now what the bleeding hell's that when it's at home? It don't sound too friendly a bugger to me.'

'Bert, for goodness' sake!'

'What?' Bert snapped at Betty. 'I suppose I can say what I like in my own bleeding house?'

Betty gave a sniff. 'It's not nice, and especially not in front of our Duncan's young lady.' Frances flushed bright red and Duncan put his arm around her.

'She don't mind, Ma,' he said. He didn't know why his mother bothered trying to check his dad. He'd always been the same and it meant nothing.

'What do you make of it all, Janet?' Bert asked.

Janet gave an impish grin and said: 'What do I make of what, the sputniks or your swearing?'

'The sputniks, you cheeky bugger,' Bert said, and everyone burst out laughing.

When it was quieter again Janet said, 'I don't think they're spying, Dad. It's a kind of race between the Americans and the Russians, isn't it?'

Bert stroked his chin and conceded, 'You could be right. People say eventually we'll have a man walking on the moon. Seems fantastic.'

'Damn foolishness if you ask me,' Betty said. 'Why would anyone in their right mind want to go up there?'

'I suppose because it's there, Mom,' Janet said. 'After all, that's what that mountaineer once said when someone asked why he wanted to climb dangerous mountains like Everest.'

'There's none left to beat now,' Duncan said. 'Everest was scaled in '53.'

'And they say there's no islands left undiscovered,' Janet said. 'I suppose the moon is the next place to explore. But it does sound incredible that people might actually land and walk about on the golden ball that hangs in the sky.'

'It'll never happen,' Betty said firmly, but Janet thought it probably would.

'I'd rather people concentrated their energies on finding out about the moon and not crushing small nations who try to protest about being controlled by a superpower,' Bert said.

Janet knew Bert was thinking of the Hungarian rebellion. It had affected him badly. 'I mean,' he went on, 'I spent six bleeding years fighting Hitler's army, and for what? He'd goosestepped his way into Austria and annihilated all the Jews he could find, but we did nothing. It was only when he attacked Poland that we got involved, and then, when it was all over, we let Stalin stamp all over us, annexing Eastern Europe, including Poland, and did bugger all about it.'

'What would you have us do, Bert?' Betty said angrily. 'Have everyone fight Russia after six bloody years of fighting Germany? Mothers and wives would have something to say about that. I know I would. Don't you think losing two brothers and risking another one and my hus-

461

band wasn't a big enough price to pay?'

Betty usually took little or no part in discussions, and everyone was silent now, watching her. Janet knew her mother was perilously near tears, but she went on, not so angry now, and looking directly at Bert.

'I saw you go off in '39 waving and cheering like you were off to some carnival. Everyone was saying it'd be over by Christmas and they'd beaten the Jerries once and they'd do it again. Well, it weren't over by Christmas and I saw some of those who came back, blind, injured, missing arms or legs or shell-shocked. I saw ordinary people trapped under rubble in the blitz, often crushed or blown to bits, and those who had their homes bombed from under them. They often had nothing but what they stood up in, and nowhere to turn either.' She shook her head at Bert and went on, 'There's no glory in war, nor solutions either. We've already had two world wars and that's two too many. We can't go on telling people all over the world how to run their countries and declaring war if they don't agree. No right-minded person wants that.'

Janet listened to her mother, amazed, and realised that Betty had had as bad a war as her father in her own way, though she'd never said much about it until now. She knew that her dad, for all his bluster, would agree with all Betty had said. He'd told Janet often enough of the carnage of war, and had only fought to try and ensure that she and Duncan and the others would grow up in a safer world. She didn't know if it was much safer for all the fighting and hardship

462

they'd endured, and was feeling quite depressed as she made her way to her grandmother's house later that evening.

She wished Simon was there – he would have made her laugh, he was good company – but he had no leave due yet. She was surprised how much she was missing him. Desperate for company, she called at Ruth's the following evening.

Ruth surveyed her friend with concern. 'You look really tired,' she said.

'Thanks,' Janet said sarcastically.

'Well, you do,' Ruth insisted. 'I'm surprised no one else has noticed.'

Janet groaned. 'Mom has,' she said. 'I keep telling her not to fuss. The point is, I am tired. The last four weeks of term we had teaching practice, which is really wearing, and then every weekend I've been coming home to help Sally prepare for the eleven-plus like Claire did for me.' She glanced at Ruth, gave a sigh and went on, 'I don't mind, I mean, I always said I'd be there for her, but it couldn't have come at a worse time for me. I can hardly let Mom and Dad know that, though.'

Ruth could see Janet's point of view and said so. 'Have you told Simon?' she asked.

'No, he's dead homesick as it is,' Janet said. 'I try to cheer him up in my letters and he's only got a few days' leave over Christmas, so I'm not going to fill one of them up moaning.'

'I see,' Ruth said in mock indignation. 'You don't mind complaining to me, though.'

'Of course not,' Janet said. 'You're a friend.

463

Simon – well, he's a mere man,' and the two laughed together as they hadn't done for some time. Janet in particular felt a lot better and she was able to talk to Ruth of other things, like the outing to see *The King and I* with Sally and the twins.

'Sally and I loved it,' Janet said. 'If I'd have allowed it, she'd have sung all the way home. Conner and Noel thought it was deadly boring. They're into rock and roll, and Elvis Presley. I like that myself too, but their renderings of "Rock around the Clock" and "Heartbreak Hotel" are guaranteed to put the keenest fan off.'

'How old are they now?' Ruth asked.

'Thirteen in January,' Janet said. 'They consider themselves big men now, nearly teenagers.' She stopped and said, 'I remember when I first heard the word teenager. It came from America, I think.'

'Most things did,' Ruth said.

'Yes, including GIs and nylons, according to my aunt,' Janet said with a laugh. She looked across at Ruth and asked: 'Are you still seeing what's-his-name?'

'Phillip, yes, I am.'

'Hasn't he got to disappear to do his national service?' Janet asked.

'He's done it,' Ruth said, 'he's twenty-five.'

'Is he?' Janet said in surprise. 'A mature man, eh, Ruth? He didn't look it, I must say.'

'Must be his boyish charm,' Ruth said with a smile, then the smile slid from her face and she said more seriously, 'I'm spending Christmas with him at his parents' house.'

'Is he Jewish then?'

'No,' Ruth said.

'But...'

Ruth said, 'It's my life and I'm choosing how I'm going to live it. I can't bring him home. You've met my grandmother, and she's getting worse. He's been for a few meals and met my parents, and they like him and he likes them. But I can't ask him to stay at my house in the middle of a festival we don't even celebrate.'

'I suppose not.'

'And his parents want to see something of him at Christmas. It seemed the logical thing to ask me to go too.'

'Did your parents say you could?'

'I didn't ask them,' Ruth said. 'I told them I was going. They're so cut up about what's happening to Ben, they're letting me run my own life.'

In case Ruth should again start relating the saga of Ben versus Therese, sprinkled liberally with Papa Steinaway, Janet broke in quickly, 'Simon is spending Christmas with us and staying for the party Christmas night. He'll spend the night on Gran's sofa like before, and the next day I'm going to meet his parents.' She made a face. 'I didn't want to go, but it's only fair, I suppose.'

'Are you still as keen on him?'

'Oh, yes, I've missed him like crazy. Really it's lucky I've been so busy,' Janet said. 'To be honest, if he hadn't been doing his national service, he'd have probably felt very neglected.'

Ruth knew why Janet had changed the subject, so she didn't mention Ben again. Instead she

465

said, 'Well, we won't see each other at all over Christmas. Shall we meet in the new year and compare notes?'

'It's a date,' Janet said. 'And now let's start the festive season the way we mean to go on, and go out for a drink.'

'You're on,' said Ruth. 'Give me a few minutes to change.'

Janet found that meeting Simon's family, who lived near Sheffield, wasn't half as bad as she'd thought. She got on really well with his two younger sisters as well, and they were soon the best of friends. Simon was extremely happy that Janet had agreed to visit his parents that Christmas. To him it meant that the relationship had moved another step forward, and he was delighted that everyone got on so well.

'They love you like I do,' Simon said as he and Janet went for a walk after dinner on Boxing Day. 'I knew they would.'

'How do you know?'

'I just do,' Simon said. He pulled Janet close and kissed her tenderly. 'I love you too, Janet Travers, but you know that. I'm crazy about you and I can't wait to be done with the army and be with you all the time.'

'Me too,' Janet said, and added, 'I've missed you.'

'I mean all the time,' Simon said. He stopped, pulled Janet round to face him and said, 'I mean marriage, Janet.'

Janet wasn't surprised. She'd guessed what Simon had been leading up to. She said nothing;

she could almost feel Simon's nervousness. 'Janet,' he said urgently, 'please will you marry me?'

Janet was moved by the emotion in Simon's voice and the love tinged with slight trepidation she saw mirrored in his eyes. She wondered at her hesitation. She loved him, for heaven's sake, and had been happy enough to wear the ring he'd given her on her twenty-first birthday, and that had been a commitment of sorts.

'Oh, Simon,' she said at last, 'I love you so much and I do want to marry, but not yet. I want to finish my probationary year first.'

'I know that,' Simon said, holding her tighter. 'We've talked about it before. I'd just like us to get engaged.'

'Okay,' Janet said.

Simon gave a whoop of joy. He could hardly believe it. Janet, the girl he'd loved from the moment he'd first set eyes on her, had agreed at last to marry him. He was ecstatic. His unbounded joy was infectious and they went back to the house hand in hand.

Both sets of parents were delighted with the news. Only Betty had misgivings, because Simon wasn't a Catholic, but she kept her doubts to herself. As a non-practising Protestant he was a better bet as a prospective son-in-law than Ben Hayman had been as a Jew. So objections were few, and by the time Simon returned to his unit a diamond solitaire ring adorned Janet's left hand. The wedding day was fixed for the second Saturday in August 1959.

After that the months passed fairly quickly.

467

Janet's second term of teaching practice was only moderately better than her first and just as exhausting. At the end of it, in April, Duncan and Frances were married at St Peter and Paul's church. Betty felt a pang of regret that Janet and Simon couldn't have a nuptial mass like Duncan and Frances, but she stifled it. Janet knew what was in her mother's mind, but she had no regrets. Simon was the man for her and she'd say the same if he turned out to be a Hindu, she thought.

Marriage seemed to be the rage of 1958. Shirley married Paul in May, before she'd even completed her course, Ruth and Phillip tied the knot in June, and Lou's wedding was at the beginning of August, in the middle of the holidays. For the first time Janet was in the flat on her own. She thought she'd be lonely, for she'd seldom been alone in her life, but she found she enjoyed just being able to please herself for once, without having to consider anyone.

Sometimes, at night, she'd wonder whether she'd been right to agree to marry Simon when she had. Shouldn't she have waited until he was demobbed? And what if he changed after marriage? Many men did; she read about it all the time in women's magazines. She missed having Lou and Shirley to talk things through with and help her laugh her worries away.

Simon often wrote three letters a week to her, expressing his love in words Janet knew he'd be embarrassed to speak if they'd been face to face. He wrote how he longed to see her and lived for her letters, and Janet would be filled with tenderness for the man so far away. If he'd been nearer she knew he would have dispersed her doubts once and for all, but he'd been sent overseas just after Ruth's marriage and she only had his letters to sustain her.

Breda was the only one she confided in, for Betty and Bert could see no wrong in Simon.

'It's just wedding nerves,' she assured Janet.

'Aunt Breda, it's nearly a year away. Surely you only get nerves when the wedding's close, like Ruth did?'

'You've got to remember you had a bad experience with the first chap you went out with,' Breda said. 'It's bound to make you a bit cautious.'

'You don't think I'm making a mistake now?'

'With Simon? No, no, I don't,' Breda said decisively. 'Course, I don't know how you feel about him – only you could say that – but I know he's a sight better than that creep Ben Hayman, who seemed so charming on the surface.' She stopped suddenly, looked at Janet and said, 'Do you ever hear from him now?'

'No, why on earth should I?'

'Well, you are friends with his sister. Doesn't she ever mention him at all?'

'Not really now,' Janet said. 'She used to tell me bits about him in the past, but I told her I wasn't interested, so she stopped.'

'So you don't think about him at all?'

'No,' Janet burst out. 'Auntie Breda, what are you getting at? This ... this uncertainty with Simon has nothing to do with Ben.'

'All right,' Breda said. 'Don't bite me bleeding head off, girl. See, human nature's a funny thing, and sometimes the more of a bastard a man is, the more he's attractive to some. That's all I'm saying.'

'Well, that's not my problem,' Janet said. 'I suppose I'm just scared of marriage regardless of the man concerned and I do get fed up with Mum and Dad and even Gran going round talking about Simon as if he's some sort of saint.' She looked at her aunt and said, 'Oh, Aunt Breda, what's the matter with me?'

'Nothing,' Breda said, putting her arms around her niece. 'Marriage is a big step. You're promising to live with someone for life, not much chance of parole and no time off for good behaviour. It takes some thinking about.'

'I do love him and I miss him,' Janet said. 'I think that's part of the problem.'

'Course it is,' Breda agreed. 'Plus this is the first summer holiday you've not worked for at least some of the time and you've got too much time on your hands. Believe me, when you start school next week, you'll have less time to think of Simon and you'll not miss him so much, and then the months will pass quicker till his demob.'

Breda, as usual, was right. Janet started at Meadowbank School in Leicester in September. The school served a large council estate which reminded Janet very much of the Pype Hayes estate where she'd grown up. She'd chosen the school because she thought she would be giving something back, carrying on the future she'd mapped out for herself at ten years old when she'd decided to be another Claire Wentworth.

470

She found, however, that it was more difficult than she'd imagined, and for the first weeks she was so confused, weary and shell-shocked that she fell gratefully into bed each night and slept deeply till morning. Neither Lou nor Shirley could understand why she'd chosen such a hard school in the first place. Only Ruth had an inkling of what was behind it all, and it was Ruth who Janet took her troubles to. 'I wish Claire was here,' she said fervently. 'Maybe she could give me some tips. There's probably a knack to it; there must be, or all the asylums would be full of gibbering teachers.'

'Maybe they are,' Ruth said with a laugh.

'Well, thanks,' Janet replied sarcastically. 'You're a great help, I don't think.'

'What about Lou and Shirley, what do they say?'

'Oh, Lou seems to be coping okay, and Shirley gets bigger every time I see her and sickeningly mumsy all of a sudden.'

'She's pregnant?' Ruth cried in surprise.

'Yes, didn't I tell you? She didn't even begin her probationary year and isn't really interested in the problems I'm having with mine.'

'What about the rest of the staff?'

'Some of them are okay, some are of the old school and don't really like probationers,' Janet said. 'You have to be careful which chair you sit on in the staff room and which cup you use for your tea in case you upset someone. I can cope with all that, but I could do with having Claire around. She'd tell me how to stop myself strangling some of the little darlings in my care and to teach them something into the bargain.'

Ruth bit her lip, wondering whether she should tell her friend the latest developments in tracing Claire, but she decided not to. After all it could all turn out to be a false alarm and then her hopes would be raised for nothing. But the fact was Ben had been trying to locate the Carters ever since he thought he'd seen Richard at the conference, and just a few days earlier she'd received a letter from him.

Dear Ruth,

Just a note to let you know I haven't given up on finding the Carters. I felt I was getting nowhere, but just last week I met an ex-colleague who'd recently met a man called Richard Carter who said he was living the other side of the Canadian border. Although he didn't get his address, I know the general area.

He says the chap speaks with an English accent, is in the mental health field and mentioned that his wife had been sick, but he didn't get her name. It's worth checking out as the details fit, but don't raise your hopes too high. It's still a long shot. I won't be able to get away until early spring, but I'll travel up there and see if it's the Richard and Claire Carter we knew. I'll be across in England on business later anyway, so I'll see you then.

Love, Ben.

In the end Ruth didn't tell Janet about the letter. She seldom mentioned Ben to Janet now, because Janet went all huffy on her, and there was no point telling her about the investigations, for they could all come to nothing. Janet had been more upset about Claire's disappearance than Ruth and she didn't want her hopes raised unnecessarily. She did, however, in her reply to Ben, include a letter for her brother to give to Claire if she should prove to be the Claire Carter they all knew. In it she'd written how everyone had missed her and would love to hear from her if she felt able to write. She told of her marriage to Phillip and her job as a cub reporter, and of Janet following in her footsteps teaching and her impending marriage to Simon Webster in the summer. She added that Janet was finding the going hard at the moment and would welcome some encouragement. She explained that Janet didn't know she was writing; she was keeping it quiet for the moment.

Ruth posted it and wondered if it would do any good. Even if the couple turned out to be the right people, would Claire get in touch? According to Ben's letter, Richard Carter had said his wife had been ill. Ill in what way? Mentally ill, perhaps? Or, God forbid, terminally ill? Well, anyway, she reasoned, the letter is sent and it can hardly do any harm, but the less Janet knows till we're sure the better.

So all she said to Janet was, 'Never mind, it will be Christmas soon and you'll have a break at least. And isn't Simon being demobbed in the new year?'

'Yes,' said Janet, her eyes shining, 'and fortunately before the January term starts again. He doesn't want me to meet him at the station but in the flat, and he'll come straight there. I think his mother was a bit upset he wasn't going home.

She was quite frosty when she spoke about it on the phone to me the other day.'

'I don't see why she should be,' Ruth said. 'It is you he's engaged to.'

'I know, but you know what mothers are.'

'Oh, don't I just,' Ruth said with a groan, and both girls laughed together.

Outside the day was blustery, grey and cold, but inside the flat it was warm and comforting. The table was laid for two with a white damask cloth and two crystal wine glasses on loan from Shirley. A centrepiece of silk flowers decorated the table, two candles stood either side and red napkins made a vivid splash of colour. Janet had been cooking all day and it was ready now just to heat up and serve. The prawn cocktails resided in their glass dishes next to the bottle of bubbly in the refrigerator Janet had just bought through the hire purchase scheme, and she was like a cat on hot bricks.

Several times she'd run to the window to watch for a taxi pulling up, but when it actually did, she wasn't there to see it and she came out of the kitchen wiping her hands on a towel to see Simon framed in the doorway. His overcoat was open, a scarf loosely tied round his neck, and his cheeks were ruddy from the wind and cold that he seemed to bring in with him.

But it was his eyes that held Janet's, and she felt her heart thudding against her ribs. Simon flung his holdall to one side, took a step forward, shut the door with his foot and held out his arms. As Janet ran across the room to him, she felt herself enfolded and held close, and heard Simon say, 'Oh, darling, how I've longed for this for months. I used to dream of holding you in my arms like this.'

Janet was so overcome she could scarcely speak for a minute or two. It didn't matter; she was happy and Simon seemed happy to stay locked together the way they were.

When he eventually released her, Janet's eyes were wet and her voice broken with emotion. 'Are you hungry?' she said. 'I've cooked a special meal.'

'Can it wait?' Simon said. 'It's not food I'm hungry for.'

Janet smiled. 'We'll eat later.' she said, and taking him by the hand she led him to the bedroom, where they celebrated his homecoming very satisfactorily and for some time.

Janet was glad that Simon didn't expect to stay at the flat after his demob. She knew that if he did, her parents would know what was going on straight away. 'I know,' he said when she attempted a stumbling explanation of why he couldn't move in. 'You don't have to make excuses. I know your family like to keep tabs on you.'

'It's not that,' Janet protested, 'it's just the way they are.' Her parents often tootled over now on a Sunday afternoon in the car Duncan had found for them. Betty and Breda had even come up on the train for a day or two in the summer and Sally liked to stay for part of her holidays.

Simon lodged with a mate, Kenny Slater, who

he met during his time in the army. Kenny told him he got engaged before joining the army and left his fiancée installed in the flat they would both live in when they got married. The flat wasn't in Leicester, but Loughborough just outside and near to Reynolds Construction, where Kenny had worked in sales and marketing before he went to do his national service, and he'd been assured that he could have his old job back after his demob. However, before the army was finished with him, the girl had written to say she was sorry but the wedding was off. Kenny was broken up, especially as it appeared from news filtered through that she'd run off with his best friend.

Simon agreed to move into the flat with Kenny, knowing he couldn't really afford to rent a place by himself. 'It's all right,' he told Janet, 'it's sorted.'

In fact Simon thought most of his life was sorted. Duncan had found him a nice little blue Ford Escort that made life a bit easier, and Kenny had wangled him an interview at his firm working in the research and development department, checking the suitability of construction materials. Simon was grateful, the job was interesting enough most of the time and the pay was reasonable. Added to that, it was fairly near to his flat, and with the car, not far from Janet, which meant she could stay where she was, doing the same job, and they'd still be able to see a fair bit of each other.

After a while he began to wonder if that was such a good thing because he wasn't totally happy about his relationship with Janet since he'd returned home. She was often tetchy and short-tempered with him. Sometimes she would apologise and blame her job, and other times she would snap that it was his fault and say he was being unreasonable.

Simon worried about it and asked Janet if she was tired of him. but she always told him not to be so stupid. Eventually he decided to take action. 'We've not been alone just the two of us since those two days we stole after the Christmas holidays,' Simon said. 'Do you remember?'

'Um,' said Janet drowsily, leaning back against Simon on the settee. She knew what he meant. Their evenings were usually spent down the pub or wine bar in the company of friends. On the occasions they did decide to have a night in, Shirley, Lou or Ruth would ring for a chat. Or other people from the block would call in for a coffee or to invite them out, or Kenny would wind up on their doorstep for a heart-to-heart with Simon, who'd usually end up driving him home later. And that took no account of Janet's family, who expected to see her often and speak to her oftener. She knew Simon had a point.

'Let's go away,' he said suddenly.

'We are, it's called a honeymoon.'

'No, before that,' Simon said. 'The Easter holidays are coming up and I can wangle a few days off, I'm sure. To be honest, Janet, you look whacked.'

Suddenly Janet was aware of how tired she really was. A holiday sounded just what she needed. 'Where?' she said.

'Well, Britain in late March and early April is not very appealing,' Simon said, 'but I believe Spain is nice at this time of year.'

'Spain?' squealed Janet. 'D'you mean it? Oh, Simon,' and she threw her arms around his neck.

He disentangled himself with a laugh. 'Don't strangle me,' he protested, then he put his arm around Janet and held her tight. 'It's fairly reasonable price-wise as well,' he said, 'and I have a bit put by.' He kissed Janet's lips gently and went on, 'And there's no one I'd rather spend it on.'

'Oh, Simon,' Janet said. Her throat had a lump in it, so she said no more and held Simon tight.

She knew her Aunt Breda was right. Simon was kind, considerate and loving and the right man for her. With him, her future would be assured, and now that he was home with her, there would be no doubts, worries or anxieties to threaten their happiness together.

Chapter Twenty-One

'Not long now,' Breda said one day, following Betty into her house after work as she often did.

'No,' Betty agreed, filling the kettle. 'Four months and it'll soon pass, but everything's in hand.'

'Is she excited?'

'Hard to tell, but I don't think so. Tell you the truth, she bites my head off if I go on, and the way she talks to Simon I'm surprised he puts up with it.'

'Well, she works hard,' Betty said. 'I mean, it can't be easy teaching in that school.'

'Well, she didn't have to bury herself away in a place like that, did she?' Betty snapped. 'Mind, I will agree, teaching can never be easy. Every teacher that had charge of the twins seemed to look strained.'

'Amazing how they've calmed down now,' Breda said. 'Pity Dad didn't live to see it. He always thought they would end up as millionaires or bank robbers.'

'Well, they'll likely be neither,' Betty said with a laugh, 'but I was so worn down with them myself, I often worried how they'd turn out.' She busied herself making a cup of tea for her sister and herself and went on, 'I always wished Bert would be firmer with them, but he always took their part. Course, he didn't see them till they were six months and then not much after that, because they were always up to bed as he came in.'

'And they've grown up so like him, both of them,' Breda said, 'except that they're taller, of course.'

'Yes, they're turned six foot and only just fourteen,' Betty said with pride, and remembered Bert saying that Conner and Noel were more intelligent than people imagined – except for Janet, who'd thought, like her dad, that there was more to the twins than met the eye. 'Janet keeps their noses to the grindstone a bit. She was telling them the other day that before they know it they'll have their O levels staring them in the face, and it was time they became a bit more responsible.'

'What about Sally?'

'Oh, who can do anything about Sally'?' Betty said. 'Janet said we spoil her and we're letting her grow up too quick.'

'You probably are, but Linda's the same and if I say a word I'm the worst mother in the world. They certainly have more than we had, or Janet either, but that's life, isn't it?'

'I suppose,' Betty said. 'Sally can twist Bert round her little finger. I mean, that racket you can hear from her bedroom is from the new transistor radio she got for her twelfth birthday, and if I go up and ask what she's doing, she'll likely say she's doing her homework.'

'With that row going on?'

At that minute they heard Sally singing 'Living Doll' at the top of her voice, and Betty gave a wry smile. 'It's all they think about, rock and roll, Elvis Presley and now this Cliff Richard Sally and her friends keep on about,' she said. 'I mean, when our Janet was studying we all had to creep round the place.'

'Well, that bleeding Luxembourg every night gets right on my nerves,' Breda said. 'Some of it's not even tuneful, and when our Linda sings along with it... Course, if I complain, Peter reminds me that we were both young once.'

'Fathers and daughters,' commented Betty, shaking her head. 'I tell you, Bert would try to take the moon from the sky if our Sally wanted it. Janet says we're making a rod for our own backs, but what can you do?'

Breda shook her head helplessly.

Sally Travers was still small for her age, petite and fragile-looking. Her perfectly oval face was lightly tanned, her eyes were a brilliant blue, while her eyebrows were dark, as were her eyelashes, which were also long and curled. She had a fine-boned nose and a wide mouth, the only feature she shared with Janet, and her golden hair hung in natural ringlets down her back.

She was truly beautiful. Bert was stunned by the lovely creature in their midst, Betty was almost awed by her radiance and popularity, and it seemed wrong to take the sparkle out of her eyes by refusing her anything. To Conner and Noel, she was the little sister they had always seen as a small and delicate baby doll. Now she was almost grown up and they were two of the most popular boys in school because their mates were always going on about their cracker of a sister. It seemed right that the lion's share of money and attention should go to Sally.

Betty was glad that money was easier now, for the new fashion items Sally always seemed to need. She had two layered lace underskirts which Betty had stiffened with sugar and which stood out so much, they wouldn't fit in the wardrobe and had to hang from the picture rail covered with sheeting. Betty thought she looked a treat with a pretty coloured cotton frock over them, or a satin one for the young people's dances in the church hall, but Bert often expressed disquiet over the length of her skirts.

On the other hand, he didn't like Sally in the tight slacks she liked. Or the large 'Sloppy Joes' she wore on top. 'She looks as if she's waiting to grow into it,' Bert said glumly.

'It's the fashion,' Betty said. 'Like those awful winklepicker shoes that I'm sure will cripple her feet, and yet Sally tells me everyone is wearing them now.'

Betty had to agree with Bert, but she liked Sally to have the latest fashions like her friends. She'd watch her with a surge of pride, knowing that her beauty stood out even among her fine-looking friends, including pretty Kate Hopkins, Sally's particular favourite.

At home, where everything was hers for the asking and she got her way in everything, Janet's approval was what she sought. She loved all her family, but between her and Janet there was a deeper bond. And yet Janet was sharp with her often and complained that she was a spoilt brat.

She wasn't charmed by Sally like everyone else, and she was often hard on her little sister, because she loved her so much and was afraid for her at times. She knew Sally was as bright as she herself had been, but partly because of her parents' laxity and partly because of Sally's own character, she was distracted easily. Fashion, music and having a good time all took Sally from her studies, and only the threat of Janet's disapproval kept her from being ruined altogether.

Sally was also almost too beautiful for her own good, and Janet was worried that it would turn her head and make her vain. She appealed to her parents to show more restraint in what they bought her, but it was useless. She knew that money was easier for them, but it still wasn't a bottomless pit to throw at Sally in huge lumps.

'You should see her,' Janet complained to Ruth, when she came over to Leicester one Saturday and the two girls went into town to shop. 'She has to have the latest this or that, everything in fashion. She had a record player for Christmas and she's after Mom and Dad for records every week, and now this transistor radio she has on and blaring all over the house all the time. It's lucky she's so small because the clothes she has, if she was bigger you'd think she was fifteen or sixteen. And I found make-up in the drawer of her dressing table the other day when I was looking for a pencil. I tore her off a strip right and proper. God, Ruth, when I think of us at twelve...'

'We were children, but we thought we knew it all, didn't we?' Ruth said. 'But don't be too hard on Sally, she is lovely-looking.'

'I know. That's what worries me.'

'All your life you've worried about your family,' Ruth said. 'I wonder what you'll do when it's your own.'

'Like Shirley, you mean?' Janet said, for they were on their way back to Janet's after a visit to Shirley and her new infant son. 'God knows, but I don't intend to have any for some years. Getting married's enough of a commitment right now. What about you?'

'I want to get myself established first. I'm really only on the very first rung of the ladder. I'd have to give up all I've strived for if I got pregnant now.'

'Hear, hear,' said Janet, getting to her feet. 'Come on, this is our stop. We'd better get in and get the tea on, or Phillip will be in and there'll be nothing made. Sure you can't tell me what it is he wants to talk to me about?'

'No,' Ruth said. 'I promised I wouldn't, so don't keep on. You'll know soon enough.'

It was less than an hour later that Janet was looking at the photographs Phillip had given her with hands that shook while she listened in horror to the tale he told of the distressed lady who'd called into his office. Her son had been born a mongol, Phillip said, like Chloe, and the woman – Greta – had eventually bowed to the pressure of the doctors and her husband and had her son sent away to be cared for. But she couldn't settle until she knew he was happy, so she went to visit him in the Elmwood Home for the Mentally Handicapped, where he'd been placed.

Phillip went on, 'The matron said they weren't used to visits from parents and they didn't encourage them as they upset the children. However, Greta insisted, and what she saw shocked her so much she had the urge to pick up her son and run. Instead she came to the paper. She said she'd never thought about children with mental handicaps before she'd had her child, and she'd be willing to bet most people were the same. She thought they ought to know what goes on in the homes.'

'But how did you get the pictures?' Janet cried, looking aghast at the rows of iron cots with babies of various ages lying flat beneath grey blankets and staring vacantly at the bare ceiling.

'I posed as Greta's husband,' Phillip said, 'and wheedled my way in. The point is, they're not being cruel to the children – they care for them in their own way and honestly think that they will never be anything more than babies, so no effort is made to stimulate them. They couldn't really do much more with the staff they have anyway. They had no objection to my taking photographs of my "son" as a keepsake. The others I sneaked in when they weren't watching me.'

'It's disgusting,' Janet declared vehemently, sifting through the pictures again. 'This could have been Chloe's fate.'

'But it wasn't,' Phillip said gently, 'and from what Ruth tells me, Chloe's short life was a happy one.'

Janet nodded and then said, 'But Phillip, what can we do about this? We can't just sit back and let children be put into these places to rot. If their parents knew...'

'The paper is willing to do a feature on the care of mentally handicapped children in Britain today,' Phillip said, 'and contrast it with the work done at Oakhurst and Ferndale. I've contacted the leader at the one Chloe attended, and she's very keen.'

'They encourage visitors – Claire always said that. She always said it helped the children to see new faces,' Janet said.

Phillip, watching her, was glad he'd not told her how upset and depressed he'd been by the home and its sour smell – a mixture of urine, cooked cabbage and bleach that stayed in his nostrils for hours. Nor did he mention the starkness of the place, the walls painted dirty cream at the top and brown at the bottom, with nothing to brighten the rooms at all.

But Janet had seen the bareness in the babies' rooms and could guess what the rest of it was like. She recalled the odd visits she'd made to Oakhurst, where all the paintwork was bright, some walls were decorated with murals and others with the children's work, and sparkling mobiles dangled from the ceiling. She felt angry that the children at Elmwood should be denied the opportunity of attending such a place.

'Older babies were sitting on potty chairs,' Ruth said. 'Phillip wasn't able to get pictures, but he told me about it.'

'Yes,' Phillip said. 'They were being fed from one big dish and they sat in a line – about six of them strapped in seats so they couldn't fall out.'

'And you are highlighting all this?' she asked.

486

'You bet,' Phillip said. 'The editor's first son was a spastic who only lived a few days, and though he now has three healthy children he told me that he always felt not enough was done for his son. He's kept quiet about it all these years. His son wasn't perfect and part of him wanted him to die, but now, years later, he is still consumed with guilt.'

Janet nodded. She knew about guilt; she had been filled with it herself all the time she was growing up. 'I suppose he feels this helps to redress the balance,' she said. 'What's this lady done with her son? I presume she's not left him at Elmwood.'

'No, indeed she hasn't,' Simon said, smiling at the memory of the determination in Greta's face as she scooped the baby from his cot, taking no notice at all of the indignation and dire warnings of the astounded staff.

'But neither of the units can take him till he's three.'

'Not officially,' Phillip said. 'But they have a register of mentally handicapped babies so the mothers can meet together, and two mornings a week a physiotherapist at Oakhurst shows them exercises they can do with their babies. Similar, I suppose, to what you used to do with Claire and Chloe.'

'Yes,' Janet said. 'I can see how that could be helpful. I should imagine that the isolation is one of the worst things when you have a handicapped child. Claire was always glad to see us, wasn't she, Ruth?'

'Mm,' Ruth agreed. She glanced across at

Phillip and went on, 'Phillip's suggested we do a book based on our experiences with Chloe – maybe just called *Chloe's Story* – and serialise it alongside the features on mental health. What do you think?'

Janet was taken aback and not very enthusiastic. 'But it's not our story to tell, is it?' she said.

'Part of it is,' Ruth argued.

'And it would show on a very personal level what could be achieved,' Phillip put in.

'But what about Claire?' Janet said. 'I mean, what if she did have a breakdown or something and she reads something like this? It could bring it all back and make her ill again.'

Ruth chose her words with care. 'I see your point, Janet,' she said, 'but no one really knows where Claire is, so why don't we go ahead with the book, and if Claire is traced she can read it and decide then whether she wants it published or not?'

'And if we finish the book and still can't find her?' Janet asked.

'Then,' Ruth said, 'we decide whether we publish the story of a lovely and very brave little child in order to honour her memory and give heart to other mothers of mongol children, or we don't bother.'

Janet could see the sense in that and agreed to at least make a start on the first chapter. For a long time after Ruth and Phillip drove back to their Boldmere home she sat before the fire, too churned up to sleep, and when she eventually did go to bed, she was haunted by the sad, hopeless faces of the children in the photographs. She was almost glad when the alarm went off so she could legitimately get up and go to work.

The next evening Simon came round after work, as he did often. Before he'd been there very long he realised that Janet was agitated about something. Over dinner she told him Phillip's story.

'Come on,' Simon soothed afterwards, as they sat in front of the television later with a glass of wine each and the silence had stretched out between them. 'Relax, you're all on edge. It isn't your fault, you know.'

'I know that and I'm all right, I'm fine,' Janet said, and then suddenly burst out, 'No, I'm not fine, I'm bloody angry and upset.'

'D'you want to talk about it?' Simon asked.

'Yes,' Janet said. 'I'm glad you're here. I wish you'd been here last night after Ruth and Phillip left. I felt so cold inside.'

'But you told me not to come round,' Simon said, puzzled. 'You said they wanted to talk to you about something.'

'I know I did,' said Janet. 'I just wished you had been here, that's all. I could have done with some comfort. What I heard around the tea table was disturbing stuff.' She turned to him and said: 'You are staying tonight, aren't you?'

'Do you want me to?'

'Yes.'

'Then I'll stay.' Simon put his arm around her and said: 'What you said about wishing I'd been here last night – there is a way I could be here for you all the time.'

'I know.'

'It would mean me moving in.'

'I know.'

Simon's heart skipped a beat. 'You mean you agree? I can move in here with you?'

'Yes,' Janet said.

Simon's mouth dropped open in an astonished gape. 'You were dead set against it before. Why the change of mind now?' he said.

Janet didn't really know. All she knew was that she would have welcomed Simon's arms around her the previous evening. She'd felt cold and abandoned after Phillip and Ruth had gone, and after all they were getting married in a few months. 'I love you and want you here all the time,' she said now. 'Is that good enough?'

'It's the best reason in the bloody world,' Simon said, his face one great beam of happiness. But although he was delighted, he knew that Janet was taking a risk asking him to move in, because her parents were sure to find out one way or the other and would have a fit. Janet didn't seem bothered by it. In fact, all she wanted to talk about was the story about the home which had so upset her.

'You should have seen the pictures Phillip showed me,' she said. 'The sterility and hopelessness of the children's lives would break your heart. What made it worse for me was knowing what they can achieve. I mean, through meeting Claire and Chloe.'

'Not every retarded child would necessarily be able to do what Chloe did,' Simon said gently.

'I'm not saying they would,' Janet said, 'but what was achieved with her means that you shouldn't necessarily give up on children like that.'

She was quiet a minute and then went on, 'They are doing a comparison – I mean, the paper is – of institutionalised care with the type of approach the units have, and how they can enrich the lives of retarded children. Phillip wants ... wants Ruth and me to write a book about how we met Chloe and what we did with her as a baby and toddler, and call it *Chloe's Story*. He says it would feature in the paper and we would easily find a publisher later.'

'And why don't you want to?' Simon asked, sensing Janet's reluctance.

'Well, it isn't really our story to tell, is it?' Janet said. 'It's Claire's, and I'd like to sort of get her permission before we start writing things about her daughter.' Simon could see that Janet had a point but knew she wasn't finished yet, so he said nothing. 'Ruth says,' Janet went on, 'that as no one knows where Claire is at the moment, we should go ahead and write the book, and then if we ever do find her, she can read and okay what we've written.'

She sighed and continued, 'The point is, I know Ruth's right in all she says. I mean, I'm not daft. I know it will add weight and a sort of personal touch to the stuff in the paper and perhaps help in the long term, and it will certainly give the mothers of other mongol children hope for the future.'

'So you'll do it?'

'I suppose,' Janet said. 'I've sort of agreed, but ... well, I still feel uneasy.'

Simon sighed inwardly, knowing that in this mood Janet could talk all night. He didn't want to waste time talking about a woman and child he'd never met and who neither he nor Janet could do anything about. He pulled Janet closer to him and kissed her gently. 'Let's talk about it some other time,' he urged. 'It's late.'

'Stop it,' Janet complained, breaking free. 'I can't think straight when you go on like this.'

'I don't want you to think straight,' Simon said. 'At least not about this business with Phillip any more tonight.' His arms went round Janet, his lips met hers, and she found she didn't want to think about the business with Phillip any more either.

Chapter Twenty-Two

'Is this how a civilised country treats the most vulnerable in our society?' screamed the headlines on Phillip's paper, and there, in grainy newsprint, were some of the pictures Phillip had shown to Janet and his account of the visit to Elmwood. He didn't mention the home's name, Ruth explained, as it would only worry parents, who could do little about the place by themselves.

There was something else Ruth could have told Janet, but she chose not to. That morning she'd received another letter from Ben. He said he'd checked the Carters out and it was the right family, but he'd tell her everything when he saw her because he was making plans to come to England immediately. He told her he'd passed her letter to Claire, who now seemed recovered from her illness, but didn't explain what it was. She'd assured him she would write to her and Janet as soon as possible.

'Tell Janet now,' Phillip said, but Ruth shook her head.

'I want to see Ben first and find out why she's kept so quiet all these years,' she said. 'You don't know how it affected Janet and I won't risk building her hopes up for nothing.'

Janet knew that there was something on Ruth's mind, but she thought she was worried about Phillip. His uncompromising headlines were

493

raising a furore amongst the professionals, who were divided as to what constituted good mental health care.

Many people wrote to the paper in support of a more liberal approach. Mothers of mentally handicapped children wrote of the achievements of their children and the importance of early stimulation.

The following week, Phillip ran a story about the Oakhurst and Ferndale units that Claire and Richard had been involved with. Janet wished the photographs could have been in colour to show the units at their very best. The children were seen working at tables with material that was, Janet knew, specially made for the Montessori schools. Others were kneading clay, painting at easels, playing with sand or using musical instruments.

Much interest was aroused by the pictures and the accounts outlining the work of the units. Many wanted to know what Montessori was and how were they able to achieve so much with the mentally handicapped. Some doctors were sceptical and expressed doubts as to whether all the children were very disabled at all, while others were concerned that they were overtaxing their brains.

Meanwhile, Ruth and Janet had begun *Chloe's Story*. Janet had written the first part, which was a short resumé of who Claire was and how she'd met her. Ruth described how she had been friendly with Janet at Whytecliff High School, but neither mentioned the bullying that went on. She said that Janet had taken her to meet her friend and ex-teacher Claire Wentworth, where she'd also met Chloe for the first time. She went on to outline many of the exercises they'd used to help stimulate the little girl.

It had taken longer than they'd thought possible to get it just right. Simon was trying to be unselfish and not begrudge the time Janet was putting in to this project. He helped as much as he could around the flat and Janet was glad that he was there most of the time.

She knew that Simon felt cramped, but they'd had little time for house-hunting. Although both acknowledged that they needed to look for something more suitable than the flat long term, Janet saw no rush to move and Simon worried about it. He'd taken to touring the estate agents on Saturdays, and was appalled at the prices properties were fetching. He was concerned they'd get nothing at all if they didn't buy soon.

'I don't see the panic,' Janet objected one Friday, about a month after Simon had moved in. 'We're all right in the flat for now.'

'Prices are going through the roof,' Simon said. 'You don't understand.'

'They'll come down again,' Janet said soothingly. 'It would be better to wait till they do.'

Simon sighed. He'd had an awful week at work and a row with his boss that day. He felt bone tired and out of sorts and was not looking forward to another fruitless trawl of the estate agents in the morning. It wasn't as if Janet was even interested. 'The flat's too bloody tiny,' he insisted irritably.

'It's not that bad,' Janet objected. 'I lived here

with Lou and Shirley for years.'

'What about when we want to start a family?'

'Well, I don't intend to do that straight away,' Janet said, and then caught sight of Simon's strained, exhausted face. Realising that he was too tired to talk reasonably that night, she said, 'Let's not discuss it now, Simon. We're both too tired. Let's make an early night of it and talk in the morning.'

Simon knew he was being brushed off and he suddenly felt murderously angry with her. 'Let's get this straight,' he said sarcastically. 'You want us both to be nearly drawing the old age pension before we have a child, do you?'

Seeing Simon's furious face. Janet quelled her desire to laugh and said, 'I just don't want to have a baby straight away. I want to wait a while.'

'How much of a bloody while?' Simon demanded. He was bitterly disappointed. He'd been certain that Janet would not want to wait too long before starting a family; he'd assumed she wanted children as much as he did.

'Oh, Simon,' Janet said. 'Can't wait to tie me to the kitchen sink, eh?'

She spoke lightly, hoping to make Simon smile. But he didn't smile. He was fed up with Janet dictating and deciding everything in the relationship and was determined to sort this issue out. 'Come on,' he said, 'it doesn't have to be like that and you know it. You can go on working afterwards if you want to. I'm not averse to that. I'll lend a hand with housework and things, you know I would.'

'Yes, of course, but...' Janet laid a hand on

Simon's arm and pleaded, 'Let's just get used to being married first. After all,' she added, 'what's the rush?'

'Oh, no bloody rush,' Simon said, brushing Janet's hand away. 'I just like to know where I stand, that's all.'

'What are we quarrelling over?' Janet burst out, exasperated.

Janet didn't know what Simon was so cross about, and he didn't really understand it either, but he suddenly felt stifled in the flat. 'I'm going out,' he said. 'I can't get my head round this attitude of yours.'

'Oh, go then,' Janet retorted, suddenly irritated. 'I can do without you moaning on all the time. You're not the only one who's had a hard week.'

The slam of the door was the only answer, and Janet flung the cushion at it in a sudden temper. 'Bugger you, Simon Webster!' she cried.

She had a desire to sweep the tea things from the table, sure that the resounding crash would help her present mood, but instead she washed them with such intensity it was a wonder they weren't all broken anyway. Then she took her bad temper out in an orgy of cleaning, the likes of which the flat had seldom seen. She'd finished, and was sitting drinking a cup of coffee and going over the row again in her head, when the door bell rang.

She knew it couldn't be Simon for he had a key, and she hoped it wasn't someone selling something, or Jehovah's Witnesses. But when she saw who it was leaning against the doorpost, the shock was so great, she actually staggered, for

497

there on the landing, smiling the smile she knew so well, that still had the power to cause her heart to thud against her ribs and the roof of her mouth to feel dry, was Ben Hayman.

'You,' she said, and her voice came out in a croak.

Ben seemed completely in charge of the situation. He took a step forward and said, 'Hello, Janet.'

Janet hadn't even known that Ben was in England. She wondered why Ruth hadn't mentioned it. Maybe she hadn't thought it would be important to her. And it wasn't either, Janet decided. The man meant nothing to her any more.

'What do you want?' Janet's voice croaked in her throat.

'Can I come in?'

'No,' Janet said, half closing the door. 'What do you want?' she said again. 'And how did you find me?' Ben smiled again, and Janet could hardly believe the lurch her heart gave. He hadn't changed much, she realised as she looked at him. Though his features had hardened slightly and his hair was shorter, he was still an incredibly handsome man.

The smile annoyed her, and so did the way her body was reacting. 'How did you find me?' she snapped again.

'Ruth.'

'Ruth wouldn't tell you,' Janet said firmly. She knew her friend wouldn't betray her like that.

'She didn't tell me, no,' Ben admitted, 'but your address was in her phone book.'

'You were snooping around...'

'My dear girl,' Ben protested, 'I was not snooping. I'm over here on business, and knowing the field I specialise in, Phillip advised me to ring this chap Trimble who he's got to know through the row he's drummed up with his series in his newspaper. He said we could compare notes, and to ring to make an appointment. Travers just happened to be on the same page.'

'Does Ruth know you're here?'

'I didn't tell her I was coming over, no,' Ben said, and added, 'Look, are we going to carry on this conversation on the landing all evening, or can I come in?'

'I don't want you here,' Janet burst out. 'Go away, you've no right to ask.'

'I have news of Claire,' Ben told her. 'That's what brought me over to England earlier than I intended, but I was coming anyway this year. Didn't Ruth mention it?'

'No, she didn't. Do you think we spend the limited time we have together discussing you?' Janet snapped contemptuously, but she stepped aside because she wanted to know about Claire, and Ben crossed into the room.

Once inside, Ben said nothing at first, but stood surveying the flat. 'This is nice,' he said at last, appreciatively, and then he walked across the room and sat on the settee.

'Yes, very nice,' he said. 'You've done well, Janet. I know you teach. Ruth used to tell me snippets about you in her letters.'

'I don't know why on earth she should,' she said.

'I asked, that's why.'

'I can't see the fascination of knowing about my life,' Janet said. 'I have no interest in yours.'

She sat down in the chair next to the settee and Ben reached out and grabbed her hand, and she felt a tingling sensation, similar to when he'd touched her at Chloe's funeral. She shook his hand away abruptly.

'Oh, Janet.'

'Say what you have to say and then go,' she said.

'Oh, Janet, don't let's be like this,' Ben said.

'How did you think we'd be?' Janet asked. 'You mean nothing to me now, Ben, you're just someone from my past. Don't offend my intelligence by saying you'd like us to remain friends.'

'Well, why can't we?' Ben asked, and went on, 'God, Janet, you don't know how often I've longed for a friend. I used to be able to tell you anything and everything. Do you remember how we talked together?'

'You have a wife who should be your friend,' Janet said icily, ignoring Ben's question. 'Try talking to her, she might be interested.'

'My wife!' Ben said, and added with contempt, 'My wife, my dear Janet, has no interest in me. She is, in actual fact, a first-class whore.'

Janet was shocked. 'That's a bloody awful thing to say.'

'It's a true thing to say.'

'Even so,' Janet said angrily. 'And anyway, why are you telling me? What interest is your marriage to me?'

'Janet...'

'You said you had news of Claire,' Janet reminded him. 'That's the only reason I let you in at all, so if you've got news, share it. If not, get out.' She glared at him and said threateningly, 'If you just said you had news to get in here...'

Ben sighed. 'Okay,' he said. 'No, I wasn't lying. I have found out where Richard and Claire are. Claire's been very ill. Apparently she had a complete nervous collapse after the funeral. She refused to accept Chloe's death.'

Janet nodded. 'I thought as much,' she said. 'Where are they now?'

'In Canada,' Ben told her. He handed her a piece of paper. 'That's the address.'

'Why Canada?' Janet asked. 'Of all places, why there?'

'It's where they were, apparently,' Ben said. 'Richard took Claire away for a holiday a couple of weeks after the funeral, thinking she needed a break to help her cope. But only a few days after they arrived she had a nervous breakdown and had to be admitted to the psychiatric wing of the local hospital. As soon as Richard realised that Claire's condition was serious and that her care would be long term, he called for her mother to come over. She arranged for her house to be sold and the Carters' house left in an agent's hands to be let. Richard was very grateful, for he had little money and the hospital bills were mounting. Eventually he accepted a lectureship when it became obvious they'd have to stay in Canada indefinitely.'

'Why did she contact no one?' Janet asked. 'Or if she was too ill, why didn't Richard or Mary write, or phone?'

Ben shrugged. 'I think, in the beginning, they were just so worried about Claire's condition and their energies were concentrated in that area. Later, Claire wouldn't allow anyone to be told. Not that she could stop Richard or Mary physically, of course, but the doctors warned them not to go against her express wishes. Her mental balance was too precarious.'

'Oh, poor, poor Claire,' said Janet with feeling. 'How is she now?'

'Pretty good, I believe,' Ben said. 'She's been wanting to contact you for some time, but thought you might be annoyed, not hearing anything from her for years. She was delighted I'd managed to track her down.'

'Why did you bother?'

'Ruth asked me to,' Ben said. 'I thought I'd caught a glimpse of Richard at a conference and I promised her I'd do all I could to find them. Claire's all for the book you and Ruth are writing, by the way. I mentioned it to her and she thinks it may help other parents of similarly affected children.'

'Oh, great,' Janet said. 'The first part's ready and she can read it if she wants. It's being serialised in Phillip's paper to start with. If she likes it, Ruth and I can get on with writing the rest.'

'Yes,' Ben said.

He made no move to leave and after a couple of minutes' uncomfortable silence, Janet said sharply, 'Was that all?'

'I suppose,' Ben said, 'I thought I might be

offered a coffee or something.'

Janet gave a hard laugh. 'I don't think so,' she said. 'In fact, I'd like you to leave now.'

'God, Janet, you really know how to make a chap feel welcome.'

'It isn't my intention to make you feel welcome,' Janet snapped. 'You are not in the least welcome and I just want you to go.'

'I don't think you really mean that.'

'I most certainly do.'

Ben leant forward, took Janet's hand in his and turned it over as if he was examining it. Janet hoped he couldn't hear her heart thudding in her chest. His touch and his nearness were sending a weakness to her limbs that she fought to control. She tried to snatch her hand from his but he held on tight, stroking it gently between his own, and suddenly she found she had lost all desire to pull away. 'Oh, Janet,' Ben said. 'You can't know how I've longed to see you and tell you how sorry I am about what I did to you. What a bloody fool I was.' He smiled wryly into Janet's eyes and went on, 'There's nothing between Therese and me any more – never was much, to be honest, just sex.'

Janet made an impatient movement and pulled her hand away. She was cross and didn't want to hear this, it wasn't her business. 'I'm not interested,' she said. 'What do you expect me to do?'

'Nothing, I suppose,' Ben admitted. 'It's just that when I evaluate everything now, I have very little. I've lost my wife and son, who now live with the Steinaways, and Papa Steinaway owns the apartment I live in, the car I drive, the nanny who looks after my child. Even though Jacob is mine biologically, the Steinaways will bring him up. He'll be given everything he wants and end up a spoiled brat like his mother, poor sod. I see little of him, what with the distance we live apart and the demands of work.' Ben shook his head and said sadly, 'If I'm honest, I never was any great shakes as a father either. I couldn't ever seem to get it together with Jacob.'

Janet remembered how life had been for Sally and the twins and suddenly felt sorry for the privileged little boy in high-society New York who would never know the love of a family like hers. 'And you want me to listen to this litany of self-pity, do you?' she said angrily. 'I think not. You want me to feel sorry for you? Well, I bloody well won't. You had free choice and you chose Therese. Now she's your wife and you don't like what you have, but that's just tough. Many people have more to put up with and complain less.'

'You don't understand.'

'No, I don't,' Janet yelled, leaping to her feet. 'I don't understand how in a few short years you can give up on both your wife and your son and blame everything on your in-laws, who did much to help you in the beginning. Grow up, Ben, for God's sake!'

'Okay,' Ben said with a resigned sigh. 'But just tell me you forgive me for what I did to you.' He stood beside Janet, put his hands on her shoulders and looked deep into her eyes. 'That's what I really came for, forgiveness.'

'My forgiveness will hardly change your life,' Janet objected crossly. She tried in vain to shrug Ben's hands from her shoulders. Her legs felt suddenly very weak and the expression in Ben's eyes was unfathomable.

'It will stop me feeling so disgusted with myself,' Ben said. 'Do you think I don't know that my life has gone downhill from the moment I gave you up in favour of Therese?'

Janet removed Ben's hands with her own, but then he held on to them as she said impatiently, 'That's not my problem, Ben, it's yours. I've recovered from your betrayal and I've found someone else; in fact, I'm marrying him in a few months' time.'

'Ruth told me,' Ben said. 'Do you love him, this man?'

Janet laughed disbelievingly. 'You really take the biscuit, Ben Hayman. It's none of your bloody business and I owe you no explanation, but for your information, yes, I love Simon Webster very much.'

She felt Ben tense before her, then he jerked her towards him so quickly she was unable to do anything about it. She felt herself crushed against him. His lips were on hers, and at the sweetness and tenderness of that kiss the memories flooded back. She felt her resolve melting and was glad her arms were pinned by his, because if they hadn't been, she was sure she would have put them around his neck and held him close. She was aware that she should fight Ben, push him away, make some sort of protest instead of kissing him back with passion, and yet she felt the old longing his kisses had always aroused, stirring within her.

Then Ben released her from the kiss and they stood still, locked together, and stared at each other, slightly breathless, both unable to believe what had happened. Janet could see the raw yearning on Ben's face and knew that it would be just as apparent on hers. She didn't struggle in the arms that held her tight against him, and heard his low moan, 'Oh, Janet.'

The clap was loud, so loud that they jumped apart, and Janet looked in horror at Simon standing in the doorway, slowly applauding the scene in front of him. His face was bright red as he said angrily, 'A good performance, should get an Oscar for that, and I'd almost believe it was real if it wasn't for the fact that Janet has agreed to become my wife.'

Simon had been to see his old flatmate and work colleague Kenny, who'd had to move to a smaller, cheaper place when Simon had moved in with Janet. He knew where to find him: the local pub near his new flat, which had become his second home. Kenny was delighted to see Simon. He'd asked him to go for a pint often enough and had always been refused before.

Simon, knowing that Kenny felt the whole female race was flawed, expected a measure of sympathy when he recounted the row he'd had with Janet. But Kenny couldn't see why Simon wanted to tie himself down to one woman, let alone saddle himself with kids. 'Love 'em and leave 'em, that's the way,' he said. 'All bitches, women, the lot of them.'

Simon felt sorry for Kenny, knowing him to be a decent bloke who'd been badly hurt. At least Janet isn't like that, he'd thought. What with her job, her family and now this famous book, she's little time for me, never mind any other man.

It was as he dragged Kenny off to the snooker table to prevent him from drinking himself senseless that he began to realise that Janet probably had a point. After all, he reasoned, they hadn't actually lived together for long. Maybe it was sensible to wait a while before they had children. It wasn't as if they were old or anything either. In this mood, he'd eventually left Kenny and gone home, to be confronted by the sight of his Janet passionately kissing a man he'd never seen before.

Simon couldn't believe his eyes, and Janet saw the hurt and confusion behind the angry words he was flinging at them. She deserved them, she thought, what had she been thinking of? Dear God, she must have been mad! Shame consumed her as she watched Simon cross the floor towards them.

Simon was restraining himself with difficulty, and a pulse was beating at the side of his head. He'd never felt such anger before. It was like red-hot sparks before his eyes. He had difficulty focusing and was almost too furious to speak.

He wants to hit me, Janet thought, and wished he would, it would make her feel better.

Simon clenched his fists by his sides. For the first time in his life he wanted to hurt Janet, but more than that, he wanted to wipe the silly smirk off the face of the man beside her. 'Aren't you going to introduce us, Janet?' he said. 'Your friend is obviously someone you know well.' Janet was silent, her head dropped in shame and he went on, 'He must have a name, this man you've been carrying on with.'

'Simon, I'm not ... I haven't...' Janet glanced across at Ben and was horrified to see a sardonic smile on his face. Did he think it was funny? And why the hell didn't he help her? she thought.

'Ben, tell Simon we didn't ... I...'

'Tell him what, Janet?' Ben said. 'Tell him we still love each other?'

The blow Simon delivered took him by surprise. It caught him between the eyes with such force, he was almost lifted off his feet. His nose was already spurting blood as he went down, cracking his head on the table with a sickening thud and crumpling in an unconscious heap on the floor.

'Oh, God,' cried Janet.

Simon gave only a cursory glance at Ben's still form before saying to Janet, 'I'll leave you to it. You can do your Florence Nightingale act.'

'Simon, you can't leave, you might have killed him,' Janet cried, and as he strode purposefully towards the door, she screamed, 'Simon, Simon, please!'

The slam of the door nearly took it from its hinges. She ran after him. 'Simon!' He continued down the stairs without looking up. It was just as if he didn't hear her screaming his name. What could she do? How could she run after him to try and make him understand anything, and leave Ben injured, perhaps worse, on her living room floor?

She retraced her steps. Ben hadn't moved and the blood from his nose was seeping into the carpet. He tried to open his eyes as she bathed his face and the cut on the back of his head where he'd caught it on the table. A low moan escaped from him. Janet was overcome with guilt, but also angry with Ben. What had possessed him to say what he had? 'Ben, are you okay? How do you feel?'

'Bloody awful. Did he hit me with a sledge-hammer?'

'Not quite,' Janet said. 'You were a perfect fool to say what you did. What did you think he'd do, congratulate you?'

'I only said what's true.' Janet was prevented from replying by Ben's moan. 'Oh, my head,' he said as he tried to raise it and failed. He opened his eyes and tried to focus on Janet, but couldn't. 'I'm seeing two blurred images of you,' he said with a smile that turned into a grimace of pain.

'I think I'd better call an ambulance,' Janet said.

'No, I'll be all right after a good night's sleep.'

'No, you mustn't sleep,' Janet cried. 'Everyone knows that. You could have concussion or even a fractured skull. You gave your head an awful crack on the table and the cut's still bleeding. It might need stitches.'

'Don't fuss, Janet,' Ben said. 'And I'd like you to know it was worth it, and I don't blame your bloke. I'd have done the same in his shoes.'

'Shut up, Ben, I'm phoning for an ambulance. You need to be in hospital,' Janet said, worried by Ben's pallor. She was also worried about how she would explain his presence in her flat to everyone

– her family and Ruth, for instance – and where Simon was and how the hell she was going to find him.

'Look,' Ben said, 'I am feeling groggy, and I think the hospital is probably a good idea, but not in an ambulance. How d'you think that will look for you? Call a taxi, and when we get to hospital I'll say I was in a fight and get them to contact Ruth.'

'And Simon?'

'For your sake I won't mention his name,' Ben said. 'After all, I've won first prize.'

'Ben...' Janet said threateningly.

'You can't argue with a sick man, darling,' Ben said weakly, and Janet knew that he was right in a way. Now was not the time to go into it. Ben needed treatment.

She wasn't sure a taxi was the safest way to take him to hospital, and neither was the cab driver when he arrived, but Ben insisted and the driver said he might as well take him as he was there and that it would be quicker at any rate than waiting for an ambulance.

'I'd say your young man needs seeing to sharpish, myself,' he said. Janet didn't bother saying that Ben wasn't her young man, but just helped carry him down the stairs to the taxi.

Ben wanted her to just leave him at the hospital, but she waited till she knew he was going to be all right. The head wound did need stitching and the nosebleed was staunched fairly quickly. But there was some concussion and the doctor said they'd keep him in overnight for observation. Much relieved, Janet went home, leaving the hospital to inform Ruth as Ben wanted.

She was so weary she could hardly climb the stairs to the flat. She didn't know what to do about Simon. It was far too late to look for him, nearly half past one. She went to bed, but lay awake, her eyes prickling with tiredness but the thoughts tumbling round in her head. Images of Ben and Simon filled her brain. She listened to the church clock chime every hour and the dawn chorus as the birds saluted the morning. She got up at seven, feeling like a piece of chewed string, and didn't know how she'd get through the day.

Chapter Twenty-Three

Later Janet was to think that that week was the longest she had ever spent. When she phoned the hospital the next morning, they told her that Ben had spent a comfortable night and would probably be discharged later that day.

Janet decided to visit him. She had to know if he'd kept her name and Simon's out of the incident, and she also had to talk to him and get him to understand that it was Simon she was in love with, not him.

He looked remarkably well, she thought, despite the two black eyes and the swollen nose he was sporting, and he smiled when he saw Janet framed in the doorway. 'You're a sight for sore eyes,' he said, and added, 'And they are sore. Simon can sure pack a punch.'

'Ssh,' Janet said, looking round at the other patients.

'It's all right,' Ben assured her. 'I told the hospital I was jumped on as I left the pub and it was too dark to see who by. I've kept you both out of it. That's the story Ruth and Phillip have too, and my parents and Aaron, who have all been to see me.'

'It was your own fault, you know,' Janet said sharply. 'To be found kissing me was bad enough, but to say what you said about loving me was just done to annoy and hurt.'

'Even if it's true.'

'But it's not true.'

'It is for me.'

'Oh, stop it, Ben, for heaven's sake,' Janet said in exasperation. 'Look, let's face facts. Once, I'll grant you, we were in love, but we were very young. I wasn't more than a child, and we wanted different things from life. Even if there had been no Therese Steinaway, there's no guarantee it would have worked out for us.'

'But...'

'Let me finish. Ben,' Janet said. 'But there is a Therese Steinaway in this. You married her and you have a son. Whether you love your wife or not is immaterial. She's your responsibility and so is your child.'

'Janet, I've never stopped loving you.'

'That's not my problem,' Janet said harshly. 'Look, you told me that Therese's father virtually owns everything you have, enabling you to enjoy a lifestyle you couldn't afford on your salary alone. Well, he might be the benevolent sort, but I doubt he'd continue to support you that way if you were to divorce his daughter to marry someone else.'

'We could work something out.'

'We couldn't do any such thing,' Janet said, 'because I don't want to. I love Simon and I'm going to marry him. What happened between us was a mistake.'

'You can't deny you didn't enjoy it.'

'I never tried to deny that.'

'So you admit there is something between us?'

'In a way,' Janet said. 'You were my first love

513

and so will probably always be special, but I don't love you deeply as I do Simon.' She hoped that Ben believed her, for she knew she was fooling herself. She *did* feel something very deep for this charming and self-centred man in the hospital bed.

'So lover boy is back, is he?' Ben said sulkily. 'He's forgiven you, I suppose?'

'Of course,' Janet said. 'I made him see it meant nothing. Look,' she added, 'I'll have to go. They just let me come in for a few minutes, and soon your family will be here to take you home, and I don't want to run into them.'

She also wanted to get away from Ben, because she had been lying when she'd said that Simon had forgiven her. In fact, he hadn't returned, and she had no idea where he was. She thought he might make contact over the weekend, and apart from the short visit to the hospital she didn't dare leave the flat, instead tried to clean the blood-stains from the carpet and the splashes from the fender and the table. When Simon returned, she wanted no reminder of Ben left in the flat.

By Sunday night she was frantic and she phoned Simon's parents to see if he was there. 'No, dear,' his mother said. 'I thought he was with you.'

'No,' said Janet in a dejected tone, 'no, he isn't.'

'Have you had a fall-out?'

'Sort of,' Janet said, wondering what the woman would say if she'd known that Simon, incensed at seeing her in the arms of another, had lashed out and landed the man in hospital.

'Well, he's not run home to mother, dear,' Mrs

Webster said with a chuckle.

'No,' Janet said. 'I don't suppose you have the address of Kenny's new flat?'

'I had no idea he'd moved.'

'He needed a cheaper place, you know ... when, um, when Simon moved out,' Janet said, hoping that Simon's parents were aware they were living together.

'Yes,' Mrs Webster said. 'I did know you were together, that's why I said I thought he was with you.'

'Well, he was, but we had a row and he walked out.'

'He'll be back, never fear,' Mrs Webster said, and Janet agreed that yes, he probably would.

On Monday she phoned Simon's office, only to be told he was on a week's leave. She had drawn a blank again and just had to wait, but she knew she had to keep away from Ben, for he was right, there was something between them. But there was something deeper and stronger between her and Simon, and she had no wish to hurt him further so she'd steer clear of Ben in the future, and if that meant keeping away from Ruth too, well, then she would. She phoned Ruth the following day to tell her that with all the wedding arrangements she wouldn't have time to go over to her house, but would work on her sections of the book at the flat and they could pool their contributions later.

In fact Janet had no wedding planning to do at all. Betty had it all in hand, with Linda, Sally and Brendan's twins Finolla and Mairead as brides-maids. Janet would have preferred a smaller affair, but Betty said she was her eldest daughter and would be married in style or not at all.

Janet knew she should phone her mother. She usually rang at least a couple of times a week, especially if she couldn't visit. She knew the family would think it strange, but how could she ring them or go and see them as miserable as she was?

She decided to write to Claire. That, at least, was something positive that had come out of Ben's visit. However, before she could get down to it, a letter arrived for her from Canada. In it, Claire explained that Ruth had written to her and told her about Janet's job. She asked how Janet was coping and congratulated her on the forthcoming wedding. They were making plans to come back to England soon, Claire continued, and she was dying to see Janet again.

Janet cried over the letter. She'd missed her friend so much and this, the first contact in years, had come when she most needed it. Janet thought it brilliant news that Claire was coming back to England, for she longed to see her again. She sat down immediately to write back. She felt she could hardly fill this first letter with an account of the argument with Simon, so in the end she hardly mentioned him at all, instead telling Claire about Meadowbank School, outlining the problems she was having and finishing by saying how much she was looking forward to seeing her again.

As she walked out to post the letter, she decided that enough was enough. She couldn't let her relationship with Simon drift on as it had

516

been doing or there would be no wedding for Claire to come back for, so she decided that if Simon hadn't contacted her by Sunday night, she'd phone him at work again on Monday morning.

Simon, in fact, had been having similar thoughts. At first he'd thought to let Janet stew for a bit, but after a week his anger had cooled and he'd realised they'd have to see each other and do some straight talking. He knew who the man was – he'd known even before Janet had spoken his name and he'd heard the slight American drawl in his voice. He was damned if he was going to let Ben Hayman come here and pinch his girl from under his nose. And as for him saying that they loved each other, that was plain stupid. The man had been in America and he was fairly certain Janet had not seen him before that night. He lived with her, for good-ness' sake, and he'd have known if she'd been carrying on with anyone. Kenny said that women were crafty bitches and past masters at making fools of men, but Kenny was just bitter.

Anyway, thought Simon angrily, what could Ben Hayman – a married man and a father too – offer Janet? He didn't want her, except as his bit of fluff on the side. Janet deserved better than that.

Janet was cautiously pleased to hear his voice when he phoned on Friday night. 'Oh, Simon, I've missed you,' she said in a voice barely above a whisper and very near to tears. Simon heard the love in her voice and it gave him heart, but he wasn't going to just pretend the incident in the

517

flat hadn't happened.

'Well, you know whose fault that was,' he said. 'What did you expect me to do?'

'I know, I know,' Janet said.

'I suppose he was all right after I'd hit him?' Simon said. He didn't much care, but he felt he had to ask.

'Eventually,' Janet said. 'I had to take him to hospital in a taxi.'

'You did?' Simon thundered.

'There wasn't anyone else,' Janet said defensively. 'I couldn't leave him lying on the floor and just step over him. I went with him to make sure he got there safely and then I left. I didn't stay.' She didn't say she'd been to visit Ben the following day. What she said was 'I'm so sorry, Simon.'

'We need to do some straight talking,' Simon said. 'I'll call round tomorrow and we'll thrash it out.'

'Yes,' Janet said, 'yes, okay.' Just before he hung up she added, 'I love you, Simon,' and he was smiling as he replaced the handset.

The next time the phone rang, it was someone called Mark Taplow from the BBC. The current affairs team were doing a documentary on the work of the units featured in Phillip's paper, he told Janet, and in view of the fact that Ruth and Janet's book was being serialised in the same paper, he wanted to do a short interview with them both.

'On the television?' Janet's voice was little more than a squeak. 'Oh, I couldn't.'

'Of course you could,' Mark Taplow said

decisively. 'Ruth is willing.'

'Ruth is?'

'Yes, and it will give the human angle.'

'Yes, but...'

'You and Ruth were in at the beginning, I believe,' Mark said. 'Viewers will be interested in seeing the people who helped Chloe and hearing them talk about their experiences with a retarded child.'

Janet could see how beneficial it could be, but she still wasn't sure she could do it. It was both exciting and nerve-racking, yet Ruth was obviously keen. She sighed. 'Okay,' she said, 'I'll try, and see how it goes. When do you want us?'

'Tomorrow,' Mark said. 'We're filming the units next week and want to get this out of the way first.'

'So soon?' Janet said. She wished she'd asked Simon for his number when he'd rung up, then she could phone him now and explain about the programme and maybe make arrangements for Sunday instead.

'Is it too short notice for you?' Mark said. 'It should only take a couple of hours.'

'No, no, it's okay,' said Janet. She could leave a note for Simon, he'd understand.

'Half nine then, at the studio?'

'Half nine!' Janet exclaimed. 'I live in Leicester. I couldn't get to Birmingham for half nine.'

'Well then, ten o'clock? Half ten?'

Janet thought for a minute and then said, 'There's a train leaves Leicester at nine thirty-five. I've caught it before and it should get me into New Street Station in less than an hour. If I

519

pick up a taxi from outside I could be at the studio by half past ten.'

'Okay, we'll say half ten then.'

'Fine,' Janet said. Her senses were still reeling as she replaced the receiver and then she made a short call to Ruth, who was so exhilarated by the whole thing she was almost incoherent, and they arranged to meet the next day outside the studio.

Janet decided on an early night, but she couldn't sleep. She tossed and turned, her nerves jangling, almost dreading the ordeal before her. She wished Simon was with her to talk over her fears and calm her down. She began composing the note she'd write to him in the morning, and his face swam before her, his eyes stern, uncompromising and as angry as they had been the day he'd walked out. Then she'd see Ben lying in a heap on the floor, and his cheerful face in the hospital. Eventually she got up to make a hot drink, and it was nearly dawn when she finally dropped off to sleep.

She woke to bright sunshine and realised with horror that it was nine o'clock. No time to write a note, no time for much but throwing her clothes on and calling a taxi to take her to the station as quickly as possible. She told herself she'd phone the flat from somewhere inside the BBC building and if Simon was there she'd explain what had happened.

But at the studio she was taken over. The hospitality lounge had food laid on, and Janet, who'd had no time for breakfast, wondered if it would make her feel better if she were to eat something, but the sight and smell of the food made her feel sick and she had a coffee instead. But even while she tried to drink it, programme planners were at her elbow, discussing the set and the format of the interview and the type of questions Mark would ask. She had hardly had time to replace the half-drunk coffee on the table before they were hurried through innumerable corridors to the set.

Mark Taplow was a nice man and an experienced interviewer, and he soon put both girls at their ease. It was hard to believe that millions of people might watch the interview at some date in the future, as today there were only cameramen, sound crews and the producer in there with them. Mark was so pleased with the end result that he took both Janet and Ruth out to lunch. Janet took the opportunity to slip away to phone Simon, but the phone rang on and on in the empty flat.

Twice during the meal she rang again, and each time there was no answer. She began to feel annoyed and was glad she hadn't just sat in waiting for him or her nerves would have been shot to pieces. He hadn't given a time when he'd be over, but she'd honestly thought he'd be early, possibly mid-morning, and had been like a cat on hot bricks because she couldn't phone him until after one o'clock. She obviously needn't have bothered.

The meal was almost over when Ruth said suddenly, 'Oh, the day is going to feel very flat after this. Why don't you phone Simon and ask him over to our place, and when Phillip comes home we'll make a night of it?'

Janet found herself replying, 'Simon isn't here, he's gone to see his parents,' and was appalled by the sudden vision of her and Simon sitting across the table from Ben Hayman.

'So you're on your own too,' said Ruth. 'Oh, come back with me. I don't want to sit in the house on my own all day.'

'Where's Phillip and Ben?'

'Phillip's working as per usual these days,' Ruth said. 'I really don't remember the last full week-end he had off. Ben's gone to Bristol to see someone – now his face is back to normal.'

Suddenly Janet wanted to be with people, not kicking her heels in the empty flat, going over and over that fateful night a week ago. And with Ben out of the way, there was no danger.

She rang the flat twice from Ruth's house, with the same result, and in a reckless mood decided to stay to tea.

Simon had in fact arrived at the flat minutes after Janet had left it, and was surprised to see it empty. As the hours ticked by, he became at first concerned and then furiously angry. He remembered the assurances of her love the previous evening and thought that obviously they amounted to nothing, for despite knowing that they were due to sort out the problems in their relationship that day, she'd left the flat without a word to him.

Betty, whom he rang first, didn't know where Janet was, and unaware of the friction between them she couldn't understand his anxiety. He also drew a blank with Lou and Shirley. It was obvious, from their manner, that Janet had not discussed any problems with them, and they were unaware of his week-long absence from the flat. He admitted to both girls that they'd had a row, but not what it was about and they assumed it was a recent thing. When Lou said that Janet could blow up quickly but it was soon over and she didn't bear grudges, Simon didn't tell her that this time it was him who'd lost his temper and gone, but thanked her for her reassurances.

There was no answer from Ruth's house and he asked himself if that was significant. Ruth could be with Janet, or out on business of her own. Suddenly his blood ran cold as he wondered where Ruth's brother was. Surely to God, he thought, Janet wouldn't do that to me, when she told me only yesterday how much she loved me.

But if she was on legitimate business of some sort, wouldn't she have left a note, or at least phoned before this to let him know where she was? She knew he was coming round today and she knew how important it was. Well, it would be a long time before he came round again. Two could play at that game. And Simon pulled his large holdall from the top of the wardrobe, quickly crammed his clothes into it and crashed out of the flat for the second time.

Despite her concern over Simon's non-appearance, Janet was glad she'd agreed to go to Ruth's. She'd missed her friend's company, as any time they'd spent together recently had centred around the book. It was nice to have time to natter and drink coffee, and Janet tried to push

523

her concern about Simon's absence to the back of her mind. After the second phone call from Ruth's house she wondered why he'd bothered making arrangements when he obviously had no intention of turning up. She couldn't understand him, but she wasn't going to allow it to spoil the rest of her day, and she went into the kitchen to help Ruth prepare the tea.

They were almost ready to sit down and eat when the doorbell rang. 'Doesn't this always happen when you've a meal about to go on the table?' Ruth complained to Janet, who was in the kitchen helping her as Phillip went to the door.

Janet had her back turned when she heard Ruth cry. 'Ben, what a surprise!' She felt as if the blood had frozen in her veins. She turned round very slowly. She could hardly believe it; it was as if they were fated to meet.

'Why didn't you let us know you were coming?' Phillip said as Ruth hugged her brother.

'I wasn't sure I was,' Ben said, 'but when Ruth phoned last night all excited about the television interview, I thought I'd try and get back today if I'd finished everything, but I didn't want to say in case I didn't make it.'

'Well, I'm glad you're here,' Ruth said. 'We can easily make the meal stretch for four.'

She glanced surreptitiously at Janet as she spoke and saw she was looking almost angry at Ben's appearance. She really does dislike him still, she thought, and was sorry that they couldn't put the whole awful business that had happened years ago behind them now. After all, Ben had a successful career in the States, even if his marriage wasn't all it should be, and Janet had made a very fulfilling life for herself and was getting married in a few months' time. And yet she still felt animosity for her brother.

Janet hadn't greeted Ben, not even when he spoke to her, and in the uncomfortable silence Ruth gave him a casserole dish and told him to take it out to the table, while she went out with another. Janet stayed in the kitchen feeling cold inside with dread, and she gripped the sink to try to compose herself.

'Janet, what's keeping you?' Ruth called through.

'I'm ... I'm just getting a drink of water,' Janet said. She splashed her face to cool it down before going into the dining room, where she avoided Ben's gaze and took her place with her eyes downcast.

She had no need to say much. Ruth regaled everyone with details of the television interview and all Janet was required to do was verify what Ruth said. She was grateful that Ruth was, for once, so garrulous, for the meal was an embarrassing one for her. Though she seldom raised her eyes from her plate and studiously avoided Ben's gaze, she was only too well aware that he was watching her with such intensity she could almost feel his eyes boring into her.

Ruth decided that going to the cinema would be a nice end to the night, but Janet just wanted to go home and sort out her differences with Simon. Another phone call, though, proved as fruitless as the earlier ones, and as she heard the phone ringing out unanswered, she felt suddenly afraid. Simon surely wanted to settle the quarrel they had had and yet he'd not returned to the flat all day. After all, she'd been ringing since dinnertime. A little voice in her head said: Then why should I go back? Simon was obviously not bothered, and it was, she thought, a dismal prospect, waiting hour upon hour for him to make an appearance. She'd already had a week of that.

He's trying to teach me a lesson, Janet thought, furious at his lack of consideration, for both her feelings and the future of their relationship. 'To hell with you, Simon Webster,' she muttered, and slammed the receiver down savagely.

She was attempting to get her feelings under control so Ruth wouldn't see how upset she was when she heard a movement behind her. Turning quickly, she saw Ben standing in the front room doorway.

Knowing that he must have seen her actions caused her famous blush to flood her face, and Ben recognised it and smiled as he said: 'Temper, temper, Janet.'

Blazing with anger, Janet advanced on him. 'Make sure you're not on the end of it then,' she spat out, 'because you deserve to be, snooping around, spying on people. And anyway, what I do now is of no concern of yours, so get out of my bloody way.'

She pushed past him and into the kitchen, where she told Ruth that Simon was staying with his parents overnight. She assured Ruth that this was not unusual and added, almost defiantly, that as she'd be at a loose end, she'd love to go to the cinema with them. She caught Ben's eyes on her speculatively, and deliberately kept her head lowered. She knew that Ben was aware she was lying, and equally she knew he would say nothing in front of Ruth and Phillip.

Eventually they decided to go into the city centre, to the Gaumont, where *Gigi* was being shown, and despite Janet's concerns she found she enjoyed the film. It was as they piled into Ben's car to go home that she realised how tired she was. Ben had behaved impeccably all evening, Janet had to admit, and she'd begun to feel more comfortable in his company. He'd realised at last, she told herself, that she really did love Simon and that the incident in the flat had been brought about by the emotion and nostalgic memories he'd stirred up in her heart.

So she leant back on the back seat of the car, quite relaxed, and listened to the others discussing the finer points of the film. She was almost asleep, lulled by the mumble of voices around her and the movement of the car, when she was suddenly jerked into wakefulness by the realisation that they were talking about Ben dropping Ruth and Phillip home first and then running Janet back to the flat.

'Oh, but...' Janet began, but Phillip broke in.

'I'd be grateful if you could, Ben. I'm shattered, to tell the truth. I've been working all hours just lately and I must go in again tomorrow, Sunday or no Sunday.'

How could Janet object after that? What was she afraid of anyway? Did she think Ben would leap on her and ravish her?

Ruth watched her friend anxiously and wondered if she should offer to go with them, but then Janet might be annoyed if she inferred that Ruth didn't trust the two of them together. You never knew with Janet.

Then there was Phillip, working so hard lately she seldom saw him. Since Ben had been staying with them – he couldn't stand the stifled atmosphere of his old home – they'd had little time alone. If only she knew how Janet felt. Ben had behaved so courteously all evening and she was certain that however he'd felt in his youth, now Janet was no more to him than a friend.

'D'you mind, Jan?' she asked quietly. 'I'll come with you if you like?' Janet looked at her friend and knew she didn't really want to come, and neither did Phillip want her to – she'd seen the disappointment flit across his face at Ruth's words and knew she couldn't ask for Ruth's protection. Surely to God she could deal with Ben Hayman if he should get out of hand? But then she remembered, he didn't have to take her anywhere, she wasn't totally bloody helpless.

'I wouldn't mind at all,' she said untruthfully. 'But really, there's no need for all this. If Ben could drop me at the station, I could easily take a train.'

'I wouldn't dream of letting a friend of ours go home alone in the dark when I have the use of a car,' Ben said, 'and it really is no trouble.'

'Oh, but...'

'No, really,' Phillip said, 'I wouldn't rest easy. You hear of horrible things happening to young women alone these days. I really would feel easier if you let Ben drive you home.'

What could Janet say after that? she thought. Should she tell these two concerned friends looking at her that she was still attracted to Ben Hayman, and her lover had fled from her the previous week when he'd caught them together in a passionate embrace? No, of course she couldn't. It was unthinkable. She gave a sigh and knew the die was cast.

And it would have been silly to sit alone in the back seat once the others had got out, Ruth and Phillip said. Janet would have felt happier to have stayed where she was, and Ben, she noticed, took no part in the urgings of his sister and brother-in-law. However, without appearing unreasonably churlish, she could hardly continue to protest, and she climbed unwillingly into the front seat. For a while they drove in silence, and Janet was glad of it, even though it eventually became uncomfortable. She sat stiffly beside Ben and watched the car eat up the miles back to her Leicester flat. Thoughts of the flat brought Simon to mind, and what had happened to prevent him returning that day as arranged to sort out their problems. She sighed softly, but Ben heard and smiled to himself. Unless he was very much mistaken, all was not rosy in Janet's life. He glanced at her out of the corner of his eye and remarked, 'Quite like old times.'

'Stop that!'

'I'm only saying...'

'Well, don't say,' Janet snapped. 'I'm not interested in anything you have to say, and I might as well tell you that I wouldn't be here at all if I hadn't understood you to be in Bristol.'

'So you're frightened to be with me?' Ben said, almost triumphantly.

'Not at all,' Janet retorted. 'God, you think a lot of yourself.'

Ben smiled. 'You're not over-fond of your fiancé either, I'd say, judging from your performance in the hall when you tried phoning him.'

'Which you shouldn't have been bloody well listening to.'

'I wasn't,' Ben protested. 'I didn't know you were there. I was just coming through the hall when I saw you hurling the phone down as if it had bitten you.'

'Yeah, well, you still didn't have to say what you did.'

'You didn't have to tell my sister lies either,' Ben said 'What was it all about?'

'It's none of your bloody business,' Janet cried.

'Okay, I'll have to guess.'

'Go to hell!'

'I was only saying...' Ben said again.

'Oh, stop this,' Janet said. She was suddenly wearied by it all and knew that Ben would have to be told a semblance of the truth or he'd just keep on. 'Okay,' she said, and sighed. 'We did have a row, and Simon walked out, but we'll get over it. People have rows and get over them all the time,' and she prayed that what she said was true. 'It's no big deal,' she went on, 'but I didn't want to tell Ruth and put a damper on the evening. Now are you satisfied?'

'Must have been some row.'

'Will you shut up?' Janet cried, totally exasperated. Suddenly she felt tears in her eyes and realised that but for the man beside her, she and Simon would be together now happily planning their wedding day. Why should Ben get away scot-free, she thought, and she cried out, 'Yes, it was some row. It happened because my fiancé saw me kissing someone else, and strangely enough he was upset and objected to it.'

'You ... you mean he's not been back since that night?'

Janet shook her head.

'But it was a week ago.'

'Congratulations,' Janet said sarcastically. 'Go to the top of the class.'

'And all that stuff about him forgiving you...'

'Was lies. He was due to come to the flat today to talk, but...' She shrugged. 'I've been ringing since dinnertime and he hasn't turned up.' She turned anguished eyes on Ben and said, 'Why the hell did you come? Why couldn't you leave me alone?' and then tears overcame her.

'You're not crying?' Ben said. 'For God's sake, don't cry,' and he swung the car off the main road into a side street a short distance from the flat and stopped.

'What are you doing?'

'I can't concentrate on driving with you crying beside me,' Ben said. 'God, Janet, you really have no idea what you do to me.'

Janet scrubbed at her eyes. 'I'm okay now,' she said. 'I'm just tired. Really, I'm fine.'

Ben knew she was far from fine. 'So he's been away all week?' he asked.

'I've already told you that,' Janet said impatiently.

'And you've no idea where he is?'

'I think he's staying with his old flatmate, but I've no idea of his address and neither have his parents. I'd just decided to ring him at work on Monday when he phoned and suggested we meet up today. Then I had the call from Mark Taplow and I had no way of letting him know I wouldn't be at the flat.'

'So you left him a note?'

'I couldn't. I overslept and didn't have time. I rang lots of times, though.' Suddenly a thought struck her. 'What if something happened to prevent him coming today?' she said. 'He'd phone the flat and when I didn't answer he'd think I wasn't interested. Oh, what a bloody fool I am!' And Janet began fumbling with the door catch.

'What are you doing?' Ben cried.

'Getting out. I've sat here too long with you already and the flat is only round the corner. I should have gone back there today. Simon might have been trying to contact me.'

'There's no rush now, though, is there?' Ben pointed out. 'After all, he'll hardly contact you again tonight, even if your theory is right.'

'He might,' Janet retorted. 'Anyway, I don't care. I'm going home.'

'I'll drive you.'

'No thanks, I'll walk.'

'Don't be silly.'

Janet strode off down the street. Within seconds Ben was beside her and draped an arm comfortably about her shoulder. 'What are you going to do about it?' he asked.

'That's my business,' Janet snapped. Ben's nearness was affecting her in a very disturbing way and she tried moving out of the circle of his arm, but he only pulled her tighter. She daren't risk a tussle that Ben could easily turn to his advantage, and she just wished her insides didn't feel like jelly and her heart wasn't thumping.

They reached the doorway of the flats and Janet glanced up at the darkened window. 'He could be ringing this minute,' she said, 'or even home by now. I haven't phoned for a while, not since before I went out to the pictures. He could be back home and in bed for all I know.' But in her heart of hearts she knew he wouldn't be.

'I'll come up with you.'

'You will not.'

'What are you afraid of?'

'Why should you assume I'm afraid of something,' Janet snapped, 'just because I don't want you upstairs?'

'You're not fooling me, Jan, I can feel you trembling.'

Janet knew Ben was right, but she said harshly, to try and disguise her true feelings, 'Don't be so bloody stupid!'

Ben wasn't deceived. He was aware that despite her concern over Simon and his uncharacteristic behaviour, she was affected by his presence, and by God, he was by hers. He sensed her emotional turmoil and knew she was in need of comfort, for she'd only made a token protest of pulling away from him. He wasn't going to let a chance like this slip through his fingers. 'Janet,' he said softly, and there was no longer anything in his face and voice but gentleness and longing and Janet felt her heart give a lurch.

She knew he was going to kiss her, and though she took a step backwards, she wanted him to. When his arms came around her, she melted into them. Nothing mattered for the moment but the throbbing excitement racing through her body. She had no thought for Simon, or even Ben's wife and child. She wanted to stay clasped to him forever, and yet she pulled away. 'No, this is wrong.'

'How can it be wrong when we both want it?' Ben demanded.

'We can't just have what we want,' Janet said. 'We'll hurt too many people. We can't.'

'Don't pretend you don't want me. I won't believe it.'

'Ben, there's different kinds of love.'

'Bullshit. There's the kind I feel for you, and you feel it too.'

And she did, God help her.

'If you can look into my eyes and tell me I mean nothing to you, then I'll leave,' he said. 'But I won't believe it unless you say it to my face.'

And Janet couldn't. She covered her face with her hands to hide her expression. She must break away from this man who had such a pull on her life, but she seemed to have lost control over her legs. She tried again, mumbling through her fingers, 'Leave me alone, Ben, please, I ... I love Simon.'

'Don't make me laugh,' Ben said harshly. 'Some love! So you'll ruin your life to avoid hurting people.'

'I won't ruin my life. I love Simon, I told you, and...'

'Oh yes, I forgot, you didn't mean to kiss me at all,' Ben said sarcastically.

'Damn you, Ben Hayman!' Janet cried. 'Now I know what it is about you I find unnerving. I don't *like* you very much.'

'I don't want you to bloody well like me,' Ben said. He seized Janet and felt her initial resistance crumble, as he'd known it would. In the short, passionate relationship of their youth she'd been able to refuse him nothing, and Ben knew that deep down she hadn't changed.

He pulled her into the cover of the doorway. For a moment they were silhouetted in the lighted hall, and as Ben's hands moved beneath Janet's clothes she moaned in an agony of desire. The door closed and they were in the relative privacy of the hallway, then Ben pulled her into the dimmer lighting of the stairwell. His probing tongue sent shafts of desire through Janet's body so intense she felt she could hardly bear it, and her nipples stood out in peaks. She pressed against Ben, feeling his hardness, and suddenly, through it all, she asked herself what the hell she was playing at. She struggled from Ben's arms. 'Don't! Stop it!'

'Don't go bloody coy on me now,' Ben said angrily, though his voice was husky. 'I know you too well.'

'I wonder if you do,' Janet said. 'I'm not just being coy. We really can't do this, Ben.'

'Course we bloody can.' Ben's hands reached out again, but Janet evaded them. If he touched her again she'd be lost, she knew. She'd not be able to resist him a second time. She had to keep away. 'I can't do this, Ben, I'm sorry,' she said. And quickly, while her resolve held and before he had time to coax her back to him, she ran up the stairs. Once inside the flat, she locked and bolted the door behind her and leant against it, panting heavily.

The place was empty and uninviting. Staggering a little, for the encounter with Ben had taken it out of her, Janet made her way to the kitchen. If she heard the car speeding away she paid it no heed. She made herself a coffee and prayed that Ben wouldn't follow her up the stairs, for if he was to knock on the door, this minute ... well, she'd never be sure.

Once she was fairly certain he'd gone, she ran a bath, scrubbing viciously at her skin, anxious to rub away the dirty feeling she had about herself and her behaviour. She hadn't had sex with Ben Hayman, she thought as she dried herself, but she felt as bad as if she had, and God only knew she'd wanted to. She cried for herself and Simon and Ben and the bloody mess she was in, and eventually she slept, curled in the chair, covered only with a bathrobe.

'I told you all women were bitches, but you wouldn't have it,' Kenny said, angry that Simon had been made to look such a fool. 'No, you said, Janet's not like that – well, she bloody well is like that. They both looked bloody cosy if you ask me.'

Simon hardly heard his friend. He was in

shock. They were parked across the road from the flats and he'd just watched Janet, with Ben Hayman's arm around her, walk down the road. In the cover of the doorway, they'd kissed long and hard, then they'd almost tumbled inside, and the light was enough for Simon to see Janet's dishevelled appearance and the way Ben's hands disappeared under her clothes.

He felt sick. He could hardly believe what he'd just seen. The night before, Janet had claimed she missed and loved him, and said it as if she meant it, and yet here she was in Ben Hayman's arms. Kenny had tried to discourage him from coming back here, but Simon had drunk enough to feel angry about how he'd been treated, and wanted to have it out with Janet that night. Kenny tried to dissuade him, but when he couldn't he agreed to drive him over.

Simon had been about to get out of the car when he felt Kenny's hand on his arm. 'Wait,' he said. He had seen the couple turn the corner draped over each other.

Simon had sat in the car and watched with horrified fascination as they approached. He seemed unable to turn his appalled eyes away from the sight of Janet and Ben Hayman clasped together. Then he sank back in the seat and said between gritted teeth, 'I'll kill the bastard!'

Kenny gave a grim laugh and started the engine. 'You tried to do that once before by all accounts,' he said, 'and that did bugger all.'

Simon had to accept that Kenny was right. God, what a fool he felt. He wondered if Ben had been in his bed all week. How she must have laughed after the phone call. She must have spent the day with Ben and they'd come back to the flat only when they assumed he'd given up waiting for her. Bloody bitch! he thought angrily.

The intense pain would come later, but as the car roared away, Kenny was telling him he'd had a lucky escape. 'The world's full of women, old son. Why make a fuss about one, there's plenty more?'

He's right, bloody right, Simon thought, and I'm not going to be caught that way ever again.

If he'd looked back as the car sped down the street, he'd have seen the dejected figure of Ben Hayman coming out of the doorway. Ben was a frustrated and angry man. What a bloody tease Janet was, he thought, working him up like she had and then pulling back. She wasn't playing him for an idiot. Who the hell did she think she was?

Chapter Twenty-Four

Janet woke, stiff with cold, just before dawn. She struggled to sit up and suddenly felt extremely sick. She barely made it to the bathroom in time. She wondered what she'd eaten to make her so ill. As she sat in the kitchen with a cup of tea she'd made to settle her stomach, she watched the dark sky lighten to milky grey and then pink and realised the short June night was over. But she wasn't ready to face the day. She was still very tired and she had no reason to get up, not yet. When the door bell rang, hours later, she was stretched out in bed fast asleep, still drowsy and a little disorientated. She peered bleary-eyed at the clock – half past ten. It could be Simon at the door, she realised; his key would be of little use as she'd bolted and barred the place the previous evening. She struggled quickly to her feet, feeling for her dressing gown.

It was as she made to stand up that the nausea attacked her again, and as she ran for the bathroom, whoever was on the other side of the door began to pound on it. 'Coming, coming,' Janet called, but when she did she was surprised by the person on the threshold. 'Auntie Breda!'

She'd never come unannounced like this; something must be wrong at home. But before Janet had the chance to ask the question, Breda snapped, 'Mother of God, child, what's the matter with you?'

'Nothing.'

'Don't give me that. You look terrible, and what took you so long to answer the door?'

'I was sick,' Janet said. 'Being sick, I mean. I must have had something that disagreed with me at Ruth's yesterday.'

'Oh, that's where you were, was it?' said Auntie Breda. 'Your mother was for having the police alerted when she couldn't reach you all day yesterday, especially after the strange phone call from Simon.'

Janet's eyes widened in shock. 'Simon,' she whispered. 'Simon phoned?'

'He phoned Betty when he couldn't find you here,' Breda said, 'and when she realised she'd not heard from you herself all week, she tried ringing the place all afternoon and evening. In the end I said I'd take a ride up with Duncan, who was coming up this way to a car auction, and see you were still living. Now what's the matter with you?' she asked, for Janet had put her head in her hands and groaned.

So Simon had been at the flat, but he hadn't stayed. Janet knew how his mind would have worked. When she hadn't been at the flat, he would have tried to find out where she'd gone, and when he couldn't, he'd have assumed she had no interest in saving the relationship. 'Oh, Auntie Breda,' Janet cried, 'I've been such a bloody idiot.'

'Don't take on, lass,' Breda said. 'You won't be the first nor the last. Let's go and have a nice cup of tea and you can tell me all about it.'

And Janet told her. She told her about Ben arriving and the kiss that Simon had interrupted, and Breda didn't comment but Janet heard her give a slight gasp at that. Janet soldiered on, explaining the punch and how she'd got Ben to hospital and the miserable week during which her energies had been concentrated on Simon and how to contact him and get him back, and how she tried his office only to be told he was on a week's leave. 'I'm phoning him again this Monday,' she said. 'I know they don't really allow personal calls and he hates me phoning there, but now I know he was here at the flat, I must ring and apologise and try and explain.'

'Did you know he was coming round?'

'Yes,' said Janet in a small voice. 'He phoned Friday and told me. I didn't know what time he'd come, though, and I never thought to ask for his number.'

'But why the hell go to Ruth's, of all places on God's earth, after that business with Ben?' Breda burst out. 'Honest to God, Janet, you need shaking. What will it look like to Simon? He finds you, his fiancée, carrying on with another man and walks out leaving you to mull it over for a bit. Then he decides that what he has is worth saving and phones, and you agree to meet the following day, and when he comes round you're out. That's bad enough, but when you ring up and tell him you were at Ruth's, where Ben might easily be...'

'I couldn't help it,' Janet cut in, 'and anyway, Ben was in Bristol.'

'Well, that's one blessing in all this,' Breda said. 'At least he was safely out of the way.'

541

Janet closed her eyes and bit her lip. She couldn't admit that she'd seen Ben again, and what she'd nearly done. Oh, dear God, even to think of it now made her blush. Thank God, she thought, no one knew about that foolhardy act but the two of them. But Breda, watching her niece, knew she was keeping something back for her face, which had been chalk-white when she opened the door, was now flushed crimson.

'Janet,' Breda said flatly, 'what do you feel for Ben Hayman?'

The eyes Janet turned on her aunt were haunted. She knew this was the one person she could tell the truth to. 'I ... I don't know, really ... I mean...' she stammered.

'How did you feel when he kissed you?'

How had she felt? Wonderful, throbbing with excitement laced with fear. She'd wanted to feel his hands on her body. She'd wanted him to make love to her. How could she say all this? 'Oh, Auntie Breda.'

'Oh, God, you still love him, don't you?'

'I ... I think so.' Janet's voice was just above a whisper. 'Can ... can you do that, love two men?'

'Course you can,' Breda said. 'Bit far-fetched to think there's just one man for each of us in the whole universe. But the bugger of it is you can only have one at a time, and Ben is already married and a father.'

'I know.'

'Is that why you went to Ruth's, to talk about it?' Breda asked.

'God, no. Ruth knows nothing,' Janet said. 'And I didn't go to Ruth's straight away.'

542

'Then where were you?'

Then Janet told her aunt about the TV interview, and how she'd meant to leave a note but had overslept, and how she'd rung as soon as she could and carried on ringing and thought Simon hadn't bothered turning up. 'I couldn't bear to just come back here and wait,' she said. 'I'd done that all week. I ... I really was very unhappy and ... and I know it was all my fault and it's no good complaining, but I do love Simon too, and very much.'

'What a bloody mess, eh?' Breda said. 'Ben is no good for you, pet, charming and handsome though he may be.'

'Perhaps I just lust after him,' Janet said, and Breda saw the ghost of a brave smile hovering on her lips.

'Perhaps,' she agreed. 'Do you lust after Simon too?'

'Sometimes,' said Janet, 'but somehow it's not just sex with Simon. It's ... I don't know, it's hard to explain. I *like* Simon, he's a great person, good fun to be with and yet considerate. He puts up with a lot, I suppose, because I'm often short-tempered and impatient with him and I know many wouldn't take it, Ben for one. He's too selfish and egotistical. So I like Simon but I don't really like Ben. I told him that too, Ben, I mean.'

'And what did he say?' Aunt Breda asked.

'He said he didn't want me to like him and then started kissing me.' And more than kissing, Janet thought, but she said nothing more.

Breda glanced at her niece. Janet had told her that Ben had kissed her just once before Simon

543

had come in on them. This didn't sound like the same incident. God forbid that it should have gone much further than that. She'd met men like Ben before – selfish, self-centred bastards with a sort of animal magnetism – and generally they were not nice people who most of the time made lousy husbands.

She held Janet's hands and said earnestly: 'Now, you listen to me. Liking is more important than loving. The rapturous thing you had going with Ben was marvellous for the short time it lasted, but believe me, it wouldn't have helped you get along together in the mundane day-to-day living most mortals have to do. Not if sex was all the relationship was based on, not if there wasn't mutual respect for each other as well. Do you remember how, much as he was supposed to love you more than life itself, he wouldn't meet you halfway about your university course?'

Janet remembered all too well.

'He's dangerous, Janet,' Breda went on. 'He's made a balls-up of his own life, but that's probably half his fault and certainly not your problem. He's probably too selfish ever to make good husband material. Now my Peter, I didn't love him – and believe me, I knew what love was, but none of my lovers survived. Who knows, if any of them had, what bloody awful marriages we might have made. Peter was just there and we went out together and had fun and I liked him, and when he proposed I thought why not, we got along all right. I found I was getting fonder of him as the years went by, and now ... well, now I'm damned if I don't love the silly bugger.'

Breda brushed the tears away from her eyes and remarked with an embarrassed little laugh, 'Must be going bloody soft in my old age.' She gripped Janet's hands and said, 'Get your man back, Janet. Phone him and do whatever it takes to convince him that you want him and only him. Get down on your bleeding knees if you have to. And now,' she went on, 'get dressed, you're coming home with me to make peace with your family.'

'I can't,' Janet cried. 'Simon might...'

Breda shook her head. 'He'll have too much pride to come back today,' she said. 'The next move has got to come from you.'

And when Janet noticed the bare place on the top of the wardrobe where the holdall usually sat, that she'd failed to see earlier that morning, she knew her aunt was right. She opened the cupboards and drawers, but they had been emptied of Simon's clothes. Somehow that affected her more than anything else and she felt the tears well in her eyes. 'Auntie Breda,' she cried, 'Simon has taken his clothes.'

Breda swore under her breath and followed her niece into the bedroom. 'He's cleared out of my life,' Janet cried.

Breda thought she might well be right, but to agree wouldn't help. 'Don't be so bloody dramatic,' she said. 'He was angry, that's all. Men do that sort of thing. I'd say you've got your work cut out to get him to believe what you say, but he loves you, you'll be all right.' And she hoped to God she was right.

'Oh, Breda, what shall I do?'

'For now, nothing,' Breda said, 'for there's nothing you can do. Let's do one thing at a time. I've come to fetch you home for a Sunday dinner with your family.'

'Oh, I'm not hungry.'

'That's between you and Betty,' Breda said grimly. 'You fight it out, I'm just the messenger. Betty was going to come herself, but she has more to see to than me, so I offered. And hurry up,' she urged, for Janet had made no move to get dressed. 'Duncan will be here soon.'

Janet seemed not to hear what her aunt said. She still sat on the bed as if stunned, and Breda urged, 'Come on, love, forget about Simon until Monday and get ready to tell your family about the television interview. You can practise on Duncan on the way back.'

Janet gave a sigh, got to her feet and began to pull her clothes on.

All the family were pleased to see Janet, and while they were interested and excited at the thought of Janet being on the telly, Betty was inclined to be critical of her not leaving Simon a note. 'Proper put out he was,' she told Janet. 'Stands to reason he'd be concerned.'

'Oh, Mom,' Sally said dismissively, 'who'd think of a silly old note when they were going to be on the telly. Simon would understand.' She gazed at Janet across the dinner table and said, 'Did you look dead glamorous, Jan? Did you see any TV stars? Did you wear lots of make-up? What a pity they didn't give you more time and you could have had your hair done.'

'Whoa a minute,' Janet said, blessing Sally for deflecting her mother's attention. 'No, I didn't see lots of TV stars, and I suppose I looked all right. It wasn't a fashion programme I was doing.'

'I know, but even so...'

Bert and the twins were more interested in how the whole programme was put together and where the cameras and mikes were positioned and so on, while Gran declared that it was all wonderful and she'd never heard the like of it before.

'Did you enjoy yourself anyway, lass?' Bert asked.

'When I got over being scared to death I did,' Janet said. 'To be honest, Mark Taplow was thoroughly nice, and there were only the sound engineers and cameramen there. It wasn't as if it was live or there was an audience; that would have been really frightening. And afterwards Mark took Ruth and me to lunch.'

'Yes, well, I hope you ate more of that than you have of my dinner that you've just moved around the plate,' Betty said sharply, for Janet had eaten virtually nothing.

'I'm sorry, Mom, I really wasn't hungry.'

'Janet, there's not a pick on you,' her gran said. 'Lord, lass, you can't be eating enough, you'll be ill.'

She looked ill, Betty thought, and she was heartsore for her daughter, for she knew she was in trouble of some sort. It was all linked to that phone call from Simon in some way, of that she was sure. Mind, she'd never liked the way Janet treated her young man. Thoughtful and considerate to all her family and friends, she'd often been offhand and less than kind with Simon, and she'd wondered sometimes how and why he'd stood it.

She'd often wondered whether Janet had been more shaken over the Ben Hayman business all those years ago than she'd let on at the time. Bert would have pooh-poohed the notion and said she read too many magazines and the whole thing was a lot of bloody nonsense, but still Betty wondered.

Something anyway was eating her daughter, for she wasn't her usual self. Many would put it down to excitement because of being asked to appear on the television, and yet Betty knew it wasn't that. There was a restlessness about her and she was jumpy, nervous. She was obviously worried, and Betty hoped with all her heart that nothing had gone wrong between her and her young man, but she was too afraid to ask her. Janet was glad when dinner was over, and explaining that she had a mountain of work to get through before Monday, she was able to escape back to the flat.

After another sleepless night of lying wide-eyed, composing what she was going to say to Simon when she rang him, Janet was unable to face breakfast and was so nervous she was sick again before she left the house. Never had a morning appeared so long, or dragged so much.

But eventually she was in the secretary's empty office dialling Simon's number with clammy hands, a dry throat and a heart thudding against her ribs. She felt weak at the knees when she heard his voice. 'Simon?' she said.

'Janet?' he replied. 'What do you want?'

He sounded so cold and distant, Janet thought. She had no idea of the struggle he had to keep his voice like that and not betray what he really felt for the girl on the other end of the phone.

'I ... I wanted to apologise,' Janet said. 'I'm sorry about everything, that time in the flat.'

'Which time now are we talking about?'

Janet was puzzled. 'Come on, Simon, you know which one.'

'Do I?' Simon was whispering, but it wasn't a gentle sound, more a savage hiss, and she guessed that he didn't want anyone to hear what he was going to say. 'I know I saw Ben Hayman kissing you in the flat the once,' he said, 'but I think there was a lot more I didn't see.'

'What do you mean? I didn't...'

'Save the lies, I'm through with them,' Simon said. 'I saw you, Janet, on Saturday, the day you made a fool of me. You weren't exactly discreet about it. He almost undressed you in the sodding doorway. Did you make it upstairs or did he have you in the hallway? God, Janet, you must think I'm stupid.'

'Oh, Simon...'

'Save the tears, maybe Ben Hayman will be interested.' Janet hadn't been aware she was crying. In her mind she was screaming, no, no, this can't be happening! 'Kenny and I were across the road,' Simon went on, 'because, fool that I was, I waited all morning and was still keen

549

to talk things through with you. I went back that night, Kenny drove me, and we saw it all. Has he shared my bed all week?'

'No, no. Oh, Simon, you've got it all wrong.' Oh, God, Janet thought, how was she to begin to explain?

'Sod off, Janet! Go back to your Yank. That's what you wanted all along anyway. Well, he can have you. I wouldn't touch you now with a bargepole.'

Janet stared at the receiver which had gone dead in her hand, too shocked to move. When the bell went for the end of the dinner hour it startled her. As she made her way back to the classroom, she was turning the conversation over and over in her mind. He'd seen her and Ben at the flat. She wanted to die with shame. There was no point in going on if she lost Simon, for now, too late, she knew that Ben Hayman's attraction was purely sexual. Breda, as usual, had been right.

The sex they'd enjoyed in their youth had been a wondrous, beautiful thing, but Janet realised now that even in that, Ben had often sought his own pleasure first, leaving her unsatisfied and unable to understand why. She'd never said anything and thought only to please him, and it was only with Simon, who set out to delight and satisfy her before himself, that Janet had found total fulfilment. And now she'd blown it. Simon had made his decision and that was that, and she was too devastated even to cry, for she felt her world had collapsed.

Later that evening Lou and Shirley both phoned. They'd been contacted by Simon on Saturday too, they told Janet, and were curious about where she'd been that she hadn't told Simon about. They were tremendously excited about the interview she'd done for the television documentary, but worried about Janet's reaction to it all. She tried to talk enthusiastically, but it was a vain attempt. She was fooling no one, and certainly not the two girls who knew her so well.

Lou put the phone down on Janet and looked at the receiver pensively for a moment or two before picking it up again and dialling Shirley's number.

'Hi, Shirl.'

'Lou. Anything wrong?'

'No. Well, I mean, I'm not sure. I've just rung Janet and ... well, she seems odd.'

'Yes, I rang her earlier,' Shirley said. 'Did she tell you about the television programme?'

'Yes, but it was like she was telling me her pet dog had died.'

'I know,' Shirley agreed. 'I asked her and Simon over for a meal, but she said they were too busy.'

'I asked her too and she said the same,' Lou said. 'Something's not right.'

'D'you think they're having problems?' Shirley asked. 'I mean, Simon said something about a row to me.'

'I don't know, Shirl. He told me that too. but it could be any damn thing really,' Lou said. 'D'you think it's any of our business?'

'Course it's our business,' Shirley said. 'She's our friend and we care about her, don't we?'

'And she is miserable,' Lou agreed. 'You don't need a man on a galloping horse to work that out.'

'So?'

'Let's get a couple of bottles of wine in,' Lou suggested. 'We'll go straight round on Friday after work.'

'With our husbands, or without?'

'Are you kidding? This is all-girls-together stuff, Shirley. Send your old man to the pub or get him to mind the baby or something. We've got to rescue Janet from whatever demons of despondency are pursuing her.'

Somehow Janet got through the week, though much of it was a blur. She realised that she was being sick a lot, which was strange, for she wasn't eating anything much, but she didn't really care what was happening to her. Afterwards she didn't remember teaching the children anything, but she must have done. She knew she looked ill, for the headmistress asked her a couple of times if she was all right, but she always said she was fine.

Twice Ben rang that week, and she put the phone down as soon as she heard his voice, and twice he called at the flat, but she recognised the hire car parked outside and wouldn't open the door. Towards the end of the week a second letter arrived from Claire.

She wrote that she and Richard intended returning home by the first week of the summer holidays, in plenty of time anyway for the wedding. She was sure Janet would be as pleased as she was about her special piece of news, she continued, and Janet read in amazement about the baby boy, Anthony Richard, 7lb 5oz and just perfect, that Claire had given birth to a couple of weeks before. She said she hoped Janet would understand why she'd said nothing till he was born. She was really looking forward to meeting Janet and her fiancé, she wrote, and ended with lots of love. Janet threw the letter to the floor and cried as if her heart would break. She tried to feel glad that Claire was coming home and dislodge the knot of misery she carried around inside her. Claire had had more than her own share of heartache and she deserved some happiness now, and Janet vowed that however she felt inside she wouldn't let it show when Claire came back. No way would she spoil her friend's homecoming.

But though she promised herself this, by Friday she was feeling so ill she was just glad it was the weekend. There was little in the flat to eat, but since she wasn't hungry it didn't matter. She hadn't been hungry for days and couldn't remember when she'd last shopped.

When Lou and Shirley knocked on the door, she'd reached the lowest point in her life ever. The two girls looked in horror at their friend and then at each other. 'Bloody hell,' Lou burst out, 'what have you done to yourself? You're as white as a sheet. You look like a walking corpse, if you don't mind me saying.'

Janet gaped vacantly at Lou and Shirley, the last people she'd expected to see. They'd been laughing, but the laughter had died as they stared at Janet. Suddenly Janet felt light-headed, and the hall began to dip and sway around her. She put her hand to her head and staggered, and swiftly Lou stepped forward to hold her and help her to a chair in the living room. 'Make a cup of something,' she suggested to Shirley. 'She looks all in.'

Shirley came in with a steaming mug a few minutes later. 'There's hardly a thing in the house,' she said. Janet made no reply, but she took the cup from her.

'When did you last eat?' Lou demanded.

Janet shook her head. 'Can't remember,' she said.

Lou jumped to her feet. 'What are you playing at, you bloody fool?' she said. 'I'm going out to get three portions of fish and chips this minute.'

'I couldn't eat them,' Janet said. 'I'll choke.'

'You'll eat them if I'm buying,' Lou said, 'and I'll see you do, if I have to ram them down your throat myself.'

Janet found herself smiling at Lou's fierce face. She'd forgotten how good her friends were. The next minute she was crying as though she'd never stop, and far from urging her not to upset herself, Shirley was holding her tight and telling her to cry it out, while she signalled to Lou to get going.

Janet was calm by the time Lou returned. As well as the fish and chips, she'd popped into a small grocer's she found still open and bought bread, butter, milk and cheese and popped them into the fridge.

'I've bought another two bottles of wine too, to go with what Shirley and I've already brought,' she said. 'I've a feeling this will be a long night.'

Janet ate the fish and chips, which she found

surprisingly good, and drank plenty of wine, and told the tale of Simon and her old lover who had entered her life again. She held nothing back, although she stumbled over the bits she was ashamed of. When she cried, often Shirley and Lou were moved to tears themselves, and they held Janet and cried together and it was, strangely, more comforting than anything. When she finished, they didn't pass judgement, or issue advice, they just looked at Janet in sadness.

'It's a bitch,' Lou said at last.

'Isn't it?' Janet said. Her sunken eyes were red-rimmed and her face was swollen and puffy from crying, and yet she felt moderately better. The two people sitting in her living room with her were on her side totally. 'The point is,' Janet said, as Lou filled their glasses again, 'now that I've come to my senses, as it were, and know I don't want Ben and truly love Simon, he's decided he's had enough.'

'You don't deserve him if you're not going to fight to get him back,' Lou commented. 'After all, he's got hold of totally the wrong end of the stick.'

'Yes,' said Shirley, 'you can't leave it there, just like that. You and Simon have been an item for years.'

'Forever,' Lou said.

'But what can I do?' Janet cried. 'I can't ring him at work again – I doubt he'd speak to me anyway – and I don't know where he lives.'

'Write to him,' Lou suggested. 'Tell it just as it was and address it to his office.'

Janet felt hopeful for the first time in ages. It

might not make Simon come back, but it would put her side of the story and maybe make her less disgusted with herself. She wondered why she hadn't thought of that herself. 'I'll do it tomorrow,' she promised.

'Great,' said Lou and Shirley together, and as they chinked their glasses, Shirley said, 'And remember, we're both for you, whatever you decide.'

Janet thanked God for her two good friends and doubted in all honesty that she could have gone on much longer on her own. Although she felt as bad as ever about what had happened between her and Simon, her friends' love and concern had given her back some measure of self-respect, and for the first time since that dreadful phone call to Simon she felt a stirring of hope.

Chapter Twenty-Five

Lou and Shirley sat on into the night with Janet, supporting her with their presence and plying her with wine till she went to bed tipsy, but happier than she'd been for a long time. She slept till morning and wasn't surprised to wake up with a headache and feeling nauseous, but at least, she told herself as she was sick into the toilet bowl, she knew what had caused it that morning and only had herself to blame.

She was immensely glad that Lou and Shirley had turned up on her doorstep, for she'd felt so ill before they arrived. As soon as her stomach stopped churning and her thumping headache had dimmed to a dull ache, helped by tablets and a cup of tea, she settled herself at the table and began to write the all-important letter to Simon.

It took a long time to write and she made several drafts. She held nothing back. She told him of Ben's first visit to the flat, which he'd interrupted, and the kiss that had so angered him. She assured him that what Ben had said was a lie – she didn't love him and she'd never said she had. She explained about the confusion on Saturday and why she hadn't been at the flat, and how she'd gone to Ruth's when she couldn't get hold of him, believing Ben to be away. But Ben had returned unexpectedly and had been running her home, after an evening spent with Ruth and Phillip, when Simon saw the second incident between them. She said she bitterly regretted what she had done, and the hurt she had caused him, as she loved him so very, very much. She assured him that what he had seen between her and Ben was as far as it had gone, but she knew that that was bad enough, and she begged his forgiveness. She had no feelings for Ben Hayman, and she loved Simon with all her heart. She signed it 'With all my love, now and forever' and addressed it, marked 'Private and Confidential', to his office.

She decided to post it straight away, and was making her way to the door when the bell rang. She automatically looked out of the living room window to see if it was Ben, but there was no car outside, so, wondering who it could be, she opened the door. There on the threshold was a smiling Ben Hayman, in total command of himself.

Had she known it was him, she wouldn't have answered the door. She'd been working on avoiding him, knowing he couldn't stay here indefinitely and must soon return to America. But as she looked at him, she knew she couldn't hide for ever. She must face him, not run away, or the business between them would always be unfinished. So she flung open the door and said, with a confidence she didn't feel, 'You'd better come in.'

Ben was furious, and controlling his emotions with some difficulty. He was no man to be picked up and dropped. He thought he knew what Janet wanted, but she was playing bloody hard to get and he'd had enough of it. He hadn't much time left to go chasing after her; he had to be back in the States in just over a week, and if she wanted to follow him out there, he would have to start making arrangements as soon as he returned. 'What are you playing at, Janet?' he said. 'Twice I've been here when I knew you were in and you wouldn't answer the bloody door.'

As Janet stared at him; she felt none of the trembling of her limbs or thudding of her heart she'd expected. Ben might be any casual friend popping in for coffee, and she suddenly realised that he no longer had any power over her. She was released and totally unafraid.

He walked past her in the doorway, so close he rubbed against her arm, and she felt nothing. From the other side of the room, he stared at her. He couldn't believe how thin she looked. Her face appeared drawn, with a greyish tinge, her eyes were red-rimmed and her hair hung in lank strands. This wasn't the Janet Travers he knew. She looked plain, even ugly, and he wondered if she were ill. Ugliness offended Ben. He liked bright, pretty things and people around him. There was something else different about her too, but he couldn't put his finger on it. Janet continued to stare at him without speaking, and the silence grew uncomfortable. Ben wasn't used to feeling uncomfortable, and in the end he had to say something. 'Are ... are you all right?' he said. 'You look...'

'I'm perfectly well, but busy,' Janet said shortly, 'so could you please tell me why you've come.'

Ben stared, open-mouthed. 'Don't give me

that,' he said. 'I'm not your bloody Simon and don't you treat me that way.'

'What way?'

'Come on, Jan,' Ben said. 'I know what we are to each other. You were ripe for it the other night, you just got cold feet. So stop playing hard to get. I haven't got time for this, I go back to the States soon.'

Janet made no reply, and Ben snapped angrily, 'Say something, for Christ's sake.' He wanted to shake her, she stood so still and mute, and he felt the confidence that she would fall gratefully into his arms begin to dribble away. 'You belong to me,' he burst out defiantly, 'and always will.'

'What exactly are you offering me, Ben?' Janet asked quietly.

'You know damn well.'

'Ah, but you see, I don't,' Janet said. 'You say we belong together. Who exactly does your wife belong to, and your son? What happens to them?'

'Nothing happens to them,' Ben said, as he caught hold of Janet's hand. 'Therese has lovers, she always has had, and plenty of them. She won't care.'

Janet shook off his hand, as if it had contaminated her. 'But you see, I do care,' she said. 'That's where we differ. I bitterly regret what happened between us. Do you know what this letter is, Ben?' and she waved it in front of his startled eyes. 'This is a letter to the man I love, begging his forgiveness. He loved me once so much, possibly more than he loved himself. He wanted me as a life partner, not a mere distraction to help him cope with a boring marriage.

You and Therese must work out your own salvation and I must work out mine. I hurt Simon badly. Maybe it will be too hard for him to forgive me, and maybe he'll never be able to trust me again. If that's how it is, I must accept it – it's my own fault, after all – but there is no reason on God's earth why I should make do with second best.'

'I'm not bloody second best.'

'You are for me,' Janet said, 'for I don't love you. You want to have your cake and eat it, Ben, and I couldn't settle for that even if I cared more for you. As it is, at this moment, I think of you only as the brother of a friend.'

'You're fooling yourself,' Ben yelled. He wasn't used to being thwarted. 'You do love me, you always have!' he cried defiantly.

Janet smiled a sad, slow smile that infuriated Ben, and said, quietly but firmly, 'Goodbye, Ben,' knowing that if they met again it would be as mere acquaintances.

'You'll be sorry,' Ben said, making for the door Janet had opened for him. His face was crimson.

'Don't flatter yourself,' Janet said, and as Ben stepped over the threshold, she shut it with a satisfying crash.

Simon was desperately unhappy and trying to prove he was having a great time. The first week with Kenny he'd taken as leave, and when he got smashed out of his brain early on in the evening and insisted on going on to a club at closing time, Kenny had gone along with it, thinking he'd eventually get over it. Since the second incident with Ben Hayman and Janet, Simon had, if anything, got worse and Kenny was worried.

He wasn't able to keep up with Simon every night and doubted that Simon could carry on at this pace. In the morning, he looked terrible, was hell to get up in the first place and late for work almost every day, but whenever he tried to talk to him, Simon told him to stay out of his life; he was having a bloody good time and it wasn't anyone else's business. Kenny would shrug, knowing he'd gone a bit wild when his fiancée had done the dirty on him, and she'd not even flaunted it in front of his nose like Janet had with Simon.

Simon in fact was getting used to waking up feeling like death, with a raging hangover and a dry throat and cough from the cigarettes he'd begun smoking again. Janet had hurt him badly and damaged his self-confidence, but he could almost convince himself he was happy when he was drunk, and he still had it in him to pull the birds. Janet might have spurned him, but there were plenty who didn't. Some, he sensed, wanted more than a one-night stand, but he always shied away, taking Kenny's advice to 'love 'em and leave 'em' literally.

There was another besides Kenny who worried and watched over Simon, and that was Sandra, who worked at the desk beside his in the office. She'd worked with him since he joined the firm and had fancied him from the start but Janet Travers had already been a fixture in his life. Now it appeared she'd blown it. Kenny had been quick to spread the tale around the office, and Sandra had overheard the telephone conversation Simon had had with precious Janet when he'd told her in no uncertain terms to 'sod off' back to her Yank. Sandra reckoned Janet Travers was a bloody fool to throw over such a great guy as Simon. She understood him and what he was doing, and knew it wouldn't last. He was hurting, but one day he'd be over the Travers bitch and then she'd be waiting. She made excuses and covered for him when he was late, and made him black coffee when he came in in a bad way, which was most mornings.

Simon was grateful to Sandra for her understanding, and occasionally wondered why he'd never asked her out. But he knew that if he was to do that she'd want more than a good night and a quick lay. Sandra wanted commitment, and he wasn't ready for that yet.

When the post came round on Tuesday morning, Simon, as usual, wasn't in, and Sandra was intrigued by the letter marked 'Private and Confidential' on his desk. She picked it up in surprise. He'd never had a personal letter before – she didn't know anyone who had – and she could make a good guess as to who the one in her hand was from. She recalled Kenny telling her how badly Janet had treated Simon in the past, and yet he went back over and over for more. If the letter was from her, it could all begin again, which would hurt and humiliate Simon and scotch her plans totally. Without a moment's hesitation she popped the letter into her handbag.

Simon came in later, his eyes red-rimmed and puffy, hardly able to hold his head up it ached so much. Sandra was furious with Janet Travers, who'd caused her man to punish himself like this by her behaviour. That morning, as she made coffee for Simon, she steamed the letter open. She scanned its contents briefly and knew immediately that no way was she going to let him see it. She could tear it up and bin it, but what if it was spotted by someone? No, it was safer to take it home with her, and she pushed it right to the back of her desk drawer, intending to deal with it later.

Janet knew she could do nothing now but wait for the outcome of the letter. Knowing that it might arrive in the office on Tuesday or Wednesday, and wanting to be around the flat from then in case Simon called or rang, she went to her mother's on Monday evening after school. She tried to eat to please Betty, but it was difficult. Her appetite had all but disappeared and she was sick most of the time.

She knew her mother was worried about her, but it was Breda who actually asked her if she was all right and urged her to see a doctor. Janet knew she would have to come clean with her aunt and tell her the whole story about her second encounter with Ben, because she wasn't one to let a thing drop. But even while she was furious with Janet and shouted at her for her naive stupidity, she was still convinced that all was not right. Janet ate so little and was sick so much, Breda was worried to death about her.

And though she pooh-poohed her aunt's concern, Janet stood in front of the bedroom mirror that night and surveyed himself, and knew her aunt had a point. Her arms and legs were like sticks and her shoulder blades and ribs stuck out. Her face was pasty white and her hair was a mess. Never mind, she thought, cosmetics could help with the face and the right clothes disguise the thinness. The hair, though, definitely needed a professional touch, and she decided to see if she could get an appointment at a hairdresser's the following lunchtime. She had to be at her best to face Simon.

She now expected a response of some sort by Thursday. By Friday she was in a fever of excitement and wondered if he would phone first, or just turn up. She stayed glued to the flat all weekend, waiting for him to respond in one way or another.

Perhaps he's going to write back first and suggest a meeting, she told herself on Sunday night, and on Monday and Tuesday she raced home from work to examine the mail. By Wednesday that hope had died, and by Friday Janet faced the fact that Simon was not prepared to forgive her and she had to look to a future without him.

Her parents had to be told by that weekend, she decided. No point in letting them go on and on with their wedding plans. It was the hardest thing she had ever had to do, even though Breda was there for moral support. Betty and Bert gaped open-mouthed as she told them that she and Simon had split up. 'I'm sorry,' she said, and willed herself not to cry. 'I'm sorry for all the trouble you've gone to and all the expense. I'm really sorry.'

'But, lass, I don't understand,' Betty said. 'Have you quarrelled or what?'

'We've quarrelled, yes.'

Betty sighed in relief. 'Lass, we all quarrel, sometimes I think life's one big quarrel. If everyone called off their wedding because of some foolish argument, there'd be very few married, I can tell you. You sometimes row more as the days draw near. Wedding nerves, that's all it is.'

'No, Mom.' Janet's voice was firm. 'This was more serious.'

'No.' Betty refused to accept it. 'Only a couple of weeks ago he phoned, distracted because he couldn't get hold of you.' But even as she said it, she remembered how she'd known that something was wrong the following day when Breda had brought Janet home, and she felt her heart sink.

'That was the start of it,' Janet said. She paused, reminding herself there'd been something before that, then went on, 'I don't want to go into it, but Simon doesn't feel the same about me any more.'

The tears were standing out in her eyes, and only her iron will prevented them pouring down her cheeks as her dad burst out: 'So this is his doing! Bugger ought to be horsewhipped.'

'Hush, Bert,' said Betty, who'd seen Janet biting her trembling lips, and the pallor of her face.

'I'll not hush. A few years ago he could be sued for bleeding breach of promise. Upsetting my lass like that. The house upside down for weeks for a sodding wedding that won't now take place.' He paced the room and began again, 'Who does he think is going to pay for it? I mean, a father's happy to pay for his lassie's wedding, but when the bugger jilts her, what then? All that material to be paid for, the bridesmaids' dresses and Janet's, cut out to fit them now so no good to any other bugger. And the woman who sewed them to be paid, and I bet we won't get the deposit back on the catering.'

'For Christ's sake, shut up,' Breda said, for Janet was sitting rocking backwards and forwards in deep distress. 'Can't you forget about money for two minutes and think of your daughter?' she demanded of Bert.

Bert was nonplussed. 'I *was* thinking of her.' He patted Janet's shoulder self-consciously. 'I'm not blaming you, pet. It's that Simon who's responsible for all this. But don't worry, he'll not get away with it. I'll go and see him and he can tell me face to face why my girl's not good enough for him.'

The 'No!', burst like a strangled yelp from Janet's throat, and then she faced her father. 'You're not to see Simon and demand anything. None of you have the right. I'm a big girl now and I can organise my own life. If you are going to lose a lot of money on this wedding, I'll try and pay you back, but Simon is not to be held responsible or blamed. It's not his fault.'

'But you said he doesn't love you any more,' Bert said, puzzled.

'That's right. People change, feelings change.'

'Not overnight they don't,' Bert said.

'Couldn't you discuss it, lass?' Betty asked pleadingly.

567

'I'm afraid not, Mom,' Janet said. 'The time for discussing is past and I don't want to talk about it to anyone, not now, not ever.'

The whole family was bemused. Only Breda knew the reason for the cancellation of the wedding. Neighbours shook their heads and said it just went to show that brains weren't everything; others went further and said they didn't think Janet would ever marry. 'Twenty-three she is, after all, and men don't really like clever girls like that, makes them feel useless.' 'Pity, though,' others commented, 'for she's a nice girl and pretty enough, and men are supposed to like them thin.'

As the weeks passed, Janet felt her life to be dull and meaningless. She seldom smiled and never laughed; the sparkle had gone out of her. The children she taught wondered what they'd done to make Miss Travers be so sharp and look at them so sternly. She was never amused any more by things they told her. She avoided her colleagues. She knew they were relieved, as they didn't know what to say. Against her better judgement, as she never met them socially, she'd invited them to the evening do of her wedding because her mother had insisted, and now she had to tell them the wedding was off. One of the other teachers, Amy Plashelt, had planned her own wedding for the first Saturday of the summer holiday, and so she in particular, found it embarrassing and kept out of Janet's way as much as possible.

The book about Chloe was finished, to Janet's extreme relief, and now there was no reason to go to Ruth's. Janet seldom phoned her friend and was brusque if Ruth phoned her. Ruth knew she was upset about the wedding being cancelled, though Janet never gave her a proper explanation and Ruth felt she couldn't ask. She wanted to offer her support but Janet couldn't accept it, for in a way Ruth was responsible for what had happened. If she'd never met Ruth, she wouldn't have met Ben and she wouldn't be in this mess now, she told herself, and she tried to forget Ruth and their years of friendship.

With Lou and Shirley, she had no such constraint. Their love and concern often moved her to tears. They descended on her every few days, sometimes separately, sometimes together. Some nights they'd bring a takeaway, which Janet could only pick at, and sometimes they'd drag her out and she'd pretend to enjoy herself. Janet was grateful, but worried that their husbands might get fed up but she needed their presence too much to make more than a token protest.

Janet also wrote to Claire to tell her the wedding was no more, but she offered no explanation to Claire either, saying only that she and Simon had proved incompatible and agreed to part. Inside and alone, however, she grieved for the loss of Simon, as if he'd died.

Three weeks after she'd posted the letter to Simon, Janet got a call from Mark Taplow to say that the programme featuring her and Ruth was due to be broadcast the following Wednesday evening, and did she want to come into the studio to watch it. Janet didn't care whether she watched it at all and declined the offer, but phoned her family and friends as she knew they'd never forgive her if they missed it.

They all urged her to come and watch it with them, but she elected to stay in the flat. She wasn't at all sure she'd tune in at all, but in the end curiosity got the better of her. It was unnerving watching herself on television, and she noticed herself displaying mannerisms and gestures she didn't know she had. But all in all it wasn't bad, thanks to the skill of Mark Taplow and the editing team, and she settled back to watch the programme on the units.

As for the family, they were most impressed. Betty had thought she knew all about mongol children, for she remembered such a boy, almost grown, from when she was still a child. He was big, fat and ungainly and went by the name of Fred, and his mother would lead him about by the hand. Saliva would drip from his wide, gaping mouth to his chin, and green mucus trails seeped from his nose, and the children would mock and make fun of him. Occasionally he would escape the vigilant eye of his exhausted mother and lope after the children, uttering strange, guttural cries, while the terrified children would run from him, shrieking. Betty could never remember a time, through all her growing up, when she was not frightened of Fred, and when Janet had told her that Claire's baby was a mongol, Betty had visualised a female Fred. She never saw Chloe, but she knew Janet loved her and imagined she'd exaggerated the claims she made about Chloe's ability. Not, of course, that she would ever have been frightened of Chloe, but she would have pitied her.

However, the children she saw in the unit, working happily with the apparatus and talking with their teachers, did not inspire pity. The interviewer said it was a shame the television audience couldn't see the bright colours of the unit, and one of the staff explained the beautiful colours they'd chosen for their paintings and other artwork that decorated the walls. Betty sat with her family and watched, aware that her ideas were being turned upside down.

Had she but known it, Simon was feeling the same way. He'd been late home every day that week, due to stocktaking, and he was in the little flat alone, because Kenny had a date. He'd brought a snack and couple of bottles of beer into the living room and turned the television on for company.

He forgot the food as he saw first Ruth and then Janet on the television. He was astounded, and wondered when they'd recorded the session – obviously after he and Janet had split up, he thought. As he watched, waves of longing washed over him, and he knew he loved Janet Travers as much as ever. But she'd made her choice and she was no longer his. He wondered if she was returning to the States with Ben – if indeed they'd already gone – and his hand hovered over the phone. But he told himself not to be such a bloody fool. Whatever she said, she didn't want him, she wanted Ben Hayman, and the sooner he realised it and got over her, the better.

The work in the units surprised him as much as it had Betty. He'd not thought much about mentally handicapped children before he met Janet, and if he passed one in the street, he felt a measure of sympathy, but also gratitude that no one he knew was afflicted that way. He imagined he was fairly typical of the average layman. Janet had told him about Chloe's short life; about the exercises she and Ruth had helped Claire with when Chloe was a baby; and about the unit she'd attended from the age of three. But hearing about something and seeing it in action were two entirely different things. The programme showed handicapped children working happily in classrooms not so very different from those which 'ordinary' children attended – and better equipped than some – and he thought Janet had a point. The children were capable of learning and mastering many skills and shouldn't be shut away in institutions.

He didn't go out that night. Instead, he tried to imagine a life without Janet. He knew he couldn't go on as he was, and he thought of Sandra in the office. She was a pretty enough girl and a good sort, and he liked her. He wondered at his reluctance to ask her out. He knew she was dead keen on him; she'd even asked him along on the fortnight's holiday she was due to go on in the second week in July, but he'd refused. He knew it wasn't fair to string her along, and he decided that he'd either have to ask her out properly, or else make it plain that he wasn't interested in that sort of relationship.

He yawned, suddenly tired, and decided to go to bed. It would be the first time in ages he'd turned in before the early hours of the morning.

Maybe, he thought, before he drifted off to sleep, maybe I'll be in before Sandra tomorrow and it will be one day when she won't have to make excuses for me.

Janet wondered what she was doing here in Fantails nightclub in Narborough, on the outskirts of Leicester, watching all the female staff from school gyrating in a circle with their handbags piled in the centre. She was restless and wondered how soon she could slip off home. She'd already sat through a crass and rather blue comedian who'd zoned in quickly on the fact that they were a hen party and directed jokes and innuendo at them.

Amy, who'd decided to have her hen night a whole week before the wedding, had simpered and giggled at the attention. Janet seethed and wondered why she didn't find it amusing when everyone else seemed not to mind, even to enjoy it. Of course, Janet hadn't gone with the intention of enjoying herself, and she told her mother and her aunt so. She knew that Amy had only asked her out of politeness. In fact, with Janet's wedding plans in complete disarray, Amy had toyed with the idea of not inviting her to the hen night at all, wondering if it would be rubbing her nose in it a bit. Eventually, however, she decided it was kinder to ask her, though no one would have been the least bit surprised if she'd refused.

However, Breda and Betty wouldn't let Janet refuse. They said Amy might think it odd, and she had to remember that she had to work with her afterwards. Eventually, Breda saying they might think it was sour grapes on Janet's part made her decide to go and show them all.

So she'd gone, and sat with a face like a wet weekend, red with embarrassment at some of the comedian's jokes and remarks, and watched the girls ply Amy with drinks in the age-old tradition of getting the prospective bride off her trolley altogether. She listened to the shrieks and gales of laughter at things not remotely funny, and wondered whether there was something wrong with her, but no one seemed surprised at her attitude. Janet told herself sternly to stop putting such a damper on the evening – after all, it was Amy's night, and she had no right to spoil it for her – but she wished wholeheartedly she hadn't come.

It was easier once the comedian was off stage and the floor cleared. Janet had been urged to join the dancing circle but declined, saying she might later. She was quite mesmerised at first by the circling lights sending shafts of colour across the dance floor, lighting up areas with their brilliance and then plunging them into darkness again.

But after a while she was bored with her own company, and the pounding beat started a nagging ache in her head and she wondered whether to kill another few minutes in the ladies' or slip away home. She was still undecided when a couple in the throes of a wild rock-and-roll number suddenly swung past her. They were illuminated for a second by the circulating orb, and Janet's gasp of shock was audible.

'Hello, Janet.' After such brightness, the darkness was total for a second or two and Janet's eyes took time to adjust, but she didn't need light to recognise Simon's voice. He stepped forward on to the carpeted area where Janet was sitting, and she felt a trembling throughout her whole body.

'H ... hello.'

'How are you?'

'Fine.'

Simon looked around the room. He forced himself to ask, 'Is ... is Ben with you?'

'Come on,' urged the girl on Simon's arm, Janet hadn't noticed her follow Simon off the dance floor. 'Come and dance. This is my favourite.'

Simon was tugged along, back to the floor, and was soon out of Janet's line of vision. He hasn't lost much time, she told herself angrily, and then was cross with herself for the thought. He's a free agent and can go out with whom he likes, she lectured herself. It was you carrying on with Ben that caused Simon to lose respect, love and any other damn emotion he ever had for you. No good yelping about it now.

But however much she told herself this, she couldn't spend the rest of the night watching some other girl cuddling up to the man she loved. Flesh and blood, she decided, could only stand so much. She gathered up her handbag, desperate now to be gone, but remembered to catch hold of one of the women in the hen party circle and tell her she had a headache and was going home, before collecting her coat and hurrying into the darkened streets.

She was outside, carried on the impetus of wishing to be as far away from Simon and the girl as possible, before she realised how stupid she'd been. Why hadn't she stopped at the foyer and asked them to order her a taxi? Bloody fool! She was angry with herself for her stupidity. She had no idea of how to get home. She stopped. She couldn't just wander around the streets hoping to find her way. She'd have to go back into the club. She was about to turn when she felt the hand on her shoulder. She jumped and would have screamed, but the voice stopped her.

'Janet, don't be frightened. It's me.'

'Simon, what are you doing? I nearly had a heart attack.'

'Sorry,' Simon said, though he didn't sound sorry, 'but what are you doing out here on your own?'

'Going home.'

'But where ... what...'

'I came with a hen party.'

'Oh, I see,' Simon said. 'But why go home now? The night's young.'

'I'm tired and I have a headache starting,' Janet said shortly. 'Go back to your date, Simon, I don't know why you came after me.'

Simon didn't either. He wasn't angry with Janet any more. He was becoming resigned to his loss, but he just knew when he caught a glimpse of her gathering her belongings and dashing out that he had to follow her. He'd left the girl he'd been with on the dance floor with the briefest of apologies. And Janet didn't seem to care whether he was there or not.

'You can't hang about here on your own,' he said. 'It's not safe. Is Ben picking you up?'

'Hardly,' Janet commented dryly. 'It's a long

way to come from America.' She turned angrily. 'I told you all this in the letter, so I don't know why you keep going on about him.'

'What letter?' Simon asked.

Janet was in no mood for sarcasm. 'Stop it,' she said wearily, 'and go back to your date before she comes out looking for you.'

She turned away from him and he swung her back angrily. 'Forget my date, for God's sake, and tell me about this letter.'

'The one I sent to you at the office explaining everything,' Janet said. She looked at him and said sarcastically, 'And now I suppose you're going to say you didn't receive it.'

'Well no, I didn't,' Simon said shortly.

'You didn't?' Janet's voice was just above a whisper. 'Then ... then what happened to it?'

Simon shrugged. 'God knows,' he said. He didn't much care. He supposed it was heartening to know that Janet had made the effort to contact him, but there was still Ben Hayman standing between them.

'But ... but when I didn't receive a reply, I thought you didn't care,' Janet said.

'God, Janet,' Simon snapped angrily, 'what I saw you doing with Ben proved to me that *you* didn't.'

'I do care for you,' Janet protested.

'You've a funny way of showing it.'

'I explained it all in the letter.'

'Oh, of course, the non-existent one.'

'Please, Simon, let me try and explain.'

'Oh, do,' Simon said sarcastically. 'I'd like to know why you can let Ben Hayman nearly

577

undress you in a doorway after making a bloody fool of me, and then say it's me you care for, not him. Don't make me laugh.'

'Why did you come running after me?' Janet demanded angrily. 'I didn't ask you to. Was it just to scream and yell at me, or what?'

Simon passed his hand over his eyes and admitted, 'I don't bloody know. I didn't mean to. I told myself that what you did was your business, but ... I found myself out here.'

Janet's heart leapt. She knew that meant Simon cared, and she took his hand. 'Just give me one chance to explain,' she pleaded, 'and I'll tell you what I wrote in the letter – well, as much as I can remember.'

Simon shrugged. 'If you like.'

They walked as Janet talked, and she told Simon everything from the beginning. He stopped her when she got to the bit about the television studio, and Janet explained the mix-up. Simon realised it was partly his fault for not giving Janet a number to contact him at, and for leaving the flat, as soon as he did, but he said none of this to Janet, complimenting her instead on the content of the programme.

Later in the story he said, 'I don't understand why you went to Ruth's.'

'Neither do I now,' said Janet, 'but I'd just spent a bloody awful week waiting for you to come back or phone or something, and when I thought you hadn't bothered going to the flat at all, I just couldn't face spending another afternoon and evening on my own. And Ben was supposed to be in Bristol, but he came back earlier than expected, otherwise I wouldn't have gone.'

'Janet, is this the truth?'

'I swear it, Simon.'

'You weren't seeing him, sleeping with him, the week before?'

'No!' Janet cried. 'I've not had sex with Ben Hayman since I was eighteen years old.'

'But you wanted to,' Simon said, and at Janet's impatient movement, he added firmly, 'Let's be totally honest here, Janet. You did want to. I saw it in your eyes that first night in the flat. And the night of the TV recording I could almost feel the desire you both felt for one another from across the street. Now unless you admit to these things and we face them, we haven't a chance.'

Janet took a deep breath. 'Okay. Yes, I did want Ben Hayman to make love to me, but I didn't give in to it.'

Simon gave a humourless chuckle. 'Oh, that makes me feel better, I don't think.' He stopped suddenly and swung Janet round to face him. 'You desired, wanted someone else,' he yelled. 'Have you any idea how that makes me feel? How it hurts?'

Janet heard the break in his voice and said quietly, 'I'm sorry, Simon. I know that's inadequate for what I've done to both of us. I've destroyed something special. I love you, and I think you love me, but you're finding this too hard to take. I understand that.' She began to walk away.

Simon hesitated a minute and then ran after her. 'You can't walk the streets all night,' he said angrily. 'D'you know where the hell you are?'

Janet shrugged. She didn't care; she'd tried and failed.

'I'll get you a taxi at least,' he said. 'There's a station round here somewhere and we're bound to pick one up there.'

Janet said nothing. If she'd opened her mouth, she'd have bawled her eyes out. She felt as if she was dying inside.

To Janet's surprise, Simon got into the taxi with her. He'd been wrestling with himself for the last few minutes of silence and eventually he said, 'I ... I need to know I can trust you, Janet, and I... We need to talk.' He held up his hand as she went to interrupt. 'Not now, we've said enough tonight and I need to get my head around it. I'll come over to the flat tomorrow.' He glanced at Janet, and even in the dimness of the taxi was aware of the tears shimmering in her eyes. 'I presume you've not made alternative arrangements with the BBC or anything?'

'Oh, Simon.' Janet tried to laugh, but the threatening tears won and the arm he'd promised he would keep by his side went around Janet almost of its own accord. It felt so right and good, but Simon told himself to be careful. The taxi drew to a halt by the door of the flats and Janet said, 'Will you come up?'

'I don't think that's a good idea, do you?' Simon said and kissed her on the cheek. She wanted to throw her arms around his neck and say that she'd do anything if only he'd come back, but she knew it would be futile, so she climbed from the taxi and watched it roar into the night, and the tears ran unchecked down her face.

Chapter Twenty-Six

In the cold light of day, both Janet and Simon were shocked by the other's appearance. Janet, Simon thought, looked ill, with lines of strain on her brow, pulling at her mouth and around her bloodshot eyes, which had smudges of blue beneath them. She had had little sleep and been very sick that morning, which was crazy, for she'd hardly eaten properly for two days, but she put it down to nerves on seeing Simon again. Simon himself looked dreadful. His face was puffy and blotched, with black pouches under his slightly bloodshot eyes, and Janet was shocked by his almost dishevelled appearance.

'Coffee?' she said as he followed her through to the kitchen.

'If you've nothing stronger.'

'I have, but...'

'No, coffee's fine,' Simon said. 'Ignore me.'

'You are all right, aren't you?' Janet asked.

'I could ask you the same thing,' Simon said. 'You used not to be so thin.'

'It's fashionable,' Janet said, with an attempt at a smile.

'It's bloody unhealthy.'

'Have you seen yourself...' Janet began, and stopped. 'Are we going to talk about our appearance all day?'

'I hope not,' Simon said, accepting the coffee

Janet handed him. He'd already had one argument that morning: Kenny had said he couldn't believe Simon could be so stupid as to go and see Janet. Looking at her now, Simon didn't know how he could be either. 'She left you high and dry that night – made a right bloody fool of you then one click of her fingers and you go running.' Kenny's words echoed in his brain, and he said, almost desperately, 'What was it between you and Ben? I have to know.'

'I can't say I know absolutely certainly,' Janet said, 'because it was as if a madness had taken me over. Love for you made me resist him, but as to what tempted me in the first place...' Janet shook her head. 'Look,' she said, 'afterwards I tried to analyse it a bit, because I couldn't handle it myself. He's a very handsome, charming man, Ben, but then the world's got a fair few of those and I don't fall head over heels for all of them. I think, I really think it's partly because he was my first love.'

'Oh, come on...'

'No, please, Simon, let me finish. I didn't love Ben; I was besotted by him. Whatever he wanted, I did, whatever plans he had, I fell in with. I thought of his pleasure before my own, gave in every time.'

'Totally opposite to the way you treated me,' Simon snapped with a touch of jealousy.

'Yes, that's it, don't you see?' Janet said. 'I was punishing you and all men for the way Ben had run out on me. The only thing I ever opposed him over was marrying him and moving to the States, and Aunt Breda said that even if I'd

582

agreed, my parents wouldn't have done, not with me being under age and Ben a Jew.'

'Get on with it,' Simon said impatiently. 'I've heard all this before.'

'Yes, but don't you see, that's the key to it all,' Janet cried. 'When Ben kissed me, I was back there, eighteen years old and anxious to please, but this time you were in the background and it was thoughts of you that kept me from going further than I would have done if I'd had nothing in my head but wanting to please Ben. Then I'd have probably gone for it.'

'You must see that this doesn't help at all,' Simon said. Kenny's words rang in his ears: 'What will happen when he's in England again? Will Janet go running from your bed to his?'

Simon didn't know if he could face that pain again. 'I mean,' he said, 'you're friends with Ruth, so what happens next time her brother comes to stay or something?'

'Simon, it's over.'

'So you say.'

'No, it is,' Janet insisted. 'Listen, my love for Ben was just based on sex.' Simon would have interrupted then, but Janet forestalled him. 'Not like our love for each other is, or was,' she said. 'Ben's idea of love was self-gratification first and last, nothing about me and what I wanted.'

Simon thought of his nightly exploits with any woman who would satisfy him, and felt ashamed.

'The point is, when I was eighteen and knew no better, that was fine. But now I know what it is to really love someone who loves me in return. I've grown out of Ben Hayman. I've matured, he hasn't...'

Janet leaned forward and kissed Simon ardently. '*You* have taught me the meaning of true love, not Ben Hayman. He came to the flat once more and offered to take me to the States to live with him there as his lover. It was laughable. You'd think it was something worth having, the way he put it. Even if I'd cared for the man I'd have hesitated, but as I don't, I lost no time in telling him to sling his hook.'

Oh, how Simon wanted it to be true. But it was easy for her to say all these things when Ben was safe on another continent. 'I want to believe you, Janet,' he cried.

'But?'

'But I'm frightened,' Simon admitted.

'Oh, I understand that,' Janet said, 'really I do.'

'It will take time for me to trust you totally again,' he said, 'and I think, until then, we should keep our relationship very casual and see how we feel in say six months or so.'

'Okay,' Janet said, ready to agree to anything that allowed her a stake in Simon's life, another chance at happiness.

'And I think it would be better if we kept this to ourselves for now,' he added.

Janet agreed, but knew it would be difficult to keep it quiet. She felt she more or less owed it to Lou and Shirley to tell them that the letter they had suggested she write to Simon had somehow gone astray. She also knew she couldn't keep the news from her family if she was to meet them face to face, for her happiness, even at the crumbs Simon was willing to throw her, would be apparent to all. She phoned them the next day and explained that as it was the hectic last week of the summer term, she wouldn't be over until the holidays began. By then, she reasoned, she'd have been out a few times with Simon and would perhaps know if things were going to work between them – and oh God, how she prayed they would. Still, at least they'd make contact and when she went to school on Monday morning, she couldn't help feeling more confident than she had done in weeks.

The talk in the staff room was about the hen night on Friday that Amy claimed she didn't get over till Sunday.

'Good job you didn't have it this coming Friday then,' someone said. 'You'd have been a wreck at your wedding.'

'Yes, what would your poor old hubby do then?' said another of the teachers. 'Waiting with bated breath for his wedding night and his wife too hung-over to perform.'

'Well, he'll have to wait another week anyway,' Amy said. 'I'm due to begin my period on Friday.'

'Oh, Amy, no.'

'Well,' said Amy defensively, 'it's not the sort of thing you work out months earlier when you're booking the wedding, is it? Mom said I should talk to the doctor, but I mean, what can he do?'

And Janet suddenly realised with horror that she herself hadn't had a period for a long, long time. She went very cold and still and the staff ceased to exist for her as she remembered back.

She was very regular usually, but the week that she and Ruth had had the television interview she was already over a week late, and with all the upset with Simon and Ben, she'd not thought of it again. Had she been aware of the changes in her body rather than her battered emotions she would have tumbled to it sooner, for the signs were there to see. As well as the nausea and sickness, she'd been going to the toilet a lot, and had been very tired of late, and then her bra had become uncomfortably tight.

Unconsciously, her hand went to her stomach, while at the same time she was suddenly aware that the room had gone very quiet. She realised that someone had asked her a question she had not heard, and now all the staff had their eyes fastened on her, awaiting her reply. 'Pardon?' she said.

'I asked if you were all right now,' Amy said. 'Someone told me you'd left the hen party early with a headache.'

'Oh, yes, no... I mean, I'm fine,' Janet said. 'It was just the music and the lights.'

The other teachers nodded sympathetically. Janet knew they weren't surprised that the hen party had upset her.

'You still don't look very well, if you don't mind me saying,' a colleague commented. 'You've gone very pale all of a sudden.'

'Er, a bit of an upset tummy, that's all,' Janet said, getting to her feet and escaping to the classroom, leaving behind her fellow teachers exchanging knowing looks and understanding nods. Without saying a word, they knew what had upset Miss Janet Travers, and it wasn't her tummy.

Janet was glad to get home that night. All afternoon the problem had been pressing on her mind and she was pleased she hadn't agreed to meet Simon that evening for she needed to get her head around this on her own. She thanked God she'd not slept with Ben, though she must have been pregnant then anyway, because thinking back, she realised that the day she and Simon had had the row – ironically about when to start a family – her period was already two days overdue. In fact, Janet realised, she hadn't had a period since the beginning of May, and it was now the middle of July, so she must be two and a half months pregnant.

'Oh, God,' she groaned, and put her head in her hands. What should she do? Tell Simon and have him marry her and feel she'd trapped him? Well, if she didn't tell him, she reasoned, he'd know soon enough. Pregnancy was one thing it was difficult to conceal for long.

And then she thought of her mother and father and the high hopes they had for her. 'Bloody hell,' she burst out. 'Bloody, bloody hell!'

Simon was annoyed. He didn't know what was the matter with Janet. She'd been all over him on the Saturday he'd called, and he could have sworn she was really sorry for her behaviour with Ben and sincere in wanting to put things right. But since then, something had changed. They'd had just two dates and both had been awful, with stilted conversation, uncomfortable silences and a curious tension between them.

The realisation of her pregnancy and not knowing what to do about it was causing a constraint in Janet's behaviour that Simon saw as withdrawal. To protect himself, certain that Janet didn't love him as she'd claimed, he curtailed their time together and put a brake on their lovemaking.

That made the situation worse, for Janet was then sure that Simon didn't want her any more. She longed to be back on their old familiar footing and had begged him more than once to go on as he kissed and caressed her, but each time he would break away, leaving her frustrated and unfulfilled. One night she'd even taken his hands and placed them on her trembling, eager body, begging him to stay the night, but he'd pulled back with an embarrassed laugh to cover his own burning desires.

The only high spot during this time was Claire's return to England. Janet was still cool with Ruth, and consequently Ruth claimed to be busy the day of the Carters' arrival, thinking it would be better if Janet met Claire by herself. Janet was pleased, though the nagging problem of her pregnancy troubled her even as she was waiting for Claire and Richard to come through customs.

But then it was all right. Claire handed the baby to her husband as she spotted Janet, and they flew into each other's arms as naturally as if they'd done it every day of their lives. When they pulled back, both of their faces were wet with tears.

'Let me look at you,' Claire said, holding Janet at arm's length. 'You've not changed much except you're thinner,' she said at last. 'And your eyes look a bit puffy. Have you been ill?'

'No,' Janet said. 'I'm fine, and I've never been fat, and I was so excited at meeting you again I didn't sleep at all last night.'

Janet thought Claire looked well, although she noticed with surprise that the brown hair was liberally streaked with silver strands, and Richard was completely grey at the sides. Claire's face, though, was still unlined and her eyes as beautiful as ever. 'Oh, Claire,' she said, 'it's good to see you.'

'How is it with you and Simon now?' Claire said, for though Janet had told her they were incompatible, the letter Ruth had written begging her to get in touch had said Simon was a great person and he and Janet were very much in love. Claire sensed a mystery, but was also very fond of Janet. In the end, Janet had given in to the urgent enquiries she made in her letters and told her of the quarrel, and what it was about, and the letter she'd sent to explain that had somehow gone astray, and how they met again anyway and agreed to give their relationship another shot.

'I'll tell you later,' Janet said, eager not to spoil these first previous moments together. 'Let me see the baby.'

Claire lifted him from Richard's arms and put him into Janet's, and she was enchanted by the beauty and perfection of him. He looked nothing like his half-sister Chloe, she was pleased to see, and aware of her own child growing within her, she marvelled at the soft skin and downy fluff on his head. The tiny toes were bare and the fingers with their minute nails were curled into fists, while his body was relaxed in the total abandonment of sleep. His eyes were closed and his fair lashes lay like perfect crescents on his pink face.

Claire was not surprised at Janet's absorption, for in the first flush of motherhood she imagined that everyone would be as enraptured by her son as she was herself. To Janet's relief, they talked of Anthony and of their time in Canada all the way home in the taxi. Janet left them alone then, back at their old Erdington home to get straight and sorted out, and promised to be round shortly.

But before that she tried to make peace with her family, who'd been horrified when she eventually admitted she was seeing Simon again. 'Have you no pride?' Betty said in pained tones. 'After what he did.'

'What are you thinking about, my girl?' Bert asked angrily. 'The man let you down once, isn't that enough for you?'

'It wasn't like that,' Janet tried to explain, but it was no use.

Even her grandmother shook her head. 'Ah, Janet, don't be going about with such a blackguard.'

'He isn't a blackguard, Gran, not really,' Janet said. 'The break-up was partly my fault.'

'Not the way we heard it,' Bert said grimly.

'And twenty-three's not old, pet,' Betty put in.

'Oh, be quiet,' Janet snapped. 'Is that what you think? God, I'm not stupid, and I'm not going out with Simon for that. It's just, I'm just... Oh, leave me alone,' she finished wearily.

Only Breda knew of the extent of the quarrel and the letter Simon claimed never to have received. 'How's it going, pet?' she asked, and to her consternation Janet's eyes filled with tears.

'Terrible, Aunt Breda,' she cried. 'We're like strangers.'

Simon decided he had to have it out with Janet. He couldn't go on like this. He couldn't even concentrate on his bloody job. After yet another awful date, he wondered if they should simply admit that it wasn't going to work. It was only the thought of Kenny's smug face if he did that kept him hanging on.

However, he was always being hauled over the coals about something at work, because he was unable to concentrate. Stupid really, because he wasn't even hung-over – or at least not so often – when he came in now. He wished Sandra was there to talk to – maybe she could have given him the benefit of her advice, over what he should do next – give the woman's viewpoint, as it were – but she was still on holiday.

Only that morning his boss had had an irate customer on the phone complaining that the estimate and samples that Simon had promised to send hadn't arrived. The boss told Simon that if they didn't go out pronto – that day – the customer would go elsewhere and Simon himself could be joining the dole queue.

Sighing, Simon got the samples and estimate ready and then found he hadn't an envelope big enough to take them. Swearing to himself, he sat back, wondering what to do. If he just sent the estimate, the customer would only ring to complain. He swung his chair round and his eyes came to rest on Sandra's tidy empty desk. Maybe, thought Simon, she had an envelope she wouldn't mind him borrowing.

Sandra's desk drawer was tidier than Simon's. The large envelopes were at the back, and as he pulled them towards him, he dislodged another, smaller envelope squeezed between them. His eye was caught by the writing on the front of it even as he was pushing it back where it had come from: 'Simon Webster, Private and Confidential', he read. What the bloody hell was an envelope addressed to him doing in Sandra's desk drawer? He drew the letter out, knowing even as he did so what it was.

Somehow the letter affected Simon more than Janet's words had. How it had come to be in Sandra's drawer could be gone into later; what Simon really wanted to know was what had happened between Janet writing the letter, when she so obviously loved him, and now, when she no longer seemed to. He left the office without obtaining permission or offering an explanation, and drove to the flat.

It was empty, but this time when he rang, Betty knew where Janet was. She told Simon in frosty tones that she was with Claire. She didn't seem surprised that Simon didn't know; in fact she sounded pleased, for the fact that Janet hadn't told him where she was going suggested that he wasn't important in her life. Simon thought it looked that way too, but this time he decided he'd wait for Janet in the flat however long it took.

Janet had spent almost the whole week with Claire. They had a lot to catch up on anyway, and she was able to tell her about the whole terrible business with Simon and the totally unsatisfactory reconciliation. Claire listened without a word, recognising Janet's deep unhappiness and feeling unable to help her.

She tried instead to interest her in a project which had begun as a spin-off from the media interest in the care of the mentally handicapped. Public awareness had been raised and debate sparked in Parliament. This in turn had caused local authorities to examine their own provision, and the Elmwood Home had been chosen to be developed as a school along the same lines as the units in the north Birmingham area.

Janet knew all about it, and she also knew that Richard had been asked to work on the project in an advisory capacity and later to stand in as headmaster, but she just couldn't interest herself in the developments. Claire was surprised at her indifference, especially after the stirling work she'd done with Ruth on *Chloe's Story* and the television interview with Mark Taplow.

Claire, however, wasn't to know of the secret Janet carried around with her, the one thing she'd been unable to share, that made other things slide into insignificance. She watched Janet's bleak face one day and wondered what it was that could possibly make her appear so despairing. She remembered the terrible days after Chloe's death when her own life hadn't seemed worth clinging on to, and the marvellous care she'd received in the Canadian hospital, and it brought to mind something she'd almost forgotten about. Maybe, she thought, it would help Janet, for she was almost out of ideas to interest her. 'I met someone in the hospital in Canada who knows you,' she said.

'Knows *me?*'

'Well, knew you, I suppose you'd say,' Claire explained. 'She was one of the psychiatric nurses. Name of Gloria Marsden.'

'Gloria Marsden?' Janet repeated incredulously.

'You do know her, then?'

Janet remembered the girl pinched with cold and walking with the aid of sticks who'd waited for her to come home from the airport to confess that she loved her brother but was setting him free. 'Yes,' she said, 'I know her, not well, but we did live close at one time.'

'I used to talk about the past,' Claire said. 'It was part of the therapy, you see, and when I mentioned a Janet Travers one day she asked to be remembered to you. She said to say she became interested in nursing as a profession after all her treatment – apparently she'd been in an accident and decided to find out more. Later she specialised in psychiatric nursing and emigrated to Canada.'

Sudden tears filled Janet's eyes, and they were for Gloria, the girl from a deprived home with neglectful and brutal parents who'd nevertheless gone on to make a fulfilling life for herself. 'Something worthwhile,' she'd told Janet, and by God she'd done it.

Suddenly Janet was angry with herself. She'd had a good start and a marvellous family who wouldn't cast her adrift on learning of her pregnancy, regardless of how Simon was to behave. It was time to stop feeling sorry for herself and start making some decisions over what to do with her life.

She took her leave of Claire shortly afterwards, needing to be alone to sort things out, and was surprised and a little unnerved to find Simon already in the flat, apparently waiting for her return.

'Hello,' she said, and glanced at the clock. It was four o'clock. She wondered what he had to say that was so important it couldn't wait until he'd finished work.

'What ... what do you want?' she asked fearfully.

'I needed to see you,' Simon said. Janet was not to know his serious tone hid the nerves that had been jangling while he sat alone in the empty flat and rehearsed over and over what he'd say. Her legs began to tremble and the roof of her mouth was suddenly dry. She was terrified of what Simon was going to tell her, but when it came it shocked her totally for he went on, 'I've found the letter you sent.'

Janet gaped. 'Where?'

Simon had already decided to say nothing about Sandra otherwise he and Janet could go off at a tangent discussing the whys and wherefores of her actions. It had to be gone into, but later. This business with Janet was, in the end, more important.

'It got mislaid,' Simon said. 'The point is, I got it today and read it. What I felt as I read it caused me to leave work to come here to talk to you.'

'Yes.' Janet's voice was just above a whisper. She was suddenly very afraid. She could barely remember what she'd put in the letter.

'What's it all about, Janet?' Simon asked sternly.

'What? What d'you mean?'

'You know, you're not stupid,' he snapped. 'When you wrote that you truly loved me, I felt it, even through the pages, but now...' He shook his head. 'What's gone wrong, Janet? What's changed?'

'Nothing,' Janet said. 'At least, my feelings for you are the same.'

She wished she had the courage to go closer to him, put her hand out, make some form of contact, anything but the way they stood, facing each other across the room.

'Then what is it? Is it me?'

'No... Oh, God, I don't know,' Janet cried. 'How do you feel about me?'

'Don't you know after all this time?'

'I think you love me, but you said you ... you couldn't altogether trust me.'

'I remember.'

'Well, I suppose that's it, if it's anything,' Janet said.

The silence stretched out between them and then Simon crossed the room, took Janet in his arms, gave a great sigh and said, 'Shall we start again? I was still chewed up when I met you at the nightclub, not ready to believe you, or forgive you, or anything really.'

'You had reason,' Janet said.

Simon was silent a minute and then said, 'I'll ask you this just once. How does Ben Hayman fit into your life now, this minute? What does he mean to you?'

'Nothing,' Janet answered firmly.

'You swear he means nothing?'

'Yes, and on anything you care to name – the Bible, my life or my mother's. Ben Hayman is history.'

She felt the relief relax Simon's tense body. 'You have no idea how that makes me feel,' he said.

'I think I have,' Janet said and turned her face up to him, and as they kissed she asked herself why she didn't tell him then of her pregnancy. But she kept quiet, and that night as she lay in Simon's arms, their lovemaking held tenderness and a sense of cautiousness as well as passion. Afterwards Janet slept deeply for the first time in a long while.

Just over a week later would have been their wedding day. Janet, aware of the new relationship with Simon, was wary of saying or doing anything to spoil it. She knew the family had planned to take her out of herself that day. Lou and Shirley had things plotted between them, and Claire said she didn't want Janet left alone, while Ruth had insisted she come to her. Janet declined all offers and to the fury of her parents went away for the weekend with Simon to a hotel in a pretty village called Fenwick, which lay to the north of Doncaster in Yorkshire.

As they lay in bed together on Saturday evening, Simon said, 'This could have been our wedding night, Janet.'

'Yes.'

'Does that upset you?'

'A little, but it was all my fault,' Janet said, 'so I refuse to feel sorry for myself. It's you I feel sorry for.'

'Ssh, I have everything I want.'

Janet turned to look at Simon in the dim glow given off by the streetlight just outside the window. The news she'd had confirmed by a doctor just before they'd left the city had been pressing on her all day. She knew that if she didn't tell Simon now, she might never find the courage to do it.

'Simon,' she said, securely held in the crook of his arm.

'Mm.' Simon had known all day there was something on Janet's mind, but he was pleasantly tired now from the long walk they'd been on, exploring the countryside around their little love nest. He longed for sleep and hoped she'd not spend half the night talking, but what came next drove the tiredness from his mind, because she suddenly said, 'Simon, I'm pregnant,' and burst into tears.

Simon was hardly aware of Janet's tears, and though he didn't withdraw his arm, Janet felt his body move away, and her heart sank.

Eventually she fell silent, scrubbing the tears from her cheeks, though they still glistened on her eyelashes. Simon lay quiet and still, and Janet was frightened of breaking the mood. At last he gave a sigh and said: 'Is it mine?'

She broke away from him slightly and hoisted herself up on one elbow.

'Of course it's yours,' she said and her tear-filled eyes flashed in hurt anger. 'I told you, I haven't had sex with Ben Hayman since I was eighteen, nor have I come anywhere near it recently. Anyway, I'm over three months pregnant already. I went to a doctor the day before we came away. This child was conceived even before Ben came back on to the scene.'

Janet saw the slow smile spread over Simon's face as he said, almost in wonder, 'A father! I'm going to be a father!'

'And I'm going to be a mother,' Janet commented grimly, and Simon stopped smiling and realised the enormity of it all.

'Why didn't you tell me sooner?' he said. 'We could have gone ahead with the wedding plans.'

'Of course we couldn't,' Janet said. 'For a start, I wasn't aware of it straight away. I first thought something might be wrong the Monday after I met you in the nightclub. We'd just decided to see each other but on a casual basis. After that, how could I say on one of the awful, tense dates we had, "Oh, and by the way I'm pregnant"?'

Simon was again quiet, then he said, 'What are we going to do?'

'Well, that's up to you, isn't it?' Janet said. 'But whichever way you look, at it, I'm going to have a child. Whether you'll be by my side or not depends on how you feel.'

'But of course...'

'Simon, there's no "of course" about this,' Janet said. 'I've had time to get used to this news, you haven't. I came to the conclusion a long time ago that I wanted your love more than marriage and I haven't changed my mind.'

'I do love you,' Simon said. 'I've told you enough times, but if you doubt it – I love you! I love you! I love you!' He took Janet's face between his hands and looking deep into her eyes said, 'And I want to marry you and look after you and Simon Webster Junior for always.'

And Janet knew that Simon meant every word he said. She was so happy she could hardly speak, and when she did it was to say something light, because she felt dangerously close to tears again. 'The arrogance of the man, thinking this child is a son,' she said. 'Let me tell you, sir, it will be a daughter to lighten my days and look after me in my old age.'

Simon took hold of Janet and rolled her gently on to her back, but the words he was about to speak died in his throat and he looked down on the girl he'd loved for so long. He bent his head and kissed her lingeringly.

'Oh, Janet Travers, I love you.'

'And I love you Simon Webster.'

Their lovemaking revitalised them, and they sat and watched the sun rise while they talked over their plans for the future.

'You're not crying?' Bert said.

'Yes, I am,' Betty said defensively, dabbing at her eyes with a lace hankie. 'Nearly all women cry at weddings, and when it's your daughter, it's almost expected.'

Bert supposed his wife was right, and truth to tell, he'd felt a prickling behind his eyes when he'd taken the arm of his lovely daughter to lead her down the aisle of Saints Peter and Paul church. He wasn't sure about Simon – after all, he'd let her down once – but then Janet had been all for it, and in the circumstances, perhaps it was just as well.

Breda was the only one who hadn't been totally amazed at the news of Janet's pregnancy. She'd seen a certain something about her niece's demeanour and a definite swelling in Janet's skirts and trousers that hadn't been there before. She was also the only person apart from Simon who asked for Janet's assurance that the child was his, and was satisfied with Janet's answer.

People reacted to the news in different ways. Ruth was particularly pleased, not least because Phillip had suggested that there might still be something between Janet and Ben. Ruth knew it was ridiculous and said so, but doubt had lingered. She was pleased to learn about the pregnancy, knowing that it was worry about it that had caused Janet to be a bit stiff and difficult of late, and it had nothing to do with either her or Ben. Lou and Shirley were delighted and declared their interest in being godparents, while Claire at last understood Janet's preoccupied manner: deciding what to do about the baby while trying to keep it a secret as long as possible had obviously put a severe strain on her.

It was nice to talk to her friends about the birth because it wasn't mentioned much at home. To tell the truth, Betty had been a little disappointed in her daughter, and rather surprised. After all, Janet was no fool and knew what was what, and yet she would have been an unmarried mother if she and Simon hadn't patched things up. Still, today wasn't the day for recriminations. She was just thankful Janet's dress still fitted or the wedding couldn't have gone ahead at all today and Janet had wanted it over before the school reopened in September. Of course, there was no fancy sit-down meal at a posh hotel, but Shirley's father had got them a room at the Lyndhurst pub on the outskirts of Erdington at very short notice. It seemed that with his contacts he could get anything. He'd arranged a firm to do a buffet too, and a band for the evening, and wouldn't take a penny piece for it, saying that it was a wedding present for the young couple. Put like that, Bert had to accept it. Before that, he was inclined to be huffy about it all, saying did the man think he couldn't provide for his own daughter's wedding? Of course, Shirley's father could afford it, Betty knew. Janet always said the family were well heeled, and yet not everyone with money liked to spend it. When everything was equal, you had to own the man was decent.

Nice child Shirley had too, Betty thought, Georgie, called for his grandad. She wondered what Janet would have and what she'd call it. It was a pity that it would arrive so soon after the wedding, though. It always amazed Betty that the stupidest person in the world had the ability to count to nine, and there would be quite a few who'd be willing to do that, she knew. But when all was said and done, a baby was still a baby and she couldn't help but be excited by the thought of a new one in the family. It might put new heart into her mother too, who was looking mighty frail just lately and had become very forgetful, but then she was getting on now, as they all were.

Breda watched Betty and guessed at the thoughts running round her head. She was well aware of what Betty thought and knew that pride and slight disappointment at Janet's behaviour would be vying with each other in her mind. Must be the only time in young Janet's life that she hadn't done what was expected of her. But she knew pride would win out, because Janet looked beautiful, Breda thought, watching her standing beside her handsome husband, and she prayed for them both to the God she scarcely still believed in.

Janet, in fact, thought that everything was splendid and far better than she deserved when she'd nearly lost Simon through her own stupidity. She loved her parents dearly and acknowledged that they were the best. She was grateful they'd never found out about her and Ben. Never would either, not from her at any rate, and she'd trust her Aunt Breda with her life. Aunt Breda was wise in ways that mattered, and what she'd said about Ben was probably true. But Janet didn't care either way really, and she certainly didn't want to think about Ben Hayman today of all days.

She was standing beside the man she loved above all others, in front of the priest who would soon declare them man and wife. And when Simon reached over and took her hand in his, and they looked at each other and smiled Janet thought she was the happiest and luckiest woman in the world.

The publishers hope that this book has given you enjoyable reading. Large Print Books are especially designed to be as easy to see and hold as possible. If you wish a complete list of our books please ask at your local library or write directly to:

Magna Large Print Books
Magna House, Long Preston,
Skipton, North Yorkshire.
BD23 4ND

This Large Print Book for the partially sighted, who cannot read normal print, is published under the auspices of

THE ULVERSCROFT FOUNDATION